TAKEN THE STARS

VANGUARD WING

J. N. CHANEY
RICK PARTLOW

VARIANT
PUBLICATIONS

LAS VEGAS, NV

CONNECT WITH J.N. CHANEY

Don't miss out on these exclusive perks:

- Instant access to free short stories from series like *Backyard Starship*, *Sentenced to War*, and more.
- Receive email updates for new releases and other news.
- Get notified when we run special deals on books and audiobooks.

So, what are you waiting for? Enter your email address at the link below to stay in the loop.

https://www.jnchaney.com/taken-to-the-stars-subscribe

CONNECT WITH RICK PARTLOW

Check out his website

https://rickpartlow.com

Connect on Facebook

https://www.facebook.com/DutyHonorPlanet

Follow him on Amazon

https://www.amazon.com/Rick-Partlow/e/B00B1GNL4E/

JOIN THE CONVERSATION

Join the conversation and get updates on new and upcoming releases in the awesomely active **Facebook group**, "JN Chaney's Renegade Readers."

This is a hotspot where readers come together and share their lives and interests, discuss the series, and speak directly to J.N. Chaney and his co-authors.

facebook.com/groups/jnchaneyreaders

CONTENTS

1

"I THOUGHT you said you'd never fly with me again," I teased, glancing over at Dani Campling just before I brought the Vanguard starfighter out of hyperspace.

The blank nothingness outside the cockpit burst like a blooming flower into a rainbow ring, streaked into multicolored tracks that stabilized a half-second later into a field of stars. Nearly a year traveling in space on a regular basis, and I still wasn't used to the utter, stark beauty of the stars. It was almost enough to distract me from the gut-wrenching jolt of a hyperspace exit.

It hit me that way every time, but this was what they called a micro-jump, coming in from the outer reaches of this system nearly into orbit of the gas giant. It loomed ahead of us, the glow off its sullen oranges and deep reds drowning out those stars as if reminding me of why we were here.

Dani glowered at me, though I think it was more at me reminding her of the battle at Haven than teasing her about her oath never to be my gunner again after I went nuts at the fear that my wife Laranna had been killed.

"Well, it was either that or sit around in one of the landers and wait for you and the rest of the fighters to clear the landing zone." She pushed a strand of red hair out of her face and tucked it under the rim of her helmet. We both wore combat armor and helmets, but our visors were up. I'd left mine up because it made me feel claustrophobic, and she probably did it because I did. "If I'm gonna have to land under fire anyway, I might as well be in on the action. I didn't come all the way out here from Ohio to sit on my butt and wait for someone else to have all the fun."

I was only half-listening, concentrating on guiding the Vanguard in an arc around a high orbit of the gas giant and keeping track of the other fighters in our makeshift wing. They all had some kind of Identification Friend or Foe transponder that showed up on the sensor screen between us in the cockpit, but counting two dozen of the things while doing my best not to fly straight into the gravity well of something at least as big as Jupiter was hard enough without carrying on half a conversation.

"I was supposed to be in the infantry," I grumbled softly, guiding the steering yoke like I was playing Galaga and going for the record high score. "Wasn't ever interested in aviation, not even Apaches, much less being a fighter pilot."

"I was a cop," Dani reminded me, holding onto the joystick for the pulse turrets like it was a life preserver, her gaze fixed on the cockpit windshield. "I sure didn't imagine *this* ever happening."

It wasn't real. I tried to keep telling myself that. Not the danger, not the enemy, but that gas giant out there, that massive, almost star-sized mass of compressed hydrogen and whatever else made it up. I wasn't a scientist and everything I did pick up was almost by accident, unless it was about how the ships or the weapons worked. I did know there was a buttload of radiation coming off that big planet, and I was happy this bird had shields.

"Why the hell do the Anguilar even *have* a base out here?" Dani wondered. "I mean, I'm not an expert, but from everything you guys have told me and every place I've been since I got here, they don't generally have bases anywhere except habitable planets."

"This is habitable," I assured her. "It's a habitable moon."

"Those exist?"

"Apparently. *Barely* habitable," I clarified. "Or so I've been told. We're still gonna have to wear our suits because of the radiation and the cold, but there's actually a breathable atmosphere. Enough that all they had to do was put up a radiation shield and insulate the place to make it livable."

"But *why* would anyone live here?" she persisted.

"They have some kind of mine in the atmosphere of this big, honking thing." I motioned at the gas giant, whose name I couldn't recall. "It's automated because even if anyone *could* live in the atmosphere, which I guess they could with enough shielding and gravity control, why would they? It kicks the processed…whatever it is out to orbit around the moon and then the Anguilar—or, more accurately, the poor bastards the Anguilar recruited into their military from their conquered worlds—load it into cargo haulers and send it back into the center of the Empire."

I didn't have to search for the comm controls anymore, which I thought was progress. It dinged at the no-look touch.

"Vanguard Flight," I said, feeling stupid using what felt like fighter-jock talk from a movie, but I had to talk to them all somehow, "this is Vanguard One. We're one orbit from Aether, and if they haven't seen us yet, they will by the time we're in visual range of the moon. We don't have any intelligence about cruisers being stationed here, and we don't expect them, but be ready for fighters. They're bound to have at least a squadron or two to meet us. Gib, you're the tip of the spear. You and your squadron take the lead. Laranna, you and your birds follow me in and provide air-to-ground fire. Everyone copy?"

"Just like the last three times you told us," Giblet drawled, earning some chuckles I could hear over the line.

My ears went warm. That was fair. I wasn't usually this nervous, but like I told Dani, I was no sort of pilot, much less a fighter pilot. Maybe these Vanguards did a lot of the flying for me, but that didn't make me any less worried about leading a bunch of barely trained recruits on their first actual combat. Laranna, Giblet, and I had taken on a whole Anguilar task force in the Vanguards, but none of the Copperell pilots we'd cross-trained from the flight crews had ever heard a shot fired in anger.

"Yeah, yeah, I know," I told him, trying to sound casual. "Humor me."

"We got it," Gib insisted. "My guys are taking all the risks, and you're having all the fun, as usual."

"Oh?" Laranna asked, and although I couldn't see her, I could almost hear her raised eyebrow. "You mean you'd rather land under fire and walk across a glacier in temperatures cold enough to freeze your lungs?"

"Naw, I'm good."

"Tighten up the formation," I told them, one of the few things I'd been able to pick up talking to Lenny about fighters. "We don't want to let them figure out our numbers right away."

It was still a risk, even with the computer safeguards. The flight-assist system didn't *want* to let us collide, but they were also combat spacecraft, and they weren't there to babysit us either. I had to consciously stop my teeth from grinding as we came within visual range of each other and then so close that the silhouettes of the pilots were visible through the windshields. The Vanguards weren't the jagged dagger shape of the short-ranged Starblades the Anguilar favored, but rather larger and more... modular-looking I supposed. The drive pods were on gimbals, which made them more maneuverable than anything else I'd flown out here, the pulse cannons at the end of the stubby wings on remotely controlled turrets.

Fatter than the Starblades, too, but that was unavoidable when each of the engine compartments had to hold half a dozen power cells, a hyperdrive, and a shield generator...or maybe the hyperdrive *was* the shield generator? I hadn't figured that out yet, but so far, I hadn't come across any ship that had shields without a hyperdrive. Either way, there was no way they'd mistake the

Vanguards for anything they'd seen before, but hopefully, they wouldn't know what to make of them.

I'd seen the terminator of a lot of planets so far, the place where the light side gave way to the dark side, but nothing on this scale. The darkness seemed to swallow up not just the exterior of the gas giant but all of creation, and it took a beat before the enhanced optics in the windshield of the fighter adjusted to the darkness and showed us the moon.

There were a dozen of them, spread all around the bulk of the planet, but only one of them was *the* moon, the one they called Aether. It was tiny compared to the gas giant but still huge, bigger than Earth's moon, nearly as big as Mars, but this world wasn't red. It was mostly white, a fraction blue and just a tiny strip green-ish. I suppose it was a miracle that it existed at all, life and a sort-of breathable atmosphere orbiting a radiation-spouting death orb, but I would have been happier if it hadn't been quite so hospitable.

Because without the atmosphere, there wouldn't be an Anguilar base, and all of this would have been so much easier.

"We got fighters," Giblet announced just ahead of the insistent beep of the warning from our own sensors.

Red dots swarming up from the moon, more likely from a security patrol in orbit around it because I doubted they could have detected us early enough to get planes from the surface. If they couldn't count us, I could definitely count them.

"Thirty of them," I announced. More than I'd thought, enough to roil my guts. "Gib, you gonna need us to stick around a little longer and help whittle them down?"

Maybe I shouldn't have offered Giblet the option because there was no way someone with his ego was going to accept the help.

"Oh, I think we'll be okay. The quality of troops the Anguilar would have out in a shithole like this isn't going to be much of a problem."

Which was exactly what I figured he'd say. I switched the comms to a private line with Laranna.

"Hang back with me until we get an idea how this is gonna turn out."

Her chuckle was soft static over the comm line.

"Giblet's barely been flying that thing for three weeks, and he already wouldn't admit some Anguilar pilot could outfly him."

No offense to Dani, but I would much rather have had Laranna in the gunner's seat beside me, even though it would have been a waste. Laranna was a better pilot than I was—not as good as Gib, but certainly too proficient to waste firing pulse turrets.

"Weapons range in thirty seconds," Gib announced. "Any reason we shouldn't let 'em have it with the big guns, boss?"

"Not one I can think of," I confessed. "It's not like they have anywhere to run."

Maybe that should have made me feel guilty, but it didn't. Not with the Anguilar.

The sensor screen demonstrated the range of our particle cannon with a red line advancing as we did, drawing ever closer to the enemy fighters, like a countdown to the start of a heavy-weight fight.

"Can you see the base yet?" Dani asked, squinting at the sensor screen. "All I can see is ice."

"Not yet. I think it's mostly underground." I made a face. "This must be one of those assignments they give to people who screwed up."

Dani's laugh was sharp and cynical.

"Maybe that's how we ended up here." She shook her head, doubt in the look she gave me. "How in the hell did we ever think this was a good idea?"

"I honestly don't remember," I said, but that was a lie.

I remembered it just fine. I still had a hard time *believing* it.

2

It had been nearly three weeks ago when I'd said the words.

"Lenny, you got some explaining to do."

And explain he had. It had wound up as dinner theater because all of us had been exhausted and famished after the battle at Haven. The surreal experience of shoveling shipboard food down while sitting next to a bunch of aliens and a medieval monk while listening to a giant, silver robot with the face of Michael Keaton telling us the history of the galaxy might not have been *the* weirdest thing I'd ever done, but it had to rank in the top five.

"My people," Lenny began without preamble, "the Creators, started out as a biological species not too different from any of you, in a galaxy far from here, so far its name would mean nothing to you. Over tens of thousands of years, we developed the technology you now take for granted...and went far beyond it."

"They developed all this technology," Valentine McKee murmured from the other side of Laranna, speaking around a mouthful of what purported to be spaghetti and meatballs, "but the food still don't taste right."

Lenny ignored him, though I was sure he'd heard the crack.

"Eventually, as our technology progressed, we realized that our physical bodies were constraints keeping us from our destiny, that each death was a loss not of knowledge, which could be stored and collected, but of wisdom and perspective. We gave up our physical forms and became part of a collective consciousness contained in ships such as this one. To interact with other species —with *you*—we built these robot bodies." He tapped his chest, metal clunking against metal. "But our full consciousness is the ship. And when I say *our*, that's exactly what I mean. I, the one you call Lenny, along with the other bodies on the other Liberators, are one. We are funneling the same collective consciousness that's existed for millennia."

I frowned, something tugging at me from a distant memory of a philosophy argument in college.

"But if you're not together, like, in communication all the time," I interrupted, "wouldn't each ship's...consciousness be slightly different than the other?"

"Briefly," he acknowledged. "But when we come together again, the databases are synchronized. Unless the gap was thousands of years long, we would never grow far apart enough to become individualized." He raised a metal eyebrow. "If I may continue…"

"Sorry." I sank down in my seat and took another bite of dinner. I was hungry enough that I didn't care that the noodles tasted like rice.

"We came to this galaxy millions of years ago"—my eyes went wide, and I wasn't the only one, but I refrained from interrupting again—"and began to spread life and intelligence as we felt was our duty, given the gifts we'd been afforded by time and nature. There were life-bearing worlds aplenty, but none had, as of then, produced sentience. Some were barely more than a sea of microbes. Through genetic and planetary engineering, we… urged them toward intelligence."

Sitting up straight, I couldn't help but blurt a question this time.

"Does that include…Earth? Did you mess with our genes?" The hair stood up on the back of my neck, and I wasn't sure if I wanted to hear the answer.

I don't know if Lenny was affecting the fond smile that passed over his face or if he was expressing the real emotion of the biological being he'd once been.

"No, Charlie. Humans evolved entirely on their own. Which is why I keep returning to Earth." He gestured at me, at Val, at Constantine and Dani. "It has been our experience that usually no more than one sentient life-form evolves per galaxy, at least on a scale of eons. Humans were the one for this galaxy, at this time. Which made Earth a huge resource for us when we went to those planets which had no life-forms higher than bacteria." Lenny spread his metal fingers like he was sifting sand through them.

"We used human DNA mixed with the local higher life-forms to create the sentient life in this galaxy, which is why, as you've wondered, Charlie, they're all so human-like." Another smile, this one positively warm. "Which also means, in case you're wondering, that yes, you and Laranna *can* have children together, if you so choose, though it will take some technological aid to avoid genetic anomalies. And the same is true for you and Brandine, Valentine."

Val rocked back in his chair as if he'd been struck, like it was something he'd never considered possible.

"It's also why we have, so far, not interfered in the societal development of Earth. Your world evolved its own intelligence, and you deserved the chance to develop on your own. We kept our existence hidden. For the most part.

"But we have made mistakes," Lenny went on, his tone growing more serious, closer to grim. "Some species are too aggressive for the sentience we gave them, the Krin for one but most especially the Kamerians. The Kamerians took the tools we gave them and used them to conquer each other. Then once their world was ruled by a single, brutal dictator, the ones who'd lost the war left their planet and conquered others, enslaving the people there to serve them. The dictator used that as an excuse to pursue them and wage war in other systems, and eventually the Kamerians began marching across the galaxy, conquering everything in their path."

Lenny grimaced, his arms falling to his sides.

"We should have intervened earlier, but we were across the galaxy, in our hubris repeating the same mistakes with other worlds, other peoples, and when we returned, for the first time in our long existence, we made war. We united the rest of our creations in a war against the Kamerians, which left the entire galaxy in ruins, a shadow of what it once was." Lenny nodded to me, to Dani. "What you see now, the anachronisms I've heard you both note, are the results of the Centennial War and its aftermath. Hyperdrives and starships, antigravity and particle cannons, and yet crops are yanked from the ground with primitive machinery pulled by beasts of burden. This, too, we could have prevented, could have aided those left destitute by the war, but…" Lenny fell silent for a moment and his gaze fixed on me. "We finally understood the extent of our hubris, our overreach, and that burden was more than we could bear. We felt that we were no longer worthy of the role to which we'd arrogated ourselves, so we decided that this would be the last time we'd ever play God…or wage war."

Lenny's caster-shaped wheels rumbled over the galley's smooth tile and he put a hand on Constantine's shoulder.

"Again, we sought you humans as a resource. We needed someone who hadn't been involved in the war, a force that could be truly neutral. So, for the first time, we sought out and recruited humans."

"The word you're looking for," Dani put in drily, "is *abducted*."

"Perhaps the Creators were wrong to take us away from our homes," Constantine put in, nodding both to Dani and Lenny, "but had we stayed, our lives would have been short and our knowledge so limited. All of my brothers were truly grateful for the opportunity to serve."

"Stockholm Syndrome," Dani muttered but didn't continue the argument.

"We created the Alahandran Monks as a check on our own delusions of godhead," Lenny explained. "We had them reprogram our operating system in a way that could never be reversed without our own destruction, forbidding us from waging war ever again. We could no longer bring harm to another sentient being."

Lenny turned away from us and stared at the wall as if seeing beyond it to infinity.

"This was, perhaps, just as short-sighted as our earlier arrogance. We abrogated our responsibility, turned away from the burden we should have seen as duty. And then, as if to bring that lesson home, the Anguilar moved into the galaxy. We'd not encountered them before, but backtracking their path, we discovered a swathe of destruction across two galaxies. Exiles from their home, they ravaged and enslaved and took what they wanted, leaving only death and devastation behind. Until they came here and decided that the opportunity to rule, to make an empire of their own was too tempting to give up. And there was no way we could fight them—we'd made sure of that.

"Yet we had, I think, finally come to terms with our responsibility. We'd created this situation and even with the limitations we'd imposed on ourselves, we had to do something to make it right. We infiltrated. We introduced ourselves as the robot slaves of the Kamerians, saying we'd collected select species for the great Kamerian Zoo." A sharp laugh. "Which had never existed, of course, except in the legends we, ourselves, spread. Our ships had been disarmed, and with a little reconfiguration, it was easy enough to convince the Anguilar that their purpose had been to collect samples."

Lenny waved a hand and an image of an Anguilar appeared on the wall screen above the galley entrance. The high cheekbones, sharp features, pointed ears, the feathered hair slicked back in a mane all spoke to the air of superiority they seemed to share.

"The Anguilar, being Anguilar, insisted on having their own version and thus, sent all of us…all of *me*…off to collect species for their own version of the zoo." A shrug. "And I did, of course. I had to collect enough that when they checked—which happened infrequently—I could show them progress. But again, we went back to Earth to find leadership, knowing that humans were the spark the original sentience came from and thus would be more likely to provide the innovative thinking we needed. First, we chose Val to lead the refugees he brought to Sanctuary because they would be living under more primitive conditions and would require someone used to that, someone who could inspire them to persevere through the harshest of trials, as he himself had done in your Civil War." A nod toward me. "You, Charlie, were chosen as the commander of our forces because we needed someone who was used to the concepts of modern weaponry, someone whose mind was flexible enough to deal with this new reality to which we've introduced you."

I realized I'd been holding my breath and let it out, then I sucked in a long, shuddering lungful of air and tried not to let the eerie, dreamlike feel of the conversation drag me away from reality.

"Why," I asked him finally, "didn't you just tell us all the truth from the beginning?"

"This wasn't our first attempt," Lenny explained. "We tried this same gambit in the past with others, and every time, those we tried to recruit for this struggle wound up hating or fearing us for what we did. They considered us gods…or devils. Perhaps with some justification. But they would never trust us."

"I don't think of you as either of those," I assured him, standing, facing him as though we were looking eye to eye, though as tall as he was, it was more eye to chest. "But I can't *trust* you either, not unless you're totally honest with all of us from now on. No more secrets. Agreed?"

"Agreed," the robot said without hesitation.

"Then tell us," Laranna insisted, standing beside me, her hand grabbing mine, then fingers intertwining, "what do you expect from us, Lenny? What's your plan?"

Lenny put a hand on my shoulder, another on Laranna's, and I had a brief, irrational fear that we'd pissed him off and he was about to break our necks. But instead, the gesture was gentle, almost fatherly.

"My plans," he told us, "have come to an end with bringing you all together. From now on, the control of your path, your fate belongs to you and no other. We are no longer your gods, no longer your Creators. If we're to be anything, it is your faithful servants."

"I don't need a servant," I told him, holding out a hand. "But I'd like very much if you were a friend."

"Hell," Giblet murmured, "I was just thinking it would be kind of cool having a robot servant."

Lenny didn't bother acknowledging the comment, just accepted my hand. His skin was hard metal, but I was always surprised when it wasn't cold. He felt *alive* somehow. And from what he'd just told us, I suppose he was.

"Now we know the truth," Laranna said, looking between Lenny and me. "That still doesn't answer the big question."

I shook my head, uncomprehending.

"What the hell do we do about it?"

3

LIKE SOME VENGEFUL god had flipped a switch, the battle was on.

Pulse cannon bursts streaked red against the dark circle of the moon, too far away to do more than singe Giblet's paint even without shields, and I imagined the lead pilot getting his ass chewed by his flight leader. Or maybe not, since the rest of the Anguilar squadrons opened up on the heels of his shots. Giblet held his fire until the enemy was so close that the scalar energy arced in a half-halo across his shields, and I was about to hit the comms and tell him to stop toying with them.

But Gib knew exactly how far to push it, and before I could thumb the transmit key, a particle blast lanced across the half-mile between the nose of his Vanguard and the wing of a Star-blade. The short-range fighter disappeared in a globe of white fire, a Christmas-tree ornament hung on nothingness, every molecule converted to energy and burning gas.

The cat was out of the bag and the reaction of the Starblades was instantaneous. Doctrine for these guys was to keep a tight formation to maximize the firepower they could focus on a single target, but all that would accomplish against ships with particle cannons and shields would be to get more of the Starblades destroyed at once. They did the right thing, scattering like cockroaches at the light.

Running away might have been the sensible thing, but they didn't have the option. There was no place out here to hide, no ship to take them to safety and landing on the moon would either make them sitting ducks or leave them stranded in frozen wastes, waiting for the cold to take them.

They knew it and they didn't give up, didn't sail off into nothingness. The Starblades regrouped into a wider formation, clustered in groups of two, a loose diamond against the blackness, their drive flares rivaling the stars.

"Go ahead and make for the surface," Gib told me. "We'll handle these guys."

"Copy that. Good luck." I turned and grinned at Dani. "Now all we have to do is follow the Yellow Brick Road."

I knew from Brazzo's lectures when he'd been teaching me to operate a lander that there were all sorts of complicated calculations involved in entering orbit around a planet and a hell of a lot more when you tried to deorbit and land on the surface. I'd watched shuttle takeoffs and landings, read about the Apollo missions, so I was familiar with the concept but had no clue how to do the math. The point of Brazzo's lessons had been that the computer-assisted flight did all those calculations for me.

All I had to do was find the spot I was looking for on the navigation board and tell the computer that was where I wanted to go, then it projected a course on the screen for me, a yellow strip across space that I'd taken to calling the Yellow Brick Road. After spending hours and hours in Lenny's simulator, I'd gotten to where I could keep to the course without yanking the steering yoke back and forth like a driving scene on a TV cop show.

The tricky part was keeping to the Road while also keeping an eye on the others. Eleven green dots strung out behind me in a double wedge with Laranna at the front, while the other twelve birds had stayed behind with Giblet, spiraling into a globular cluster. The fire between their fighters and ours didn't show up on the sensors, but I inferred its existence by the way the red icons kept winking out.

"Not a fair fight," Dani mused, her eyes on the sensor screen as well.

"I'd feel worse if it was," I confessed.

"Isn't that a little cold-blooded?" She wasn't exactly glaring at me, but I could feel her look even if I was trying to pay attention to our course on the screen.

"You didn't see Peboktan." My lip quivered at the thought of an entire world, just as big and green and living as Earth, reduced to molten rock. "You weren't on Copperell, or on Strada before we liberated it. The Anguilar have enslaved entire worlds, killed tens of thousands of civilians, and killed a whole planet. I don't like war, but I'd like losing this one even less."

"I guess I'm just coming from a time when we've been fighting a lot of wars and not bothering to win them."

I winced. She'd told me about what had happened the last twenty years or so back on Earth, and I didn't like a lot of what I heard.

"Maybe things would be different," I said, "if you'd been fighting for your right to exist. Losing isn't an option."

"We have fighters peeling off from the main body to come after us," Laranna told me.

I checked the tactical sensors and spotted ten of the red dots heading our way. The Vanguards had the advantage for a long-distance race, but the Starblades were sprinters. They were going to catch us before we hit atmosphere. And maybe they couldn't take us one-on-one with their light pulse cannons, but the problem was, with them in the air, we couldn't land. The Vanguards might have shields, but our body armor didn't.

"Damn," I murmured. "No choice. We're gonna have to turn and fight."

I'd opened my mouth to give the order when space ripped open behind us, right at the edge of safe jump distance, the tattered edges of the rainbow ring disgorging a starship the size of a New York City skyscraper. The *Liberator* roared after us on pillars of fire, her particle cannons slashing across a mile of open space and erasing one of the Starblades from existence.

"Sorry we're late," Val drawled over the cockpit speakers. "Didn't want to send the birds scattering from the nest too quickly."

"You're just in time, *Liberator*," I assured him.

Val wasn't actually flying the ship, of course—that fell to the

Copperell flight crews and the Peboktan engineers. But Lenny not only couldn't fire the weapons due to his programming, he couldn't even give the orders to take the ship into battle. Which was damned inconvenient in some ways, but now that he'd told us his story, I could understand it.

If the Anguilar pilots had managed to keep their heads and stay in the fight even in the face of the superior Vanguard wing, no one could blame them for breaking off now. They might not have grasped yet how heavily shielded the starfighters were, but they had to know that nothing except an Anguilar cruiser could take on something as big as the *Liberator*.

"Where the hell are they going?" Dani wondered, twisting around as far as she could to watch the fighters spinning and banking to run from the huge ship.

"I'd bet they don't even know."

"Charlie," Val called, "you want us to go ahead and launch the landers?"

"Not yet," I told him. "Hang in geosynchronous orbit and wait for our call. No use risking the ground troops until we're sure."

"We got an orbital defense platform coming around the terminator," Laranna reported, nearly stepping on my transmission.

Cursing under my breath, I tapped the red diamond on the sensor screen, and it obliged by zooming into the symbol until it became an actual shape rather than an icon. Squared off on the top, it narrowed into a second platform beneath the first, then further into what looked like a spike pointing toward the surface. I'd studied the identification files for Anguilar ships and platforms, and I recognized the model immediately.

"The fighters launched from there," I said, pointing at the second platform and nodding to Dani. "It's like an orbital aircraft carrier."

"What's that big phallic looking thing sticking down from it? Overcompensation?"

I barked a laugh.

"Sort of. It's a big-ass particle cannon."

"Then why's it pointed at the planet?" she asked. "Shouldn't it be aimed out here if the thing is meant to defend against attacks from"—she waved around us—"out here?"

"Just watch," I told her, pointing at the platform.

It was turning. That should have surprised me, but I knew from the files I'd read that it was designed for it, and it wasn't as if it had to worry about planetary gravity, since it generated its own.

"All right, hang on."

It meant turning away from our Yellow Brick Road, but I figured the navigational computer would understand. I tapped the platform's icon, held it down until it flashed three times and moved to the navigational display. The Road shifted, and I pulled the steering yoke up and to the left to follow it. There were two red lines across the tactical screen now, the one for our particle cannon and another for theirs.

"Um, Charlie," Laranna called, "perhaps you should let one

of us take care of that for you? Seeing as how you're our *commander?*"

"Nope," I muttered, lining up the targeting reticle, keeping one eye on those range lines. "Either I'm leading or I'm not, and I don't lead from the rear."

"Dammit, Charlie Travers…"

She didn't bother to finish the thought, probably because she knew it wouldn't do any good, or maybe because she didn't want to distract me. We were close enough to the moon now that the darkness of its night side swallowed up everything else, blocking out not just the stars to one side but the gas giant to the other. But against that darkness was the glint of the sun around the terminator off the edge of the platform and even without the light, the cockpit optics showed us the lines of the massive orbital structure as it slowly swiveled in place.

The weapon that, thanks to Dani, I now couldn't think of as anything but a *dick cannon* turned inexorably our way, *my* way, as if it had a grudge specifically with me. The Vanguard's shields were tough, maybe tough enough to take a shot from a particle cannon at extreme range, but I had no desire to test the theory. Those red lines were getting damned close to intersecting, and I licked my lips, my mouth suddenly dry.

A sharp pull up on the steering yoke just as the two firing arcs touched, and we were adding degrees to the turn the platform had to make to target us. It wasn't natural for me, not the way it might have been for someone actually trained on a bird like this. I had to think about it, but it also wasn't that hard a thought. Slide my finger across the throttle to kill the drives, then turn the yoke sideways, the maneuvering thrusters banging emphatically against the fuselage like stomping feet keeping time with a song.

Oh, shit. I forgot to put on some tunes.

Too late now. The targeting reticle floated across the widest section of the orbital platform, and I pressed the firing stud. Coruscating white energy crackled out from the nose of the Vanguard and burned its way through the superstructure of the defense satellite. If it had been a ship that size, I wouldn't have expected one shot to take it down, but starships have shields. It's part of having a hyperdrive, and no defense platform was going to come equipped with a hyperdrive, particularly not one dropped way out in the middle of nowhere in a base barely worth maintaining.

The particle blast ripped the hangar bay apart and penetrated straight down into the thing's power core. The platform swelled, coming apart at seams rimmed with white fire, a balloon filled with gasoline and set aflame. A cascade of glowing metal expanded at the edge of plumes of burning vapor, destined to shower down upon the moon like a swarm of fireflies. I wondered if the enemy troops looking up would realize what the light show meant.

"We're clear," I reported, just in case any of the others had missed the explosion. "Follow me down."

The dive through the moon's atmosphere would have been suicidal in any spacecraft NASA had ever built, would have burned us up if it hadn't crushed us to paste from the *g*-forces. Thank God for the technology Lenny and his robot brothers had brought with them from some other galaxy a long time ago, though, because shields and gravity resist kept us alive. Even that wasn't enough to keep us comfortable. As near as I could figure after meandering conversations with Mallarna, the inertial dampeners that kept gravity and acceleration from smashing us into the floorboards worked kind of like a shock absorber, taking in all that kinetic energy until it bottomed out and had to pass some on to the poor suckers in the spaceship. And the larger the ship, the bigger the shocks it could absorb.

The fighter was pretty small by comparison to something like the *Liberator*, which meant even more of that shock got past, and it was enough to slam me back into the padded seat with a feeling not just like being punched in the face but like someone was continuously punching me in the face for the better part of five minutes. It was all I could do to keep hold of the control yoke and stay in the middle of that yellow line. We could have gone down an easier route, of course, could have done a few orbits and never even spilled our drinks, but that would have made us easy targets for whatever might be shooting at us from the ground.

It was hard to pay attention to the details on the surface with the weight of a jersey cow resting against my chest, but I got the impression of snow-capped mountains and distant glaciers, of tall evergreens, or the local equivalent thereof, and half-frozen rivers flowing down from the glaciers to the ice-rimmed sea. I would have missed the base altogether if I'd only been counting on my eyes to find it. It was half-buried in the snow, only corners sticking out of the winter wonderland of Aether's equator, the warmest spot on the moon. But it glowed on thermal, a bonfire amid the blizzard, even before the Anguilar garrison was kind enough to send up a signal flare by opening up on us with ground-based pulse turrets.

A spider-web of cross-hatched crimson energy sliced across the night sky, searching for us, fired from the four corners of the Anguilar base. The fighter shuddered as the shields converted scalar energy into momentum and some of it fed back through the fuselage, arcs of angry red forming in a sphere around the Vanguard as it speared straight toward the ground, the galaxy's biggest lawn dart.

I had to pull up, but I had one of those gun turrets lined right up with my particle cannon, and I wasn't going to waste the opportunity. If the base was a medieval castle buried half under snow, the gun positions were the turrets, crenelations rising above the rooftops, each with a quad-mounted pulse cannon. Begging to be taken out. I tapped the trigger, and it was gone, erupting in a volcano of billowing smoke and flame, and before the mushroom cloud had the time to rise above the surrounding trees, I was pulling up.

The yoke resisted, not hard but insistent, and I had to argue with it, then slide the throttle open, the Vanguard tilting upward, the exhaust from the drives sending twisting billows of steam rising up as snow melted a hundred feet below us. My stomach swirled with the steam, and I twisted the yoke, spinning us toward the other turrets.

"Fire!" I snapped at Dani, but she was doing it already, traversing our pulse cannons left to right.

Threads of fire tied us to the other turrets and ripped into the roof of the base along the way, but before Dani had the chance to finish off the last, a particle cannon lanced out of the sky and blew it and a corner of the roof into ashes and molten metal.

Four Vanguards rumbled overhead while Laranna's plane side-stepped into a hover less than a hundred yards from us.

"We'll finish up here," she told me, the words punctuated by her gunner sweeping bursts of pulse fire across the front of a column of armored vehicles as they burst out of double doors at the front of the base. Snow and ice transformed into a veil of steam, hiding the ugly reality of their fate from the rest of the world. "You two get to the objective. We don't want to stick around here any longer than we have to."

"Copy that," I told her. "Tell Lenny to get the landers launched. Hopefully by the time they hit the atmosphere, we'll be able to tell them where to go."

"Be careful."

"You, too," I said, already feeding power to the belly jets, taking us up another few hundred feet and heading west.

"Where is this place, anyway?" Dani asked, speaking up to be heard over the climbing roar of the drives.

"I mean, I see it on the map, but I couldn't make out anything on the way down between you flying like a maniac and the clouds over the ocean."

"I didn't see it either," I admitted, keeping our speed as high as possible without gaining too much elevation. There probably weren't any other fighters down here, but I felt better staying low. "But it's on the nav screen…" I squinted at the readout beside the uneven blob to the west of the continent. "Two hundred and fifty miles offshore. Hop, skip and a jump."

At least for a Kamerian starfighter that could hit something close to Mach 12 in the atmosphere, and might have gone faster if it weren't for turbulence. I didn't push it quite that hard, but even at a sedate Mach 3, the flight over the clouded, ice-rimmed ocean brought the hackles up on my neck the way flying through open space never had. In space, no one might have been able to hear you scream, but there was also a lot less shit to run into. Down here, every cloud bank could hide a mountain, some island that wasn't on the maps from Lenny's database. The Vanguard's shields might be able to protect us from an energy beam, they wouldn't do a damn thing about running straight into a mountain at supersonic speeds.

The clouds hid nothing but snow, and it took less than ten minutes before a break in the clouds showed the same thing as the naked eye—the island. As islands go, it wasn't much, just a big slab of white that I could have mistaken for a huge iceberg if it hadn't been on the map. Wisps of fluffy white dipped low over the jagged cliffs, barely a hint of rock showing beneath the snows of decades or centuries. It never melted here, or so I'd been told.

Backing the throttle almost to a stall, I hit the belly jets and hovered in a gentle arc around the rocky, frozen coastline. No waves broke against it because the ocean itself was trapped in the grip of the ever-winter, subdued and gentle, lacking the wild nature of a warmer clime.

"It's there somewhere," I mused, gaze flickering back and forth between the snow-covered plateau and the sensors. "There's gotta be a…"

"There!" Dani said, pointing at the screen. It wasn't much,

just the barest hint of a temperature difference on thermal, something buried deep under that hill.

"…power source," I finished, grinning. My finger tapped against the side of the control yoke in contemplation. "Well, we can bring the landers in and try to dig through all that with an excavator, or do it the easy way."

"Anything that doesn't put me out there for hours in that death-cold sounds better," Dani opined, leaning back with her arms crossed.

"It's settled, then."

Just a few ounces of pressure on the controls, circling back around the island until that thermal reading was at its strongest, then back to a hover. A flick of my thumb on the arming control and a targeting reticle floated red just a couple degrees away from the power source down there. I pulled the trigger.

The particle cannon was a lightning bolt crackling between clouds, an explosion of superheated air that drove a concussion wave in every direction, including back at us, and I struggled with the controls to maintain our position as the entire fuselage bucked and shimmied. Curtains of steam billowed off the mountain, ice and snow melting for the first time in centuries…but not the first time ever.

Steam condensed into a brief deluge of rain and snow, and once it had cleared, a crater bigger than an Olympic swimming pool had been blown into the side of the mountain. Except it wasn't a mountain, was no sort of natural feature. Gray metal showed through where it wasn't charred to black, hard edges and straight lines, visible on either side of that crater for a hundred yards.

The mountain was the remains of a starship, crashed on this island centuries ago. I hunted along the base of the artificial plateau, found a likely flat spot and hoped it would support the fighter.

"Get buttoned up," I told Dani. "It's about to get cold."

4

"Let's think about what we need," I said, tossing my fork down on an empty plate during that fateful dinner conversation weeks ago, trying to answer Laranna's question.

Everyone else still seemed in shock from Lenny's explanation of their own history, even Val, to whom it surely mattered less than the non-humans at the table, particularly the senior officers from the Copperell and the Strada. Watching their reactions, I was grateful we hadn't included the entire ship's complement in the meeting. I considered Mallarna one of the most stable and level-headed people on our crew, but the Peboktan looked as if she were torn between disbelief and rage at the story. Best to get them thinking about something else.

"We need a shower," Giblet opined dryly. Okay, not *everyone* was in shock. "And a change of clothes. Couldn't we talk about this later?"

I offered him a scowl and a meaningful tilt of my head toward the others. Giblet sighed and settled back into his chair.

"We have warships," Laranna said. "We need to use them."

"No, we don't have warships," I corrected her and earned a raised eyebrow for my trouble. I jerked a thumb over my shoulder in the general direction of the hangar bay. "We have *starfighters*. There's a difference. We have an entire flight crew of Copperell who know how to run the bridge of a cruiser and an engineering crew of Peboktan who could maintain it. These aren't cruisers." I looked around the table. "How many people here ever flew a fighter before?"

Giblet raised his hand a bit smugly, and I waved acknowledgement.

"And Gib's experience consists of exactly one flight in a short-range Starblade…and that ended in a crash."

"Hey, any landing you can walk away from…" Giblet said with a defensive scowl.

"Look," I said, shaping the argument with my hands, "any of us can learn how to fly the things, how to shoot the guns. With a little practice, we can use them for hyperspace travel, though I sure as hell wouldn't want to spend a whole week cooped up in that cockpit, especially with someone I didn't feel comfortable taking a sponge bath in front of, because it would get pretty ripe."

Chuckles at that, as I'd intended. I was trying to loosen them up *and* get them thinking about something other than Lenny and his people basically creating all their species.

"But the real issue is using these things to their full potential.

We can blow up enemy fighters with these things all day long, but to go up against cruisers, to use them like we intended, to take the fight to the Anguilar strongholds, we can't just be each of us fighting our individual battle. We have to fly like we've been trained for it."

"Well, that's the problem, right?" Giblet asked. "There ain't no one left to train us. The last pilots to get trained to fly these things died during the war."

"I doubt there are even technical manuals left after all this time," Mallarna lamented, her hands wrapped around some kind of hot drink that smelled too bad and looked too thick for me to even think about trying. "These planes…from what I've read in their on-board documentation, they were introduced just before the end of the Centennial War, less than five years before Kameria was laid waste."

"What happened to Kameria?" Dani asked, leaning on her chin, tapping her fork against the table. "Was it destroyed? Like…" She reddened as she realized what she was about to ask but had to follow through now. "Like Peboktan?"

"No," Mallarna replied, just a slight downward flicker of her eyes indicating she'd felt any fresh grief because of the reference. "No one had the capability or the will to commit such an atrocity before the Anguilar arrived. The Kamerian cities were laid waste, their society destroyed, but the people still survive. Those on the planet have regressed so far into savagery that not even the Anguilar would recruit them for cannon fodder. And the ones who escaped the wrath of their victims are like Seraph Nix, violent and bloodthirsty, selling their services as mercenaries since they lack a home to return to."

I rubbed my thumbs against my temples, trying to think.

"Well, that sucks. It sounds like not only do we not know how to use these things, but there isn't anyone alive who can teach us."

"That," Lenny said, speaking up for the first time since his confession had ended, "may not be true."

All eyes turned his way, and though a robot couldn't blush, I felt as if he shrank under the attention.

"Enlighten us," Laranna said, an edge to the words that said she still wasn't quite over the revelations he'd shared with us.

"Centuries ago," he explained, "near the end of the war, we received intelligence of a last-ditch Kamerian effort to set up new bases farther out from their homeworld in the event they needed to transfer their military and political command structure away from Kameria. They never got the chance, of course, but they tried. I sent one of our ships—one of the five we have in our fleet now—to investigate a report that an Anguilar cruiser was taking several squadrons of Vanguard starfighters to Aether, the habitable moon of a gas giant in Alpha Sector. We intercepted the cruiser and destroyed her drives. Her course brought her into the gravitational pull of the moon, and she crashed on an island in the northeastern ocean."

"So, there might be more starfighters on this…Aether place?" I asked, leaning forward, curious now.

"No. Once the cruiser had impacted, we flew low over the island and scanned the wreckage. If we'd left the fighters intact, there would have been a chance that the Kamerians would come back and try to salvage them. The hangar bay was totally destroyed, along with everything in it."

"Well, damn," I murmured, settling back into my seat.

"But." He rolled to the other side of the room, then back, as if pacing. "We *did* detect a faint energy signature. Just enough to power a handful of stasis pods. And from the position of the pods and our knowledge of the disposition of the personnel in Anguilar cruisers, there's a good chance that the stasis pods were in the section of the Vanguard flight crews."

"I don't get it," Dani admitted, frowning. "You knew there were survivors, but you didn't go down and try to rescue them?"

"What would we have done with prisoners?" Lenny asked, staring at her without comprehension.

I squirmed a little, feeling bad because I hadn't even considered the question. And remembering what I'd done when the matter had come up for us with the Anguilar. Apparently, Lenny wasn't quite as dense as I'd thought, because he at least recognized that the matter required further explanation.

"These ships did not have crews, Deputy Campling. It was just me. I would have been required to personally send this body down into the ship and make multiple trips into orbit, leaving myself open, during that time, to possible counterattack by the Kamerians."

Dani grunted, not sounding satisfied with the answer but not pressing the matter any further. I decided to change the subject before she changed her mind.

"Even if the stasis pods were the flight crew, could they have lasted this long? I mean, I know Val was in the freezer for like a hundred and fifty years, but this is a lot longer than that and they're in the middle of a wrecked ship. Wouldn't the power have run down by now?"

"Unknowable. The only way to find out for sure is to go there and see for ourselves."

"Hold on a second," Laranna said, hand slashing crossways as if cutting through the conversation to halt it. "Even if those pods are still intact, we're still talking about Kamerians. They were assholes then and, from what we've seen of Seraph Nix, they're assholes now. What makes you think a bunch of assholes from *then* are going to want to help us *now?*"

"I certainly wouldn't trust Kamerians with our most powerful weapons," Mallarna declared. She shrugged. "But it might be possible to question them, press them for insights into the Vanguards."

"And offer them *what* in return?" Val wondered. He hadn't said much, and I thought it was probably because he had no desire to fly or even ride in one of the fighters. He tapped his chest. "I got a fair idea of what they're going to experience when you thaw them out. Their home doesn't exist anymore, everyone else they know is dead, they have no purpose. I tell ya what, if Lenny had woken me up and offered me that kind of life without me meeting Brandy and Maxx first, I'd have turned him down flat."

"So," Giblet said, shrugging, "you're saying all we gotta do is find these guys girlfriends and they'll sign right up?"

Dani sighed heavily and Laranna smacked Giblet in the back

of the head, saving me the trouble. Giblet winced and shot her a dirty look.

"You're right, Val," I acknowledged. "They're not going to have much motivation to help us…unless we give them one." I nodded to Mallarna. "You said Kameria has fallen into savagery, that no one wants to bother to take it over because the natives are too violent." I tilted my head in a shrug. "Sounds like just the kind of place that would be easy to take over for a few motivated Kamerians."

I thought it was clever, but the others just stared at me with doubt in their eyes.

"You really think that'll work?" Dani asked.

I stood, grabbing my tray and taking it to the recycling bin as a way of shutting down the discussion. I'd listened to their concerns, but someone had to make the final decision, and they'd decided that was me.

"There's only one way to find out."

"Shit, it's freezing!" Dani exclaimed, stepping out into the tightly packed snow.

She wasn't wrong. The external temperature monitor in my helmet display put it at negative fifty, not counting the wind chill factor. And there was a hell of a lot of wind chill. It shoved me around even with the added weight of the armor, and I dug the spiked soles of my boots into the snow and ice to keep my footing.

"Turn your heat up," I told her. "Control is on your left wrist, second menu."

I'd cranked mine up before we got out of the fighter, risking being uncomfortably warm for the last few minutes to avoid the biting cold…though I couldn't avoid it entirely. Every time the wind hit me, my toes and fingertips went numb, the armor's heating coils notwithstanding, and my faceplate's defogging circuits couldn't quite keep up with the condensation.

I'd never been on a glacier. George told me that his parents had gone to Alaska once and taken a chartered bush plane that landed them on a glacier, that they'd considered it a life-changing experience. This was impressive all right, but life-changing, I wasn't so sure of. Life-*threatening*, that I was convinced of.

Everything was white, covered in snow. Even where the particle cannon blast had scoured away centuries of ice the snow was already blowing in to coat the bare metal, as if nature were embarrassed by the presence of the Kamerian cruiser and wanted to erase it. Which I wouldn't have had a problem with if I hadn't been standing on top of the thing. It might have been scenic as hell, but all I could see was what was twenty feet in front of me.

I knew the direction I had to go…up.

"Use your spikes," I told Dani. "One hand for you and the other for the mountain."

"It's not a mountain," she informed me.

"Close enough."

There was only one obvious way up to the ragged hole in the side of the cruiser and it still wasn't a great way. Spikes dug in, fingers followed, and I braced myself for the snow to give way, but there was hard ice beneath it and if that wasn't ideal, it was better than my hand sinking into nothing. The saving grace of Aether was that the moon was smaller than Earth, about the size of Mars. The gravity was heavier than Mars, though, because the moon was denser at its core. Maybe two-thirds Earth gravity, which was a very good thing since I never could have made this ascent in full body armor if I was lugging around my normal weight.

Up and up and still up and I had to force myself to check back over my shoulder to make sure Dani was still there because I didn't want to look down. It hadn't looked like this long of a climb from the base, but it was a good twenty minutes before I reached the edge of the hole I'd blasted from the fighter. There'd been enough time for it to cool down, thankfully, but the edge was smooth, like molten rock that had resolidified. Three feet of it and somehow, I had to get up onto it.

There was only one way and I hated it. I knelt down and jumped. If I screwed it up, I was going to wind up tumbling back down the cliff and I'd probably survive because of the armor and the snow, but I would look so freaking stupid. But I got one foot up on the edge of the hole and pushed forward with it, the spikes barely giving me enough purchase to slide into a seated position.

"You know there's no way in hell I'm about to do that," Dani said, staring up at me.

Sighing, I shifted onto my belly, extended my arm out, hand open.

"Don't worry, I got you."

By the barely audible muttering over the helmet comms, she wasn't convinced, but she did it anyway. As embarrassing as falling myself would have been, missing her hand would have been equally, as Dani had told me it was called in 2023, cringe. I almost did. Her jump didn't carry quite as far as mine, probably because she wasn't used to wearing the armor, and I had to lunge forward to catch her forearm.

And slid. That ledge was just as smooth and polished from one side to the other, and if it had been hot enough for a few minutes to keep ice from forming, that just meant it was wet with melted snow.

"Shit!" I blurted, digging a heel into the metal and pulling for all I was worth, the spikes on the bottom giving me just enough friction to pull Dani's center of gravity over the edge.

My heel was less than an inch from sliding all the way off. I collapsed backward, arms aching, and gasped for breath until I had the energy to move again.

"How're we gonna get down?" Dani asked, looking back over the edge as I carefully got to my feet and ice-skated across the slick section of hull until I reached the interior of the ship.

"Getting down is easy. Lighter gravity, thick snow." The deck was four feet below the edge of the hole, and I demonstrated by jumping down to it. My boots clomped loudly on the metal. "Getting the stasis pods down is going to be the hard part. Probably have to rig up a pulley system with a winch when the landers get here."

The corridor was as dark as death and I flicked on the helmet lights, not satisfied with the dim, green twilight of the enhanced optics. Charred metal, molten rolls where the beam had pene-trated all the way through the hull and into the passageways, melting and then solidifying into modern-art sculptures that were still red hot. It might have been uncomfortably warm if the external temps hadn't been so frigid.

The footing was easier than it had been on the ledge but not by much. Fragments of metal had fused with the deck, putting up an obstacle course of jagged punji sticks interspersed with smooth, slick patches of glassy deck plate.

"Careful," I said.

"Yeah, got that, thanks."

Picking our way through the metal minefield took longer than climbing up the cliff and was probably more dangerous, though it hadn't felt like it. I had to stop and check twice on my forearm display to make sure we were going the right direction, and it was a relief when we hit the intersection to turn left away from the wreckage. Sort of.

The wreckage had, at least, been a distraction from the nature of the ship. Kamerian cruisers, it turned out, shared pretty much the same layout as the Anguilar versions, form following function, but there were subtle differences. The lines were broader, harsher, more aggressive in ways where the Anguilar had gone for pure efficiency. The Anguilar didn't see themselves as conquerors the way the Kamerians did, didn't revel in the violence, in showing their prowess in battle. The Anguilar saw the rest of the galaxy as resources to be exploited, sort of like the Belgians in the Congo back in the 19th Century. The Kamerians were more like the Mongols, or the Huns, and it showed in their architecture.

We hit the first bodies about two hundred yards in. Well, I should say *mummies*. These had died in the crash, I guessed from the way their limbs were twisted and broken and from the lack of burn marks on their spacesuits. They wore pressure suits but no helmets, and despite the dried and shrunken skin wrapped over their skulls like masks, I could still tell they were Kamerian. There was no mistaking the strong jawline, the slightly pointed teeth. The symbol emblazoned on their suit chests was familiar, the same one I'd seen on the *Revenant*.

"Hope those weren't the pilots," Dani murmured, her light playing over the gruesome remains.

"The stasis chamber is this way," I said, waving her toward a hatch to the left.

It was closed and, I discovered when I tried the lever to open it, locked. I pushed harder on it, thinking it might just be frozen after all this time, then slammed my shoulder into it, which only rewarded me with a sore shoulder.

"I hope we have a key," Dani said drily.

By way of reply, I swung the pulse rifle off my shoulder and waved her back, then leveled it at the lock.

"That only works in movies," she objected, "not in real life."

"*Bullets* don't work on door locks," I corrected her. I pulled the trigger.

I wouldn't have tried it without the armor and I ducked back reflexively even with its protection as a spray of sparks shot back toward my face. Smoke curled up from the blackened and fragmented remains of the lock and the hatch swung inward with a plaintive creak of age and corrosion.

The compartment inside the door, unlike the rest of the ship, was *not* completely dark. A subdued, green glow shone from the far end of the chamber, casting an eerie glint over the lines of transparent cylinders in double rows against the walls. Most were empty, their lids yawning open, but as we passed by those, the next few had been sealed up, their interior hidden behind a layer of frost. I rubbed at the built-up ice with the heel of my hand and another mummy stared up at me, better preserved than the others, a female with those golden eyes intact.

The pod was just as dead, the control panel dark. So was the next bank of stasis tubes, and I didn't bother wiping those clear, already having given myself enough nightmare fuel for the rest of my life. Instead, I bypassed the pods with dead controls, searching for the source of the green glow.

"There," Dani said, pointing to my right. "That group of four at the very end."

She was right. The double row still had power, the only ones in the entire compartment, the small control panels at the head of each of them still lit up with a gentle green glow. I leaned over, read the display.

"Life signs are active," I told Dani.

I wiped the frost off the surface of the cylinder and beneath the ice and the glass-like whatever it was that made up the tube was a face. Eyes closed, not breathing, but clearly alive, not a decomposing mummy. The golden skin, the high cheekbones, the hint of a pointed tip to the ears, half-concealed by his long, dark hair. He was Kamerian, and if I remembered the insignia guide I'd read from Lenny's database, the markings on his uniform said he was a fighter pilot.

"Hey there, handsome," Dani said, looking over my shoulder. "What's your story?"

5

"WE SHOULD EJECT THEM INTO SPACE," Brother Constantine said, no rancor in his voice, as casually as if he was advising me which laundry settings to use.

I looked up from the stasis pods, offering the monk a disapproving scowl. The older man shrugged.

"They're Kamerians," he elaborated, as if that explained everything. "You could no more trust them than you could a wolf."

"Domesticated dogs descended from wolves," Dani pointed out, glaring at Constantine with her hands on her hips, which looked even sterner and more threatening since she was still in her combat armor, rifle slung across her chest. "And by the way, I didn't think I was joining the side that was into war crimes."

The medical bay of the *Liberator* was crowded, not just with the four Kamerian stasis pods and the portable generator that we'd used to keep the things working once we got them loaded onto a lander, not just with the Peboktan and Copperell techs and medical crew, but us as well. The team, Laranna, Val, Giblet, Dani, Mallarna, and me, all of us armed and watchful. And Constantine and Lenny, of course, though I had my doubts about that.

"Should you be here?" I asked Lenny. "I mean, you did kind of destroy these guys' civilization and kick their asses in the war. Maybe we should hold off on rubbing their noses in that."

"No," Giblet declared before Lenny could answer. I thought he might be about to make a wisecrack, since that was his usual MO in inappropriate situations, but his manner was dead serious, and his eyes burned like coals. "Dani was right...the Kamerians are more like dogs than wolves. When you want a dog to behave, you show him right away who the alpha is. They lost the war, and they need to know it right away unless you want them to have the upper hand."

I nodded. That made sense. I motioned to the head medical tech, a Copperell woman named Mara.

"Go ahead and wake them up."

The crew moved in and worked the control panels, scrolling through menus until their efforts paid off in a series of high-pitched beeps. As they worked, I frowned at a thought.

"Hey Lenny," I said, "how come these guys got to ride out their stasis with their clothes on but I woke up naked?"

"These pods were specifically designed for Kamerians," Lenny explained. "The ones aboard the *Liberator* were made to adapt to multiple species."

I wasn't sure if I was convinced but the time for conversation was over. Air hissed out in wisps of condensation as the lids of the stasis pods cracked, swinging aside. I moved forward next to Dani, bringing my pulse rifle to low port. It would suck to have to shoot these guys after going to so much trouble to find them, but coming out of hibernation was confusing and Constantine was right. These guys *were* Kamerian. Well, three guys and a girl. One of them was obviously female in all the glorious ways that mammalian, humanoid bipeds were, although the look of the Kamerians was too predatory for me to find her anything but deadly.

Nothing happened for long seconds, and I looked at Laranna and then Dr. Mara, wondering if we'd wasted our time after all. A loud gasp from the pod to the right brought my rifle up reflexively, and when a hand grasped the open edge of the pod, I nearly pulled the trigger.

It was Handsome, the first one we'd found on the Kamerian cruiser, his golden eyes going wide as he looked around him. Intelligence flickered behind the shock, and I noted the order of the way he took in his surroundings. First me, the muzzle of my pulse rifle trained on him, a slight narrowing of his eyes, probably because he didn't recognize humans. Then Giblet and Laranna, just the hint of a nod at the familiar, peoples his Alliance had conquered. Lenny and eyes and nostrils flared with instinctive anger, but I also saw him fighting the reaction, realizing that flying off the handle would be a bad idea with all the guns trained on him.

And finally to Dani and the twitch of an eyebrow that spoke

not of anger or surprise but…interest? I suppressed a chuckle. This guy *was* a dog. *And* a wolf.

His hands raised slowly and carefully.

The others roused slower, their reactions more pronounced. One of the two other males was shorter, obviously younger, and shock overrode every other reaction on his face, while the female was completely under control, a perfect poker face. But the last of them was huge, taller even than Handsome, his features pronounced and exaggerated, as was his expression when he saw Lenny.

"Demon!" the big Kamerian bellowed and lurched upward out of the stasis pod, more agile and full of energy than I'd been when I first woke up from stasis.

I'm not sure what he thought he was going to do with his bare hands against a seven-foot-tall robot, but it was possible he was confused and hadn't thought it through. In retrospect, maybe I should have let him have a go at it, just for shits and giggles, but reflexes took hold, and I swung the butt of my rifle across his face. Also in hindsight, that might have been a bit too violent a response, since if it had been a human, a blow like that would have had a good chance at breaking his jaw, if not his neck.

I certainly *thought* I had when I felt the impact of the strike up my hands and into my upper back, heard the solid, metal-on-bone *thock*. His head jerked backward, and he slumped into the stasis pod, but these Kamerians were made of sterner stuff because he immediately shook his head and rubbed at his jaw as if I'd punched him instead of butt-stroking him. Amber eyes glared at me hard enough to burn holes through my chest, but the muzzle end of the rifle kept him immobile.

"Calm the hell down," I told him. "I just went to a lot of trouble to pull you out of the wrecked cruiser, and I'd rather not have to shoot you and make all that a waste of time. Go ahead and sit up…*slow*."

They did, Handsome the slowest of all. He was a thinker. Gears were turning behind his eyes, and he would have made a hell of a poker player, not giving anything away with his expression. He worried me.

"I'm Charlie Travers. What are your names?"

From the stubborn set of their eyes, not one of them was going to say a word. Except Handsome.

"I'm Tamura Tel," he said, offering what I thought was a salute, touching his right hand to his left shoulder. "Captain in the Kamerian Alliance. This," he went on, motioning at the big guy, the one I'd hit, "is Lt. Dothan Abur, my second in command." A nod to the female. "Junior Lieutenant Sainrastil Gant." Then the younger male. "And Jr.-LT Fenris Osa."

"You're all pilots," I said, gesturing toward the symbol on the chest of his uniform. "Vanguard starfighter pilots, right?"

A waft of air reached me from the pods and my nose wrinkled. These guys needed hundreds of years' worth of showers, and quick.

"We are," Tamura confirmed. He looked as if he wanted to stand up from his pod and I nodded to him, backing up a step to give him room…and so I could still cover him with my rifle. "I take it you are forces of the Coalition and you've taken us prisoner? That's not the…usual way of your people in this war."

"The war is over," Lenny said. I was surprised that he spoke. I hadn't had the impression that he wished to deal with the Kamerians at all. "It's been over for hundreds of years. While you've slept."

"I don't believe you!" Dothan Abur snapped, jumping to his feet, but this time staying his motion at the sight of a half-dozen pulse rifles pointed his way. He eyed Tamura. "This is a damned Coalition trick, Captain! You know you can't trust these demons!"

"You know the Strada, Kamerian?" Laranna asked, stepping up beside me, meeting the pilots' eyes without flinching. "You've fought us, have you not? So say the legends of my people."

"Aye, we know of you Strada," Tamura agreed. He smiled toothily, and when some of those teeth are pointed, that's the toothiest of toothy you can get. "Though I, fortunately, have not had to face you, since you're well known as foot soldiers, not fighter pilots."

"Then you know we do not lie," she said, ignoring his attempts at charm. "It would violate our honor."

Tamura shared a look with his fellow pilots and eventually, each of them nodded.

"Yes, we have heard that."

"Then believe me when I tell you," Laranna said, "that the Centennial War ended hundreds of years ago, not long after you crashed. You've been in stasis ever since. You can check the readouts on your pods."

The female, Sainrastil, clambered out of her pod and tapped

at the display of the control panel, froze there for several seconds, blinking rapidly, as if she couldn't believe what she was reading. I couldn't imagine a Kamerian weeping, but when she finally looked up at Tamura, a tear glinted in one eye.

"They're telling the truth."

"How long?" Fenris, the youngest demanded, features falling as if he'd just realized what the truth meant.

"Long enough. Long enough that the Alliance is gone, along with everyone we ever knew." Sainrastil wiped a sleeve across her face, her shoulders sagging as she leaned against the stasis tube. "You should have left us to die."

"Yet they didn't," Tamura said, not nearly as moved by the loss of family and friends. Maybe, I thought, he didn't have any. Or at least any he cared about. "You need us for something."

Yeah, this dude was smart.

"Things have changed since the war," Giblet told him, but now Tamura came as close as I'd seen yet to losing his cool.

"No!" he snapped, raising a finger, glaring at Giblet and then at me. "Whatever you want, you're not going to get it unless the Varnell keeps his mouth shut. I know what they're capable of, and I won't have my mind twisted by his words."

"Racist," Giblet said, scowling.

"It's okay, Gib," I told him, waving it away. "He's right, though. Everything has changed. The galaxy you left behind fell right along with your Alliance."

I was recalling Lenny's explanation and wished I could let him give it, but I doubted the Kamerians wanted to hear from one of the robots that had brought down their civilization any more than they wanted to be mesmerized by a Varnell.

"Everything crashed, not just your ship," Laranna said, taking up the explanation. "The Creators abandoned us." She eyed Lenny. "However well-meaning their reasons for doing so, they left us to our own devices. With the losses we'd all taken during the war, trade routes fell apart, and the Coalition dissolved as if it had never been. It was every system for itself, and with the disappearance of the Creators and most of the industrial base of the galaxy…" She shook her head.

I finished it for her. Sometimes it was easier to get to the point when you hadn't lived through it.

"No one makes anything anymore. No more gravity control, no more power cells, no more hyperdrives. Everything gets reused, salvaged, pirated, sold on the black market. No one could build up their fleet beyond what they had left after the war, and no one watched anyone else's back. Which made this whole galaxy just ripe for the picking."

Lenny glanced at the large display on the far wall and an Anguilar appeared there, haughty and superior.

"They're scavengers," Lenny explained. "Exiles from outside this galaxy. They came here to loot and pillage but stayed to build their own empire. To enslave worlds…and destroy those who wouldn't submit."

Tamura stared daggers for a moment at the robot, but then sighed, as if reaching a conclusion.

"And what do you want with us?"

I looked them over, finally noticing the fatigue I'd expected from the beginning.

"You're tired, hungry and"—I shrugged—"being honest, pretty damned grimy after all that time in the tube. I'm gonna have our people escort you to the showers, get you some fresh clothes and then give you some food. After that…" I smiled tightly. "We can do a little show and tell."

"WHERE IN THE name of the Blood God," Dothan rumbled, his voice like boulders crashing on a field of gravel, "did you find these?"

He ran a hand down the flank of a Vanguard starfighter, as gentle as a man caressing his lover. Probably as gently as this big lunkhead had ever touched anything in his whole life.

He and the other pilots looked out of place in the generic gray fatigues our people used, and I'd assured them that the *Liberator* had the capability to duplicate their flight suits, but I was having second thoughts about that. Maybe the constant reminder of their past wasn't such a good idea.

"A cache," I answered his question. "Preserved by the Creators and their Alahandran monks on an isolated world called Haven."

Tamura's quick glance showed me he'd heard of the place, but he made no comment. He and the rest of the Kamerians walked down the line of fighters in the hangar bay and I followed, the group of us flanked by Strada guards, keeping their distance but ever-vigilant. Laranna led them personally, taking no chances, and for some reason, Dani had tagged along as well, walking just behind me. For obvious reasons, Giblet had come, too, though he hung back with Laranna.

"They're in beautiful shape," Tamura admitted, swiping a finger along the wing tip of the nearest bird as if searching for dust. Then he cast an eye toward Dani. "*Very* beautiful."

I was twenty feet away from Giblet and I could still see the bristling of the feathers at the nape of his neck.

"You want to use the Vanguards against these Anguilar of yours," Tamura said, turning abruptly to face me, making my escort nervous enough for their rifles to come up a fraction. "And you want us to…" He spread his hands. "Fly for you? Fight for you?"

"Not quite," I told him, thumbs hooked in my gun belt, looking casual but keeping my right hand next to my sidearm. "We can fly them. We can even fight in them. I've destroyed two Anguilar cruisers in combat already, and I'd never even piloted a fighter of any kind before. What we *can't* do is use them to the full extent of their capabilities. Because we have no one to train our pilots."

"Ah," Tamura said, smiling broadly, genuinely, as if finally grasping the situation made him more comfortable. "Now I see." He waved at the other three pilots. "And what do you offer us in return? Besides our continued existence, I mean." He peered closely at me, a jeweler looking through a rouge to gauge the worth of a stone. "You're young, but you're not a stupid man. You wouldn't be the leader of this bunch if you were. That's why

I know you wouldn't just threaten us. Unless we have positive motivation, you'd never get the best out of us, and since there's no one else to check our work, you'd never know it."

"Damn," Dani murmured, not in disappointment, I thought, but more in admiration.

Damn smart. Seraph Nix had been as well, and if that was at all genetic, I'd have to be very freaking careful dealing with this guy.

"What do you want more than anything?" I asked him, gambling I knew the right answer, afraid it might be *revenge*.

He thought for a moment, his expression softening, and proved me right.

"To go home again. Back to the way things were."

"I can't give you the way things were," I told him, "but I could give you the chance to rebuild them how you want them. Kameria is still there. The people are still there, leaderless, reverted to savagery and barbarism, without trade, without technology. Seems like four pilots could make a lot of that if they were given a few short-range fighters, weapons enough to arm their own militia, medical supplies…" I shrugged. "It wouldn't be easy, but Kameria could be a place worth living again. If that's what you want."

The glint in Tamura's eye was mirrored in the faces of Fenris and Saimastil, the first hope I'd seen from them. Not Dothan. Dothan's glint was something darker, closer to the revenge wish I'd worried about.

"Of course, you'd only allow us short-range spacecraft," Tamura said, not missing that detail. "No starships." He grinned.

57

"Wouldn't want to risk a repeat of the war in another few decades."

"I am of the opinion that you shouldn't even be allowed the chance." The voice seemed to come out of nowhere and I fought not to jump in surprise like an idiot. Brother Constantine emerged from the shadows behind one of the fighters, his dark robe like a cloak of invisibility, his hood pulled up so that just his eyes were visible. "Kamerians very nearly destroyed everything worthwhile in this galaxy and I believe it an insane risk to bring any of them back. The few who survived have caused enough trouble, as my comrades well know." The monk locked eyes with me. "I hope very much you don't regret this."

He spun on his heel and stalked away and I offered the Kamerians a shrug.

"There you go. This is the best deal you're going to get." My eyes narrowed as a nasty thought struck me, no doubt thrown by Constantine's rant. "By the way, if you should get any ideas about saying yes, then stealing the fighters you're training in, I'd like to remind you that four starfighters and the four of you aren't nearly enough to take on the Anguilar Empire. And the Anguilar don't allow any competitors, don't have partners. You offer to ally with them, they'll take your starfighters and turn you into slaves. To them, you're inferior, useful only as front-line disposable troops who they wouldn't trust with an armed starship. You don't believe me, well…there's a bunch of documentation of it in the ship's database. You're welcome to take a look yourself."

Tamura nodded slowly, then turned to the others. Sainrastil mirrored the nod immediately, while Fenris took a moment longer to decide. Dothan…he was so obviously seething that I wouldn't have been surprised to see smoke pouring out of his ears.

"It galls me," Dothan growled, "to be forced to work with the metal demons who stole our chance at eternal glory." His shoulders sagged in a heavy sigh. "Yet what this scrawny pink weakling says is so. We have no other choice."

"Then it's decided," Tamura said, offering me a hand. "We are at your service."

I shook his hand. But when I got it back, I counted my fingers, just to be sure.

6

"It would have been treason to say it back in the day," Sainrastil mused, toying with the bottle of clear liquid that Lenny had informed me was the liquor of choice for discerning Kamerians, "but I'd long thought that continuing the war was the worst sort of overreach."

"It's damn near treason now," Dothan said, the words carrying the jagged edge of a threat despite the fact that the big man made no move to leave his couch. "And I care not how many centuries have passed."

Tamura shot Dothan a quelling look and motioned for Sainrastil to continue, then took the bottle from her and drank straight from it, not bothering with the glasses we'd provided. The small lounge Lenny's worker bots had created between the suite of compartments the Kamerians had been given for living quarters wasn't elaborate, just a couch, a table, and four chairs, but the pilots had spent more time there than they did their rooms in the few days we'd spent in hyperspace. Right down to practicing martial arts and doing calisthenics in the lounge instead of taking us up on our offer of using the ship's gym.

"We'd conquered half the galaxy," Sainrastil went on at Tamura's encouragement. "Built a wall around Kameria that none could have breached. Had we paused then and built up our defenses, taken the time to integrate those worlds into the Alliance, accepted their populations as full citizens in another generation or so, made it in their interest to defend our state…" She shrugged, grabbed the bottle back from Tamura and downed a long swig, then sighed and wiped her mouth. "Not only would none of them have risen up against us, as they *did*, you may remember, but even the Creators could never have turned back what we'd accomplished. When they returned, as they *did*, they would have had to accept our conquests."

The woman bared her teeth and spat. Which I thought was bad manners in someone else's house, but whatever.

"Instead, Autarch Canso felt compelled to cement his place in the legends of our people by finishing the job his mother had started. He went too far, too fast, stretched our forces too thin. And now, we see the results."

"Any soldier with sense saw them even before we went in stasis," Tamura agreed, looking around at the others. "I was not shocked to awaken and find we'd lost the war, because the war had been lost years ago, even before the first Vanguard had come off the line. Kameria had the best weapons and the best soldiers, but even before the Creators returned to oppose us, the Coalition outnumbered us, outproduced us. It would have ended either way, even without the Creators and their god-ships laying waste to our fleets." He shrugged, perhaps with a hint of bitterness but still with definite acceptance. "That just hastened our end."

"Either way," Fenris said with obvious hesitance, glancing furtively at Dothan's disapproving glare, "it's a moot point now. The Alliance is gone and it's not returning."

"Not unless we *make* it return," Tamura agreed. "The four of us are nothing, a spot of oil in an ocean of water, not enough to accomplish a damn thing by ourselves."

"What?" Dothan scoffed, throwing his head back and barking a sharp laugh. "You think if we're good little servants for the metal demon and his underlings, they'll reward us with a throne ruling over dirt-farmers in mud huts back on what's left of Kameria? You want to build your own empire out of the shit-heap?"

"No," Tamura admitted, the corner of his mouth turning up in a wry smile. "Though that's very much preferable to the second prize in this contest, which is likely death. I've accepted their terms because we have no other option, but I hope to turn things our way in time." He shrugged. "Training them will be a long and drawn-out process. Many things can happen."

I leaned toward the display, fingers gripping the back of my chair at the command station on the bridge. This was why we were monitoring the Kamerians' suite of rooms, as dirty as it made me feel, as much as it meant I had to waste hours sitting around and watching them.

"You do not need to do this," Lenny reminded me again and I glared at him for interrupting. "I am quite capable of carrying out surveillance of the prisoners without your presence and reporting anything significant."

"So you've told me," I acknowledged. "But how would I know what you consider significant is the same as what *I* would consider significant?" I put a finger over my lips. "Now shush."

"What do you have in mind, Captain?" Fenris wondered, caution in his expression, as if he was afraid of what Tamura might say.

"Who are we, Fenris?" Tamura spread his hands to include all four of them.

"Pilots?" the kid guessed, shaking his head.

"Close." His gaze shifted to the female. "Sainrastil?"

"We're the best fighter pilots in the entire galaxy, sir!" she snapped, grinning back at him.

"You're damn right we are," Tamura agreed. "Once we demonstrate that to them, once we prove that they're a lot better with us fighting with them than stuck on some backward-ass world fighting for scraps, they won't be so quick to get rid of us." He leaned back in his chair as if revealing his plan had taken a burden off his shoulders. "We'll become part of their inner circle."

"*What* inner circle?" Dothan grumbled, arms crossed, obviously unconvinced.

"The ones on this ship, Dothan. You've seen the mix here. Strada, Peboktan, these *humans*, whatever they are, a Creator, even a Varnell. This isn't a normal ship's crew." He pointed at the floor demonstratively. "This resistance of theirs, whatever they want to call it, started on this ship with these people. They're the ones who make the decisions or they wouldn't be here, wouldn't be the ones talking to us. That Creator, the metal demon…it's not the one in charge. The kid is, Charlie Travers." He pointed at Fenris. "He's barely older than you, yet he's the leader of their resistance."

"That's crap," Dothan mumbled without conviction. "There's no way."

"He's a soldier," Tamura went on, ignoring his second-in-command's doubts. "However young, I can see it in his eyes. He's a lead-from-the-front type, someone who'll be carrying a gun or flying a fighter when the battle starts. Not a politician, not a windbag. The way to convince him that we can be part of their government, part of the decision-makers once this is all over, is to do what we do best, fly those damned fighters and kill the enemy."

"What makes these Anguilar *our* enemy?" Dothan wanted to know. "I've never even met one."

"You never had a problem killing a bunch of other enemies you didn't know because the Autarch demanded it. Well, the Autarch is long dead and so is the Alliance. If any of us hope to be something more than tribal warlords on Kameria, you can damn well kill Anguilar for the resistance."

I found myself nodding. Tamura wasn't a Varnell, didn't have any special resonance to his voice that could hypnotize people into doing what he wanted, but he could have sold used cars in any lot in town. Or raised funds for a political campaign. Hell, *I* believed him and I was the one he was talking about having to convince.

"We do that, we make sure these guys win the war, not only will all of us be heroes…" He smirked. "Again. But we'll get them to trust us. Enough that they won't exile us out of fear of what we might do. We'll get a say in what comes after. And one of the things we can make happen is rebuilding Kameria." He sniffed in disdain. "Not with a few fighters and medical supplies, but with a *real* army, people who'll be willing to reconstruct cities, build schools and hospitals…build *spaceports*. By the time all of us have settled down to watch our children grow up, they might be doing it on a restored Kameria, a Kameria that'll be a factor in what-ever interstellar coalition grows out of this war."

"Then we'll try again?" Sainrastil asked, frowning. "Try to recapture the Alliance, conquer all those worlds again?"

She clearly wasn't crazy about the thought, but Tamura was already shaking his head.

"No. Even if I wanted to, it would be an insane thought. The galaxy hasn't recovered from the last war yet. What would we conquer? More poor dirt-farmers, more ruins? We could have that on Kameria. No, my friends. What we have to aim for is to conquer from within. To convince these people that Kamerians are natural leaders…because we are. That they can trust us to help rebuild the galaxy. We'll have power the right way, the way the Autarch *should* have done from the beginning. By uniting the galaxy, tying us all together through trade, through trust."

"Sounds freaking boring," Dothan said, punctuating the comment by draining the last of his bottle. I'd tried the stuff, and it was strong as hell, yet he'd downed an entire fifth of it and was still coherent. Sort of. "Couldn't we just blow the hell out of everyone and take it all over?"

"Just the four of us?" Sainrastil pointed out.

"The four of us by ourselves can do nothing," Tamura declared, thumping his fist on the table. "But the four of us with the entire galaxy behind us…"

"Why the hell are we spying on them?"

I turned, gaze flickering back and forth between the Kamerian on the screen and Dani stalking up behind me, irrationally concerned about the aliens hearing her.

"What do you mean?" I asked her, genuinely confused. "Why wouldn't we spy on them? We're trying to figure out if we can trust them with our starfighters. Of course, we're gonna spy on them."

Apparently, Dani didn't see the logic in that argument, or at least that's what it looked like to me from the stern set of her jaw and her hands on her hips. Of course, I wasn't a great judge of women, having had a grand total of four girlfriends in my life, getting dumped by three of them and marrying the fourth.

"Listening in on their private conversations isn't a way to build trust. It's not right."

I goggled at her.

"You were a cop, right? Didn't you ever wiretap anybody?"

"I was a small-town sheriff's deputy," she told me, rolling her eyes. "And you don't actually wiretap cell phones, and even then you need a search warrant, but that's beside the point. We're not cops…not even me, anymore."

"No, we're not. We're soldiers in a war. And you don't need search warrants to bug people in a war."

"Even your friends?"

"We don't know they're our friends yet," I pointed out. "And this is a lot more important than some guy who knocked over a liquor store."

"Knocked over a liquor store?" She eyed me in disbelief. "Sometimes I forget you're from 1987, and then you say shit like that."

"Whatever people do nowadays. It doesn't matter. We need to know these guys aren't stringing us along and if I have to watch them go to the damn bathroom every day, three times a day, to make sure they don't take off with four of the most powerful weapons in the galaxy, then I'll do it."

"It doesn't feel right," Dani insisted. "I want to feel like the good guys, and this doesn't seem like a good guy thing to do."

"The good news is," I said, trying to derail the debate, "from what we just heard, I think they may be ready to be good guys, too. Or, at least, ready to do good things for"—I shrugged— "kind of selfish, morally questionable reasons. I can work with that, though." I looked at Lenny, who'd been watching the exchange with an artificial expression that might have been amusement. "We can't take them to Sanctuary, obviously. I don't know if I'll ever trust them *that* much. We need a training area, someplace we can fire live rounds and blow stuff up. You got anyplace like that?"

"Of course. We could go to Strada, but that's a long journey and I assume you'd rather do this sooner than later."

"Before they have the chance to do their own thinking," I agreed. "Right now, they're still treating this Tamura Tel guy as their CO, but at some point, they're going to figure out that the fact the Alliance doesn't exist anymore also means that he's not their superior officer anymore."

Dani's eyebrow went up.

"That's actually pretty smart."

"You sound surprised." I grabbed my chest, pretending I was wounded. "Anyway, somewhere within a few days' flight."

Which, I'd found out the hard way, wasn't as easy as it sounded. Hyperspace connections went where the gravity lines pulled them and that wasn't always the nearest system or one you wanted. For all I knew, everything within a few days' flight of here might be Anguilar strongholds.

Lenny pulled a star map up on the bridge central display and highlighted three systems.

"These three are close enough," he told me, "and there's been no report of Anguilar activity in any of them."

"Any habitable planets?" I wondered, stepping closer and peering at the projection.

"These two have habitables." Lenny pointed. "No major population centers, but there might be trade, possibly smuggling or pirate activity." He indicated the last one. "This system has no terrestrial worlds, merely two gas giants and an ice giant, plus a large asteroid belt."

"Any mining activity?" It wasn't common to find asteroid or gas mining in systems with no habitables, mostly, I'd been told, because the cost of building space habitats for housing workers was too high to justify it when livable planets were so plentiful and every system with a living world also had rocks for digging in.

"No," he gave me the answer I'd expected and made my choice for me.

"That one, then. What's the travel time?"

"Fifty-six hours."

I nodded to Dani.

"Just enough time, then."

"Enough time for what?" she asked.

I smiled.

"To work up a training schedule. And figure out who gets to keep an eye on these guys in the cockpit."

7

"Cut left!" Tamura snapped. "You're under fire!"

I hadn't seen the sensor warning, much less spotted the drone on optical, but *he* had, and by this point in the training, I'd learned to listen to him. I twisted the steering yoke a half a second before the tracer rounds cut through where my Vanguard had been, invisible on optical but clear on the scanner.

"Now back," he told me, "get it in your gun sights."

Which was an easy thing to say but took like six different steps. Twist and push the wheel to the right, the maneuvering thrusters banging against the fuselage, then spin 360 degrees and hit braking thrusters, turn again, and by that time...

"No good. He's on the other side of that rock."

The rock was an asteroid about the size of an office building, tumbling through the two thousand miles between my fighter and the drone, one of the natural obstacles out here. Just to make things harder. And the unmanned target drone wasn't coming out, either. Damn Lenny for making the things too smart.

"He's hiding back there," Tamura observed. The Kamerian wasn't *exactly* back-seat driving because he was beside me, not behind me, but he was certainly micromanaging. "Gonna use the rock to keep you from employing your particle cannon because he knows you outrange him. What're you gonna do?"

He spoke fast and urgent, totally unlike how he'd been back on the *Liberator*, when every word had been smooth and commanding. Now, he was trying to pressure me, and it reminded me of Colonel Danberg walking back and forth between training stations during field exercises, snapping questions at the cadets.

I knew what to do, but that didn't mean I had to like it. I brought up the navigation screen and touched a point two thousand yards on the other side of the tumbling asteroid, then pulled down the lever to take us into hyperspace. I wished the damned thing could have taken us out of hyperspace automatically because that would have been so much easier. Instead, a beeping warning alerted me that it was time to do it myself.

That was the hard part. Jumping into hyperspace was a physical and psychological lurch, like trying to step off the last stair and finding out there were actually three more, an impact, a pressure, a sense of shock even though I knew it was coming. It took me a few seconds to shake that off but I didn't *have* a few seconds. Gritting my teeth, I forced my hand to move despite the psychic inertia of the jump.

Too late. I pushed the levers up and we popped back into existence, another shock just as jarring, but it had taken me too long to react and we were a good fifty miles past the asteroid, well out of particle cannon range.

"Damn it!" I blurted, opening the drive throttle to chase after the drone.

Too late again. The drone had already boosted away, staying ahead of me.

"It took me a long time to get used to the short jumps," Tamura said, calm and steady now that I needed instruction. "There's a trick to it. It's not just in your mind, you understand, but your mind can help you get over it quicker."

"I'd love to know what it is," I said, impatient and annoyed, mostly with myself. "Because every time we short-jump, I pretty much want to puke my guts out."

"You have to visualize yourself." Tamura shaped the scene with his hands. "Think of diving off a cliff into a lake. Have you ever done that?"

"Close enough." I suppose a flooded rock quarry counted.

"Good. You're diving off into the lake…concentrate on your form, on keeping your body in line, and as you do it, tense up your stomach muscles and keep your body tight until you come back to normal space, then let everything loose and exhale, empty your lungs." Tamura motioned at the drone, still outpacing us. There was another rock spinning lazily through space a few hundred miles away. The thing was likely heading for it. "Go ahead. Get ahead of the target."

I shook my head. This would be even trickier…I had to figure out how fast the thing was going and where it would be when I came out, and I didn't even have time to use the navigational computer to do it, just Kentucky windage. I made my best guess and stabbed at the screen, took two seconds to prepare myself mentally and physically. Getting ready to jump off the bank into the pond, hips flexed, up on the balls of my feet, clenching my stomach muscles.

Hit the levers. It wasn't as bad. The pressure washed over me instead of slamming into me and when the warning told me to exit, I was able to slap the controls the second the beeping started.

Relax. Exhale. Yank back on the control yoke. The reticle spun with the ship and floated down over the red triangle of the drone. My finger stroked the trigger and the particle cannon lashed out, white and crackling.

"Splash one drone," I murmured, grinning proudly, chest puffing up like a rooster.

"Satisfactory," Tamura said, clearly unimpressed. "We should try it again."

"Satisfactory?" I repeated, motioning at the fading glow of the cloud of vapor where the drone had been. "That's the fastest I've ever recovered from a short-jump!"

"Yes, and I'm sure you'll improve with practice." He gave me the same sort of look that Sgt. Redd had after I'd scored Expert for the first time at the rifle range and thought that meant I was sniper material. "I'm afraid you'll never be an instinctive fighter pilot, Charlie. You'd have to keep at it for years and it's nearly too late to start that sort of training. But you're definitely on the track to be serviceable."

I stared at him for a second, outrage rumbling like a volcano inside my chest, getting ready to erupt at the slight. The challenge emerged without conscious thought, and I spoke it before I could pull it back.

"I'd like to see you do it."

"Of course," Tamura accepted without hesitation, gesturing between us. "If you'd care to trade seats with me?"

It didn't occur to me until I'd unstrapped and squeezed aside to let him take the pilot's controls that this all might be a ploy. Maybe he was being overly critical in the hope of getting me to do just this, to let him get a chance at the controls. He could jump us out of here and take his chances with me one-on-one, without having to worry about the *Liberator* or the other fighters coming after him. My right hand moved almost of its own accord toward my chest holster, to the compact handgun there, but I interrupted the motion and instead touched the comm controls.

"*Liberator*, this is Vanguard One, requesting another target drone in our AO."

Which was probably unnecessarily specific and cryptic given that ours was the only Vanguard flying right now, but it was good practice for the real thing. Getting lazy and sloppy in training was a good way to train to be lazy and sloppy.

"Launching," Val reported.

Not that he was personally launching the drone—that would be done by one of the Copperell techs. Nor was he flying the *Liberator*, nor would he be targeting the main guns in the case of a fight. But someone had to be in command of the ship since Lenny couldn't, and I trusted Val more at that job than anyone except Laranna…and she was down in the hangar bay, waiting for her turn at this.

Laranna with Dothan because he was a big, dangerous son of a bitch and she was the toughest fighter I knew. Dani with Sainrastil, not because I expected Dani to be a great pilot but I had to give her the chance. Giblet with Fenris because if I'd put him with Sainrastil, he'd be too busy hitting on her to notice if she tried to steal the fighter.

The *Liberator* wasn't close enough for me to separate her from the other glittering dots in the asteroid belt, but she was a bright and shining arrowhead of red on the sensor screens, far enough back from us that no one would start chasing a drone back into her and put a round into the shields. A much smaller crimson dot broke off from big red and darted toward our position, moving frantically, randomly, not making things easier for us.

Whoever was guiding the drone, whether it was one of the Copperell techs or Lenny himself through the autonomous programming, had noticed the trouble I'd had getting to the other side of the asteroid and ran the target into the nearest cluster, about two hundred thousand miles away. That was one thing that had disappointed me about real-life asteroid fields as opposed to the kind they showed in movies and TV shows and video games—just how big a distance there was between them. No waves of rock floating around banging into each other, just individual fragments an average of half a million miles apart.

But there were clusters, places where the fragments had drifted together, falling briefly into each other's individual orbits, sometimes colliding. Kind of like people. This particular cluster was in the middle of a collision that would probably take years to complete, surrounded by a ring of debris still spinning and tumbling, a perfect place for a little drone playing fighter to hide from us and our bigger weapons.

"Damn," I murmured, annoyed even though I'd been trying to show Tamura up. "That's gonna be a tough nut to crack."

"Not so difficult," he said, the picture of cool, Maverick and Iceman rolled into one arrogant package. "Hold on, it's going to get a little rough in here."

I expected a heavy burn, something that the inertial dampeners couldn't handle, but instead, Tamura's fingers flew over the nav screen, and he flipped the jump levers casually. Nothingness swallowed us up, the canopy turning black at the presence of the Nothing. For all that I'd been warned, I wasn't ready for the hyperspace entrance and was even less prepared for the exit.

The fighter's fuselage rang like a handbell as fist-size chunks of rock banged off of it, and massive shadows spun across the canopy. I barely had time to grasp that Tamura had jumped us right into the debris cloud, in the middle of the cluster, with rolling remains of asteroids the size of Anguilar cruisers surrounding us on every side. And right in the center of the whole mess was the target drone, sitting happy as a clam, safe and secure from us and our big gun.

If there'd been a pilot inside that drone, he would have been shitting his pants, and I hoped if anyone was watching from the bridge of the *Liberator*, they at least had to be feeling a little surprise. As much as I was. Tamura hesitated just a moment before he pulled the trigger and I got the sense it was a dramatic pause more than any attempt to make sure of the targeting.

White lightning snapped out from the nose of the plane, reducing the drone to burning vapor. I shook my head, about to offer Tamura congratulations, but he wasn't done yet. I barely noticed him work the control lever before we were back in, then back out of hyperspace in the blink of an eye. I did *not* throw up, but it was a near thing.

"Next time," Tamura said, cracking his knuckles, "you should have them use three drones so it will be a challenge."

"I don't think *you* need the challenge," I told him, wiping at my mouth. I'd managed to preserve my lunch, but my pride was certainly splattered all over the floor. "Trade places with me and you can run me through it again." I sighed in resignation. "I got a lot to learn."

I HAD so much to learn that we spent ten full days on individual training, which was about three days more than I'd intended and maybe a year less than I needed. By the end of it, everyone was ready to get the hell out of this lifeless system and the desolate asteroid field...but we didn't. Because now it was time for squadron training.

"There are more than four planes in a Kamerian squadron," Tamura pointed out, his voice not even breaking at the sudden punch of thrust as we burst free of the hangar bay, the last of the group.

"You're training us," I said, pointing at Laranna, Gib and Dani, their Vanguards hanging off the bow of the *Liberator*, waiting for us to catch up. "Then we have to help train the others. Before we can do that, we have to know what we're doing."

Tamura's grin was knowing and cynical as he watched me guide the fighter to the front of the squadron wedge. We were aligned with the ecliptic and the system's star shining through the dust cloud of a nearby cluster of rocks threw a golden glow across a small section of the black expanse.

"What you mean is, you want to be able to watch us train them to make sure we don't screw it up on purpose."

"Maybe," I admitted, giving the fighter half throttle, getting some distance from the sharp-edged lines of the *Liberator*. "But it's also important for us to train them because you learn things better when you tell other people how to do them."

"Very wise for one your age," he admitted. I took the compliment without clarifying that I'd stolen that bit of wit from Sgt. Redd. "But what if we've been deliberately teaching you incorrectly? How would you even know?"

I met his eyes for a moment, searching for the truth in them. It was a good point. Everything he'd taught me had worked well in training against the drones, but that didn't mean it would work as well when going up against enemy pilots who knew what they were doing.

"Among the other stuff that I need to be an expert at to do this job," I told him honestly, deciding there was no point in being cagey about it, "is figuring out whether I'm being lied to. If I can't do that, all of us are probably going to get killed. No use putting that off."

Tamura nodded, said nothing else.

"Val," I called, "launch them."

This was a different scenario. Luckily for us, Lenny could run these drones out by the dozen in the ship's fabricators because we'd gone through nearly a hundred of them so far. This time, a stream of the things poured out of the ship's hangar bay, sixteen in all, and rather than running for cover in the rocks, they converged on the four of us, making a run for weapons range. Four squadrons of four each and even if Kamerians usually had six planes in their squadrons, the Anguilar didn't and that was who we were fighting.

Whoever was guiding the drones had a good plan, and I'd made sure they didn't clue any of us in as to what it was going to be. This was supposed to be training for real combat, not an attempt to impress anyone with how well we did. A pincer movement was what I would have called it on land, except this was a three-dimensional version, with the four squadrons splitting up to surround us from every side except the front, making sure we could either fight or turn and run,

If we actually had been in real combat with Anguilar fighters, it wouldn't have been a problem. Their pulse cannons couldn't have penetrated our shields, and I wouldn't have been afraid to run directly into their guns to get a shot. But that would have been too easy, so we'd decided to "arm" the drones with simulated particle cannons, powerful enough to penetrate our shields if we let them take potshots at us.

They were behind us, gaining but still about ten thousand miles back. No one said anything, but I could hear the unspoken question. *What are we gonna do?*

I didn't think about it. Thinking had gotten me killed by the drones more times than I could count in the last week and a half.

"Turn into them," I ordered, cutting thrust and spinning my Vanguard end-for-end.

My hand hovered over the throttle, waiting until the others had turned as well before I fed power to the drive pods in a fierce deceleration, hard enough to push Tamura and I back into our seats. The pressure forced a grunt from me but Tamura made no sound, his face as impassive as if this was a Sunday drive.

"We'll be in weapons' range in ten seconds," Laranna warned me.

"Micro-jump three thousand miles relative north, now!"

That was something else that had taken me some time to grasp. In the movies, everyone talked about directions with vague numerical values. "Turn to point three five" or some such crap, but in real life, we had to use some universal value to describe well…which way was up. And that reference was the ecliptic of whatever star system we happened to be in, the plane that the planets revolved around their sun. Above that plane was north, below it was south and if that seemed arbitrary, well… it was.

The bottom line for us was that when I pushed the jump levers, we popped into and out of hyperspace and reappeared *above* the drone fighter group relative to the plane of rotation, while their notional particle cannons were all pointed down.

"Fire!" I ordered, though no one had waited for my command.

Our formation was tight enough that the particle blasts interacted with each other, crackles of electricity like lightning forking between clouds in a thunderstorm. Half the drone group ceased to exist before their controllers scattered them, every imaginary man for himself…or at least each two-drone team for themselves, since they all had cybernetic wingmen.

"Split up and take them down," I said, and wasn't sure if I imagined the slight downturn at the corners of Tamura's mouth that meant he was concealing a frown of disapproval.

I was making a mistake, apparently, but I was right in the middle of it and didn't have time to second-guess myself. The two-drone team I'd followed made a run for an asteroid cluster, unimaginative, the same thing they tried every time, and I reacted as Tamura had taught me. Another micro-jump, another dive head-first off the bank into that flooded rock quarry, landing like an Olympic diver just ahead of the two drones.

Flipping the bird end for end was just as instinctive as the jump now, as instinctive as firing the particle cannon. They were too close together, close enough that the blast I'd aimed at one of the two drones clipped the other, sheering off its port drive pod, the spray of burning gas sending it tumbling. Right into one of the rocks they'd been seeking out for cover. There wasn't much to the drones beyond the drives, certainly no armor, and when the thing smacked into the asteroid fragment, it came apart like a model airplane.

I grinned, pretty happy with myself, but Tamura's frown hadn't changed.

"Where's the rest of your squadron?" he asked.

I spun the Vanguard and eyed the sensors, finding them scattered over a good two or three thousand miles, chasing down their quarry. Giblet had already nailed his targets and was heading back toward the center of gravity between us, while Laranna had taken out one and was hot on the heels of the other. Dani's bird spun through a tight arc, trying to stay on the track of the two drones she'd been assigned.

A little spread out, but everything was going well, and I didn't know what he was worried about. Until the warning flashers filled the cockpit and the sensors screamed at me what Tamura's frown had been trying to say.

Sixteen more drones heading our way...

8

"WELL, *THAT* WAS A FIASCO," Giblet drawled, then tossed back a shot of something flame-orange.

None of the rest of us said a word, particularly not me. The galley was as silent as a tomb other than the clink of glasses and the occasional muttered curse. I'd left the lighting dimmed to something that didn't make my head hurt and probably still wouldn't even after I had as many drinks as I intended. Just us in the galley this time, though we'd eventually have to share the lessons learned with the rest of the pilots in training.

I didn't want to look at the Kamerians, particularly not Dothan, whose disdainful sneer hadn't left his oversized face since we landed. Probably before that. Laranna wasn't afraid to look at him though. She'd been glaring at him for an hour, barely touching either her food or the drink I'd poured for her. I hadn't asked what had happened on her fighter, but I could imagine.

Tamura was the one who broke the silence, standing from the table where he and his fellow Kamerians had congregated and walking to the center of the galley.

"Does anyone know," he asked, motioning expansively to include all of us, "what went wrong out there?"

"We all got our asses killed," Dani ventured, swirling her drink around inside its glass before downing the last of it.

"That's a symptom," Tamura said, shaking his head, "not the disease."

"We thought there'd be sixteen drones and there were thirty-two," Laranna snapped. She got angry when she failed, and he was the nearest target. "I'd like to know how the hell *that* happened!"

"Because I asked Lenny to do it."

That brought even Laranna up short.

"Why would you do that?" Dani wondered. Unlike Laranna, she didn't seem upset, just curious.

"Because for some reason," Tamura replied, a glint in his eye that I couldn't read, "I've convinced myself that you're worth keeping alive. And taking it easy on you, letting you keep making baby steps, is not the way to do this."

Laranna sighed.

"Why are we making such a big damned deal of this?"

"Because you're not going to be fighting drones out there," the Kamerian clapped back at her, showing more daring than most people, including me. "You're not going to be going after short-ranged fighters, either. You brought us here to train you to take on multiple enemy cruisers, ships with guns that could take you out, ships with hyperdrives, just like yours. Your only advantage over them is speed, agility…and teamwork." Tamura stalked over to my table and slammed his palms against it, rattling the dishes, then stared me straight in the eye. "Tell me, *commander*, what went wrong out there?"

I knew. I probably knew all along, but it hadn't clicked until that moment.

"We split up. I shouldn't have ordered us to split up."

"Almost." He nodded. "You never leave your wingman. You never go off by yourself with no one to watch your back." Tamura turned to the others. "When I fly in combat, who's with me always, no matter what?"

"I am," Dothan said with a smirk. "No matter how stupid you get."

"And when Sainrastil goes into combat, Fenris is flying at her five o'clock because your wingman never leaves you, always watches the shit you *can't* watch on your own. And it's a damned good thing you learned that lesson now, when the only casualties are your pride, when the only thing you've killed are some brain cells drinking your blues away."

I nodded.

"He's right. This was my fault."

"Your fault, my fault, *nobody's* fault," Tamura interrupted, waving it away. "It's why you're here, why *we're* here. To learn, to teach." He pointed my way with what Sgt. Redd would have called a knife hand, all his fingers and thumb, toward me. "You're the commander. Tell us what we do now."

I took my drink and raised it to Tamura.

"We go back out." I laughed softly. "We do it again until we get it right."

THRUST, turn, jump, exit, turn, thrust. Fire.

Over and over. It was my life, all of our lives, for the last three weeks. So much longer than I thought, longer than I'd planned, but we were cramming what Tamura had insisted was months of basic fighter combat training into a few weeks and that meant spending eighteen hours a day in the Vanguards.

Thank God the flight suits had equipment for waste management, though *that* was something I'd never counted on when I'd been abducted by a UFO. All day, every day, one drill after another, one flight of drones after another, one cold, tasteless field ration after another.

I dreamed about flying, had nightmares of drones sneaking up from behind clusters of asteroids and barely talked to Laranna when we both dragged ourselves into the cabin at the end of training. And this was the last day. According to Tamura, anyway. Dothan had been of the opinion that we were all useless and would get ourselves killed if we ever went up against a *real* fighter pilot, but had at least acknowledged that except for the four of them, there probably weren't any real fighter pilots anymore.

"Ready to launch, Commander?" Tamura asked, the hint of a sadistic smile visible through the open faceplate of his helmet.

"Whenever you call me that," I told him, "I know things are about to suck."

"At least you're learning something."

"Launch," I snapped, opening the throttle.

Roaring in my head, pressure against my face, my chest, familiar by now, like the handshake of an old friend. Assuming I was tired as hell of that old friend and wanted to punch him out every time I saw him. We were free of the hangar, silver metal spitting us out like a watermelon seed, back in black.

Three more Vanguards, Laranna to my right, my wingman, Giblet and Dani on the left. No talk yet. We didn't have to. We'd been through this too many times and we just fell into formation without thought, without effort.

We didn't tell Lenny to launch the drones anymore, either, because knowing when they were coming was too predictable. Just cruised in silence, except Tamura. He hummed, always the same damned tune, and it bugged the hell out of me.

"Don't you know any other songs?" I asked him, not looking away from the sensors.

"It's a Kamerian tradition," he informed me. "A hymn to the god of good fortune. It brings us luck in battle."

"Well, this fighter isn't part of the Kamerian Alliance anymore." I fished out my comm and scrolled through the menu with one hand, saving the other for the steering yoke. I found what I wanted and pushed the play button. "Maybe it's time for a new tradition."

A synthesizer rang through the cockpit speakers and for the first time since he'd woken up from stasis, I saw confusion in Tamura's eyes, discomfort. Then the guitars started and Sammy Hagar's voice belted out lyrics about the world turning black and white. The song had come out in 1986, which was decades ago now, but for me, it was two years. I'd listened to it every morning in George's car on the way to school because he couldn't get enough of it, because of that video with the Blue Angels.

"Contacts!" Laranna's voice came over the speakers, overriding Sammy for just a moment. "Drones on the way!"

"Let's go get 'em," I said, shifting the control yoke to the right and pushing the throttle close to the red.

The others shifted with me, the four of us banking as our drives swung on their gimbals, and we joined battle with our automated enemies once more, but this time with Van Halen's *Dreams* belting out in the background.

"Dry your eyes," I murmured along, touching the trigger. "Save all the tears you've cried...'cause that's what dreams are made of."

Lightning ripped apart thin metal, Laranna's joining with mine while Gib and Dani broke the other direction and caught the targets in a crossfire. Six down, ten to go.

"Vanguard Three"—that was Gib—"take Four and jump south. Two"—Laranna—"with me and jump north. Catch them in a pincer."

Jump, dive off that bank into the water far below. Exit. Spin, brake, fire. Do it again.

"Vanguard squadron, form up!"

Jump again, this time coming together. I didn't look at Tamura anymore. I had the first ten or twelve times we'd done this, watched him carefully to make sure I wasn't screwing up again. Then I'd made a point of *not* looking at him, which was almost as bad as the staring. Now, I might as well have been alone, and the only way I would have acknowledged him at all was if he'd actually been operating the pulse turrets he could have controlled from his seat.

Fat chance. I'd asked once.

"That's not my job," had been his response. "I'm an observer."

And here I thought his job had been to train me, but whatever. I didn't need advice anymore.

"Contact thirty degrees north by northwest!" Giblet said, not talkative at all anymore on the comms, which was a tribute to the repetitive tedium of the last month. "Twenty drones at three thousand yards, coming in hot off that cluster of rock fragments!"

Same thing as always. Not the same time, not the same place, but always more.

"Back to front." That was shorthand. Jump past them, turn, fire.

We did it twice, back to front, front to back, side to side until they were gone.

"Form up."

Jumping again. It didn't even make me want to puke anymore…or maybe it did, but I'd become inured to the sensation by now, so wanting to puke didn't make me puke. We lined up together again, shoulder to shoulder, like gunfighters in a spaghetti western, ready for whatever enemy lined up along the streets of that cardboard western town.

Nothing did.

"Vanguard squadron," Val said, his voice breaking the spell of combat, echoing into the last few lines of a song called *Drown You Out* by a band that hadn't been around for twenty years after I was born, "this is *Liberator*. Scopes are clear, exercise is over."

"That's *it*?" Giblet demanded. "After all this, that's it? I was expecting something more apocalyptic."

"We can only do so much with drones, Vanguard Three," I reminded him. "Come on, squadron, let's get back to the ship. I'm looking forward to some hot food and a shower. Vanguard One out."

"He's good," Tamura said quietly, barely audible above the *bang-bang-bang* of the maneuvering jets.

"Hmm?" I grunted, glancing over at him. He sat back in the gunner's seat, legs stretched out like it was a living-room lounger, fingers steepled in front of him. "Who's good?"

"The Varnell. Giblet." Tamura pointed out the canopy like he could tell one Vanguard from the other. "He's a natural pilot." He nodded toward me. "I mean, you're...adequate. You and Laranna both. Don't get me wrong, you're likely better than anything these Anguilar can produce, at least from the combat footage you've shown us. It's part of their battle strategy, overly dependent on capitol ships, short-range fighters as an afterthought. So, when I call you adequate, it's compared to us."

I shrugged, choosing not to take it as an insult.

"But Gib isn't just adequate?" I assumed, turning my attention back to the controls, setting a course for the ship.

"He's as good as any of us, or would be with another few weeks of practice."

"What about Dani?"

A long pause and I eyed him curiously, wondering if he was about to tell me she was horrible and there was no hope, but instead, he was smiling.

"She's not as good as you, nowhere as near as good as Giblet, but she's useful. Not a liability."

"You…" I clamped down on my words, refusing to sound like a high schooler and ask him if he *liked* Dani. "You're interested in her, right? I mean, I'm not the brightest guy when it comes to relationships, but you aren't exactly trying to be subtle, either."

"Subtlety was never my strong suit," Tamura admitted. "And yes, she has…spirit. Spirit I'd not thought to find in someone not of Kameria."

"Then you're gonna have a problem with your best pilot. Giblet's better at reading people than I am, and he knows just as well that she's interested in you, too."

"Oh, for the love of the Blood God," he sighed. "Don't tell me the Varnell is in love."

"Love, I don't know. But he's jealous. Maybe it's just as well that we're done with the one-on-one training. A few more weeks to train the other pilots, but I'd like to switch things out and put you and your people in your own birds for that, use you guys as OpFor."

Tamura's brows went up.

"You're trusting us in the cockpit alone?"

I grinned at him.

"I'm not quite that stupid. You'll still have an escort along with you in the gunner position. For now. If we get through the training and you're still around and haven't killed your babysitters and taken off with the fighters, then your babysitters become actual gunners and you fight right alongside us."

"Is that so?" He turned his chair toward me. "Well, at least the goal is in sight. And tell me, once all this training is complete, how long will it be until we actually get to fight these Anguilar of yours? How long until we tackle an actual objective?"

"I haven't had either the time or the mental energy to think about it," I told him. "Not with this cycle of fly-eat-sleep-repeat we've been going through. I still can't say for sure, not until we get an idea of how good the rest of the pilots are. But if you can get them into the same sort of shape we're in, then there's no reason to wait. Meet us in the galley for dinner. We'll talk about it."

Which meant that the rest of us would have to get together *before* dinner and discuss it first. Because like I told Tamura, I wasn't stupid.

9

"I THINK we should go right for the jugular," Val said, smacking a palm down on the table with a vehemence that surprised me. Valentine McKee was as consistent as the tide, rarely losing his cool, and that only made this eruption more notable.

The rest of us stared silently, clustered around the card table and chairs we'd hauled into our compartment. The quarters on the *Liberator* weren't small, but seven people and a giant robot made the room feel that way. Besides Val, Laranna, Lenny and me, we'd called Dani, Gib, Constantine and Mallarna for the pre-meeting meeting. Just the existence of that idea made me feel like a colonel.

"Copperell," Val went on, meeting each of our eyes. "The Anguilar don't know we have this Vanguard wing. We hit them at Copperell before they're ready for it, we can take that damn planet and cut the empire in half before they know what hit them."

"Seraph Nix escaped from Haven," Laranna reminded him. "You don't think she'd tell the Anguilar what we found down there?"

"Not unless she thought it was in her best interest," Val said, crossing his arms, jaw set in a picture of stubbornness. "I still say even if she told them, they wouldn't listen to her. She's not Anguilar."

"He may have a point," Giblet conceded, sprawled out over the end of our bed. I wanted to glare at him but there were more important things to worry about. "You know how Anguilar are. Stuck-up buttholes who won't listen to anyone else. She's the hired help. Even if they believe her, they won't make any big changes yet."

I wanted to sit down, wanted to lean against something. I was already exhausted physically, and now I was getting burned out mentally trying to process the many arguments from all sides. But every chair was occupied, every inch of bare wall already a resting spot for someone's shoulder. I could have backed up against Lenny's chassis, but that felt a little too intimate.

So I just stood at the center of the room and tried not to sway back and forth from fatigue.

"Y'all are making good points," I acknowledged. "And I think, if we really wanted to press things and brought all five Liberator ships and all our ground troops, we could take Copperell."

Surprise in a few expressions, eagerness in others, but I raised a hand to forestall protests and encouragement.

"We could take it, but then we'd have to *hold* it. And to do that, we'd tie down every single ship and all our ground troops, and then what? All we could do at that point is sit there and wait for them to counterattack because even with the fighters, we still can't make more ships. Lenny, how many ships do you think we'd lose taking Copperell?"

"Of our five Liberator ships," the robot said, "likely three. Of the Vanguard wing, at least ten."

After that, I could have heard a pin drop in the room as everyone realized what that would mean.

"So," I continued, "we'd barely have enough to defend the world and we'd still have those remaining forces attrited as time went on."

Murmuring all around and none of it satisfied.

"What's the point of having the fighters if we're not going to go on the offensive?" Val demanded.

"I know nobody's going to like this," I said, "but I think our only option is island-hopping."

Confusion from every face except Dani, who knew enough history to figure out what I meant, and Laranna, to whom I'd explained the concept.

"During a war on my planet," I explained, "one that my grandfather fought in, my country was fighting an empire, an island nation that had taken over all the key islands in the South Pacific. A lot of our people wanted to bypass their strongholds on those islands and head straight for their homeland, put all our effort into taking it over. But what we wound up doing instead was island-hopping. Going from one island to another, taking back what they'd seized and isolating them on their home islands, cutting them off and pounding them with airstrikes until they finally surrendered."

And yeah, I was simplifying the hell out of World War Two and skipping a bunch, including the two atom bombs we'd dropped, but this wasn't a college history course.

"As it turned out, a lot of people think it was a good thing we did it that way because our forces were inexperienced, young, our weapons systems old, obsolete and we didn't even know it. We lost a lot of troops in those island landings, but if we'd tried to invade the homeland directly, we would have taken so many casualties. We might never have recovered."

I wasn't sure if I was getting through to them or not, not least because I doubted any of the non-humans had ever even heard of a war between nations on a single planet, fought with ocean-going ships.

"Okay, cool," Gib said, eyeing me in confusion. "What the hell does any of that mean?"

"It means we start small, with systems far enough away from the center of the Empire that the Anguilar won't be able to retake them without overextending themselves. Systems that we can hold with orbital defense platforms and short-range fighters even after we pull out with the Liberators. Systems that will give us logistical bases on all four corners of the Anguilar Empire that we can use to supply and stage larger operations."

"Like what?" Val wanted to know.

"Lenny," I said, motioning at an empty section of wall. "Show me a map."

"RIGHT HERE," I said, tapping the system on the star map.

Dothan peered at the screen with only one eye open, his feet propped up on the table, the soles of his massive boots only a few inches from the plate I'd left behind while I explained the plan. Served me right for trying to sit with the Kamerians.

"What's that say?" Dothan mumbled. "Thalassia? Never heard of it."

"Join the club," Giblet murmured.

He wasn't happy, Val wasn't happy, Dani hadn't seemed happy since we'd started training, and I doubted the Kamerians would be happy, either.

"Thalassia," Lenny said, "is a former Copperell colony settled centuries ago before the Centennial War and occupied by the Anguilar less than a decade ago. The population is middling, only about three million residents spread out across farms and mines on three continents, and the Anguilar only bother occupying the largest city, Philos, on the northern continent, where the only spaceport and the largest seaports are."

"Seaports?" Dani repeated. "That sounds so…"

"Primitive?" I guessed, smiling lopsidedly. "We've gone over that before. Just because the Anguilar have plenty of starships and air cars doesn't mean everyone can afford to use those for things like moving cargo. Especially not way out here. People make do with what works and what's cheap." I waved it away and took up the narrative. "Anyway, the upshot is, the Anguilar don't feel like they need a lot of troops on the ground because the population is so thinly spread and there's no way to get a lot of them together quickly, no history of military training for anyone to recruit vets for a rebellion. The estimates Brandy gave us in the last intelligence update were maybe six thousand troops, almost all of them stationed in the capitol. How many ships and fighters they'll have is a bit more iffy…we could catch them between patrols and there'll be nothing or during a rotation change and they'd have twice as many ships as usual. But it won't be more than we can handle, either way."

"So, it's easy," Tamura deduced. "But if it's that easy, is it worth doing?"

"Fair question," I allowed, then went back to the table and retrieved my plate before Dothan could knock it off the side. There was still about half the helping of chicken teriyaki and I shoveled the rest into my mouth, talked around it. "First off, the Copperell flight crews need combat experience before we try anything on a large scale. Second, we need a staging base on this side of the Empire. The nearest one we have is Strada and it's weeks from here. It all comes down on what we want to do. Do we want to just keep doing hit and run strikes or do we want to cut deep into the heart of the Empire? Because if we do, we need to surround them, start eating away at the peripheries of their territory, boxing them in, which means we need strongholds. The fighters are a start, not the goal. We need more ships, more soldiers, more food sources, and we're not gonna do it with a couple hidden outposts and Strada as our only real operations center."

"Also," Laranna added, "if our only stronghold is Strada, that makes it more attractive to the Anguilar to build up their forces and keep trying to retake it. If they think they can dispose of the entire resistance in one attack, there's no disincentive."

Dothan laughed raucously, throwing his head back.

"You seriously believe you can take down an empire with a handful of ships, a couple dozen fighters, and a few thousand infantry? You're all fools."

"Then what are *you* doing here, ugly?" Dani snapped at him, coming to her feet, her right hand straying toward the sidearm at her hip. "If you're not interested in flying again, if you're not interested in fighting the Anguilar, you could stay the hell in your cabin and concentrate on training people with more balls than you."

Dothan growled deep in his massive chest and exploded out of his seat, the metal legs scraping against the floor with a screech like fingernails on a chalkboard. Laranna and I both moved, though my biggest worry wasn't Dothan hurting Dani but Dani shooting him between the eyes. Neither of us got there in time because Tamura was closer.

He didn't raise a hand, didn't reach for a weapon even if he had one. He just interposed himself between the two of them and stared up at Dothan without even a hint of fear in his eyes.

"Dothan," he said, as calm as if this sort of thing happened every day, "could you do me a huge favor and sit back down?

You're my best friend in the entire galaxy, and it would be a tragedy if I had to watch this beautiful woman splash your brains all over the galley before I've even finished my lunch."

Dothan stared at his commander for a taut, silent few seconds before falling back into his chair, the metal groaning in protest. Dani watched him sit, and her hand slipped off the butt of her gun. I cleared my throat to get her attention.

"Dani, why don't we all sit down and relax?"

She scowled at me but took a seat, still glaring at Dothan.

"You know what, Dothan," I said, pacing between the two of them, standing beside Tamura, "you're right. We're not going to bring down an empire with a handful of cruisers and a couple dozen fighters. What we're gonna do is use what we have to get more. You remember what the Alliance was like?" I asked the question of both of them, looking between Tamura and Dothan. "You remember why you lost the war?"

"We lost because of *them*," Dothan snapped, pointing at Lenny, nearly coming out of his chair again. "Because the Creators returned and led the others against us!"

"No." I pointed back at him. "You lost because all those other worlds out there, all those other people *hated* you. Because you treated them like shit, Dothan. You conquered their worlds and put your own people in charge, taxed the hell out of their farms and mines and conscripted them into your military. Just that was enough to piss people off so much that when Lenny and his other"—I rolled my eyes—"*Lennies* came back, it didn't take much to turn them all against you. They fought you to the point where their entire society fell apart, and they didn't care because it was a good enough reason to lose everything."

"Are you trying," Tamura asked, raising an eyebrow, "to get him torqued off again?"

"I'm trying to make a point," I said. "What you did was enough to unite the galaxy against you, even though you were one of them, even though you'd dealt with all those other races and worlds and governments for centuries. But what the *Anguilar* are doing makes what you and your Alliance did look like a family quarrel."

"The Anguilar have enslaved entire worlds," Laranna interjected. "They've slaughtered hundreds of thousands of innocent people and allowed others to starve from lack of food because they take everything they grow. They let them die in the mines and then drag men and women and sometimes children out of their homes to replace them. They make things so god-awfully bad that the young people on these worlds join their military voluntarily just to get out. And even then, the Anguilar don't trust them as anything but frontline troops and strong backs."

"That seems…short-sighted," Tamura said, his words carefully chosen, as if he detected the rage roiling just beneath the surface in Laranna.

"Not as short-sighted as what they did next," Mallarna took up the story. She didn't stand from her chair, just sat, arms on the table, fingers interlocked and her eyes staring straight ahead. "Their tactics were so brutal that multiple systems rebelled, including mine. The Peboktan were so desperate, they contracted out to pirates to kick the Anguilar fleet out of the system. But the Anguilar had already made a plan for what they'd do if any system dared to fight back against their rule. Rather than use their resources for building automated mines or farms, they threw them all into a planet-killer. They…" Mallarna swallowed hard. "They destroyed my world and would have done the same to Strada."

"We boarded the ship," I told him, "and blew it up. Lost one of my best friends in the world doing it."

"I think I understand," Tamura said, eyeing me with what might have been respect. "These Anguilar…they're brutal. Stupid."

"They were exiles from their home," Lenny said, an echo of what he'd told them when we first thawed them out, and if a robot, even an artificially intelligent one, could be said to have real feelings, this one seemed to be feeling regret. "They came here as they had other galaxies before, to strip it bare and then move on. But it was already defenseless, and the fault for that was my own. They decided to stay, to make a new home for themselves, but this home will only truly be theirs once every other competitor is cleansed from the galaxy. The rest of you are only useful as slaves."

"To make a long story short," Giblet cut in, making a come-along motion, "we don't *have* to beat these sorry assholes ourselves. All we have to do is give everyone else a chance, an opening, and they'll throw themselves into the enemy guns just for the chance to kill them." He hadn't said anything up until now, just kept giving the stink-eye to Tamura, but the cynical anger behind his words wasn't directed at the Kamerians.

"They laid waste to our worlds centuries ago, butchered my people and hunted down the ones who got away." His eyes locked on Tamura. "I made my life swindling people, conning them out of their money with not a single altruistic thought the entire time, not even a notion, a daydream of striking back against the Anguilar. Because I thought it couldn't be done. Because no one had the balls or the brains to fight the Empire. Until I met these guys." He waved at me, Laranna. "They didn't give a damn how hopeless it was, they just did it anyway. And once I saw it could be done, that was all I needed. It's all most of us need."

"My wife," Val added, like this was one of the Pentecostal church services Jill used to take me to and we were all giving testimony, "is Copperell. The first ones conquered by the Anguilar. They've been beat down so long, thousands of them have volunteered for the Anguilar military. But when the Anguilar came after me, she helped me anyway. We have thousands of Copperell in the resistance now. And tens or hundreds of thousands of more will join when they see there's hope."

"All right, I get it," Dothan said. "I still think you're all suicidal chumps, but…" His massive shoulders shrugged. "If I get to fly again, I guess that's a better way to die than in my sleep in a stasis pod."

"We *will* get to fly, won't we?" Tamura asked pointedly, tilting his head toward me.

He wasn't the only one looking at me. They all were.

You asked for this, Travers.

"Yeah, you will. Val, contact the other Liberators. Tell them to pick up four thousand Strada and have Nareena come with them. And enough landers to carry them all."

"We're gonna do this?" Dani asked, her smile tight and thin. I thought she might be eager…and nervous.

"No more reacting." I grabbed Laranna's hand and squeezed it tight. "Now we take the fight to them."

10

I WAS NEVER any sort of mechanic. As a teenager, I'd been too busy with athletics to work a lot of hours, so I'd never earned enough to buy my own car, and my parents weren't about to buy me one. Or anything. So I didn't have the experience my friends did rebuilding engines and switching out transmissions from junk-yard salvage. I certainly hadn't done any electrical work, even in a car, much less an airplane.

Which isn't to say any of that would have been adequate training for maintaining a Vanguard starfighter, but maybe it would have given me at least a false sense of confidence. I didn't even have that, just a tablet with a technical schematic, a test kit, a tray of replacement power couplings, and an all-purpose wrench that looked like Dr. Who's sonic screwdriver.

And a headache from jamming myself under the pilot's station in the cockpit with my legs hanging out the side and the open maintenance panel banging against the back of my skull every time I shifted positions.

"Damn it," I murmured, forcing myself not to rub the side of my head, instead concentrating on touching the test module to the next in a row of power couplings.

The tester beeped plaintively, and I sighed, then tossed down the tablet and grabbed the sonic screwdriver. I worked the prongs at the end around the edges of the coupling and squeezed the lever at the side, locking it in place, then yanked. The first few times, I hadn't pulled hard enough, and I'd had to go hunt down Tamura in one of the other Vanguards on the far side of the hangar bay and ask him what I was doing wrong. Listening to Dothan laugh at me had been incentive enough not to go back again.

Sure, I could have let the Peboktan engineers maintain my bird, but everyone else was working on their own fighter and I had to set an example. It wasn't as if there was anything else to do on the flight to Thalassia. I couldn't even go over the attack plan with the Strada because we wouldn't rendezvous with them until we jumped into the outer system.

Setting the bad coupler beside the tray, I found a replacement, checked the diagram again and pushed the new one in place partway by hand before I used the tool to seat it correctly. I hoped. Another check on the tester and the light showed green, no annoying beep.

Who would have thought that several-hundred-year-old fighters would have so many worn-out parts?

"You need any help, Charlie?"

I sat up at the question, then cursed as I banged my head on that damned maintenance door again. It was Dani, standing beside the open hatch of the fighter, balanced on the steps.

"Don't you have your own bird to service?" I grinned. "And no, I don't mean Giblet."

"That's not funny," she said, scowling. "I…um…handed mine off to one of the Copperell trainees."

"Dani," I sighed, setting down the wrench with a clatter, "to set a good example, we should all work on our own…"

"I don't want to fly."

I didn't realize my mouth was hanging open until I closed it.

"What?" Not the most intelligent comment, but all I could manage with the pounding in my head.

Dani said nothing for a moment, her expression racked with emotion that might have been shame or guilt before it firmed up into something closer to the resolve I expected from her.

"Charlie, I've always had the gift of being able to make a pretty fair and objective assessment of my own strengths and weaknesses. If I stick with this for a few more years, I could probably be a fair pilot, but right now, I kind of suck. And that's just compared to you guys, not the Kamerians. I've watched the Copperell train and any one of our spare pilots Tamura and the others have been testing are better than I am. They give you a better chance at pulling this off than I do, and as much as I fricking *hate* benching myself"—she slammed her fist into the fuselage beside the door with a solid thump, gritting her teeth—"I think it'd be better if I wasn't behind the stick for this battle."

Dani sagged against the side of the hatchway, lip trembling

almost imperceptibly. I'd only known her for a few months now, but I had an idea of how much pride this had cost her.

"Okay," I said, nodding slowly. "In that case, you can either head down with Val and Nareena—they'd make you a company commander for one of the ground units—or…" I grinned and motioned to the right-hand seat. "You can go back to being my gunner. I know you hate it, but it's nice flying with someone who appreciates my taste in music."

"There's no one under the age of fifty who appreciates your taste in music, Travers," she assured me. "But okay. Besides, I'm good with a gun but I wouldn't have the slightest idea how to command a company."

"Well, you're gonna have to learn that, too. Because whether or not either of us is qualified to do it, the people we're leading, the Strada and the Copperell, believe in us and we can't let them down. On the bright side, it's a hell of a lot easier to learn than flying a starfighter, and I can actually teach you something about it. So can Nareena if you get any time with her. She's a badass."

I picked up the bad couplings I'd found and motioned back at the disassembled panel.

"Since you're officially my flight crew now, do me a favor and keep looking for burned-out couplings while I throw these away."

Dani scoffed but slid into position between the pilot's seat and the control panel anyway.

"You're just using me for grunt work so you can slack off," she accused, though I didn't think she meant it.

"I'll be back," I promised. "Watch your head." I'd barely

gotten the warning out when I heard the metallic *bonk* from the maintenance hatch.

"Dammit!"

"Have fun," I called over my shoulder, trying to drown out her cursing.

The recycling bin was all the way on the other side of the hangar, far enough for a nice break, and even better, right beside the break room. That was a recent addition, commissioned by me and constructed in a day by Lenny's builder bots. I'd watched them build it, one of the first opportunities I'd had to see them at work, and it was honestly among the freakiest things I'd ever seen. The things were about the size of a skateboard if a skateboard had a dozen grasping arms with interchangeable hands, and watching them disassemble and reassemble the interior walls had reminded me of termites constructing a mound. It gave me a chance to grab a cup of coffee and let my head rest.

Well, I *called* it coffee, but it was more like herbal tea with lemon, and it had taken me months to get used to the stuff. It was hot and it had caffeine in it, which was all that counted right now. Better still, there was no one else in the break room at the moment, which meant I wouldn't have to answer questions. That's the thing no one tells you about being a commander, the constant stupid questions that people should be able to figure out on their own. I'd gotten spoiled with our own small team and the general competency and self-reliance they showed. That had all ended when we took on the Copperell and Peboktan recruits.

"I don't like Sgt. Handel. Can I get assigned to a different platoon?"

"My gunner snores during long flights. Can you transfer him to another fighter?"

"Clarassa ate my leftover Kep-mok bloodticks! I was saving them for lunch!"

And on and on and on. I took my steaming cup to a table, then leaned over it to breathe in the vapors, which tasted better than the actual drink itself, and savored the silence. The door opened from the hangar bay, and I was all set to cringe at the intrusion when I saw it was Laranna.

"Already shamming, Charlie?" she asked, offering a grin to take the edge off the words as she grabbed a cup for herself and sat down beside me.

"I got Dani to do the work for me," I said, slipping an arm around her. She kissed me, which was a much better pickup than the caffeine. "She's decided she doesn't want to fly this run, says she's not ready for it. Wants to stick with being my gunner this time."

Laranna frowned, her lip curling in disappointment.

"She didn't strike me as someone who would give up so easily."

"Dani says she needs more stick time before she's ready for combat," I explained, shrugging. "I don't think she's giving up, she just doesn't want to be a liability on this operation. We know she can handle herself on the ground. It might just be that this isn't something she's wired for. It's not just the actual mechanics of flying one of these things, there's something about being on your own, isolated like that…" I looked around. "I mean, it gets to me a little, too. If I wasn't dumb enough to have volunteered for this, I'd probably be happy to just haul a rifle around on the surface, where the air is breathable."

Laranna chuckled.

"Perhaps that's the problem. She has the same sort of mindset you do, that of a primitive. You think it's somehow safer to be running around on the ground in a free-fire zone where any stray shot could kill you than it would be to fly a starship with shields and a hyperdrive."

"Well, when you put it *that* way," I admitted, scowling at her only half-seriously, "it feels a lot like an insult."

"Not at all." She smiled around a sip of her drink. "It's easy to find a leader who'll sit behind shields and a hyperdrive and tell the people on the ground to charge the enemy. Much harder to find one who's happier with a rifle in their hand."

"I think you're happier with just a knife."

"It *is* a more personal way to do battle." Laranna sighed. "Sometimes I wonder if I've abandoned the warrior ideals I was taught as a youth. We Strada are comfortable with firearms, but there's something honorable about the blade."

I scoffed, sitting back in my chair, shaking my head.

"Jeez, and you call *me* a primitive…"

Laranna's expression was gearing up for a spirited response to that but she was interrupted when the door swung open again. Brother Constantine stepped through, still wearing the same robes. I wondered if he even washed them. I mean, he *had* taken to bathing regularly at my insistence, but those clothes still had a ripe stench to them.

"Hey Constantine," I said, raising my mug in salute. "You want some coffee?"

I hadn't expected to see him here in the hangar, since he was neither a pilot nor a mechanic, but I'd given up trying to figure out the medieval monk weeks ago. There was a mysterious purpose to everything he did, and I couldn't shake the idea that discovering what it was would reveal the secrets of the universe.

"I have not come to drink," he told me. "I came here to find you." Constantine eyed Laranna. "I need to speak to you privately."

I felt Laranna tense up beside me and had a premonition that Constantine was about to experience first-hand exactly the sort of combat Strada warriors considered honorable unless I intervened.

"Laranna is my wife," I told him, putting a stern edge to the words, "as well as my second-in-command and the one person I trust most in the whole galaxy. Anything you have to say to me, you can say in front of her."

Constantine still had doubt in his eyes, but he nodded curtly. He made no move to sit down, standing as stiff and unmoving as Lenny, which might have been because he was trying to emulate the robot or maybe he'd noticed Laranna still close to a boil, her hand wrapped around the hilt of the knife at her belt.

"Very well." He pushed his hood back, revealing thinning gray hair, and glowered down at us like a fire-and-brimstone preacher. "I understand you intend to take the Kamerians into battle with you."

"That's right. They'll be the lead squadron." Which meant

we could keep an eye on them, but I didn't say that, either to Constantine or the Kamerians. "What about it?"

"You're making a grave mistake," he declared. "I was against the Kamerians being here, but you've kept them under close watch, which was wise…perhaps you've managed to extract some use from them. However, out there you'll be trusting your life to them, and they are not worthy of your trust." Constantine sniffed, nose wrinkling as if he'd smelled something rotten. "You don't understand their history."

"Well, you're here," Laranna growled deep in her throat, still eyeing him with the promise of violence. "Why don't you tell us about it?"

"You can sit down if you want," I added, motioning at the chair across the table from us.

"Thank you, I prefer to stand." The corner of his mouth turned up. "Though all the world stands against me."

"Oh, whatever." I restrained myself from rolling my eyes. "Get on with it, Constantine."

"I had access to all the records of the Creators in my office as an Alahandran," he said, not seeming to notice the sarcasm. "The Kamerians were the most primitive of all the races of the galaxy, the ones most in need of the help of the Creators. Their society was racked by violence and war, ravaged by famine and catastrophe, and when the Creators came, the Kamerians benefited more than any other world from their gifts. In a matter of years, their world had been rebuilt, their cities grown to marvels of technology that could house and feed millions. They became leaders in the new alliance of worlds, explorers, soldiers. They'd come the farthest…yet they had the least appreciation for the gifts they'd been given."

Constantine did move, then, pacing across the small break room like a caged lion, his strides long and powerful, as if he thought he were about to leap into battle. Though I wasn't sure if he thought he was about to fight the Kamerians or us.

"When the Creators moved on to find more worlds to aid, the Kamerians saw their opportunity. They had the advantage of starting out from a more primitive society…which meant they retained the aggression of a more violent culture. The only world they considered a threat was Strada, but they were able to secure a treaty with the Strada Council. They didn't need their help, just their inaction."

"My people did that?" Laranna asked, her eyes wide.

"You didn't know?" I asked her, surprised.

"There's not a lot of history left from before the war," she admitted.

"They did," Constantine confirmed. "They had no desire to become involved in what they saw as a conflict between the Kamerians and the Copperell."

"Damn," I murmured. "Poor Copperell…they always get the worst of it."

"That's probably why they fell first to the Anguilar," Laranna guessed. "But I know Strada fell to the Kamerians…"

"Once the Kamerians had Copperell," the monk told us, "they took a few years to consolidate their gains before they went after the Krin. The Strada had no love for the Krin…no one did. So they didn't interfere. By the time the Alliance moved on to the next world, the Strada finally moved against them, but by then, it was far too late."

"This was all a long time ago," I reminded him. "That war lasted decades." I motioned out at the hangar bay. "These guys wouldn't even have been born when it started. You can't blame them for what happened."

"A Kamerian is a Kamerian," Constantine insisted with a sneer of disdain. "They can no more change than a leopard can change its spots."

I said nothing for a beat, wondering how to read this guy. He'd been raised in medieval Germany, trained as a monk at a time when people didn't debate things like this, they just *knew* them. But on the other hand, he'd also been taken to the wider galaxy, met aliens, read histories no one else retained, lived for over six hundred years. In the end, I decided I just had to tell him what I really felt.

"Back when I come from, some really bad things happened because we judged people based on nothing but their race. We still had problems with it when I left, and if Dani is a good judge, they're not over yet, thirty-six years later. If I have anything to say about it"—I arched an eyebrow—"and I *do*, we're going to be judging people as individuals, not based on where they were born or what they happen to look like. You are what you do, the choices you make."

"That's a wonderful sentiment, Charlie. But it's just as likely to get you killed. And this resistance of yours right alongside you."

"Maybe," I conceded, shrugging. "I'm pretty new at this, and

I know you've been around a long time, Brother, but I think I've learned a little."

Pushing up from the table, I faced him, not giving an inch, facing him eye to eye.

"A resistance that doesn't give everyone a chance to fight for their freedom doesn't deserve to survive."

11

"Only two," Tamura said, sniffing in disdain. "I was hoping for more."

"Oh, I think two Anguilar cruisers are plenty," I assured him, tapping a finger against the console. "You gotta walk before you can run."

"I don't like being out here this long," Dothan grumbled, staring around at the bridge. I wasn't sure if he meant sitting in the outer reaches of the Thalassia system or being on the bridge of the *Liberator*, but I could tell he didn't feel comfortable with either. "We need to get this thing going. We don't need the other ships to take two cruisers and a few squadrons of fighters."

"We had to wait for the other ships," I reminded him, "because we're not just blowing up some cruisers, we're taking this planet. And to do that, we need troops."

"Well, I hope they're freaking ready now."

So did I, though I wasn't going to give him the satisfaction of letting him know that.

"Nareena," I said, leaning over the audio pickup, "you read me?"

"Loud and clear, Charlie."

Which was no surprise, given how close the *Flying Fortress* was to us. She was visible on the optical cameras, a floating mountain blending in with the dark shadows of the asteroid we were all hiding behind. The *Fortress* and the *Marauder* couldn't have been more than a mile away, which seemed pretty far, but out in space, for ships this size, it was practically spitting distance.

"Are your people all caught up on the operations order?" I asked her.

"We're good to go," she replied, though I thought I still heard a little amusement in her voice at the American military term. The Strada were more traditional when it came to battle, warriors more than soldiers, and getting them to adapt the discipline and organization of the US Army had been a long battle. Hopefully, a rewarding one. "Ready to board the landers at your signal."

"The *Liberator* will jump in first," I reminded her, "drop the fighters and start taking out the orbital defenses. Once we get all their attention on us, I'll tell Val to bring your ships in."

"It might be easier to break down those defenses with two more Liberators," Giblet pointed out.

"What, Varnell?" Tamura asked, his tone mocking. "You don't think we can handle them ourselves?"

"I think," Giblet said, glaring at the Kamerian, "that if I had the call, I'd send just you four in and see how well you do all by yourselves."

"That'd be fine with me," Dothan said. "The rest of you are all dead weight, anyway."

"Why don't both of you shut up?" Dani suggested, which was as close as she'd come to a conversation with Giblet in days.

"We're holding the other two ships back," I told Gib, ignoring the bickering, jumping in before one of them wound up trying to kick the other's ass, "because we want the Vanguard Wing to get some experience, and because the Liberators are irreplaceable. We lose one, or even get it damaged bad enough, we lose our troop transports."

"Oh, good," Giblet sneered. "I love being expendable."

"If it helps," Tamura said, smiling with saccharine sweetness, "I'll always think of you that way."

Dani barked a laugh, but Giblet didn't seem amused.

"Get to the fighters," I told them. "Gib, make sure the flight crews are loaded up and ready to launch once we jump in."

"Yeah, I'm all over it," he said, still glowering at Tamura... and Dani to boot.

Tamura watched him and the other Kamerians go before he turned back to me.

"It won't mean much to you," he said, "not being Kamerian, but..." He made a complex gesture with one hand, then touched his chest and forehead. "May the Blood God keep your honor and grant you a good death."

He was right, it didn't mean much to me, but I could tell by his expression that it did to him. Maybe Constantine was right, maybe the Kamerians were playing me for a sucker, but if I couldn't trust my instincts enough to figure this right, then I wasn't much of a commander.

"Thank you." I smiled. "And I know this won't mean much to you, but…" I raised a hand in a Vulcan salute. "Live long, and prosper."

"I don't know that a long life is in the cards for someone like me," Tamura admitted, "but I appreciate the sentiment." He pointed at me sternly. "Don't forget, Charlie Travers…your fighter has a hyperdrive for a reason, and it's not just to get you from point A to point B. It's a tool and a weapon and you should use it as such."

"I won't forget. I hope to see you and your squadron at the end of all this."

"You mean you hope we don't steal your fighters and run off in them," he said, eyeing me sidelong as he turned to leave the bridge. "That's why you've assigned your Copperell gunners to us and made sure they're armed." I opened my mouth to say something reassuring, but he waved it off. "I wouldn't respect you if you didn't. Once we've shed blood and risked our lives together, things will be different."

I hoped he was right.

"Lenny, give us half an hour to get strapped in and ready for launch, then jump in as close as you can." The robot didn't reply, but I didn't worry that he hadn't heard. Lenny heard everything. "Val, you sure you want to come down with the landing force? We could still use you up here for command and control during the battle." I raised a hand at the scandalized expression on the face of the chief of the Copperell bridge crew. "Not that I don't completely trust you guys to run the ship, but Val knows infantry fighting and would be more savvy about the type of support they'd need."

Which was half-true. I trusted Val more because he'd proven himself when I needed him, whereas the most these guys had done was take a few easy potshots in a battle that was already won.

"No," Val insisted, his expression mulish. "I trained those Copperell troops and they need someone they're used to following. No offense to Nareena, but the Strada have their way and we have ours."

I frowned, a little because I was hoping to keep him out of harm's way so I could deliver him healthy and whole again to Brandy and Maxx, but mostly because I'd spent months trying to turn the Strada way and the Copperell way into the military way.

Walk before you run, Travers.

"All right," I told him. "But your landers don't launch until I say."

"We need to get to the fighters," Laranna reminded me. "Half an hour, remember?"

I tossed Val an offhanded salute and followed her off the bridge, matching her long strides.

"The Kamerians seem to think this is going to be a cakewalk," I said, "barely worth our time."

"Do you trust them?" she asked.

"I want to. I gotta admit, I like Tamura, for all that the Kamerians are like frat boys mixed with a high school football team. And believe me, that's not something I ever thought I'd say about one of them after meeting Seraph Nix."

Laranna grunted softly.

"You're not the only one who likes him. Though I'm fairly certain Dani's feelings toward him are of a different nature than yours."

"Have you thought about what Lenny said?" I blurted, the thought coming out of nowhere, storming out of the back of my head unbidden.

Laranna shook her head in confusion.

"Charlie, I know you've told me that married people can read each other's minds, but…"

"The part about how we could have kids." I motioned expansively. "I mean, he said it would take some technological intervention, whatever that means, but it's possible."

"Yes, I remember," she said, which seemed awfully noncommittal to me.

"Is that something you want?" I pressed. "I mean, it's a big step and we're at war and constantly throwing ourselves into life-or-death situations, but…I'd like to know."

Laranna stopped abruptly, oblivious of all the crew passing us in the corridor, grabbed me by the neck, and yanked me into a kiss so fierce it took my breath away. She didn't completely let go, just pulled away enough to look me in the eye.

"I wouldn't have married you otherwise, Charlie Travers." She shrugged and started walking again, leaving me scrambling to keep up, suddenly interested in other things than flying. "However, you're right. We're at war, and perhaps it would be wise to wait until things settle down."

"I don't know when that'll be," I confessed once my big head was working again. "You know, back on my world, there've been times like when Rome fell—they were kind of like the Kamerians—when everyone was in constant danger of starvation, disease, and invasion for decades. Things didn't settle down for hundreds of years. But life still had to go on."

Laranna peered at me from beneath raised brows.

"You want to have kids right now?"

"No, not right now," I sighed. "I just don't want to put it off until everything gets normal…because I'm not sure if things ever *will* be normal."

"Warning," an automated voice announced against a background chorus of alarm buzzers and flashing red lights, "hyperspace jump in ten minutes. All hands to battle stations."

"You have odd timing, my love," Laranna said.

She grabbed my hand and dragged me off to battle.

ONE THING I'd learned out here was that sci-fi movies are full of crap. Maybe that's ironic coming from a guy who got abducted by an alien robot, who fights space pirates and goes to bed every night with a green-skinned warrior woman, but what I was thinking of specifically was the idea of desert planets and jungle planets and ice planets and water planets, or any world that had just one kind of weather or environment. That's not how things work.

The closest I'd seen to that was Aether, and that was only anything close to habitable because of hot springs and volcanic activity caused by its proximity to the gas giant. Everywhere else…well, there'd been worlds with more desert than others, and some with more oceans than others, but they all had mountains and valleys, seas and wastes and everything else that made up a world because if they didn't, they wouldn't be livable and there wouldn't be a settlement there.

Thalassia was a little more green and a little less brown than some, with shallow seas winding their way among two vast continents, the ice caps smaller than Earth's but larger than other worlds I'd seen. It had the look of a living planet and a pleasant one…until the sensor scope flashed red with the icons of the enemy. Two big ones, the Anguilar cruisers, wedge-shaped in their crimson avatar as they were in real life, and streaming out of them a swarm of smaller craft that could only be one thing.

"The cruisers are accelerating," Dani told me, competent by now at reading the sensor screens after weeks of training in the cockpit. "And launching Starblades. I'm picking up six squadrons of them from the cruisers. Don't know if there'll be more launching from the planet."

"Not yet," I guessed, maintaining our acceleration and course. "By their way of thinking, the *Liberator* is hanging back and sending out a fighter screen to clear a path to the cruisers. They saw us launch out of her, figure we're just some kind of short-range craft, probably kludged together by pirates. They're thinking those Starblades are gonna cut us to pieces and then the two of them'll move in and take out the *Liberator*."

Dani regarded me with a skeptical tilt to her head.

"They are, huh?"

"Let's hope so," I told her, "because there's nothing between them and us but…nothing."

That was the part about flying a fighter that bugged me, the part Laranna didn't get because she'd been raised with all this as normal. To me, the getting shot at part wasn't nearly as terrifying as the whole floating in blackness with nothing around for hundreds of thousands of miles. Nothing except the enemy.

If there was any consolation, the training *had* made a difference. The micro-jump in the *Liberator* hadn't bothered me at all and, as long as I pictured the incoming flight of Anguilar fighters as the target drones I'd been facing for weeks, I could look at that scope and not have my confidence waver one bit.

What gave me even more confidence was the arrowhead formation of fighters behind me, arranged by element, flight, and squadron. We'd considered, early on, whether to go with the Kamerian designation of a squadron as six planes or the Anguilar one of four fighters, but I'd decided that if I was remaking the military in the image of the one I knew the best, that of 1980s-era America, I was going to stick by that organization.

Two Vanguards to an element, two elements to a flight, two flights to a squadron. And given the number of fighters we were pretty much stuck with, three squadrons to a wing. Which made me the wing commander, although Dani laughed uncontrollably whenever I mentioned that and asked if Freddie Prinze Jr. was going to play me in the movie. The only Freddie Prinze I knew had played on Chico and the Man, but I didn't bother to ask for an explanation since my head was already stuffed too full trying to remember everything that had changed since I left.

In practice, though, Laranna led First Squadron and Giblet led Second, while I'd put Tamura and the Kamerians in Third, which I was technically also in charge of but had put Tamura as the tactical leader. That allowed me and my wingman, a Copperell pilot named Donnell, to go wherever I needed to if anyone else needed support. I'd rather have had Laranna on my wing, but that would have been a waste of one of our better pilots and one of our best tactical leaders.

I take it back. The worst part about flying a fighter wasn't the nothing, it was the waiting. We were burning at a good clip toward the Starblades while they were doing the same straight at us, and it still dragged on into minutes of nothing but the roaring in my ears.

"Can't we just jump on top of them?" Giblet asked. I double checked to make sure he was calling on our private frequency rather than whining in front of the entire fighter wing and sighed with a little relief when I saw he was at least wise enough for that.

"No," I insisted. "You know the plan. The idea is to *not* give the cruisers enough time to make a run for hyperspace. The less warning the Anguilar get about this base going down, the more time we have to fortify it before they try to counterattack. No micro-jumps until the fighters are fully engaged."

He didn't reply, unless the soft burst of static from the cockpit speakers was a grunt.

"We'll be in firing range in two minutes," Dani warned me.

The Anguilar didn't think much of us. I could tell that because they weren't trying anything fancy, not spreading out to take us at the flanks, determined to hit us head on. Which we could have done very easily, but letting the enemy know we had shields wasn't in the plan, either. We were just ordinary fighters, nothing special…that was what we wanted them to think.

"Vanguard squadrons," I said, watching the red range line moving toward us, "execute."

"Always gotta do things the hard way," Giblet murmured just to me, but when he switched to his squadron frequency, he was all gung-ho. "Second squadron, follow me over the top!"

Again, direction was a relative thing in space, but Gib and his squadron broke toward the north side of the system compared to the ecliptic while Laranna led hers downward, leaving the Kamerians and my element all alone in the middle. It would have been too much to ask for the Anguilar pilots to just come straight on into Third Squadron like the bait we were. Instead, they blossomed, flowering into three petals, aimed at each of our elements.

"Only pulse turrets," I cautioned, risking distracting my pilots to preserve the plan. "No particle cannons yet."

Gib didn't grumble this time, but that might have been because he was too busy spinning his fighter, trailed by the rest of his birds, hitting braking thrust just long enough before they turned back into the enemy Starblades. It wasn't a fair fight, not the way I'd set it up. The Starblades had the advantage on us when it came to short-range speed and maneuverability, and I was pulling our punches. During the discussion of the battle plan, Dani had called it "nerfing." Unlike most of her slang, this term actually made sense to me.

Like my father had used to tell me when he spanked me as a kid, "this is going to hurt me more than it hurts you." Dad had been lying, but I wasn't. I had to fly my Vanguard straight into the muzzles of a squadron of Starblades, pretending I couldn't have blown them apart ten seconds earlier. Like the *Flying Fortress* earlier, the fighters were a stone's throw away, close enough that I could make out the Anguilar stencils on the wings by their drive flares by the time we crossed that red line.

"Break left!" I ordered, yanking the steering yoke even as I spoke the words.

Streaks of red scalar energy seared through the space I'd just vacated and even if I knew in my head that the pulse blast would have spent itself on my shield, my gut had accepted the necessity to hide those shields as a matter of life or death and reacted accordingly.

Donnell followed my lead, but the Kamerians had me beat by a fraction of a second, were already spinning on their axes by the time I twisted the wheel. The roar of the main drives fighting each other on their different gimbal headings was nearly drowned out by the drumhead vibration of the steering jets swinging our fighter around to bring the lead Starblade into the firing arc of our pulse turrets.

"Dani…"

"I got it," she said quietly, twisting the twin joysticks of the turret controls and jamming down the triggers.

A cascade of red energy connected us to the enemy fighter, catching the bird in mid-turn, its maneuvering thrusters flaring across one side, its drive cut off for a quicker change of direction. Glowing darts of power pierced the cockpit while another shower of scalar force chopped divots from the wing before sparking off the main engine.

I spared the dying fighter a single glance before kicking in our drives again, the momentum edging past the cushion of the inertial dampeners enough to shove me against my restraints. Natural instinct for self-preservation tried to drag my attention back to the other Starblades engaging my squadron, but the burden of command anchored my eyes in place on the sensor screen, trying to get a sense of the rest of the wing…and the status of our strategy.

It had worked. The Starblade squadrons were spinning in place, engaging with the Vanguards, their momentum spent in braking burns that had left them drifting tens of thousands of miles from the Anguilar cruisers. The capitol ships were at station, keeping just at minimum safe jump distance from Thalassia, waiting for the *Liberator* to make a move, cautious because they'd heard about the former zoo ships.

They hadn't heard about us.

"Vanguard Wing!" I called, tapping the nav controls almost without thought, the movements automatic by this point. "Jump!"

I wasn't the first because the Kamerians were faster than the rest of us at everything and Gib was still the best pilot in our group, so I had a momentary glimpse of rainbow rings tearing holes in space, a brief burst of energy as the other fighters entered hyperspace. The hand of unreality came for me, then, grabbing me by the shirt front and yanking me out of our universe and into another for a single heartbeat before dumping me out again on the other side.

If star cruisers had faces, these would have been gaping in disbelief as an entire wing of Vanguards appeared out of hyperspace less than two thousand miles off their bow. Now, the battle would *really* begin.

12

Despite the training, despite the visualization and the high-dives and the stomach-clenching, there was still a half a second's recovery time that none of us could get around, and by the time I blinked the haze away, the Kamerian flight had already opened up on what we'd decided to designate cruiser Alpha. I'd thought about just calling them one and two, but that didn't seem dramatic enough, and if I was going to be flying a starfighter in a space battle, well, dammit, I wanted it to be dramatic.

Tamura and the others made it dramatic as hell, concentrating their fire exactly where we'd planned, targeting the sensor array with four perfectly aimed particle cannon shots. The curved metal plate described an arc across the front of a ridged section of the dorsal hull of the Anguilar ship…until it didn't. Nothing was left except a charred, molten line, and still the four Kamerians rocketed toward the center of the cruiser. I opened my mouth to shout a warning but before I got the words out, all four Vanguards vanished into nothingness, the rips in space they'd traversed closing behind them.

"Oh, hell yeah," I muttered.

"Oh, no," Dani insisted, shaking her head, her hand raised in warning. "You're *not*…"

"Vanguard Sixteen," I called to Donnell, "follow me in and do exactly what they did."

"Do I *have* to?" the Copperell moaned.

"You can stay here if you'd rather, but I'm going in!"

The Kamerians had totally destroyed our squadron's primary target, so I switched to the secondary, a ring of maneuvering thrusters on the port bow of the ship. The cruiser tried to help, firing those thrusters, trying to spin upward, raising its main guns into a firing arc that would have torn me apart, but all it did was expose the target even more.

Pulse turrets had already bracketed us, firing a spray of energy across our trajectory, but I ignored the incoming rounds except a passing thought that the violet halo of the shields was beautiful, particularly since it meant I wasn't dying. Despite his protests, Donnell had fallen into formation with me, and the actinic whiplash of his particle cannon reached out alongside my own, both of them striking the thruster module.

I couldn't have sworn to what the thruster ran on, except that it wasn't unleaded. Not a rocket like the space shuttle, I assumed, because I didn't recall Lenny mentioning a need to refuel anything, but it also didn't need a power cell to operate because we'd been able to use the maneuvering thrusters even when our power had been close to drained. Whatever it was, it blew up real good. Sprays of white sparks and a cloud of burning gas billowed out from the wreckage of the thruster pod, but I couldn't afford any more time to gawk at it, not with the massive bulk of the cruiser only a half a mile away.

It didn't take much, and I'd had plenty of practice, but I only had seconds, and that seemed to make me even more thumb-fingered, but I managed to push the levers forward just before I would have smashed into the side of the hull. God slapped me in the back of the head and then kneed me in the groin while I was distracted, but I was alive and on the other side of that ship.

I whooped an involuntary yell of exultation and when Donnell emerged behind me, he was screaming as well, though possibly not for the same reason.

"You're a maniac, Charlie," Dani said, though I was almost certain she was hiding a grin.

I didn't try to hide mine, spinning the fighter in place to join the Kamerians, putting the bulk of the cruiser between us and Second Squadron as they attacked from the other side. My particle cannon slashed across the ventral spine of the ship like a pirate's cutlass, joined by five others, ripping glowing chunks out of the ship despite its shielding glowing white in a desperate halo, as if an angel from on high were doing his best to protect the Anguilar...and failing.

The shield couldn't keep the particle cannon blasts from penetrating, but it was still absorbing energy...a lot more energy than it could manage, and that halo grew with every passing second, every shot. I had a gut feeling and acted on it without wondering if I was wrong.

"Second and Third," I snapped, fingers already tapping commands into the navigation console, "jump away from him, minimum distance! Now! Get out!"

Another reality shift and Dani put her hand to her mouth, retching fitfully but trying to keep it contained. We were maybe five or six thousand miles from the cruiser, but I couldn't see it anymore. Not because we were too far away but because it was concealed behind a coruscating wall of white, the shield glowing like a streetlamp.

The sphere of energy collapsed in on itself, and I gasped at the sight, at the inevitable rebound that followed, the cruiser disintegrating as all that stored energy fell in on it. Our own shields glowed with effort as the waves of power washed over us, sending Vanguard One bobbing and shaking like a ship in a storm.

The second cruiser wasn't going to put on a show for us, I judged. Laranna and her squadron had battered and broken the thing, but in discrete blows, not a constant barrage that overloaded the shields. Bits of the cruiser had splintered away, the edges of the breaks glowing white, atmosphere gushing out and briefly burning until it dispersed. I knew if I looked close enough, I'd see bodies tumbling out of those gaps, but I didn't try. Some things couldn't be unseen and even if the Anguilar all deserved it, which I tried to convince myself, that didn't mean I had to like it.

"Second and Third, we're hitting the ground defenses," I

said. "First Squadron, once you've finished the cruiser off, circle back and take care of those Starblades."

"Copy, Vanguard One," Laranna replied. "See you down there."

The starfighter rumbled at my touch on the control yoke, the throttle, like the engine of a classic muscle car from the 60's, and I guided the magnificent beast in toward the blue-green face of Thalassia, knowing the fire that would be pouring up at me and not fearing it.

I was still infantry at heart, but I had to admit…there was something to be said for flying.

———

"Follow the yellow brick road," I hummed, guiding the control yoke gently, just a nudge here and there, keeping the fighter's icon aligned on the navigational pathway. "Follow the yellow brick road…"

"If you only had a brain," Dani lamented softly and I couldn't help but laugh, remembering a line from one of the movies I'd watched courtesy of Sheriff Dobbs' cell phone.

"I understood that reference."

"Be cautious, Charlie," Tamura radioed.

He'd cooperated with every other measure I'd put in place, from the new-to-him organizational tables to what I'd considered pushing the envelope, not putting him in charge of his own squadron, but he just wouldn't do the whole "Vanguard One, Vanguard Two" thing and every time I brought it up, he would simply state that our comms were secure enough that we didn't need call signs.

"We'll be in range of their ground defenses in another minute," he went on, "and if they have particle cannon emplacements…"

He didn't have to finish. As devastating as the weapons were in a vacuum, they were a hell of a lot worse in an atmosphere, where they had something to conduct their thermal and electromagnetic energy. All it would take was one hit and, shields or no, I'd be toast.

That atmosphere buffeted at the fighter as if teasing me with the implicit threat, and damned if Philos, Thalassia's capital and the largest city on the planet, wasn't on the night side. It didn't really make a difference, not with the enhanced optics in the fighters or our combat helmets, but there was something claustrophobic about fighting at night that no amount of technology could change.

At least the darkness made the air cooler, the ride smoother… and the thermal signatures of the air defense turrets easier to see.

"Remember," I told them, not because they would have forgotten but because it would go against every instinct they had, "we want those emplacements intact, if at all possible. Don't get yourselves killed doing it, but if you can make it down past the defenses, plan A is to land and attack on foot."

"It's still a stupid-ass plan," Dothan insisted. "We're pilots, not soldiers."

"Big boy," Dani teased, "you're trying to tell me that you don't think you can take out a few Anguilar conscripts without some Strada foot-soldier holding your hand? You? A Kamerian fighter pilot?"

She shot me a grin and I offered her a thumbs-up in return. Dothan, for his part, growled in a deep, bass rumble that vibrated the speakers.

"These Anguilar wimps couldn't defeat a Kamerian kindergarten class."

"Second Squadron," I called back to Giblet and his birds, spread out behind us in a double wedge formation, "you're pulling cover. We're gonna be busy with evasive maneuvers, so don't shoot us by accident."

"No worries, Charlie," Gib replied, a hard edge to his tone. "If I shoot anyone, it's not gonna be by accident."

"What the hell is his problem, anyway?" Dani asked, shaking her head. I checked to make sure she hadn't just blurted that out on an open mic and was relieved to see it had been muted. I did the same to mine before I replied.

"You can't seriously tell me you don't know," I said, rolling my eyes. "I think it's pretty clear that he's attracted to you."

Dani spluttered a derisive laugh.

"For God's sake, Charlie, Gib is *attracted* to pretty much anything female with two legs. Mallarna told me he tried to hit on her when she first got to the *Liberator*, and she's half a *bug*. Not to mention, he has *feathers*! I've had a few weird boyfriends in my life, but I never dated anyone who evolved from a damned bird."

"You asked," I reminded her, shrugging the exchange off, concentrating on the ground rushing up below us.

Philos was a seaport, built on a river delta, and the land

around it was flat until it reached rolling hills and thick forests, but the space around the river was cleared, bridged, crisscrossed with roads and development. They could have put the air defense emplacements anywhere, but the thermal readings told me they were on alternating sides of the river just outside town. And if that white glow building up just below the surface meant anything…

"Evasive!" I snapped, barely getting the word out before I threw the Vanguard into a barrel roll.

Lightning flashed not from the clouds but up from the ground, turning the air around it to plasma, static electricity crackling for miles around the particle beam. St. Elmo's fire glowed around the metal of my bird and probably everyone else's, but for the moment, I couldn't worry about anyone else, couldn't be a commander. I had to survive to get down to the ground, if that meant leaving my stomach behind at 30,000 feet, well…so long, stomach.

This was one of those times when I wished for a Starblade. Despite the lack of armor, the light weaponry, the short range, the damned things could really *move* down here in the air. Flying the Vanguard in an atmosphere was like driving a truck, and only the gimballed engine pods saved us from being fried as one thundercrack after another shook the fuselage, fat snaps of electricity leaping off any metal surface in the cockpit to nip at my fingers.

The bird didn't have enough wing surface for a real evasive course, but when one engine pod could vector away from the other, the Vanguard could power through some pretty nifty maneuvers. Not painlessly, though. I'd pushed the compensators to their limits and they pushed right back, crushing me into the seat as it spun wildly on its own gimbals, mirroring the drive pods to keep me from being thrown out of the seat.

Not that it was much worse than riding the Scorpion roller coaster at Busch Gardens, but no one had ever asked me to operate the coaster at the same time I was riding it. Even the seat groaned in protest at the *g*-load I was putting on the plane, unless that was actually Dani. Or maybe even me. It was hard to tell because my entire focus was on keeping my eyes open, watching the emitter of the particle cannon swinging back and forth, desperately seeking a target.

And of course, I was worried sick about Donnell. Not the Kamerians—I didn't know them well enough and also figured they could handle themselves. But Donnell was my wingman, my responsibility, and he had less combat flight experience than I did. Not by much, but it was still enough to make me feel guilty about dragging him along on this, despite the fact that we'd barely been nodding acquaintances before he'd been assigned to me.

The descent went on a lot longer than any rollercoaster, dragging for minutes that felt like hours, and I'd lost count of how many bolts had blasted into the air from the air defense turrets. Enough that the air was supercharged with the raw, bristling energy, low-hanging clouds glowing bright with stored static electricity, discharges striking the ground like the worst lightning storm I'd ever experienced.

I didn't realize I'd been clenching my teeth until the tactical computer informed me with a cheerful ding like a microwave timer that we were below the firing arc of the turret and could just relax now. I didn't relax much except my jaw, twisting the wheel and the fighter into a tight spiral around the base of the turret.

"Vehicles in the open," I told Dani, the announcement almost preceding the conscious realization of what I'd seen, armored cars or tanks or APCs or whatever the Anguilar called them, parked on either side of the flower-pot curve of the air defense turret.

We hadn't trained for this as much as we had the space combat, but Dani, for all that she wasn't the best pilot, was one hell of a gunner. Her pulse guns spoke their displeasure at the presence of the tanks in our LZ, coughing out raging gouts of raw power at the objects of our irritation, blowing the vehicles off the ground in fountains of vaporized dirt. Tons of metal flipped and tumbled and neither had hit the ground before Vanguard One touched down on landing gear that had barely had time to lock in place.

Impact jerked me forward against my seat restraints, forcing me to hit the quick-release twice before the thing would let me loose. I stumbled out of the chair before the gimbals had a chance to set it straight, paused at the rack beside the hatch, and grabbed a pulse rifle for myself, then handed the other back to Dani. Dark outside. I pushed down my helmet's faceplate, the image in the enhanced optics flickering green for a fraction of a second before it settled back into almost midday brightness.

I gave Dani a thumbs-up and got the same motion back from her, then palmed the hatch control, snugged the butt-stock of the rifle into my shoulder, and ducked through before it had the chance to fully open. Charred soil crunched like shattered glass under my boots, and an impenetrable haze of white smoke swallowed me up, pulling a veil over even the enhanced optics.

My gut clenched at the thought of a shot coming out of that curling, drifting smoke, putting an end to my adventure. Just some random Anguilar soldier stumbling around blind, getting lucky. Not that I panicked. I might have, a few months ago, might have just held down the trigger and sprayed a couple dozen rounds off in every direction to keep any notional enemy's head down. It would have been reckless and stupid, but I hadn't been above either of those when I'd first arrived here, never having heard a shot fired in anger.

The fear hadn't gone anywhere, was still solidly in place, fluttering in my stomach, but I'd at least learned enough to keep it from expanding out from my gut to my head. Fear was good, panic was not. I didn't know who was out in that smoke, but I knew *what* was there. The turret. Due north, maybe fifty yards away. I wanted to sprint toward it but loped instead, long strides carefully placed, watching for those holes Dani had chopped in the ground.

Flames crackled to my right, the remains of one of the armored vehicles burning fiercely, the main chassis upside down, half buried in dirt, throwing up even more smoke. Fifty yards seemed to take a lot longer than I thought it would and I was certain I'd missed the entire structure and was about to run off the side of the bank into the river before the smoke cleared.

I didn't see the wall until I ran into it. Gray, featureless, much like the haze surrounding it, and I slammed into it shoulder first with a crash of metal on concrete and bounced off. No way to tell which way the entrance was, but the turret base was generally round so I just kept my left hand on the wall and circled to the right.

Gaps in the smoke teased at the edges of my vision, showing me glimpses of the river, of the burning vehicles, the fighter. Overhead, engines screamed as the other fighters came down under fire, thundercracks echoing up the river valley like it was the end of the world. I wanted to call up to them, get their status, make sure everyone was okay, but I couldn't. Not yet. Right now, taking this turret was my only job.

I was beginning to think the entrance was on the exact opposite side of the structure, that I'd have to circumnavigate the thing to reach it, when a handy guide showed up to tell me exactly where the door was located. He wore Anguilar combat armor, though this far out on the edge of the Empire, he probably wasn't one of what they called the *bloodline*, the families who had left their home thousands of years ago. Just some poor schlub who'd lived so long under the thumb of the Anguilar that Stockholm Syndrome had set in, and he figured he should throw his lot in with the winners instead of working on a farm or in a mine.

If I could have captured every one of the pitiful bastards who'd fallen into that trap, I would have treated them like cultists, had them deprogrammed and forced to face the truth. But there were only about twenty thousand of us, only twelve thousand of those combatants, and the best thing we could do was make sure that men and women like this guy had an alternative.

I shot him before he saw me.

The door into the turret swung back and I threw myself forward just in time to catch it, stepping over the dead trooper, his legs still kicking in one last galvanic response. Light from the inside of the turret sent rays through the smoke like a sign from above, and I, like the wandering spirits in my favorite ghost movie, went into the light. Two more of them, neither wearing armor. Technicians, the guys shooting off those blasts over and over, their field utilities revealing that they were Krin. They were also armed, one of them clawing at his belt for the pistol holstered there while the other lunged for a comm unit.

They didn't have a chance, but they were Krin and from what I knew of Krin, surrendering wasn't their M.O., which was probably why the Anguilar used them for cannon fodder. The red flare of my pulse rifle outshone the interior lamps for just a moment just as the *crack-snap* of the discharge drowned out the dull thud of their bodies hitting the floor.

No one else. No *room* for anyone else in the cramped control room, barely room for me to stand without stepping on the dead Krin. I kept the muzzle of the rifle on them for a long second, watching for motion, for breath, but they'd never be moving again.

"Clear!" I said to Dani, sensing her coming up behind me, then repeated myself into the comms. "Vanguard One objective clear. Third Squadron, check in with your status."

"Vanguard…Sixteen here," Donnell replied, apparently having to think a second about what his call sign was. "We've taken the turret but Aerik is wounded. He may need to be transported back to the *Liberator*."

"Copy that." It sucked that Donnell's gunner had taken a hit, but I was so relieved that the Copperell hadn't been shot down, I almost didn't notice. "Tamura, what's your status?"

"Higher than yours, undoubtedly," Dothan replied unbidden.

"Dothan," Tamura chided. "We've all captured our assigned objectives with no casualties, Charlie." I couldn't see his grin, but I swear I could hear it.

"And we didn't even steal your fighters in the process."

13

WE MIGHT AS WELL HAVE HUNG signs around our necks reading "shoot me."

I knew we'd taken out everything on the planet and in orbit that could bring down a Vanguard, but hovering above the city gates on columns of fire from the belly jets, just hanging there fifty feet off the ground, seemed reckless.

Only the five of us this time. I'd sent Donnell back upstairs with Aerik. Now that the *Marauder* and the *Flying Fortress* were dropping landers full of troops, there'd be plenty of hangar space for Donnell to dock and get his gunner medical treatment. The first of those troops were already on the ground, driving their own armored vehicles toward the gates with infantry marching behind them like this was World War Two France.

The tanks at the air defense emplacements hadn't been the only ones...the wreckage of another dozen of them poured black smoke on the road between the gates and the river. They'd come out to meet the landing troops and paid the price for it. Dani had taken out three of them herself and from the grim expression on her face, this first experience of real war had taken its toll.

"You okay?" I asked, keeping my eyes on the gates. No Anguilar troops had come through them to meet us once the armored vehicles had met their fate, but now the heavy, metal barriers were closed, a symbolic gesture given that the city walls were nothing but concrete and local brick, but one that would have to be countered.

"I thought I was ready for this," Dani said in a dull monotone. "After what happened on Haven, I figured this would be nothing."

"That was survival," I corrected her. "Same as if you'd been in a shooting as a cop. This is war. It's different." I risked a glance to the side. She wouldn't look at me. "If you can't handle this, there's no shame in it. There's plenty you could do that doesn't involve…this."

"If I couldn't handle it," she ground out, anger replacing numb shock, "then I wouldn't be here."

"Good to know." I switched to the comms. "Val, Nareena, you ready for me to knock on this door?"

"Not gonna get any readier," Val assured me.

The particle cannon was already lined up with the huge, metal double doors of the city gates and all it took was a touch to make it do what it so badly wanted. The thunderbolt of Zeus struck the gates and blasted them inward along with a good section of the walls on either side. Dust and smoke billowed upward, curled into the breeze of the pre-dawn morning.

Still no troops poured through.

"Take them inside," I called down to Val, then switched to Tamura's frequency. "Slow and steady to the center of the city. I'm going right up the middle. You guys watch the flanks, space out a half a mile on either side of me, then half a mile past that and watch for troop concentrations. If you find them, do *not* fire unless they're in the open and easily identifiable. We don't have a fix on where the civilians are taking shelter and I'm not looking for collateral damage here. Call any sightings in and I'll have the ground troops recon it first."

There was no response for a moment and I put an edge to my tone when I spoke again.

"I want to know you heard me."

"I copy your transmission, Vanguard One," Tamura said, with only the inclusion of my call sign a hint that he was being sarcastic. Sarcastic or not, that was going to have to be enough.

Flying over the wall after blowing in the gate felt ridiculous, though not as ridiculous as advancing at barely twenty miles an hour, just fast enough to keep ahead of our APC's and barely fifty feet above the street. Rooftops forced me up another twenty yards, but even from that height—it seemed odd to call a hundred feet "altitude"—I finally spotted the civilians.

Furtive, terrified, but too curious not to look, they popped out of doorways and windows, wearing no armor, carrying no weapons. All Copperell, which made me feel more secure they actually *were* civilians and not just Anguilar troops hiding in plain sight, acting as spotters. I'd considered that possibility but I'd figured that the locals would know the collaborators and wouldn't let them get away with it.

I was more concerned with the Anguilar forces taking shelter in civilian buildings. That could get messy in ways I hadn't had to deal with yet. I was young and inexperienced, but I'd also studied military history and knew all about human shields. The Japanese had used the native Okinawans as shields against the Marines during the battle there in 1945, had forced the civilians to carry explosives or to walk in front of their troops during assaults to try to make the Americans hesitate. So far, the Anguilar had been too dismissive of the resistance to even try that, but these guys knew who we were and had known for a couple hours that we'd be coming.

The first sign of opposition inside the walls came less than a mile from the city center, from what looked like an industrial district, rows of warehouses and factories and parking lots filled with heavy construction equipment. That equipment apparently looked like cover to the Anguilar troops because a few hundred of them had attempted to conceal themselves between the rows, which I might have missed if they hadn't popped up to fire at me with crew-served pulse cannons.

A *lot* of crew-served pulse cannons. Enough that the air above the parking lots shimmered with the heat, crackled with static electricity, and the front shields lit up bright red, the transformation of heat energy to kinetic shaking my Vanguard like a bone in a dog's mouth. Ideally, I would have let Dani take care of them with the fighter's turret-mounted pulse guns, a measured response, but the fire was too intense to wait, and I pulled the trigger by instinct.

The particle cannon blast vaporized a dozen of the heavy construction vehicles, tossed another handful into the air, streaming flame, and what it did to the enemy soldiers who'd used them as cover was, thankfully, hidden from my view by the fire and smoke. Movement on thermal caught my attention, an attempt by the survivors to retreat back to one of the factories, and I didn't want to take the chance they might have civilian workers in there as cover.

I fired again, aiming at a point just beyond their line of retreat, the last two rows of bulldozers and earthmovers. A line of yellow metal erupted in an inferno of raw energy, sending the things spinning off to the side like toy cars scattered in a fit of pique by an aggravated toddler. A few squads of stragglers squirted out the sides, but Dani found them, cleaning up the leavings with precise bursts of scalar fury.

Nudging the Vanguard forward, I tried to summon guilt for what I'd done, empathy for the troops on the ground, but I just couldn't. Peboktan had been a world filled with civilians, with innocents, mothers and children, and the Anguilar's solution to a rebellion there had been to turn the entire planet to slag. In the face of that, holding back against these guys would be murdering their future victims.

Particle cannons and pulse guns fired to my flanks, the Kamerians having their own encounters with the enemy, and I hoped to hell they were following my instructions because there wasn't a damned thing I could do about it at the moment if they weren't.

Columns of smoke rose above a dozen spots along our line of advance, some of them caused by our air to ground fire, some behind us, the work of the infantry.

The battle even from this close to the street seemed different, distant in the cockpit. More impersonal, and I was sure I didn't care for that. I had to be able to maintain detachment, but it shouldn't have come this easily. When a staggered column of Anguilar vehicles rolled up the central avenue, laying down a stream of fire at Val and Nareena's infantry, no thought passed through my head before I pulled the trigger.

The pavement erupted in the midst of them, not lava swallowing them up but a storm of electromagnetic destruction. Two more shots, at the center of the column, at the end, and a dozen armored vehicles were on their sides, flipped on their roofs, burning...the ones that weren't disintegrated outright.

Infantry had advanced behind them, but without the cover of the armor, hundreds of troops in the gray and black armor of Anguilar turned and ran. Not an organized retreat, not a fighting withdrawal, just a rout. This time, I let them run. Panic in the enemy should be encouraged. I forgot who'd said it, but a quote came to mind.

Never interrupt your enemy when he is making a mistake. It sounded like something Napoleon might have said, so I mentally attributed it to him since I had no way to look it up other than going back to Earth and visiting a library. Or maybe that internet thing Dani was always talking about.

If Napoleon *had* said it, he was smarter than my military history professor had given him credit for, because it worked.

More of their infantry pulled out from behind businesses and government buildings and parked cargo trucks, turning their backs on us and running toward the center of the city, toward the fortified administration center we'd spotted from orbit.

It was as close to a redoubt as the Anguilar had on this world, ten stories tall and surrounded by high walls, protected by pulse turrets at each corner. They probably thought they could hold out in there, and I realized I had to cure them of that illusion before they dug in and forced us to come in and pull them out.

I pulled up on the controls, gaining a little altitude and speed, high enough for the turrets to see me. And target me. Tamura and the other Kamerians were converging on either side of me. Better if this went quickly.

"Third Squadron, take out those turrets."

I did my part, again letting Dani save her ammo because impressions and theatrics mattered when you were trying to intimidate the bad guys into giving up. The particle blast didn't just blow up the turret at the southwest corner of the building, it shattered the tower, bringing it crumbling in a rain of brick and concrete, dust rising as the structure fell.

The Kamerians took their hint from me, their main guns cutting off the red streams of anti-aircraft fire with claps of thunder.

It's just overkill, to quote Men at Work.

Enough overkill to bring the corners of the building crashing down and spook all those panicking foot soldiers from trying to race inside the building for perceived safety. Instead, they huddled just inside the walls, pressing against them as if *that* metal and cinder block would prove less vulnerable to our guns than the metal and cinder block in the towers.

More tanks were arrayed outside the walls, their gun turrets traversing to target the Strada and Copperell infantry and armor advancing up the road. Still needing a lesson.

"The vehicles," I ordered. "All of them."

Tamura and the others needed no further explanation. Lightning strikes laid waste to the Anguilar tanks, the street outside the fortress and sections of wall behind them. Smoke rose alongside billows of dust, destruction and death and the promise of more. Unless.

"I'm going down," I announced.

"Are you sure that's a good idea?" Tamura asked, sounding as if I'd just told him I intended to dive naked into an Antarctic Sea.

"Yeah," Dani agreed, her eyes wide. "That sounds pretty stupid...not to mention suicidal."

I didn't argue with either of them, barely even listened, already bringing the Vanguard down on the vertical-take-off belly jets outside the main gates of the fortress. They were already open, having been used by the Anguilar troops to retreat through, and on the other side of them, enemy soldiers huddled and watched, terrified, panicking.

The landing gear touched down on cracked and broken pavement, settling in with a lurch. I didn't get out immediately, of course. Despite Dani's accusation, I was neither stupid nor suicidal and there was a method to my madness.

The Vanguard was equipped with external speakers for just this sort of scenario, which was either preternaturally foresightful by the Kamerians or else simply arrogant. I was going with the latter and hoping I wasn't making the same mistake. I switched the speakers on and leaned over the audio pickup.

"This is Charlie Travers of the Resistance Military Forces. You have two minutes to surrender unconditionally, or we'll bring the entire building down around your ears. The only guarantee I'll give you is that if you do surrender, you won't be harmed, and you'll be given food, water and shelter. Anyone who surrenders and then attempts violence against us will be shot but otherwise, you won't be punished other than by being confined under guard until such time as we can arrange your disposition to another planet. Again, two minutes or we open fire."

Dani scoffed loudly.

"You can't honestly believe they're going to surrender."

"If this were closer to the center of the Empire, maybe not," I admitted. "But out here, with no hope of reinforcement for weeks, if ever…" I shrugged. "If not, we do what we have to do. But I'd rather not be known as a butcher. It makes it harder to get the enemy to give up, and if he won't give up, then we have to kill them all. I'm not sure there are enough of us to do that."

She still didn't look convinced, but she didn't argue it further, just waited. Tamura and the Kamerians did the same, their fighters hovering above the fortress in implicit threat. Whether it was the Vanguard fighters or the advancing army or maybe the knowledge of who we were and what we'd accomplished against them already, something pushed the needle across the red line.

The figure who emerged from the wreckage of the fortress' front entrance was an Anguilar, one of the bloodline. An officer, from his uniform and the look of haughty superiority, though the whole air was thrown off by the rips on his tunic and the smudges of dust and ash on his face. The others looked to him, their faces hidden but their body language plain to see. He was the commander and they wanted him to save their lives…somehow. The same way that a child looks to his father to make everything right. They needed him to surrender, though I wasn't sure if any of them were thinking clearly enough to realize it.

"I want to talk!" the officer called, waving at us. "Don't shoot!"

I considered wearing my helmet but discarded it at the last second. It was still pre-dawn but the street lighting—and the fires —would be bright enough to see by. And I wanted them to see my face.

"Don't do it," Dani warned, leaving her own helmet on and grabbing a rifle from the rack by the door. "You can't trust this guy."

"I have four Vanguards and a few thousand heavily armed troops backing me up," I reminded her, hitting the control to open the hatch. I paused there as it opened outward, then grabbed the comm unit off my belt. "Tamura, keep your eyes open but don't fire unless I tell you. Clear?"

"Crystal."

I didn't bother with a rifle for the same reason I hadn't worn a helmet. Optics. It needed to be clear to these guys that I was in charge, and if it came down to shooting, having the rifle wouldn't save me.

The stink of burned metal and plastic washed over me as I

stepped down to the pavement, the early morning breeze pulling it out of the courtyard through the open gates. Breaking down in a coughing fit would have ruined the image I'd been trying to maintain so I made sure to breathe shallow and fight the tickling in my throat.

Anguilar troops stared at me but made no move to raise their weapons, taking their cue from their commander as he stepped forward to meet me. A few of the enemy soldiers pushed up their visors, revealing Krin and Copperell and more actual Anguilar than I would have thought. Not the majority by any means, but maybe a quarter of what was left. Which might have meant that this place wasn't as backwoods as I'd thought, but another, darker possibility occurred to me. It might have been that all those troops that had attacked us and been slaughtered had been the non-Anguilar, sent to give their lives to delay us until the *important* people made it back.

The gentle crackling of fires and the occasional crash of collapsing bits of wall were a muted undertone to the whine of the jets of the Vanguard fighters overhead, a flight of avenging angels hanging at my shoulder, a reminder not to screw with us. I hoped this guy wouldn't need it. He was older than I'd thought he'd be, old for his position, which might mean he'd been exiled here for pissing off the wrong person. Or maybe he just *looked* older because he'd been beat up during the attack on the fortress, because he sure as hell looked beat up.

"You're Charlie Travers?" he asked. He had a sidearm at his waist but made sure to keep his hand well clear of it.

"I am. Who am I talking to?"

"I'm Major Ad-Lok Kin, the commander of the Thalassia outpost." No bloodline, no relatives listed, which confirmed that he was a nobody, stashed away here on purpose. "I've heard of you." His lip quirked upward in a wan smile. "The stories say you're ten feet tall and breathe fire, that you walked into the Imperial Administration Center on Copperell and kicked a general in the chest, then walked out just as brazenly. That you personally boarded the Emperor's pet project, the one that had consumed enough resources to construct another fleet, the *Nova Eclipse*, and destroyed her."

"I'm obviously not ten feet tall," I said, shrugging. "And I actually had to *run* out of the Administrative Center on Copperell, but the rest is close enough."

"And why do you, the legendary Charlie Travers, grace us with your presence?" he asked. Not scared enough. Maybe he'd been out here so long, he'd simply given up? "This is hardly the Imperial headquarters, and we seem to be fresh out of secret weapons."

"That's simple, Major," I told him, gesturing expansively. "We're invading the Anguilar Empire. We're going to take it back one system at a time. We started with Strada and you're next. Nothing personal, but you need to surrender if you don't want all your troops killed."

"You know why I'm here, don't you?" he asked. "You're an intelligent man, if the rumors are true. You look at me and I see the judgment in your eyes. I'm too old for this position and my rank. My family is unimportant, my career unimpressive. This is my last stop unless I somehow excel here, and what are the odds of that in a place such as this?" Major Kin shook his head, motioned at the troops filtering in through the gateway, Val and Nareena at the head of them, at the fighters. "What could one such as I do in response to the force you've shown us here?" A glint shone behind those defeated eyes. "I suppose the best I could do for my family is to die valiantly, but it's even too late for that…"

"Charlie!" Tamura's voice came small and tinny from the comm on my belt. "Get down, now!"

14

I DIDN'T QUESTION HIM. I wasn't sure why, since I had every reason to, but I dropped, hands going over my head. Heat. Raw heat like the surface of a star come down to the planet to show us what we were missing, a searing wash of it that burned the exposed skin of my neck in the tiny slivers I hadn't covered with my armored gloves. The sound came after the heat, deafening, hitting me like a physical blow, a weight against my back, coming apace with the shock wave running in the opposite direction of the sound. It picked me up in the hands of a giant and tossed me negligently back, the breath leaving me like I was back in the surf at Cocoa Beach, being tossed by waves.

I landed next to Dani, who'd been standing about twenty feet behind me and had still been knocked down by the blast, the impact on the pavement cushioned by my armor, though my ears were ringing, my mouth was full of cotton, and my head felt like someone has used it as the clapper for the Liberty Bell, and I was sorely regretting the decision not to wear a helmet. Besides the headache, the streetlights had gone out and plunged the court-yard into darkness.

For a moment. Until the flames shot out from what was left of the fortress and I turned toward them, raising a hand instinctively to shield myself. Where the Anguilar major had been was nothing but a dark smear, and the entrance hallway, which had once been half-crumbled was nonexistent. The entire front of the five-story building had crumpled to a pile of children's building blocks—if some psycho child had splashed gasoline on them and lit them on fire.

The whole structure was near collapse, propped up by charred splinters and good wishes, and that prop was kicked out when one of the Kamerian fighters lanced another particle blast into the back of it, the flare of white light blinding, flashing after-images across my vision. Another wave of heat and concussion and I almost didn't notice the pulse fire from the rifles of the Strada and Copperell troops gathered around me until dozens of the Anguilar soldiers that had huddled inside the walls had already fallen.

"Cease fire!" I tried to yell it but there was no moisture in my mouth and it came out as an inaudible croak.

And then it was too late. In retrospect, I understood what had happened. The attack by Tamura and his people had spooked the Anguilar hiding out in the perceived shelter of the courtyard and they'd opened fire on our ground troops. Val and Nareena's people had returned fire and the whole thing had spread from one side of the courtyard to the other. There was nothing I could do to stop it and the Kamerians had already taken up the fight, their gunners raking the lines of Anguilar on both sides of the wall, blowing bits of the wall out as well.

Cursing, I grabbed my comm unit from my belt and cleared my throat until I could yell into it.

"Cease fire! Cease fire and get your asses on the ground now!"

The pulse turrets cut off slowly, like a hose losing its pressure after the water spigot had been closed, but once the red streaks ceased, the ground troops stopped firing as well. I had no trouble seeing the carnage left over from the exchange, not with the fires crackling all around the fortress…all around what was *left* of it. Hundreds of Anguilar soldiers were down, their bodies smoking in desultory silence, only a few here and there still moving, and even those survivors charred and blackened by the overwhelming wave of pulse fire. If any had gotten away from the massacre, they hadn't stuck around.

I didn't have to worry about getting the Anguilar troops to surrender anyway…there were none left here to do it. I also had no need to check the fortress for civilians. Anything inside that building was dead. All I had left was a roiling stew of rage inside my gut, steaming, boiling over. I should have tried to control it, but instead it controlled me and I stalked out through the gate, giving no orders, taking no reports.

The Vanguards from my squadron descended on jets of red and yellow flame, touching down in a tight formation just behind where mine had landed, off to the side of the long column of our troops. Hot wind buffeted me as I approached, debris smacking into my face, and I squinted, raising a hand to shield my face but didn't stop walking. Hatches descended from the fuselage and helmeted figures stepped out. I recognized Tamura's bird and aimed straight for him even before he'd even taken off his helmet.

"Who did it?" I demanded. "Who opened fire?"

"I did," Dothan said casually, striding over from his plane as if it was nothing, his helmet tucked under his arm.

He was taller than me, had a jaw like an oaken bucket and I thought nothing of it, leaping into the punch, plastering my right fist across Dothan's face with every ounce of force I could muster. It was like hitting a brick wall, and only the armored plates over the knuckles of my glove kept me from breaking my hand into tiny pieces. Dothan didn't go down, of course, but he did stumble, a cut open on his cheek and a look of surprise on his big face.

"What the hell is wrong with you?" I bellowed at him, ignoring the pain in my wrist, pointing at him, barely able to keep from drawing my gun and putting a round between his eyes. "You just got hundreds of people killed! You could have gotten my ground troops killed and you damn near blasted me to atoms! What the hell did you think you were doing?"

Dothan growled deep in his chest and surged toward me, and my hand went to my sidearms, but Tamura interposed himself, putting one palm against the big Kamerian's chest and one on mine.

"Stop," he said in a commanding voice and Dothan did, but I could tell it was a near thing. Tamura turned to me, his expression grave. "Charlie, you're right, we disobeyed your orders to hold our fire and check with you if there was a threat, but there was no choice." He jerked his head toward the Vanguard. "Come, let me show you something."

Kaison, Tamura's Copperell gunner, stood in the open cockpit hatch, his eyes wide, jaw working as if he wanted to tell me something but couldn't summon the wherewithal to actually speak. Tamura gently pushed him out of the way and ducked through, leaning over the pilot's station and bringing up an image on the sensor screen. It was a thermal image of the fortress... before it had been destroyed. I didn't know my own thermal signature but I recognized myself and Major Kin standing just apart from each other just out from the entrance.

And behind Kin, concealed by the partially collapsed entrance hallway in an alcove not visible from outside, was a tank, the muzzle of its main gun pointed through the wall directly at me.

"It was a trap," Tamura told me, firm but not sounding angry. "The commander lured you there and kept you talking until he was sure he could kill you, die with honor rather than surrendering."

I blew out a breath, the rage pouring out of me.

"You gave him the order to fire?"

Tamura nodded and I frowned at him.

"Why didn't you do it yourself?" I wondered, and the corner of his mouth turned up in a wry grin.

"Because Dothan can take a punch better than me."

I didn't laugh. Too many people had died for me to laugh. But I returned the half-grin. How could I not?

"You were wrong," I told him. He cocked an eyebrow in an unspoken question. "You did what you thought was right, but you don't know the Anguilar. They don't throw their lives away for honor because they don't have any." I shrugged. "Oh, they'd be more than happy to let a Copperell or Krin recruit sacrifice themselves in a grand gesture if it would let them get away clean, but this guy wasn't going to kill himself."

"You're sure of that, are you?" he asked, not seeming convinced.

"Let me put it this way." I leaned against the inside of the hatchway, regarding him with cool equanimity. "When we infiltrated the *Nova Eclipse*, I convinced not one but *two* Anguilar officers to conspire against their own people with just the promise of letting them go so they could tell a story that would make them a hero in the eyes of their government and advance their careers. Then the first one killed the second one just so there'd only be his story told."

Tamura barked a sharp laugh, throwing back his head, exposing those slightly sharpened teeth.

"All right, I'll grant you that." He shrugged. "I went with my instincts, but perhaps they were honed fighting a different foe. Do you want to be the one to tell Dothan or should I?"

Scowling deeply, I considered the question.

"No, I don't want to tell him at all," I decided after a

moment. "He wouldn't accept it—he'd just think I was making excuses."

I bounded down the steps, straight up to Dothan. No use putting it off.

The big guy watched me with pure hatred in his eyes and I couldn't blame him. None of this had been his fault.

"Dothan," I said, "I apologize. I was wrong. You were following orders and Tamura was just trying to save my ass." Not a damned thing changed behind those golden eyes and I sighed. "Look, if it makes things right, you can hit me back just as hard as you want."

I offered my chin and he stared at it hard, as if seriously considering the offer. But in the end, he shook his head and snorted scornfully.

"If the punch you attempted against me was any indication of your strength, human...then were I to hit you as hard as I wanted, it would break your scrawny neck."

With that, he turned on his heel and stalked back to his fighter. He didn't go inside, just tossed his helmet to the floor and sat down on the steps to the cockpit. I sighed, shook my head. Tamura clapped me on the arm.

"He'll be all right. Just let him work through it on his own."

Val jogged toward me and I turned away from Tamura.

"What's the status?" I asked him, looking around. "Where's Nareena?"

"She grabbed a ride on one of our personnel carriers. There's about a thousand enemy troops surrendering on the west side of the city."

"Good." I waved around us. "We need to find the civilians. They had warning so I assume they're hiding out somewhere around here. Spread your people out and hunt me up someone willing to be their leader. We're gonna need them to start rebuilding some kind of local government but more important right now, we need a place to confine those prisoners and the locals should know the best options. We also need to know where they store food and other supplies. I don't want anyone starving because we 'liberated' them from the Anguilar or we could wind up with a bunch of pissed-off locals ready to fight us when they wouldn't fight the Anguilar. Food, shelter, clean water and power are our priorities, and we need to get that done in the next twenty-four hours, even if that means none of us get a minute's sleep." I pointed outward. "For the prisoners, too. Well-fed prisoners are complacent. Starving ones are willing to die to kill us and break out."

Val stroked his beard, which was growing out again after he'd shaved it a few weeks ago.

"There are a lot of non-Anguilar. Among the prisoners, I mean. Lot of Copperell in the ones who surrendered. Nareena told me she thinks that there's a chance a lot of them might be willing to switch sides and sign up to fight for the resistance if we give them the chance. I mean, we're gonna run into the whole problem with food and supplies, but if we can get Thalassia producing for us, it could work."

He grinned as if this were the way we'd all planned for things to go instead of a huge Charlie Foxtrot.

I glanced over at Dothan, who was still sulking on the steps of his fighter's hatch while Tamura, Sainrastil and Fenris spoke quietly to him. They all looked back toward me every few seconds, with varying degrees of resentment and possibly anger.

Great.

"I'll tell you what, Val," I said to the old marshal, shaking my head, "let's hold off on that for now. Changing sides isn't as easy as it sounds."

15

I KEPT WALKING because it was the only way to stay awake.

I'd told Val that no one was going to sleep until the prisoners and civilians were squared away but I decided I might have to revise that and go to fifty percent security because if I was the walking dead then a lot of our troops had to be close to the ragged edge, too.

I wasn't even sure where I was. I mean, I knew I was on the west side of the city because it was mid-morning and the position of the sun made it obvious, and from the look of the buildings lining this street, I was in a residential district. But if someone had called me on the comm and told me to run back to the front gate, the only way I could have found it was to go straight until I found a wall and then follow it around.

It was probably irresponsible, but I thought it was important that I showed these people my face. The Copperell hadn't come out of their hidey-holes until dawn, despite encouragement from my people, but now they were wandering about the city, gawking like tourists in their own home. Most of them seemed hesitant to approach me and I didn't force the issue, nodding politely to them and waving hello.

They were, like most subjugated populations I'd encountered, ragged and afraid, their eyes hollow and haunted, the common denominator on a sea of different faces, young and old, male and female.

I walked beneath a clothesline strung between multistory apartments and looked at the garments hanging there. The clothes were mostly the usual work-a-day fare I'd seen among Copperell everywhere, including their occupied homeworld, but in worse shape, patched and repaired too many times, cleaned by hand with unpowered washtubs too many times.

Just another need to keep in mind when I got the report from Val and Nareena about the food supplies. Along with getting some of these people into the buildings the Anguilar had been using as barracks for their troops. Those were all in better shape, roomy enough to house hundreds of families. As for the survivors of the Anguilar forces, I hadn't yet found a perfect place to imprison them in my meandering walk, but I'd made a mental note of a couple empty industrial spaces that could be secured with a little elbow grease. Add whatever cots we could scrounge up, some makeshift pallets and bedding and it could work.

So lost in thought about the possible EPW—Enemy Prisoner of War—camp was I that I didn't notice the Copperell girl standing in my line of travel until I'd almost run into her. She stared up at me with eyes the size of saucers, her mouth dropping open in shock. Her hair was jet black, twisted into a braid, and one hand clutched to her chest a ragged lump of cloth stuffed with rags that might have passed for a doll if I squinted hard at it.

"Hey," I said, kneeling down in front of her to get at eye level. I nodded to the lump of cloth. "Is that your doll?"

"That's my kitty," she told me, blurting the words out like she hadn't meant to speak to me at all but my error was so egregious she couldn't remain silent. "He keeps me safe from the rats."

I knew the translator goo was turning her words into concepts I'd understand, but I hadn't seen any cats since I left Earth and I wondered what the local equivalent looked like. Ditto rats… though I *had* seen scuttling little lizard-looking things that might have been mistaken for rats on a dark night if I'd had a couple drinks too many.

"Does your kitty have a name?" I asked her, grinning. Kids, it seemed, were the same everywhere. Maybe. I hadn't met any Anguilar kids…or Krin. For all I knew, they both hatched full-grown out of eggs.

The little girl couldn't have been older than four or five and she gave me the sort of look only a child that age could, one that asked *how are you so stupid at your age?*

"Her name's Kitty!" she said as if it was obvious. She gave the cloth doll a kiss. "I named her after my real kitty." She pouted a frown. "I don't know what happened to the real Kitty. She ran away one night and I didn't see her again."

"I'm sorry to hear that," I told her sincerely, then looked

around. I hadn't noticed any stray animals walking around. "Maybe you can get another real kitty somewhere?"

"I looked," she insisted. "My mom told me there weren't any left in the city. That they all went somewhere there was more to eat."

I gulped, finally understanding the truth. There were no pets in the city because all of them, including hers, had been turned into stew.

"Where did the metal men go?" the girl asked.

"The what?" I shook my head, not understanding, though I might have if I hadn't been so damned tired.

"The metal men who own the city," she clarified. Again that look of superiority. "The Angry people. Mom always says to stay away from the Angry people."

"The Anguilar?"

"That's what I said. What happened to them? Vella, the girl from the next building over, said that you killed them all."

She'd said it so casually that I didn't respond for a long second, taken aback by the indifference she showed.

"Umm...my name's Charlie," I told her, hoping to change the subject. "You didn't tell me yours."

"I'm Maya. But you didn't tell me what happened to the Angry Metal men. Did you really kill them all?"

Damn.

"Maya! What are you doing?"

The Copperell female scooped the girl up like an osprey grabbing a fish out of the surf, coming out of nowhere and startling me enough that I nearly fell back on my ass. I caught the fall on my knee instead and pushed to my feet, leaving me just a long step away from the mother. She was young-ish, I judged, though worn by the work and the weather and probably the lack of food, the sort of look I'd seen from pictures and paintings of women on the frontier from the 19th century. Except for the bronze skin.

"Sorry," I told her. "Didn't mean to scare you. I was just talking to Maya about…her kitty." Which wasn't entirely accurate, but I didn't want to go into the whole business of discussing how many people I'd killed.

The woman's eyes narrowed in what I took for suspicion but might have been fear.

"We don't want any trouble," she told me, turning to put her body between me and her daughter. "Please just leave us alone!"

"I'm not gonna hurt you," I said, holding my hands up, palms out. "My name's Charlie. We came here to help you and your people, to get rid of the Anguilar."

"So, you *did* kill them!" Maya exclaimed, eyes brightening in enthusiasm. "Vella was right!"

Uggh.

"Some of them didn't want to surrender," I admitted. "But there are still a lot of them we're keeping as prisoners. We don't want to hurt anyone if we don't have to."

Not strictly true. I had no problem hurting the Anguilar leadership and if I ever got Seraph Nix in my sights again, it'd be the last time. But mostly accurate. The woman looked me up and down, as if seeing me for the first time.

"You don't look like anyone I've seen before," she admitted. "Who are you people?"

"We're the resistance," I told her, not for the first time thinking we *really* needed a better name. "We've been fighting against the Anguilar for about a year now."

"What do you want with this place?" she scoffed, bitter amusement replacing her earlier fear. "I'm not even sure why the Anguilar bother with it. We barely grow enough crops to feed ourselves and the occupiers..." She smiled wryly. "The *former* occupiers. The mines are the only thing we have, and they've already worked half our men to death in them." The smile fled. "Including my husband. I was grateful our only child was a girl because the Anguilar don't consider females worth the effort to enslave in the mines."

"We don't want your mines," I assured her. "Or, if we do wind up working them, we'll bring in free laborers to dig for pay. Your people too, if they want it."

Being honest, I had no clue whether we'd need whatever they mined here. One of the many areas I needed to learn more about was the economics of all this. I'd been so caught up in the military aspect, finding troops to fight, getting them weapons and ships, and then figuring out how to feed them, I had no idea if we needed raw minerals for anything or not.

"What we want Thalassia for," I continued, feeling a little more certain now, "is to use it as a base to strike at the Anguilar. We want to arm and train any of your people who want to fight, build this place up with more farms, spaceports, defenses, make it so tough a nut to crack that they won't bother to try to take it back."

"You're going to do that *here?*" she asked, eyes going wide. I still didn't know her name.

"If you'll help us. Look…" I laughed, closing my eyes for a second, then having to pry them open. "I've been wandering around here since we took the city, trying to get a sense of this place, of the people here. I'd like it if you could spread it around that we want to get you people out of this"—I waved around us—"out of these broken-down buildings, get you someplace nicer. Get food to everyone, if we can find out where the Anguilar were keeping their stores. Then we want to get everyone working for themselves, get people out to the farms so they can start bringing food into the cities and letting you eat what you grow. We can't do that without your help. There just aren't enough of us. Can you do that for me? Can you tell them?"

She nodded slowly, and when she smiled, she looked a lot younger.

"I hope you're telling the truth, Charlie. I haven't had much hope that my daughter would grow up to do anything but work in the Anguilar processing plants, storing the food they stole from us, until she died young, like my mother, and her mother before her."

"Are you sure the Angry men won't come back?" Maya asked, eyes flickering to the sky, as if expecting their ships to descend any second.

"They might," I admitted. "But if they do, we'll be right here waiting for them."

"Charlie!" I turned at the call and was surprised to see Laranna jogging my way. She'd left her combat armor behind and was dressed in her customary Strada clothes, though she still had a rifle slung across her back. "Dammit, why don't you have your comm on?"

"I don't?" I pulled it off my belt and winced when I saw the power switch set to off. "Shoot. I don't know when I did that."

And maybe it was just an indication of how badly I needed sleep.

"I had to send people out looking for you," she told me, then frowned as she looked into my face. "Have you been looked at by the medics? You were hit pretty hard by that shock wave. You might have a concussion."

"It's certainly a possibility," I admitted, flicking the switch back on. "But they had more important things to worry about. What's up? Is there a problem? Oh." I turned back to Maya and her mother. "Maya, um…" I frowned. "I never got your name."

"Wendra," the young woman volunteered, looking at Laranna like she'd never seen a Strada before.

"Maya, Wendra, this is my wife, Laranna." I grinned broadly. "She's beautiful, smart and kicks major ass and I still have no idea what she sees in me."

"You *are* concussed," Laranna sighed. "Charlie, we've found the city…elder, or whatever they call them here. He has some ideas about what to do with the prisoners and you need to meet with him."

"While I'm concussed?" I asked her, scratching my head. I needed a haircut. Plus there was dried blood from a cut I hadn't realized I'd picked up during the explosion.

"It's not ideal," she admitted, "but this guy won't be working with us at all unless he meets you first."

I went along with her, waving back to Maya.

"Bye Charlie," she called.

I didn't know who this city elder guy was, but, concussed or not, I felt like I'd already made my best ally on this planet.

NOVO WAS A FUSSY OLD WOMAN.

That was my first impression of the Copperell elder as he paced back and forth in the temporary operational headquarters we'd set up inside what looked like it had been some kind of administrative office at the edge of the swathe of destruction Dothan and the other Kamerians had left where the fortress had stood. Unlike the spartan work garb most of the Copperell I'd seen here wear, Novo was dressed in gray robes with a high collar…not fancy, but clearly ceremonial, a sign of his office. The fact they and his Bouffant hairstyle made him look like a Victorian noblewoman was purely coincidental.

"There aren't enough adult men!" he insisted, whining at Val and Nareena when Laranna led me into the central offices. "Most of them are dozens of miles away, in the mines! If the Anguilar guards there haven't just killed them already!"

"We'll send as many troops as we can spare to the mines in our landers," I told him, not waiting to introduce myself. Novo spun around like a cornered rabbit, eyes wide. "From what we saw on the way in, they can't have more than a few dozen troops there and given the quality we encountered here in the city, I'd be surprised if they haven't already shucked their armor and taken off into the woods."

It was more coherent than I'd sounded in hours and I thought maybe I was catching my second wind. There was no power yet in the offices, or anywhere else this close to the destruction, though Mallarna had sent along a few Peboktan to see about getting the place up and running again before nightfall. The office doors had been left open, which was why none of them had heard me come in, and the noonday sun streamed in through tall windows, miraculously intact unlike any others within three blocks.

"And you are?" Novo asked plaintively. He seemed to do everything plaintively. The word elder fit him, though, because he was most certainly *old*, perhaps the oldest Copperell I'd run into. If he were human, I would have judged him to be in his seventies, but given that I didn't know how long Copperell lived in general and the harsh nature of life here, I just settled on *old*.

"This is Charlie Travers," Laranna told the man, "the one I told you about."

"And thank God *you're* here," Val sighed, settling back on a low railing that separated one section of the office from another, "so I don't have to deal with this anymore."

"Val," I said, "do you have a clear idea of where the mine guards are stationed?"

"Yeah, Novo here laid it out pretty good for us," he admitted, though he sounded as if he grudged even giving the Copperell elder that much credit.

"You're in charge of the op, then. Take as many of your

Copperell troops as we can spare and run your landers nap-of-the-earth, don't give them a chance to see you and react."

"I'll get it done," Val promised, looking eager to be out of the room.

"I suppose that will help," Novo said, hands clasped in front of him as if in prayer. "But even if we get our men back from the mines, none of us have ever even been allowed to *touch* a weapon. How do you expect them to become soldiers?"

"Val has trained a lot of Copperell," I assured him. "Half the troops out there, the ones who took this city, are Copperell just like you, refugees from Anguilar-held worlds. It'll take some time, but he can do it. Look, Elder Novo," I said, "we have a problem. We have over a thousand enemy prisoners and we need to find a secure facility to hold them in while we decide what to do with them. Someplace we can keep them under guard but where they'll have adequate shelter." I shrugged. "It doesn't have to be a five-star hotel or anything, but we need it fast. Any suggestions?"

The man snorted disdainfully.

"Yes, I suggest you put them in a quarry pit outside town… then fill it in. What good are Anguilar prisoners?"

"Most of them aren't bloodline Anguilar," Nareena reminded the older man. She was quiet and stiff-backed, which, knowing the woman for the last few months, I read as her disliking Novo's company almost as much as Val did. "In fact, most are Copperell just like yourselves."

"Not like us!" Novo insisted, hands bunching into fists. "They joined our oppressors! When our miners staged a work stoppage to protest conditions in the pit, they obeyed their Anguilar officers and executed the leaders…including my son! When our women and children marched peacefully outside that accursed fortress, *begging* merely for enough food to live on, those soldiers who are *just like us* waded into the crowd and struck down mothers holding their babies with the butts of their rifles, kicked them on the ground, fired their weapons at their feet to disperse them."

Lost in a fit of righteous indignation, Novo looked less like an old lady in a house dress and more like what he was—a bitter, broken old man, living in the wreckage of the colony his grandfathers or great grandfathers had come to with hope for a new life. A wave of pity replaced my initial scorn, and shame was on its heels. An accident of birth was all that had kept me from being in the same position as any of these people.

"I understand," I told the old man. "But if we just slaughter these soldiers after they've surrendered, what makes us any different from them? How could you and your people believe we'd treat you fairly if we did that?"

Novo huffed, dissatisfied but his rant short-circuited.

"There's a place," he admitted. "Down by the port. It used to be a grain storehouse but it hasn't been used since I was a boy, not since the new silos were built. It's large enough to house that many people. You can buy food for them from the independent fishing boats, at least for the short term." Novo scowled. "Until you can get them off this planet. Your wish to keep your hands clean is admirable, but don't expect my people to respect it forever."

"Noted," I said, deciding not to argue the matter. "Now, what about food? We're going to get the farms running supplies out to the city as soon as possible but for the next few days, we need to find the stores that the Anguilar had ready for shipment and get those distributed. Do you know where the food is?"

"Everyone knows that," the old Copperell sneered. "The Anguilar make no secret of it. The storage silos are at the spaceport, kept there in plain sight, under guard, waving the food we've grown and processed under our noses as they ship it out to their own people."

Nareena looked up sharply at that.

"*Everyone* knows that?" she repeated, her voice going up with every word. She turned to me, eyes wide. "Charlie, if all the people here know where that food is and it's spread that the Anguilar are gone…"

"Charlie, do you read me?" It was Dani, her voice small and distant over the speaker of my comm unit. I grabbed it off my belt, spurred by the urgency in her voice.

"Yeah, I'm here, Dani. Where are you?"

"I'm standing out past the front gate, where Tamura and the others landed their fighters, and there's like…a *swarm* of people going out of the gates and every hole in the wall. Women, kids, old men, all of them are heading out to the spaceport, it looks like. Are we evacuating the city and nobody told me?"

"Oh, shit," I muttered, realizing exactly what was happening. "Hold on, Dani." I used the comm unit as a pointer, extending it toward Nareena. "Can you get some people out there? We have to make sure they don't strip the storehouses dry or we'll be going door-to-door confiscating food to make sure the people who didn't grab their share get fed, and you know how messy that's gonna get."

I thought about Wendra and Maya and their reaction if I sent troops into their apartment to take back the food they considered rightfully theirs. It would be a damned disaster.

"Val took the Copperell to the mines," Nareena said, shaking her head. "Along with all the landers. If I strip troops away from guarding the prisoners...they're all just sitting out in the open right now. We don't even have enough restraints for them all if we pull enough soldiers to make a difference."

I cursed under my breath and stripped off my armor as quickly as I could, tossing it to the floor, leaving my rifle with it. Nareena stared at me like I'd gone nuts, but the look in Laranna's eyes told me she understood.

"Your fighter?" she asked as I threw down the last segment of body armor, metal clanking petulantly off the tile floor. "It's still sitting right outside the fortress."

I nodded wordlessly and followed her out the office's open door.

"Wait!" Nareena called after me. "What are you gonna do?"

"Win their hearts and minds," I tossed back over my shoulder, then finished the last part of the old joke quietly, to myself. "So I don't have to burn their damned huts down."

16

THIS WAS, I realized, the first time I'd flown the Vanguard with Laranna sitting beside me. Not that I wasn't romantic or anything, but I didn't have the correct headspace to appreciate it.

Tens of thousands of heads turned up to watch us pass overhead, hands shielding their eyes from the early afternoon sun. They were gabbling, yelling at the roar of the jets, and I thought I could read the terrified looks on their faces even from a couple hundred feet up. The Vanguard was a weapon of war, and they were used to those being pointed their way.

"This isn't going to be easy," Laranna warned. "You heard Novo. He's just the most eloquent of the Copperell here, not the angriest."

"I know. But if I can't do it, who's going to?"

The storage silos were two klicks down the paved road from the city gates, massive, concrete structures that I hadn't noticed on the way in, at night, under fire, except maybe to note that they weren't weapons emplacements. Half a dozen of them, each at least sixty feet tall and nearly as wide, loading docks surrounding the silos, cargo trucks parked beside them, either having brought in the food from the seaport or ready to take it out to the cargo ships. No drivers, whether they'd been civilians pressed into duty or Anguilar military, because they'd been smart enough to get while the getting was good during the battle last night. No workers, no loaders, no one left to run when we touched down in the shadow of the nearest silo.

"Charlie, this is Tamura." I glanced around at the speaker, sharing a look with Laranna.

"Go ahead," I replied, not sure what the Kamerian wanted.

"Do you need us in the air to back you up?"

I clamped down on my initial response, which was to tell him that no, I did *not* want him and his goons to scare the crap out of the civilians and make everything much worse. Or, worst-case scenario, blow a bunch of them to vapors. That wouldn't have been fair, though, and wouldn't have been smart, either, and the warning look from Laranna would have been clue enough to how I should react.

"Negative, I'm going to try to do this low-key. If I need backup, I'll give you guys a call."

"You might wind up needing backup," Laranna warned as I hooked my comm unit up to the fighter's external speakers and stuck the earpiece in. I hated that thing. Beyond the fact that it wasn't very comfortable, it made me look like a Secret Service agent.

"You *are* my backup," I reminded her. "If they swarm over me and try to tear me apart, you get this thing up and fire a warning shot into one of those trucks with the particle cannon."

"That's a hell of a warning," she told me, eyes widening a hair.

"If I ask for it, I'll be in a hell of a lot of trouble."

I'd touched down only a couple hundred yards from the leading edge of the mob, which gave me a couple minutes to find the most dramatic place from which to address them. Standing in front of the fighter was my first thought, but there were so many of them, that would mean most wouldn't see who was talking, which would defeat the whole purpose.

I could have stood in the open hatch, but that might not be high enough, either. Which left only one possibility, though it seemed very Eva Perone or Che Guevara. Sighing in resignation, I found a foothold beside the hatch and pulled myself up onto the roof of the fighter. It might not have been a good idea on a jet fighter back on Earth, as thin as their skin was, particularly on top, but the Vanguard was meant for work in a vacuum and her fuselage was as thick as the hull of a submarine.

It was also pretty damn slick up there and my foot slid a few inches, nearly sending me right off the edge, but I managed to catch myself, my stance widening like I was about to spar in the *dojang*.

And there they were, close enough now that I could make out the individual faces, the fear and confusion and bemusement and anger evident in their expressions. All of them staring at me.

"I'm Charlie Travers."

I'd shouted by instinct and winced as the speakers took it as a challenge, blaring the announcement out way louder than I'd intended, my name echoing off the storage silos and the cargo trucks. The Copperell shrank back from the storm of sound, children putting their hands over their ears. Taking a deep breath, I started again.

"I'm Charlie Travers, the leader of the…Vanguard Wing." I don't know why I chose that name, but I was tired of saying "the resistance." "We came here to set you free of the oppression of the Anguilar, and we've done that. The Anguilar here are either dead or our prisoners. You've seen this."

Nods all around, though they still seemed angry. They probably still worried they were just trading one set of oppressors for another, which wasn't an unreasonable assumption in this galaxy.

"We just arrived," I went on, "and we're trying to get things organized, make sure you're all taken care of. We're going to get everyone fed, clothed and housed adequately, but we need some time to do this. We've been talking to Novo, your city elder, trying to find out where the resources are and how to distribute them."

"Novo!" a middle-aged woman scoffed. "He's worthless! He never did anything to help his people, just cowered like a whipped dog under the boot of the Anguilar."

"He doesn't have to be a soldier," I reasoned. "He just has to help us to take care of all of you."

The closest of them, an older man, stooped over as if he'd been crippled by a lifetime of backbreaking work and dressed in rags, raised a fist and yelled up at me.

"We're hungry!" he insisted. "We can't wait for you to *organize* everything! We need food and the food is right here!"

A rumble of agreement rolled through the crowd punctuated by angry shouts every few hundred people in the crowd. Butterflies invaded my stomach at the sheer size of the crowd. It was like playing a concert at Carnegie Hall…I assumed, since I'd never played any sort of concert.

I closed my eyes and tried to overcome the exhaustion and the headache and just think.

"How many extra meals do you need to tide you over for the next few days?" I asked.

Murmurings and arguments went back and forth, starting right in front of me and passing back and forth all the way down a line of people one hundred across and a quarter of a mile deep. I thought I would be standing up there for hours, waiting for them to come to some conclusion, but after a few minutes, a woman pushed her way to the front, holding a child in her arms. It took me a second to realize the woman was Wendra and the child was Maya.

"Charlie!" Maya crowed, waving at me. I waved back because what else was I supposed to do when a little kid says hi?

"I can't speak for all," Wendra called up to me, her voice firm and carrying, "but all the families I know could get by with three meals per person." She pointed at the silos. "These storage buildings are loaded with processed and packaged individual meals meant to be shipped to their troops offplanet. Three of those for each person in the family would be enough for now."

I sighed. Thank God, finally something concrete. The roof of the Vanguard was getting hot in the afternoon sun and sweat had started to trickle down my back. Now, though, there was another problem. There were somewhere around ten thousand people out here and more would probably come once the word went out. I wasn't going to stand out here and hand the meals out personally and we didn't have the troops to do it.

"Wendra," I said, motioning her toward me, "come up here with me."

She blanched, staring at me askance.

"What? Why?"

"Just trust me," I told her. "I need your help."

The Copperell woman stepped forward hesitantly, stepping up the stairs to the hatch, where Laranna waited.

"I can watch your daughter for you," she offered, holding out a hand.

If Wendra had looked doubtful about joining me atop the fighter, she was twice as reluctant to trust her little girl to a complete stranger.

"I trust Laranna with my life," I told Wendra. "She'd die before she let anything happen to your daughter."

"Do you have children?" Wendra asked, setting Maya on her feet, regarding Laranna in frank judgment.

"Not yet. We've talked about it." She smiled up at me. "But I had to hold *this* one's hand when he first arrived here, until he learned how to take care of himself."

I might have objected to that if there'd been more time, but I guess it was enough for Wendra because she knelt down eye to eye with her daughter.

"Maya, stay with her until I come back, okay?"

"Can I fly the spaceship?" Maya asked brightly, grabbing Laranna's hand.

"Not with my husband and your mom on the roof," Laranna told her, "but I will show you how it works…"

They disappeared inside the cockpit and I went down on a knee and offered Wendra a hand. Her grip was firm and rough, the hand of a woman who worked hard for a living, and she scrambled up beside me with surprising agility. The crowd had started to grumble at the long pause but I waved at them, then whistled loudly, the sound sending feedback blaring from the speakers. The people in front covered their ears while the rest took a step back.

"Listen up!" I told them now that I had their attention. "This is my friend Wendra! She's one of you! She lives in…" I turned to her, raising my eyebrow in a question.

"Southtown," she supplied.

"…Southtown, and she knows what you need. What's going to happen is that Wendra is going to pick"—I did quick calculations in my head—"fifty of you to help her, and then you're going in there." I pointed back to the silo behind us. "And you're going to hand out three meal packages for each member of each family. No more!"

Another dissatisfied rumble and some individual cries I could barely make out that it wasn't enough and I whistled again to get their attention.

"It *will* be enough," I insisted, "because we're going to have people out here before the end of the day to distribute the food to all of you, to everyone, not just the people who came out here. And we're going to make sure the farms start running out to the cities, too. You have to trust us…we came here to help you. Trust us and your friend Wendra, and we'll get you fed."

I took the earpiece out and handed it to her, motioned to her to put it in place.

"I am Wendra," she said, then started as if she didn't expect her voice to be so loud. "I am Wendra of Southtown, and I have lived here for my whole life, as my mother and father before me, and theirs before them back to the time when this world was free. Now, thanks to Charlie and the Vanguard Wing, we are free once more." Wendra gestured toward me. "I trust them and you should, too. Now, who will volunteer to help me hand out food? Those who would help, step forward…but know, you and yours will be fed last, after all the others. You have to be willing to help others first."

There was a pause, a hesitation just long enough for everyone to look at each other, and then an entire rank stepped forward, hundreds of people. Wendra shot me a confident smile and handed back the earpiece. I put a hand up.

"Keep it for now." I took the comm unit off my belt and passed it over to her. "We'll stay here with the fighter for now, until you get everyone organized."

"How did you know you could rely on me to do this?" she asked, tucking the comm unit into a pocket of her dress. "We just met. For all you know, I could use my position to steal food and sell it."

I shrugged, then climbed back down from the top of the

fighter, helped her off the roof as well before I attempted an answer.

"I guess I give people the benefit of the doubt," I told her, "until they show me they don't deserve it anymore."

"Really?" She sounded skeptical. "And how has that been working for you?"

Laranna came out of the cockpit, holding Maya's hand, and I slipped an arm around her waist, then pulled her into a kiss.

"Sometimes," she whispered to me, "you're brilliant."

"What do you mean *sometimes?*" I murmured back to her before I turned to the Copperell.

"I don't know," I replied to Wendra's question. "So far, so good."

17

"Hey, Charlie!"

"Good morning, Charlie!"

"Hi, Mr. Charlie!"

My arm was getting tired from waving, and nodding was starting to give me a headache, but I couldn't *not* say hi back, not without seeming rude. And anyway, the smiling faces made me feel like all this was worth it. Like when we'd freed Strada, except better because so many people had died in that battle, the celebration had been bittersweet. We'd gotten there too late to help Peboktan, too late to do anything except keep it from happening again, and Copperell...

My smile faded thinking about Copperell. There'd been no chance to do anything meaningful there other than accomplishing the mission, and the last memory I had of the place was getting Grenalane killed. No, that wasn't fair to her. She'd made a choice, sacrificed herself to let Val and me get away. Still, it had left a cold knot in my gut, one I'd never quite gotten over.

Walking through the streets from the makeshift living quarters we'd set up near the office building that had become our administration headquarters, the morning sun warm on my face, the smiles of the Copperell civilians even warmer, something of that cold knot loosened.

They looked better. It had only been three weeks since we'd arrived, but every man, woman and child who passed us wore new clothes, made on the fabricators that the Anguilar hadn't shared with the general population, and they were all filling out now that the food was no longer rationed. And there *were* actually men among them now that Val and his people had brought back several thousand from the mines. More still were still out at the farms, helping voluntarily now rather than as forced labor, working to get food to the city.

Families walked together, hand-in-hand, probably for the first time in months.

Laranna bumped my shoulder with hers, bringing my attention back to what she'd been saying.

"Are you even listening to me?" she teased. "Or are you too busy basking in the accolades for Good King Charles?"

"I'm not their king," I protested, still nodding and waving, though my smile wavered at her subtle mockery. "As soon as we can arrange it, they're going to have some kind of elected government."

I made a mental note to talk to Novo about that, then made a mental note to make a physical note of it because I already had too damn many mental notes. It hadn't even been a month and there were so many other problems to solve that seemed more pressing…

"And what if that elected government tells us to piss off?" Laranna asked, arching an eyebrow at me. "After we spent so much time and so many resources getting rid of the Anguilar to make this place an outpost? Do we do what they want? Even though we know the Anguilar will come straight back and enslave them again?"

"They know that's what would happen," I protested, looking away from the greetings, from the construction crews already getting to work repairing the buildings that had been damaged during the battle. "They're scared shitless of the Anguilar…they wouldn't kick us out."

Laranna shrugged, offering a mischievous smile.

"Oh, I know. I just wondered how far you're willing to go with this democracy thing you keep talking about."

I was disturbed at times by how unknown representative democracy was out here. It probably had something to do with the destruction and instability after the Centennial War, followed by the invasion of the Anguilar. Every society we'd come across not ruled by the Anguilar seemed to be run by a strongman, a warlord, or else some inherited position like this elder, Novo. Still, it was a point. Were these people ready to govern themselves after generations of servitude?

The American in me wanted to say yes, but then I thought about Vietnam. Trying to make South Vietnam into a liberal democracy had only resulted in a corrupt, authoritarian dictatorship because the country was too unstable and had no tradition of individual freedom and representation. Or that's what my military history professors had said. I'd been eight years old when we pulled out of Vietnam and hadn't spent much time watching the nightly news. Dani had told me similar stories about American wars in Iraq, which I barely even knew the existence of, and Afghanistan, which I was only aware of because of the Soviet invasion.

Were the Copperell here more like Europe after World War Two or like Vietnam? I was afraid it might be the latter, but we'd cross that bridge when we came to it. The first thing we had to do was make sure we had go-betweens people would listen to. Novo was one, although some of the residents here still resented him as a do-nothing, and Wendra was another. She'd brought in a few of her friends who she said she trusted, and they'd brought in some of *their* friends, and I'd put them in charge of food distribution, transportation and clothing manufacture…

And damned if that wasn't just starting a government based on patronage and nepotism and I hated so much having to make every one of these stupid decisions that could wind up having lasting effects for decades. Laranna must have noticed the shift in my mood because she grabbed my hand and squeezed it.

"Sorry, I didn't mean to get you all sulky and pensive," she said. "Come on, cheer up. These people have a chance now because of what we did."

I nodded but didn't reply. The relocation center loomed in front of us, the skeleton of an unfinished warehouse on the edge of the industrial district, draped with tarps by hired locals to keep out the rain and sun. We'd hauled in tables, chairs, computer displays, cameras and printers for ID cards and started processing people through. I felt a little uncomfortable with the whole business of taking everyone's photo, putting their faces, biometrics and stats on file and handing them ID cards they needed to carry, but it came down to the fact that if we were going to integrate some of the ethnic-Copperell EPWs into their society, working on the farms and in the mines for room and board at first until they proved themselves trustworthy, we needed to make sure we knew who everyone was.

So far, no one had complained about it, not while they were too busy getting their food and new clothes. Well, no one except Giblet.

"Boss," he whined the second I came into the processing center, squeezing through an unorganized gaggle of locals and stepping around an orderly line of Copperell EPWs, being watched over by Strada guards.

Giblet hopped out of the chair he'd been lounging in and jogged over to me as if this couldn't wait for me to make it across the chamber. I shivered even with my leather jacket in the shade of the flapping tarps. It was, as close as I could figure, still early spring here on the east side of the northern continent and while the high-forties temps didn't feel too bad out in the sun, it was downright chilly in here. The locals didn't look uncomfortable, but the EPWs were shivering. I made another mental note to ask about getting space heaters in the processing center.

"What's up, Gib?" I sighed, stuffing my hands in my pockets to keep them warm.

"How long am I gonna be stuck with this"—he grimaced as if the very act of saying the word was about to make him physically ill—"*clerical* work?" Giblet threw up his hands, the vestigial feathers on his arms flapping around like he was about to take off. "I'm a lot of things, Charlie…a damned good pilot, a fair shot and not too bad at convincing people to do things my way, but what I am *not*, and never will be, is a damned secretary."

Wendra spared me a look from the head of the line for the locals and rolled her eyes.

"He's right about that," she said. "He's horrible at it and we have to do most of the work."

Maya wasn't there and I assumed she was either staying with the woman's friends or maybe at the makeshift school we'd encouraged them to set up for the children. That was taking more effort to get rolling because they had a tradition here of kids accompanying their parents to work and learning on the job. Again, maybe it was just me trying to be an American on an alien world, but the whole child labor thing didn't sit right.

"Gib," I told him, grabbing at patience, "I know this isn't what you want to be doing but it's something that has to get done and it's important that we"—I made a circle with my finger encompassing Laranna, Gib, and me—"be seen contributing to it." I leaned in closer to him so the Copperell around us couldn't overhear. "Do you really think the locals would be bending over backward to get food and clothes for the prisoners working in the mines or on the farms if we didn't keep track of them? How many do you think might just disappear?"

"And what do *I* care if they do?" he insisted. "How come

Valentine and Nareena aren't in here taking care of this? I mean, this working with the locals stuff is supposed to be their gig, right?"

"Sure," I told him, starting to lose all that patience I'd been attempting to hold onto. "And when I send them here to supervise this, I'm sure you'll take over for them while they organize food shipments from the farms and transportation to the mines and back? You'd rather do that?"

Gib bit down on whatever reply he'd been about to snap at me, visibly shifted tactics.

"Okay, then…what about the rest of the pilots? How come Dani's not in here taking her turn at handing out licenses to eat? Or those Kamerian a-holes? Do they get a pass because they're such hotshots?"

"They get a pass," Laranna interjected, probably because she'd noticed how close I was to chewing Gib out right in front of everyone, "because they *are* a-holes who'd probably wind up smashing someone's head in the first time a Copperell prisoner mouthed off at them. We're keeping them busy running the other pilots through training up in orbit all day long so by the time they come back down for dinner, they'll be too tired to cause trouble."

And because the other pilots needed training and the Kamerians *were* hotshots, but Gib didn't need to hear that. The answer seemed to mollify him, at least on that subject, maybe because I'd made it clear that the Kamerians were up in space and Dani *wasn't.*

"Fine. Well, we're almost through the last lot of EPWs you're sending out to the farms. Not that any of them are that bright," he added, sighing theatrically. "You'd think it was hyperdimensional physics just getting these geniuses to give their names and planet of origin, but they should be processed by the end of the day."

Wendra had walked over while we were talking, and had apparently caught the last part of Gib's status report. She leaned in close to us, glancing around to make sure the prisoners couldn't hear her.

"Do you really think they'll work for us, Charlie?" she asked. "I know they're Copperell, but most of them have been here for months if not years, their boots on the back of our neck." Wendra stole a look at the line of prisoners and shuddered. "If I were out at one of the farms, I'd worry about them slitting my throat in the dead of night."

I nodded in understanding, if not agreement. There was a qualitative difference between the ethnic-Copperell prisoners and the local civilians, despite their shared ancestry. The Anguilar recruits shared a regulation-short military haircut, of course, but beyond that, they also had in common a hard detachment behind their eyes. Fear, too, fear of us, probably fear of the resistance. *The Vanguard Wing*, I corrected myself. These guys wouldn't know what that was, but everyone was going to find out. The fear had started out as their overpowering characteristic while they'd huddled together in the face of aerial bombardment and an invading army, but now it had faded to a secondary feature behind the detachment.

Maybe I needed to change that. I raised my voice, pitched my answer to Wendra's question so everyone could hear it.

"No, Wendra, I'm not concerned about the former Anguilar soldiers relapsing to their old ways and causing trouble for their Thalassian employers." I offered the prisoners a broad, toothy smile. "I'm sure every single one of them is smart enough to realize that making a new life here is the only choice they have. If they tried to go back to the Anguilar after having worked for us voluntarily, they'd be executed. The Anguilar don't mess around when it comes to what they consider treason, after all."

The line of former Anguilar recruits shifted back and forth uncomfortably, like every single one of them had discovered the urge to go to the bathroom at the same time. Murmurs ran up and down the column, as if some of them hadn't considered that.

"Beyond that, of course," I went on, "we're not just going to dump them off and not check in on them. I plan on leaving a couple platoons of our troops out at the mines on a rotational basis in case anyone becomes...dissatisfied with their new job. As for the farms, well, they're all going to have their adults of fighting age sworn into the militia and they'll all be trained and armed by our people. Now, I won't put up with any of them abusing their authority or harming any of their new workers unprovoked. But if any of these fine, upstanding workers has the bad judgment to do anything violent, well...I also don't plan on trying too hard to disprove self-defense in that case."

Adam's apples bobbed and faces blanched, eyes darting sideways as if they were reconsidering their choice. I'd given them the stick...it was time for the carrot.

"But I meant what I said. Any of them who can adapt to their new life here, work hard and not cause trouble for a whole year can either volunteer to stay in their current job or apply to join the Vanguard Wing. It'll be hard work, but it could mean the difference between being on the winning side or the losing one." I grinned at Wendra as the murmuring among the prisoners took on a different note, perhaps a more hopeful one.

"We have to go," Laranna reminded me. "You still have to check in on the militia training and then you're scheduled to go out to three of the farms to show the flag."

That was an expression she'd learned from me since neither the Anguilar nor any of the major societies out here used flags. I sighed and motioned to Giblet.

"You see, you think *you* have it bad. I'm gonna be doing this all day, just like the last two weeks. I barely get done with the scheduled stuff by dinner time and then I have people bugging me with questions the rest of the night. I am *not* cut out to be any kind of administrator and if you want to change jobs…" I spread my hands.

"No, I think I'm good here," Giblet admitted. But then he jerked his head to the side and we followed him away from the others, including Wendra, into a corner of the building where the edge of a pair of overlapping tarps flapped in the breeze. This close, I caught a whiff of Giblet and wondered if there was a diplomatic way to tell him he needed a shower. "Hey man, I know you got this plan to set up outposts and squeeze the Anguilar from the outside in. It sounds good but…" He made an expansive gesture. "Look at all the damn work it is just to get this Podunk colony running on its own. We're gonna be doing this for *months* before these people can take a dump without one of us there to wipe their asses."

Laranna scowled at him, storms darkening behind her eyes.

"These people were enslaved for decades, Giblet. You can't expect them to be able to just step in and run the government…" But he was already shaking his head.

"I *know* that," he insisted. "That's not what I'm saying. What I'm saying is, this is just *one* planet. What happens when we try to take someplace bigger and they take some serious damage? Someplace like Wallow or Graycliff or Copperell itself? How long do you expect this island-hopping campaign of yours to go on for? Hell, it's taking us about half our ground troops just to guard prisoners and even if you get the ethnic Copperell to sign up with us, that still leaves a bunch of Krin and a few Anguilar who'll *never* join our side. At this rate, we're all going to be old and gray before we get anywhere near the Anguilar capital at Martinet."

That…was a good point. I wanted to fire back at him, tell him I knew what I was doing, but the truth was, I was a twenty-five year-old playing general, and for all the World War Two analogies I threw around, this was *not* WW2. We had maybe twelve thousand people, five cruisers and two dozen fighters. The Anguilar had a hell of a lot more than that but still nowhere near what any military in the 1940s had. The only reason they'd been able to conquer this galaxy was that everything was in shambles after the war.

"He's not wrong," I told Laranna, sighing heavily. "This is going to take a lot longer than I thought."

"But we'll be growing, too," she suggested. "Just because we only have a few thousand people now doesn't mean we're going to be stuck at that forever. The more victories we win, the more recruits we'll get. And this is the first time we've had to set up the local government on our own. Strada had a resistance movement of their own that could take over. We'll learn from this, and next time, we'll do it faster and better."

"Or," Giblet suggested, "we do it a different way." Enthusiasm entered his voice, brightened his expression for the first time in weeks. "We have our whole force intact right now. Everyone has combat experience and if we needed to, we could probably recruit some more warriors from Strada. We do something big...and we do it right now."

I considered the idea for a second, then decided it was too big for me to make a snap decision...or to make a decision by myself.

"Laranna," I said, "can you get the entire leadership together tonight after dinner?" She nodded, pulling out her comm unit and taking a step away, making the call immediately. I turned back to Giblet. "Get ready to make your case. We'll hear you out tonight."

18

I LIKED WATCHING the sunsets here.

They were pretty back on Sanctuary too, of course, but it felt like I hadn't been there in forever. It was a home for other people, for the people we saved, not a place I got to live. Not a place I'd *earned*. I felt like I'd earned this sunset.

The best place to watch the sun set over the western hills was up on the wall…which was also a little dangerous, since the wall had been shot to hell during the battle. But there was one solid section on the western side of the city, an intact staircase leading to the battlements at the top. The whole thing was very medieval and I wasn't sure why they'd bothered. Wendra would probably know. Maybe it dated back to before the Anguilar, had been around as long as Philos. Maybe there was some dramatic story behind it, a war between cities or dangerous natives that they'd had to guard against when they first settled here.

It was easy to imagine, staring out at the rolling hills, cloaked in green mystery. The sun shone gold over the mountains at the horizon, showing just a hint of white snow caps at the peaks. Planets were *big*. I mean, I should have known that already, being from one of them, but it was easy to forget when I only had time to visit one or two cities on each of them. Even on Sanctuary, I'd rarely gotten any farther away from the main settlement than the hiking trails in the hills a few miles away.

The problem was one of population, though I hadn't realized it until a long conversation with Lenny. If planets were big, the galaxy was freaking *huge*, and the percentage of people who were willing to give up the familiar surroundings of home to settle on a strange world was vanishingly small. Most colonies had two or three cities max, with farming settlements or mining operations between them, and the smaller worlds like this barely had a million people in total.

The settlers would build a city around their initial landing zone and spread out from it, and there'd be no reason to build a second city until the farms and mines had extended so far away that another source of supplies, services and transportation was needed. They hadn't reached that point on this world, yet. They probably wouldn't have if the Anguilar had stayed in charge. Hard to have a population explosion when most of the young males were worked to death as slaves.

That was short-sighted on the part of the Anguilar, but then, from what I'd found out, this was their first try at conquest, here in our galaxy. Lucky us. I took one last look out at the sun-kissed hills, then clambered back down the stairs...carefully. It had rained in the early afternoon and the stone steps were slick, coated with algae and lacking any sort of handrail. OSHA would have had a field day with any of the worlds we'd visited, but of all the things I missed about living in America in…God, it was hard to think of it as the 1980s. For me, it had just been the *now*, but I had a different now…now. But of all that I missed, all that I wanted to bring out here to these worlds, the bureaucracy wasn't one of them.

I sighed in relief when I got back to the street, almost missed the giggle.

No one lived out on the west side of the city. It had been used as a parking area for the Anguilar armored vehicles and cargo trucks and now, both were gone. The tanks were gone forever, blown apart by our fighters, while the trucks had been put to good use, hauling raw crops to processing centers so we could get a handle on the whole food supply issue.

It was just a bunch of empty space and unused maintenance garages and there shouldn't have been a giggle. I didn't make a sound, not wanting to scare some poor local kid who'd come here with the aim of getting out from under their parents' eye, but it didn't take long to figure out this wasn't a kid.

Two adults walking hand in hand, silhouettes at first because my eyes had yet to adjust from watching the sunset. Tall, both of them, broad-shouldered, even the woman, and they weren't dressed in the typical rough work clothes of the Thalassians, dress-like robes for women, loose, broad-ended pants for men. Instead, the woman wore jeans and a brown jacket, while the man's clothes were even more distinctive, a blue-gray flight suit with knee-high boots. Blond hair waved at his shoulder, blown by the evening breeze, and as the last light played across their faces, all became clear.

Tamura and Dani. Dani had *giggled*. That was a sound I never expected to hear, nor had I expected the broad, bright smile. She and Tamura were a good fifty yards away and still her grin was plain to see, as was his. They walked together in the general direction of the chow hall…or what we'd designated the chow hall, what had used to be some kind of rec room for the Anguilar military here. It had been full of weird board games that none of us knew how to play, though the Copperell recruits had recognized them and taken them back to their barracks. We'd turned it into a chow hall and a roomier meeting room than the offices and I'd been about to head there myself.

So, they were friends. It wasn't that big of a deal. They had a lot in common, both of them strangers in a strange land, torn from their homes and shoved into a situation not of their own making. Kind of like Laranna and me.

Shit. That wasn't the example I wanted to use.

Another giggle, louder this time, and Tamura swept Dani into his arms and kissed her, and that pretty much removed all doubt.

"If I'd known you were a peeping Tom, I probably wouldn't have been so quick to marry you."

I did *not* jump out of my skin, but that was only because I recognized Laranna's voice so well. She was so damned stealthy, I hadn't heard her walking up behind me.

"I wasn't spying on them," I said softly, making a shushing

motion. "I was out looking at the sunset and they were just… *here*."

"I don't know what it is with you and climbing up that rickety wall," she murmured, eyeing the steps dubiously. "Nor do I know why you're surprised at this. I saw it happening almost from the minute they laid eyes on each other."

"Yeah, but I was just really hoping it wasn't going to happen." I sighed and watched the two of them disappear around a corner.

"Why? You still don't trust him? Or are you just not a romantic at heart?"

"I was thinking more about how Gib is gonna react," I confessed. "Things are hard enough as it is, trying to get everyone acclimated to the Kamerians. If Gib finds out that Tamura and Dani are involved…"

"Think and walk," she told me, nudging me with her hip. "We have to get some dinner."

"Yeah. But I'm not looking forward to what comes after." I shook my head. "I wish I knew what Giblet had in mind."

"Copperell."

"You can't be serious," Val said, rocking back in his seat.

I'd waited until everyone was done with dinner—all the way done, so there'd be no more talking with mouths full like some of our strategy meetings—so at least when Valentine McKee's boots rattled the table, it didn't knock over any dishes.

"Deadly," Giblet said.

And in fact, he was. Giblet was serious about his flying, serious about not getting killed, but rarely serious about anything else. Not this time, though. That sharp, angular face was etched with determination and his stance was set in stolid stubbornness like he was getting ready to meet a charge.

"We were there," Val reminded him, motioning toward where I sat at the edge of the cluster of tables. "The two of us. We saw the defenses they have there, and that's just around the administrative headquarters. There's no damned way we're taking that whole planet!"

"We don't have to *take* it," Giblet told him, throwing up his hands as if it was the most obvious thing in the world. "That's the difference between what I'm talking about and what Charlie wants to do with the whole island-hopping plan. We don't *take* anything. We just destroy."

"Now you have my attention," Tamura admitted, cocking an eyebrow. Giblet returned the expression with a glare, perhaps because Dani sat beside the Kamerian pilot, their shoulders touching.

"What do you mean, Gib?" I asked, trying to drag him back to the point before guns came out of the holster.

"We don't have enough people yet to hold planets." Giblet explained, his eyes shifting back to me only reluctantly, and even then still glancing back toward Dani every few seconds. "And even if Laranna is right about us recruiting more troops, that's not gonna happen fast. In the meantime, we don't have to spin our wheels on nothing outposts like this. We can keep hitting the Anguilar where it hurts. The Vanguards are our secret weapon and we can use them to jump in, destroy any Imperial cruisers on patrol, jump back out again."

"I guess blowing up Anguilar cruisers is good," I granted, "but why is that a strategy?"

"Because Copperell isn't just their administrative HQ...they have a big-ass shipyard there. We could take it out. Destroy the whole damned thing. Any ships under construction, the drydocks, everything." He grinned, his slightly pointed teeth showing. "And we keep doing that, over and over. The Anguilar can't have more than a half a dozen shipyards total capable of turning out cruisers."

"Not a bad idea," Laranna said, nodding slowly. "If we destroy their capability to manufacture new ships, they'll stop risking the ones they have, withdraw back to their core systems and try to hold them."

Giblet nodded enthusiastically, pointing at her.

"Exactly. And leaving a bunch of places just like this open and unguarded. We won't have to *take* them because they'll *give* them to us."

"That would solve another problem you guys have been bringing up," Dani said. She still seemed disgustingly happy, which Laranna was right about, should have been a good thing except that it still worried the hell out of me. "We're all worried about how we can protect this place once we move on to the next one, whether we can bring in enough of those orbital defense platforms to keep them safe from attack after the Liberators and the fighters are gone."

I nodded. That was the reason Lenny wasn't down here

participating in this meeting. The Liberators were on their way back to Sanctuary, picking up the platforms. The *first* shipment of platforms. We'd need at least three trips back and forth before we had enough, which would take months.

"But if we do what Gib says," she went on, "then we wouldn't have to leave this place for more than a couple weeks at a time, not enough for the Anguilar to make a run at it."

I would have expected Gib to be happy Dani liked his plan, but instead, resentment flared behind his eyes as he stared between her and Tamura, and he said nothing.

"I like it," Dothan said, slamming his palm on the table. Another change, since Dothan didn't like much of anything in my experience with him. "Action! Not just sitting around training sub-par pilots and eating crappy food!"

"It's a daring plan," Tamura agreed. "I only see two downsides."

"What?" Giblet demanded, sounding even more outraged that the Kamerian objected than he had when they'd supported it.

"First of all, casualties…birds and pilots." Tamura shrugged. "Normally, back in the day, that would have been expected. You can't fight a war without casualties. But back then, we had ship-yards to build more fighters and cruisers, schools to train pilots. If we lose any of these starfighters, we won't be getting another."

"That's a danger whether we go with my plan or Charlie's," Gib protested, sullen and defensive.

"It is. But his plan also involved building up our forces before we took on any harder targets. Seizing cruisers, fighters, recruiting new troops. If we stay here and launch precision strikes, we're stuck with what we have."

He was saying *we* a lot lately. That was a good sign, as long as it was earnest and not just to impress a girl.

"We could...try to hijack cruisers at their shipyards," Giblet suggested, not sounding quite so certain anymore. "Before we blow everything up, we could insert a team to steal the ships there."

"We could," Tamura acknowledged. "But that would take longer, and the longer the mission drags on, the more casualties you're bound to take."

"What's the second thing?" I asked, interrupting before the argument had time to take us on a long tangent. "You said there were two."

"Well, the other is obvious," Tamura said, shrugging, using the motion to slip an arm around Dani's shoulder. "This place."

"I thought one of the main positives was that we wouldn't be leaving it defenseless," I pointed out. "We wouldn't be gone that long."

"True. But if we're jumping from one world to another, we don't make a particular target out of any one of them. If we're using this place as our main base, launching every attack from here, then before the enemy pulls in their horns and battens down the hatches at their more fortified systems, they'll throw everything they have at this world. And even if we win that fight, Thalassia loses."

Shit. He was right.

"We're rebuilding this world for them," Val mused softly. "But if we use this as our one base, it'll get destroyed. The bombardment would take out this city, burn their farms. They'd be constantly running to shelters, in fear, constantly building things back again."

"Not to mention," Nareena put in, "that this militia we're training is going to take a long time to turn into anything even capable of defending this place, much less using as an expeditionary force. There just aren't enough fighting-age men and women who don't have families depending on them."

"It sounds like everyone's telling me why *neither* of these ideas are going to work." I interjected. "Not mine nor Giblet's."

"No, to the contrary," Tamura said. "Both could work, or some combination of the two. But as the commander, you need to be aware of the possible worst-case scenarios. You don't fight a war without risk. It's your job to decide which risks are acceptable…and survivable."

"Anyone else have suggestions? Objections? Anything?" I looked around. "Because whatever we're gonna do, we have to start prepping for it now, which means this decision has to get made tonight. Recommendations?"

"I say we stick to the original plan," Val said immediately. "It's slow, but it's better for the people here and probably for the other worlds we plan on liberating."

"Agreed," Nareena declared. And she would. The two of them were the ones most involved with training the locals.

"I like Gib's idea," Dani said. "Yeah, it's got a possibility of blowback, but this is a war, and the idea isn't to come out of it with clean clothes, it's to win."

"Well put, Dani," Tamura said, offering a small clap. "And I agree. The plan is daring and kinetic. You'll win the war quicker this way and that is the single best way to reduce casualties, civilian and military."

"And you speak for all four of you?" I asked, glancing at Dothan, Sainrastil and Fenris.

"Tamura is our captain," Dothan said, a certain smugness in his words. "If we didn't trust his judgment, we wouldn't follow him."

That left Laranna, since Mallarna had gone back to Sanctuary with Lenny to pick up the defense platforms. I looked to my wife and she didn't answer immediately, her expression deliberate and thoughtful. Which wasn't like her. Not that Laranna wasn't intelligent or thoughtful, but she was also decisive, a woman used to combat where every choice had to be made in the fraction of a second. Normally, I would have expected her to have weighed the options while we were debating it and already have her answer, but not this time. Her grimace looked as if she felt physical pain.

"I'm torn on this one, Charlie. You told me about the difference between strategy and tactics. Tactically, Gib's plan is superior. It'll mean fewer casualties and a greater chance of immediate success. But strategically, well…consider, beyond just how it's going to affect Thalassia, what it'll do to the other worlds we're trying to free. If the populations there see us freeing them, *see* us defeating the Anguilar on their worlds, they'll join us. Even if they can't provide us with ships, they can grow food for us, mine raw materials, provide troops."

She spread her hands.

"But if we just strike out from here and start blowing up Anguilar shipyards, even if it works the way we intend and they *don't* manage to root us out of here, what's the best-case scenario? That they abandon those worlds without a fight? What do the people on those worlds think? Do they give us the credit or when we go ask them for help, for volunteers, for food, do they tell us to go piss up a rope because they've spent the last forty or fifty years as slaves and where were we the whole time?"

And again…wow.

"Sometimes I think you should be in charge," I told her.

"If I were," she said, her smile rueful, "then I'd be the one who had to make this decision…and the one who'd get blamed for it if it was the wrong one."

"Yeah, there is that." I tapped my fingertips together, staring at the far wall. There was a mural on it, painted by the Copperell long before the Anguilar invaded. Wendra had mentioned it was religious in nature, though to me, it looked like a third grader doodling in their notebook during class. "We're gonna do both." Questioning looks from everyone, of course. "We have the Liberators. They're pretty useful for mobile defense and once we take a colony like this one, they can secure it. But the fighters…look at what's happening here. Once the Liberators are back, what are the fighters gonna be doing while we're getting this planet buttoned down? Training? Maintenance? No, we're gonna use them to make those long-range strikes Gib is talking about." I shrugged. "It's not going to be the most comfortable ride stuck in that cockpit for days, but it's gonna distract the Anguilar from coming back and trying to retake the worlds we liberate. We keep moving, keep striking and pretty soon, there'll be too many planets for them to concentrate on any one of them."

"It'll be hard on the pilots," Tamura warned. "We'll have to train new crews or else they'll get burned out from spending that much time in hyperspace. But it's the best use of our assets."

"What do you think, Gib?" I asked him.

"I think it's the worst of both plans," he grumbled, "and it makes more work for all of us. It's no wonder you want to do it."

And with that, he slammed through the exit door and left us there.

"What's wrong with him?" Dani asked, frowning. Laranna stared at the woman askance, said what I wanted to.

"Dani Campling, for a smart woman, sometimes you're as dumb as a box of rocks."

19

"WHAT THE HELL WAS THAT?" I demanded.

At least I hadn't had to chase Giblet too far. The city didn't have much in the way of streetlights yet and the chow hall was a tiny circle of illumination in a sea of blackness and shadow. I had a flashlight on my gun belt, but I didn't really want to go hunting for him in the dark with a flashlight like Diogenes looking for an honest man.

But there Giblet was, pacing furiously in the alley between the chow hall and the next building over, staring at the ground like the secrets of the universe were concealed there. He didn't look up at my question, nor did he attempt to answer it.

"Gib," I said, stepping into his path to force him to pay attention to me, "I let you have your say, let everyone weigh in on it, then I made my decision. Are you pissed off because I didn't just agree to your plan right away? Hey, man, got news for you.

You're not the star of this show—it's an ensemble cast. I'm the commander, but even I wouldn't make a decision like that without consulting everyone first."

He eyed me from under hooded brows, still pissed off but maybe, I figured out, not at me.

"This is all just a waste of freaking time!" he blurted, throwing up his hands. "This shit is just building up people's hopes for nothing! We're telling the Thalassians they're free, that they can rule themselves and we'll keep them safe, but you know as well as I do that if the Empire comes after this place in full force, we're not going to be able to keep them out. All this"—he waved around him—"will be nothing but ash."

I took a step back, feeling as if he'd slapped me.

"If you believe that," I said, "then why the hell are you here? Why did you even stay with us in the first place? Did you never believe we could pull this off?"

"I'm just as big a sucker as the people here," he snarled, turning away from me, hands stuffed into his jacket pockets. "I should have known better. I'm a Varnell, for God's sake—I *do* the conning, I don't *get* conned. But I really wanted to believe. You know that? After so long believing in nothing, just taking whatever people would give me and not looking back, you came along, kid. You came along and you conned me into believing there was hope."

"It wasn't a con, Gib." I put an arm around his shoulder and turned him back to face me. He tried to pull away, but I didn't let him. "Look at me, man." His eyes weren't angry, they were hurt, and it was a punch in the gut. "We're in this together. I never lied to you. You're part of this, and you have been from the beginning. Remember what I said? Varnell don't just con people out of their money. You're supposed to be our diplomat, but you haven't been very diplomatic lately. In fact, it seems to me like you're mostly feeling sorry for yourself because the girl you like doesn't like you back."

"I never lacked for companionship before," Giblet snapped, pushing my arm away from him. "Before I threw in with you lot and got all worried about shit like ethics and morals and doing the right thing. Look what good that's done me. I can't...*persuade* Dani the way I used to be able to because I respect her, because I want her to respect me. And what does it get me? Rejected. She thinks I'm a joke." His lower lip quivered. "What's the point of being one of the good guys if your life's going to suck?"

"The point," I told him, putting my hand back on his shoulder and not letting him push me away, "is being able to look yourself in the mirror every morning, man. Being able to live with yourself without constantly running away from the bad, selfish shit you did. As the Strada say, being able to die well and be mourned by the people who love you. And we love you, Gib. You're my best friend and I love you like a brother. We already lost Brazzo, and it's been damned hard to keep things going without him. We can't do this without you."

Giblet's face worked through emotions I hadn't seen much from him before settling on the mask again.

"Stop being so damned treacly," he scoffed, pushing me away again, but only half-heartedly. Gib sighed. "You know I'm with you guys till the end. What the hell else am I gonna do?" He grinned slyly. "And anyway, this whole city is full of single moms looking for a new dad for their kid. They might not be so picky about whether or not Dad has feathers. Maybe I should take a walk."

He headed off into the darkness and I watched him go, just shaking my head.

"Now that," I murmured to myself, "is the Giblet I know."

My shoulders sagged, dragged down by weariness. I needed some sleep.

"Why am I not in bed?" I asked, rubbing at my face, barely able to feel it. "I should be in bed."

My eyes focused again, this time on Valentine McKee, who didn't look much more rested than I was. His clothes were rumpled, hair and beard in tangles and red rimmed his eyes. Not to mention the nascent bruise on his cheek.

"Hell, Charlie," he mumbled, wincing as he spoke, "we all should be. But these bastards had other ideas."

The bastards were lined up against the wall of the former grain storehouse, hands secured behind their back, two dozen of them, all Krin and Anguilar. There were bruises on their faces as well, along with cuts seeping red. The smell of their body odor fought for supremacy with the fishy stench from the docks outside and I decided to let the fish win to preserve the dinner I'd had earlier.

The Strada guards watched over them with pulse rifles

leveled, some of them sporting bruises as well, and all of them wearing expressions that said they wouldn't mind too much pulling the trigger if one of the prisoners so much as twitched. I thought they might do it. The Krin still snarled even through the black and blue and red all over, too damned stupid to be afraid, and the half-dozen Anguilar survivors were...well, *Anguilar*. Narcissistic, haughty, pissed off at us for having the temerity to kick their asses and stick them in a box where they belonged.

"Where are the others?" I wanted to know.

"Being taken to the medical center," Val told me. "Ethnic Copperell, all of them. They got into it with the Krin over some of their people going over to our side and the Krin, just like always, ganged up on someone weaker and beat the shit out of them. I was on watch tonight—me and Nareena take turns on the night shift—so I got to lead the guards into the mess and bring out the victims and these varmints."

"You look like you could use a visit to the medics yourself," I told him, raising an eyebrow. "Brandy's gonna be pissed at me if I ruin your rugged good looks."

He snorted, then winced again, raising a hand to his cheek.

"Dammit boy, don't make me laugh right now."

"How many Krin and Anguilar left besides these guys?" I asked, nodding toward the group lined up against the cracked and faded paint on the wall. It had been yellow once upon a time, but it was nearly white now. It was easier to look at the wall than look at the Anguilar without wanting to shoot them myself.

"There're five more Anguilar officers and senior NCOs," Val

said, brow furling as he retrieved the numbers from memory. "Another eighty-seven Krin."

"Well, they can't be held in the general population with the Copperell, obviously," I reasoned, shrugging. I racked my brain, trying to recall the layout of the town. "There's a building not too far from the fortress, I think it was some kind of"—I grimaced at the thought—"interrogation center. Probably some of these Krin worked there, keeping a lid on anyone who might cause trouble. It's not big enough to hold all the prisoners, which is why I didn't consider it earlier, but it'll hold this group. I want this bunch here moved over immediately, and you can call some more Strada troops out here and escort the rest to the building in the morning. And make sure they lock it up tight." I shrugged. "We'll see about getting them food and water." My lip curled as I gave the Anguilar a look. "Eventually."

"You're going to regret this, you hairless ape," one of the Anguilar spat. Literally. The glob of blood he spat came within inches of my boot even from ten feet away. "You're all going to suffer, die slowly for what you've done. The Anguilar will hunt you down like the vermin you are and rip you apart one piece at a time!"

I sighed and rubbed at my temples.

"I have a headache already," I told the officer, "and you're just making it worse. You know, every time I've gone head-to-head with you dumb sons of guns, you get your asses handed to you, but every time, you act like everyone's just so damn inferior. You know what you remind me of? The rich kids I used to go to college with. Frat boys who lived off their parents' money, looking at a guaranteed job at Daddy's company once they graduated college and thinking that somehow, being born into a rich family means they accomplished something."

Two long strides took me face to face with him and I pushed him back into the wall, my hand at his throat. I squeezed just a little, enough to make his eyes bug out.

"But you know what, you birdbrain a-hole, you didn't hit a damned home run. You were born on third base. You came into this galaxy after it had been torn apart by war, when no one was ready for you. Guess what? We're ready for you. You're going to leave here just the way you came in…on the run, kicked out. You hear me?" Squeezing just a little harder made him grunt assent.

"Charlie," Val said, a warning rumble.

I let go and the Anguilar sank down off his tiptoes, gasping for air, glaring at me.

"I don't like losing sleep," I told them both, though I was still looking at the Anguilar. "And I am the *only* thing keeping these Anguilar you've been using as forced labor for the last few decades from burying all of you in a shallow grave outside town. Don't piss me off."

I didn't wait to hear an answer since I knew better than to think any of them would listen, just stalked out onto the docks, my steps hollow, echoing across the flats of the river delta in the still of pre-dawn. A cold breeze blew off the gulf and I stuffed my hands in my jacket pockets and glanced upward. The stars were probably out, but the dock was well-lit and I couldn't see anything past the glare of the floodlights.

"Were you just making a point in there?" Val asked from a

few steps behind me. I hadn't realized he'd followed me out. "Or were you really that fired up?"

"Oh, I guess a little bit of both," I admitted. "You've been fighting the Anguilar longer than I have, Val. Don't tell me they don't piss you off just as much."

"I gotta admit," he said, raising his hands, palms out as if in surrender, "before you came along, I'd never actually had the chance to talk to any of the critters. I shot a bunch of them, but never stuck around long enough for conversation to result, polite or otherwise." Val shrugged. "Brandy knows them better than I do, of course. She lived under their rule just like these people did. Brandine isn't a woman given to hate, Charlie, but she purely hates the Anguilar. She saw them destroy so many families, leave so many kids orphans…"

"I wonder where their families are," I mused quietly. Val cast me a curious stare. "The Anguilar. I haven't yet seen any of their kids. Not very many females. They must have them somewhere, right? I mean, look at this place…look at Strada. The Anguilar kept troops on both worlds for decades, but from what I've been told, they never once brought families to either place. I guess they rotated troops in and out, but…" I shaped the thought with my hands. "For instance, I was gonna be an Army officer. If you're active duty in the Army as an officer, and you get assigned some-place that you aren't allowed to bring dependents, like South Korea, it's a year assignment, maximum, because they don't want to keep families apart that long."

"I see what you're saying," Val told me, nodding. "I don't know how long Anguilar soldiers are assigned to posts like this, but it's more than a year. You thinking they don't mind leaving their wives and kids?"

"I'm thinking they're not like us. Not just us humans, but all the other races in this galaxy, the ones Lenny and his robot friends created." I took a step outward toward the edge of the dock, the water lapping on the pilings, and tried to look at the stars against the darker backdrop of the ocean. "Even the Krin and the Peboktan, who aren't based off mammals, still raise their kids, have a family, because that was the way the Creators designed them. To be like *us*. But the Anguilar aren't designed. Or at least not designed by Lenny. Maybe their kids are…like larvae or something. Maybe they're all raised together on the same world by the mothers, and they don't leave until they grow up."

"Is this really the most important thing we need to be considering right now?" Val wondered. He motioned toward the Strada guards escorting the two dozen troublemakers up to the bed of a cargo truck parked outside the entrance to the storehouse. "Ain't we got bigger concerns?"

"I'm not sure we do," I admitted. "Sun Tzu said 'know your enemy and know yourself and you need not fear the results of a thousand battles.' We're just starting to know ourselves, I think, but what the hell do we know about the Anguilar?"

"How much do we *need* to know? They're the enemy. They're exiles pushed out of their home and they came here to scavenge what they could, then realized what a damned shambles the place was in and decided to stay. Isn't that enough?"

"It might have been enough when all we were doing was

hitting and running, kicking them off worlds that they barely held anyway." I motioned around us. "Like this one. But if we're going to be taking down their empire, trying to make them give up and leave this galaxy, we need to know what it'll take to do that, right?"

Val shook his head, though whether in annoyance or admiration, I wasn't sure.

"Maybe that's why you're in command here," he said. "And maybe you just need to go back and get some sleep."

"I think you're right about that," I acknowledged, yawning in surrender. I waved at the groundcar I'd used to drive out here from the city. "Want a ride back?"

"I wish I could," Val groaned. "But I gotta get this place settled down first. I'll grab a nap in the morning after Nareena takes over. I'm surprised Laranna isn't out here with you."

"I told her to stay in bed. One of us has to get some rest."

20

I still couldn't sleep.

Two days later, the EPW situation taken care of, I still stared into the darkness, Laranna snoring gently beside me without a stain on her conscience or a care in the world. The prison riot thing had even worked out to the good, in a way. More of the ethnic Copperell among the EPWs had volunteered to work for the locals, and most just wanted to bypass that and go straight into our infantry. Laranna, Val, Nareena, and I still had to have a long talk about that. I wouldn't trust someone we'd recruited that way to go anywhere near Sanctuary, but now that we were branching out, maybe there'd be a place for them.

A base here would take time to build, just like Gib had complained about, so maybe a little reform time working on a farm would be a good thing. Gib had settled down, though I thought that was more because I'd started sending him out on training patrols instead of leaving him in charge of the ID process. Wendra had taken over that duty, for which we'd compensated her with the use of a vehicle and personal training in weapons and hand-to-hand combat by Laranna on their off-duty hours. Wendra had very little interest in ever going back to servitude to anyone. The militia was coming together as well, though they wouldn't be anything resembling real soldiers for months.

Everything was proceeding about as well as could be expected and the *Liberator* would be leading the *Flying Fortress* and the *Marauder* back from Sanctuary with the first load of defense platforms in a couple days. So why couldn't I go to sleep?

I felt like I'd forgotten something. It nagged at the back of my thoughts like a sore spot on my tongue and I debated whether I should go find something alcoholic to turn my brain off. That was a dangerous habit to get into, though, and maybe a couple nights of missed sleep were preferable. I checked the time on my comm unit and hissed in exasperation. Just past midnight. Too early to just give up, get up and go take a shower. But I just couldn't bring myself to lie here any longer.

I glanced over at Laranna, made sure she was sound asleep before I slid out of bed as smoothly and quietly as I could. She was a light sleeper, usually, prone to waking at the slightest noise or movement, but she'd also gotten used to sharing a bed with another person in the last few months, and that had inured her to the slight movements I made in my sleep. Pausing at the edge of the bed, I watched her carefully. No reaction, no sign she would wake up.

I didn't try to dress in the bedroom, just grabbed my clothes and slipped through the door to the small living room that had once belonged to the Anguilar base commander who'd died so spectacularly at Dothan's hands. His taste in art and furniture had been bizarre enough that we'd tossed it all out into the street and replaced it with simpler stuff fabricated for us by the local Copperell, based mostly on my recollections of my grandparents' house. The floor lamp in the living room was based on the one outside the hallway to their master bedroom and I made sure the bedroom door was closed before I turned it on.

A yellow glow suffused the small chamber, reflecting off the frilled white drapes in a homey feel. The couch was real leather, though not from a cow, with a slightly scaly texture to it, and the rocker in the corner was an exact replica of the one Papa Chuck had spent his final days in. I was halfway dressed before I realized I'd left my gun belt in the bedroom.

"Damn," I murmured, pulling my jacket on as I glanced at the bedroom door.

I'd managed to get it shut without waking her, but I was dead certain sure I couldn't get away with going back in. I'd gotten so used to carrying a gun the last year, the lack of the weight on my hip felt unnatural, and I very nearly risked waking her up again but shook it off. We'd had control of this place for weeks now and the only trouble we'd had with the locals was a few fights over women between the males who'd returned from the mines. There'd been no street crime because no one had anything worth stealing. There shouldn't be any danger for me walking in the streets near the headquarters unarmed.

I slipped out the door and pulled it shut as quietly as I could. The chill in the air was bracing, waking me up almost immediately, although that hadn't been the plan. At some point, we were going to hit summer…I hoped. If we were still around by then. In the meantime, I zipped my jacket up, tucked my chin down to keep my ears under the collars and walked. No voices interrupted my walk, no one crossed my path, not a civilian and not one of our people. The city was as dead as if it had been deserted.

No voices except my own. That one I couldn't shut down no matter how hard I tried.

Should we set up a guard at the gates at night?

Why bother? There are so many holes in the wall, they'd have to surround the city to do any good.

Why can't we use robots? Like with cameras on them? Like Lenny does for working on the *Liberator*?

You've already asked Lenny about that. He doesn't have enough spares or the material to make them. Not to mention that the Strada and the Copperell don't like robots all that much…including Lenny. And besides that, robots cost money and time to maintain. You wouldn't be saving any resources in the long run, and if you're gonna take the time to make the locals fabricate robots, you might as well just recruit a couple hundred of them to stand guard and save the raw materials.

I grunted, unsatisfied with my own explanation but unable to come up with anything better.

There's no real point in guarding the walls anyway. There's nothing to steal except the same food and clothes we're giving to everyone.

As if that wouldn't be enough for some people to kill for after decades with not enough. At least it would have been back on Earth, and nothing I'd seen out here said that the Strada or the Copperell were any different from the humans they were so closely related to. If two people each have two shirts and food for two days, one could kill the other and have four shirts and food for four days, and that was the mathematics of desperation.

Then we need to get them to police themselves. That's what the militia is for. It'll just take some time. We don't have enough troops to do everything.

We'd put up guards at a couple places, of course. Food storehouses, fabricators, vehicle parking lots. Plus the communications center. That had survived the battle, and so had the hyperspace transceiver in orbit, which was almost a miracle. Or, more accurately, a total screw-up. If I'd been on the *Liberator*, or Laranna, it would have been the first target taken out, even before the defense platform. We didn't want the Anguilar calling for help and bringing a bunch more cruisers here before we were ready to take them on. But Val wasn't used to the technological angle of this war and Nareena had no experience at all in space battles, and I guess the Copperell bridge crews didn't have the same tactical sense that we did. No one had thought to blow the thing up.

After the battle, after my poorly thought-out punch of Dothan and the chaos that had followed, I'd found out about the satellite from Lenny and would have been royally pissed if it hadn't been for everything else that had happened. But since the thing was still there, I figured we might as well get use out of it. We'd left a rotating guard on the ground control center for the satellite, two Strada and one Peboktan engineer to run the equipment, because I didn't want anyone getting it into their head to strip the place for valuable metals or computers.

I don't know how I wound up at the place. Maybe it was because it was the only bright light in this part of the city, the security floods left in place by the Anguilar. A beacon in the depths of the night beckoning to me, tired, poor and huddled, yearning to breathe free. Or just yearning for sleep, but settling for something new to distract me from the thoughts that wouldn't stop banging against the inside of my skull.

What about kids? Do you still want to have kids when you're looking at a war that could last ten years?

You're the one who told Laranna that you didn't want to put off having a family just because things were bad.

Yeah, but she's not going to sit back and be a stay-at-home mom while you're off fighting. Those kids could be orphans in one battle. Is that smart?

Dammit, I hated arguing with myself. I couldn't come up with any debate points I didn't already know. Lacking any better argument, I told myself to shut the hell up. Maybe a surprise inspection of the radio shack would give me something boring to not think about.

There was only one entrance to the comm shack and instructions had been to leave one guard outside at all times, having them switch off every hour. The light from the floods bathed the solid, metal door in a harsh yellow, making it obvious that it was cracked open a couple inches…and that there was no one around. No guard.

I sighed in disappointment but tried not to get mad. The Strada were excellent warriors in combat but this kind of thing, military discipline, was new to them. I couldn't let myself get pissed off every time one of them dropped the ball. Still, the lapse deserved a chewing out or at least a stern talking-to and I tried to remember what the names of the Strada on duty were. Normally, I would have had no idea but I'd written out the watch schedule myself and I've always had a pretty good memory for stuff I'd written down.

"Lancet?" I tried. No reply. "Braxon?"

I'd kept my voice low because...well, I don't know why. Because it was dark and someone, somewhere might have been sleeping, but mostly because it was nighttime and instinctive to keep my voice down.

No one answered and I considered yelling before I just went busting in through the door, but something caught my eye. The radio shack was concrete the same gray color as the pavement, reflecting back all that floodlight glare, but there was one pocket of shadow. A storm drain built into the side of the building under the covering branches of a decorative tree, just like all the others I'd passed the last few weeks, day and night, barely noticing...not consciously.

I guess I'd been seeing them subconsciously though, because I knew there was something different about this one. It was... lumpier. Probably nothing. Probably just some branches or moss that had gotten washed down with the last rain. But I was already wasting time out here so what was a couple minutes more?

The dark lump coalesced with proximity, going from possible branches and moss to...legs.

"Shit." Again, I could have yelled it, wanted to, but instead I hissed it in a tense whisper and pulled the body out of the drain.

It was limp, deadweight. I'd read about rigor mortis and from what I remembered, it set in after a couple hours. This body was fresh. I didn't have a flashlight and couldn't make out anything in the shadows, so, as disrespectful as it felt, I dragged that leg into the light. The green tint to the hands marked him as Strada, and when I saw his face, I recognized him immediately.

Lancet. His throat had been cut.

I turned halfway to the door and that was the only thing that saved my life, just a glint of light off the edge of the blade coming straight at my face. There was a drill we practiced in Taekwondo class every time at the end, when we did street self-defense moves. Some of it was, I'd found out since, utter bullshit, like the one where someone stuck a rubber gun in our face and we did this stupid slap move that never would have worked in real life.

But the one I'd always paid attention to was the one where someone came at me with a plastic knife. There were different defenses, and I couldn't remember all of them, but one thing I did remember was, grab the knife hand, pull it close to my chest, control it no matter what. One of the other black belts who used to run the drill with me was a big guy named Drake who outweighed me by at least twenty pounds, and he'd try like hell to pull his arm free, even managed it once in a while, but I had some pretty good footwork.

Whoever this guy was, he wasn't near as heavy or as strong as Drake and he wasn't getting that hand free. He must have known that because before I could make another move, he wrapped his other arm around my neck and squeezed. That was a problem. I couldn't hold his knife hand in place with one hand and I also couldn't breathe.

Time for some footwork. I danced backward and tried to catch his knee with a heel, but he was just as agile as I was and faster…and apparently, a better dancer. My throat burned, my vision swam with flickering lights and narrowed into a dark tunnel. I only had a few seconds before I blacked out.

The funny thing was, I didn't panic. A year ago, I definitely would have. Even with all the martial arts training, I'd never actually been in a real fight before then, and the thought of someone choking me out while simultaneously trying to knife me in the throat would have sent me hyperventilating. My brain didn't work the same way, I guess, because all I could think was weapons of opportunity. The knife for one. But to get it off of him, I needed to shake him up.

The wall. He was a good dancer, able to get out of the way of any of my kicks, but there was one partner he couldn't out-dance. The wall. I shuffled backward and slammed him into the side of the building. The whoosh of breath had a sickly sweet scent, something I'd smelled before. Anguilar.

The arm around my throat didn't let up, as if he knew that it was his only chance, but that cost him--the knife loosened in my grip and I pulled it out of his hand, flipped it around and stabbed backward. Now the arm around my neck went slack and the Anguilar took a breath, ready for a scream. Spinning, I pushed my arm against his throat, choking off the cry and stabbed again just under the sternum. The light went out behind those golden eyes and the Anguilar officer slumped against the wall. Pulling my arm away, I let him slide down.

Another way I'd changed. I barely looked at him. Instead, I kept my eyes on the door while I patted him down, searching for a gun. There it was, tucked into his belt, a compact pulse pistol. Not ideal, but it would have to do.

I could either go for help and chance letting them get away with whatever they were trying to do inside that building or risk handling it myself. Thinking about it wouldn't make it any easier, so I yanked the door open and threw myself inside.

I had time for a flash of data, a photograph, one frame of film projected on the screen inside my head. Two bodies on the floor, surrounded by puddles of red, one Strada, one Peboktan. The other guard and the engineer. Two Anguilar, one of them sitting at the controls of the transmitter, the other pacing, frozen in mid-step with his eyes wide when I burst through the door, a pistol in his hand.

That was all the time I had because that pistol just happened to be pointed directly at my head. Momentum was my friend, the momentum I'd gained coming through the door, and I used it to keep moving forward, ducking into a shoulder roll just inches under a burst of pulse fire that wanted very badly to take off my head. The burning sensation across my neck was all-too-familiar, the sting of static electricity and air heated to a plasma by the scalar energy pulses.

The sting was lost in the impact of the concrete floor on my shoulder, and in the second it took me to fall into a crouch and get turned around toward the shooter, I would have been dead...

but he didn't shoot me. Instead, the Anguilar twisted toward the control board and poured a stream of crimson energy into the transmission tower's instrument panel. The explosion of sparks and burning metal sent the other Anguilar tumbling backward, the chair sliding out from under him and gave me the opening I needed.

The little gun wasn't much for power, but it pointed nicely in my hand, just like shooting a squirt gun when I was a kid. A thread of energy connected us for a half a second and the Anguilar pitched forward, trailing smoke from his burning clothes.

One left. He'd had a gun—I saw it on the edge of the console, left behind when he'd fallen. Still alive, though, thrashing around on the bare floor, patting out smoking hotspots on his uniform where the sparks had landed. Where the sparks had touched, his feathery, white hair was charred, burnt down to the gray skin beneath, leaving him with a sort of plucked-chicken look. He was distracted, hurting, in no condition at all to even notice me when I came up behind him and clocked him in the side of the jaw with the butt of the pistol.

His head lolled, though he didn't go unconscious, and I rolled him into his belly while he was stunned, twisted his arms around behind his back and pinned him with a knee between the shoulder blades.

It was only then that I let everything catch up with me, gasping for breath, my heart pounding in my chest like a triphammer, hands shaking. I sucked in a couple deep breaths, held them for a second and exhaled slowly, a trick Laranna had taught me. I didn't have a comm unit, but Braxon did. My first attempt to pull it off the Strada's belt while still keeping an eye on the Anguilar prisoner ended with my hand splashing into Braxon's blood and I cursed reflexively before trying again.

Grimacing at the sticky warmth on my palm, I switched the comm frequency and keyed the mic.

"Laranna, this is Charlie."

A long second passed in silence, but I knew she'd pick up and I didn't bother repeating myself.

"Charlie, where the hell are you?" Not a trace of grogginess in her voice. Just instantly awake.

"The radio shack. I need security out here." I looked around at the bodies and the wrecked equipment, coughed at a curl of smoke from the shattered control panel. "We have a problem."

21

"WHERE THE HELL did you come from?" Nareena demanded, holding the Anguilar's narrow, long-nosed face tightly between her fingers and thumb. The prisoner tried to jerk his head away but the Strada woman was broad-shouldered and powerfully built and her grip was unyielding.

This place wasn't much of an interrogation room, nothing like the chamber of horrors the Anguilar garrison had maintained, but we were using that one to hold the remaining Anguilar and Krin prisoners. Of which, apparently, this guy and his late partner were not among.

"We know you weren't with the other prisoners," Nareena went on, her vice-like grip tightening enough to elicit a pained gasp from the Anguilar. "So, tell us…where've you been hiding out?"

The prisoner's heels kicked, but the chair we'd tied him into was bolted to the floor, the remains of what had apparently been a Copperell barber shop—or beauty salon or whatever. No one had used it for decades, but the chairs remained, high backed and far enough off the ground that the Anguilar's feet didn't touch. The lights hadn't worked, but we'd hauled in some portable lamps, aiming them directly into his eyes.

The Anguilar said nothing. Val walked around behind him, waited until Nareena let loose of his face before grabbing him around the neck and yanking him back into the chair's padding.

"What's wrong, pardner?" the old cowboy drawled. "You didn't seem to have any problem talking on that transmitter. Why don't you tell us who you were calling?"

From my experience with Anguilar, I expected the prisoner to at least cackle and gloat, maybe tell us that we'd find out soon enough or some such cartoon-villain bullshit, insanely confident and narcissistic like all the others. Instead, this one played it smart, which worried the heck out of me. Not that he looked particularly tough, with dried blood caking the side of his face and half his hair burned off from the blast that had destroyed the interstellar communications hardware.

Ragged or not, he showed no sign of being intimidated by the show Val and Nareena were putting on, said nothing even when Val tightened his arm around the Anguilar's neck for a few seconds, cutting off his air briefly before letting go. The captive wheezed, said nothing.

Nareena leered at the Anguilar as she pulled a curved knife from the sheath at the small of her back.

"I wonder if you ever heard about what your people did to

mine on Strada?" She rested the tip of the blade against the Anguilar's chin, put just enough pressure on it to draw a single drop of blood, and the captive winced but was very careful not to move his head. "If you ever heard how many Strada they executed, how many they enslaved? They killed my mate...*you* killed my mate." Her features twisted in rage and I wasn't totally sure if she was play-acting anymore. "What do you think I dream about every night, Anguilar? I dream about having one of you in just this position so I can cut you into little strips and feed them to the dogs while you're still alive to watch."

"Go ahead, savage," the Anguilar said, voice even and calm. "I've accomplished my duty. My bloodline is secure."

Nareena pulled away, shifting the knife in her grasp as if she was thinking about whether to carry through with the threat. I kept one cautious eye on her, only half-turning when the door creaked open on ancient hinges.

Laranna walked in from outside, the morning sunlight pouring in behind her before she let the door swing shut. I nodded her to the shadows in the far corner of the room and spoke in a low voice.

"He's not talking," I said.

"Have you tried smacking him around a little, getting him scared?" she suggested, eyeing the Anguilar with disdain. "They're not that tough."

"This one is." I gestured at his injuries. "He has to be in some serious pain from those burns and we haven't offered him any treatment yet, not so much as a shot of the local moonshine. He hasn't complained, hasn't moaned or asked for painkillers.

Plus…" I shrugged. "I'm not really comfortable with going any further than we have already. Did you get the guards to double-check the counts?"

"I did," she confirmed, accepting the change in subjects as my decision on the whole torture thing. "Then I checked them again myself. There are no Anguilar prisoners unaccounted for. Every single one taken alive was listed by rank, if not name, had their photo and biometrics recorded and kept on multiple data-bases. None escaped."

"That's bad," I sighed. "That means some got away during the original battle. Did we ever get our hands on their personnel records?"

"No. From what we've been able to find out talking to the ethnic Copperell who've switched sides, that data was all stored in the fortress…and it's nothing but rubble and ashes now."

"Maybe some of them were out at the farms," I speculated, only halfway paying attention to the tag-team intimidation Val and Nareena were still attempting. Val had pulled out a heavy pulse pistol and kept ejecting and reinserting the magazine dramatically. "Or the mines…or even off-duty somewhere. There's not much security at the gates. They could have snuck in and tried to call for help."

"That wouldn't be the worst-case scenario," Laranna said, stifling a yawn. Which made *me* want to yawn and I covered it with my hand. She glared at me. "You aren't sleeping. That's not healthy."

"It's my guilty conscience," I told her, half-grinning…and half-serious. "And yeah, you're right. I guess I always assumed the

Anguilar would find out about this place and try to take it back. I was just hoping we could get the defense platforms in place first."

"The Liberators should be back in a few days. They can't have any major force here before that."

The door banged open again and Nareena glowered over at us, like we were interrupting her interrogation. If she'd been accomplishing anything, I might have felt guilty. Instead, I nodded to Giblet, Dani, and Tamura, waved them over to us.

"You check out the radio shack?" I asked Gib.

"It's toast," he told me, shaking his head. "The short-term memory storage got fried in the shootout. There's nothing there but ash."

"We checked the satellite," Tamura interjected, motioning between himself and Dani, "but apparently, the Anguilar sent a command that cleared the on-board caches after transmitting their message." Dani nodded agreement.

"From the records on the databases we transferred to the Vanguards, it looks like the transmitter was aimed at an Anguilar-controlled system only a week's jump from here. No information on how many forces they keep there, though."

"We could send out a scouting mission," Tamura suggested. "Two fighters, no more. Perhaps me in one, Giblet in the other. Jump to this system where the transmission was aimed and see if there are any forces marshaling there for an attack."

"And maybe take some of them out," Dani agreed. "Delay their response until we're more ready for it."

I discovered I was scowling and forced myself to stop. I didn't like the plan. It felt wrong deep in my gut, but I had to give it a fair evaluation, which was easier said than done as tired as I was. Talking it out would help and would also let them know I was giving it a fair shake.

"Best and worst-case scenarios here," I said. "Best-case, you find a bunch of unsuspecting Anguilar cruisers sitting with their pants around their ankles and you kick them in the ass. It delays them for weeks, gives us enough time to get the first group of defense platforms set up and we take no casualties." I looked around at them. "Anyone wanna take a crack at worst-case?"

"Worst-case," Laranna chimed in, knowing what I was thinking better than anyone else could, "we lose one or both fighters for little to no return, we let them know that we have the Vanguards and give them a head start on how to combat our tactics while reducing our ability to project force or turn back an attack."

"I'm not gonna get shot down," Gib scoffed almost exactly at the same time as Tamura expressed the same sentiment. The two of them glanced at each other, the Kamerian laughing softly while Gib looked like he'd just taken a big bite out of something sour.

"Let's say you don't," I conceded. It wasn't unreasonable, given that Tamura and Gib were our best pilots. "Let's say you do some damage and get out unscathed. You're not gonna take out everything they have, not with two fighters, not even with a dozen. There'll be videos, reports, sensor readings. They'll know exactly what we have. Those Anguilar who sent that message, even if it got through and someone listens, they were here on the ground and all their sensors here would have picked up would have been a couple Liberators launching fighters. If we want this plan of Gib's to work, with the long-range strikes to keep them off-balance, we need surprise on our side, right?"

Gib harrumphed, arms crossing.

"Well, it's not *completely* my plan, but…"

"Close enough." I shrugged. "Look, I'm not a dictator here. I lead by the unanimous consent of the forces I command. Not that I plan on taking a vote before making a decision, but I can only command you guys for as long as you agree to have me give the orders. I'm willing to listen to suggestions and if everyone thinks I'm wrong, then I'll step down."

"No one wants you to step down," Giblet insisted.

"You don't think we should send the scouting mission," Tamura said, and it wasn't a question. "Not even if we don't attack their forces. Would you care to explain why?"

I would not, I thought hard back at him but couldn't say. I wasn't going to be able to get away with not telling him. The others, maybe, but not him.

"Would you accept it if I just said I was going with my gut?" I asked him. "Because I'm about to give you whatever logical reasons I can come up with, but I'll tell you straight up, the real answer is, my gut says no. And I haven't gone wrong listening to it yet."

Maybe. Depending on how things worked out with the Kamerians.

Tamura stared at me with clear, discerning eyes, and I thought for a moment he was going to tell me that no, it *wasn't* good enough and he *wouldn't* accept it, and I prepped myself mentally for a long, drawn-out argument and perhaps a compromise. But he just nodded.

"You don't know much about Kamerians, Charlie Travers. What you would call our religion, for example."

I blinked, unsure whether this mental bypass would actually deposit us back on the train of thought we'd started off on.

"I've heard you mention it," I said.

"To outsiders, it sounds primitive, atavistic," he admitted. "But the priests of the Blood God aren't simply religious figures. They're a combination of therapist, behavioral psychologist and anthropologist, the teachers for our educated classes." Tamura laughed softly. "Of course, some of them are full of it, but one who taught me in the Academy told me something that stuck with me. What people think of as their intuition, their *gut instinct*, is actually a function of their brain's subconscious thought working puzzles in the background, unseen by the conscious. Every waking hour, you're taking bits and pieces of your experiences and arranging them into a cohesive image." He shrugged. "Often, our instincts are wrong because we're working with incomplete knowledge, or because our experience is inadequate to make the necessary judgments."

I had no reply that wouldn't have sounded inane, so I decided to take Abraham Lincoln's advice just this once in my life. *Better to remain silent and be thought a fool than to speak out and remove all doubt.*

"I trust you, Charlie," Tamura said. "Until you give me a reason not to."

I guess that was going to have to be good enough.

"Nareena," I said, loud enough for the Strada woman to hear

me over the ineffectual threats she was still attempting with the prisoner. "Val." They both looked up at me and I made a dismissive gesture. "This isn't getting us anywhere. Put him in solitary confinement with a guard on him round the clock. Give him water and medical treatment but no food yet. Not unless he gets more talkative. We'll have a go at questioning him again later, after he's had some time to think about his situation."

"Charlie," Val said, alarm in his expression, "if they sent out a warning, we may not have that long…"

"We're gonna behave as if there's going to be an attack," I cut him off. "Whether he talks or not doesn't matter." Not that I believed that, but it was what I wanted the prisoner to think. This approach wasn't working, and I didn't want to discuss alternatives right in front of the Anguilar soldier. "Between the two of you," I told Val and Nareena, "I want a round-the-clock patrol schedule drawn up. We need soldiers on the streets, patrolling the perimeter every hour of every day. The only reason we caught this bastard was because my guilty conscience wouldn't let me sleep." I laughed sharply and pulled open the door. Sunlight hit my tired eyes and I squinted, unable to keep them open.

"Even *I* don't have enough shit on my conscience to keep that up."

22

"Tell me again," Dani said, "why exactly we have to do this?"

I didn't answer immediately, returning the greetings of a family of local Copperell as they passed. The city was becoming busier with each passing day, which I took as a good sign. Buildings had been repaired, some in the process of being rebuilt, and work crews labored at patching the gaps in the walls, all funded by us. Sort of. We paid them with basically IOUs and fabricator time, for the moment. Once the economy was up and running enough to make it work, we'd work with them to establish some sort of monetary system.

That'll have to wait until there's something worth buying.

I was so lost in the bustle of activity that I almost forgot her question, and only a glimpse of the dirty look she was giving me reminded me.

"Because the patrols are for everyone," I told her. "And because I want to take a turn in any duty I assign to my soldiers."

"Yeah? Is that something they taught you in the Army?"

"It was something one of my ROTC cadre told me," I said, not responding to the sarcasm in her voice. "Captain Fields served with Special Forces in Vietnam. Started out as a sergeant, E5, but got field-promoted to first lieutenant since second lieutenants couldn't be in SF. Then, once he rotated back, they made him go to college and get his degree and he went infantry before getting sent to ROTC."

The fact that Colonel Danberg disagreed with Fields about that only made me more inclined to practice it.

"Vietnam, huh?" Dani cocked an eyebrow at me. "Not quite the War I'd want to take as an example."

"Yeah, well, we're all doing it anyway. Look at the bright side, it could have been worse. You could have gotten stuck with a night patrol."

"Who's doing that one?" she asked with an amused snort.

"Val and Giblet."

This time, she laughed louder.

"Well, Gib deserves it the way he's been sulking and pouting. I'm just glad you didn't put me on patrol with him."

I tried really hard not to get pissed off at her, but she wasn't making it easy.

"You do know that he's in love with you, right?" I blurted. I hadn't meant to get in the middle of this, but neither one of them was giving me a choice.

Dani stopped in her tracks, staring at me with her brow furled in disbelief.

"You can't be serious. I mean, I knew he was hitting on me, that's the same whether it's some scumbag in a bar back in Columbus or an alien, but *love?*"

I checked around us in the street, making sure no one was listening.

"Look, you know that the Varnell, people like Gib, have an ability to persuade people—*most* people, not Kamerians for some reason—to do whatever they want. It's this harmonic thing in their voices, I think. It's why they have a reputation as con artists. Now, anyway. Before the Anguilar came, they were known for being diplomats." I shrugged. "It also means they have no trouble finding partners among other species."

Dani's look went from confusion to outrage.

"That's not right! That's like drugging people!"

"That's just the way it's always been for his people. He didn't know any better, because his people have been hunted down and killed or shunned and exiled for centuries just for who they are. He's trying to do the right thing, and it's hurting him that someone he cares about as much as he does you isn't even giving him a chance. Anyway, he doesn't do it anymore. Not since he joined up with us." I chuckled. "Not that he hasn't kept hitting on girls—hell, he tried to cozy up to Mallarna after her *planet* was destroyed. But he hasn't used his abilities on any of us, and he hasn't tried to use them on *you*. Because he knows it's not the right thing to do, because we've taught him that, and because he respects you."

"I'm glad to hear that," Dani said, "but it doesn't change the fact that he's a damned *bird*-man, with freaking *feathers*! I mean, it's hard enough to get used to Tamura having sharpened teeth, but as long as he's gentle with them…"

I raised a hand, wincing.

"Please, I *really* don't want to know. But I get it. I mean, I lucked out with Laranna, found someone really close to human, but I understand that you might be…freaked out by the idea. All I'm saying is, you really should think about having a talk with him, explain how you feel."

"He's never explained it to *me*," she protested, throwing up her hands, which looked more threatening with a rifle in them. "Why should I be the one to have to bring it up to him? That's not fair…"

Dani wasn't wrong, and I was trying to come up with a good reason why she should do it anyway, when the bomb went off.

"What the hell!" Dani exclaimed, going to one knee as the explosion shook the ground beneath us.

I knew immediately that it wasn't natural, wasn't a lightning strike. I'd heard explosions before, both in the National Guard and ROTC training and many times since I'd arrived here.

I kept my feet and kept my mouth shut, scanning the skies with my rifle at my shoulder, my first instinct that it was a fighter or an armed aircar. Nothing zipped across the blue except a small flock of birds, but a black billow of smoke rose up nearby, over the top of the buildings on the next street. I knew exactly what was over there.

"That's the trucks," I said. "The place where all those Anguilar trucks and construction vehicles are parked."

I waved for her to follow and took off running. It was more difficult operating the comm unit while sprinting than I'd imagined, and we were nearly to the end of the block before I'd managed to pick up Laranna's channel.

"Explosion at the truck park," I told her, gasping the words out. "Meet me over there with some troops as soon as you can."

"On my way," she said tersely. I noted she didn't bother telling me to be careful, probably having got to know me better than that.

Civilians were coming out of street entrances, sticking their heads out of windows, rubbernecking and gabbling in fear and curiosity.

"Get back inside!" I yelled as we ran. "Stay inside and get under cover!"

Which was good advice whether the threat was some accident like a fuel tank going up or an attack by some of the Anguilar holdouts who we hadn't forgotten might be out there, waiting for the help they'd called. Either way, we didn't want a bunch of lookie-loos out in the streets getting in the way of rescue crews or reaction teams, whichever was appropriate.

For just two blocks over, it took a lot of running to get around those buildings since there was no obvious way through them, and by the time we reached the parking lot, the smoke had spread vertically and horizontally, choking the entire lot with black clouds and flame. The fumes stung at my eyes and I coughed reflexively, holding a hand over my mouth as we approached. I couldn't do that and keep my rifle at my shoulder, so I slung it and pulled my handgun instead.

Cargo trucks—mostly flatbeds but a few with sloped buckets like dump trucks—formed line after line across the lot and the first few were intact, unbothered except for charred spots where debris had struck them, blocking the rest from view. Weaving between them, I tried to pinpoint ground zero, following the red flicker of flame. The closer we came to the source of the blast, the harder it got to make anything out through the smoke and fire, and I rubbed at my eyes, trying to clear the grit and tears.

"There!" Dani said, pointing with her rifle, then breaking into a coughing fit before she continued. "There it is!"

I followed the barrel of her rifle and saw the ignition point. I even remembered which vehicle it was because I'd remarked to Laranna that it was an internal combustion engine, fabricated locally to run on distilled alcohol because that was less expensive and less trouble than importing batteries.

Just the one vehicle. The trucks on either side poured smoke, flames licking at the canvas covers over their beds, but neither had blown up, just the one flatbed. I stopped, Dani beside me, and scanned around the vehicle, searching for movement.

Phantoms teased at the edges of my vision, wisps of smoke that my mind wanted to identify as Anguilar troopers, but nothing cohered into reality. I spun at the scrape of boots on the pavement and lowered my gun just before it came into line with the face of my wife.

"Anything?" she asked as Nareena shouted orders at a platoon of Strada, directing them around the edges of the parking lot to set up a perimeter.

I shook my head.

"Just the one truck exploded," I said, stifling another cough, then backed away a few more feet from the smoke. "You think it's an accident?"

"What does that thing run on?" Dani asked, motioning at the burning vehicle.

"Alcohol."

"Then it's no accident," she declared. "Alcohol doesn't burn that color. That's some kind of petroleum burning. It has to be a bomb."

"Are there any security cameras here?" I asked, looking at the corners of the buildings surrounding the lot. "Maybe we could check the tapes and see who…"

"No, nothing," Laranna interrupted, making a slashing gesture. "The Anguilar cameras all got torn down by the Thalassian Copperell less than a week after we freed them. I can't blame them. They were a symbol of the Anguilar occupation."

"Damn," I murmured. "But if this was deliberate, what was the point? What does blowing up a single truck halfway across town from us accomplish?"

Laranna's eyes narrowed in suspicion, and she pulled her comm off her belt.

"Val?" she called. "Do you read? Is anything happening back at headquarters?" We shared a worried look when there was no immediate answer. "Val, this is Laranna over at the truck park. Is anything happening on that side of town? Please respond."

Fear squeezed at my gut, a gone feeling like the bottom had fallen out.

"This was a distraction," I realized. "To draw our reaction force away from the headquarters buildings."

I'd just run half a mile and inhaled a bunch of smoke, and the HQ was a good two miles from here by foot. But the trucks…

Jogging away from the ones still wreathed in smoke, I jumped in the first I came to, an open-cab model that, like the rest of them, started with the push of a button, no key required. Another alcohol-fueled model, it rumbled to life, shaking like an unbalanced washing machine, but it would have to do. Dani and Laranna clambered into the cab beside me, and I thought about taking off immediately but decided it would be reckless.

"Nareena!" I yelled, leaning out of the cab. "Get as much of your platoon that'll fit on the back of this truck now!"

The Strada woman frowned at me, confusion passing across her expression.

"Why? What's going on?"

"We've lost comms with Val," I told her. "We have to get back."

And hope to hell we weren't too late.

23

VISIONS of dead bodies and smoking ruin haunted my imagination for the entire drive across town. Val was there. If I'd let myself get suckered, if I found him with his throat cut like those Strada soldiers, I'd have to be the one to go back and face his family, tell them what happened.

But there was no smoke rising up from our HQ buildings as we came within a few hundred yards of them, no sign of fighting at all. Strada and Copperell troops nodded to me as we drove by, glancing at the truck curiously since it obviously wasn't built for the narrow roads at the center of the city, not one of them showing alarm. I barely remembered where the brakes were on the vehicle, cruising halfway past the front entrance to what had been the office building before the truck squealed to a halt, jerking me forward.

Laranna and Dani clambered out the opposite door of the

cab before I even had the thing parked, and the Strada who'd hitched a ride on the flatbed were already hopping off on either side, flashing by in the mirrors. I cursed the unfamiliar controls for the parking brake, turning a dial to set it and jumping out the driver's door without attempting to use the step down the six feet to the pavement. My knees flexed to absorb the impact, but the wind still whooshed out of me when I hit, my rifle rattling across my back on its sling. I pulled it around and sprinted inside on the heels of the others.

And skidded to a halt with two dozen sets of eyes staring at me. Well, me, Dani, Laranna and most of an armed Strada platoon all standing in the center of the conference room, trying not to point our guns at the Copperell and Peboktan technicians and clerks working at their stations.

"Charlie?" I turned, saw Valentine McKee walking out of his private office, confusion writ in his expression, one hand on his holstered sidearm. "What's goin' on? Is everything all right?"

I shook my head, slung my rifle and threw my hands up.

"What the hell?"

"They could have been trying to draw our attention away from the prison," Laranna suggested. "Or the holding facility for the Copperell." She had to make a distinction since we'd separated the Krin and Anguilar, who'd likely never be rehabilitated or repatriated, from the ethnic Copperell, most of whom already wanted to switch sides now that their Anguilar overseers were gone.

"I'll check," Nareena said, keying her comm unit. "Barathan, this is Nareena. Is there any activity at the prison?"

Again, just as when we'd tried to call the headquarters here, no response. I turned back to Val.

"You didn't receive our transmission a few minutes ago?" I asked him.

"Not me." Val shook his head, then looked around the office at the workers still staring at us. "Did anyone else get a call?" Heads shaking all around. Val frowned and pulled out his comm unit, then touched the control. "General call, general call, does anyone hear me?"

No comms beeped, certainly not mine. I met Laranna's eyes and saw the same thought reflected in them.

"Listen up!" I barked. "Everyone who's armed, spread out and check every room in this place. We're searching for an Anguilar jammer."

The building had three stories up and one down and Nareena quickly sent her own people to check the upper floors. I nodded for Laranna, Dani, and Val to follow me and headed for the basement. It wasn't like a building back home, where the stairwell was a straight line up the side, from roof to basement. Whoever had built this structure had put each staircase at opposite corners, the one from the first to the second floor at the northeast, the steps from second to third southeast, and so on. It seemed like an inefficient use of space to me, but I supposed it was a cultural thing.

The three of us had to go down a side hallway to reach the basement door, and I paused beside a decorative sculpture in a corner beside it. I'd seen what the Anguilar considered art so I assumed the rampant serpent was a product of the Copperell society, but the sixteen-inch long gray cylinder stuck behind it was definitely Anguilar.

"Dammit!" Laranna snapped, reaching for it.

"Wait," I said, holding up a hand. "It's probably *not* booby-trapped, but…"

Both of them backed away as I pulled my heavy pulse pistol. A storage room off to the side provided cover and we all squeezed into it, pushing aside boxes of cleaning supplies. I aimed carefully, not wanting to put a hole in the wall needlessly, and squeezed the trigger. I'd only exposed a sliver of my face and my gun hand, but I still fought an urge to duck back, knowing the follow-through for the shot would keep me from flinching. As it turned out, I needn't have worried.

The cylinder blasted apart in a spray of spark and smoke, but there was no explosion. I waited a second just to be sure, then holstered the pistol and pulled my comm unit.

"General call, general call. This is Charlie. Does anyone copy?"

"I read you, Charlie," Nareena answered immediately. "We haven't found anything upstairs."

"Yeah," I said, scowling. "I think the action is in the basement."

I unslung my rifle, but I didn't believe I'd need it. Whatever had happened, I had the sense that it was over and had been long before we figured out it was happening. The door should have been locked, but wasn't, just squeaked open at my push. The tap of our boots against the concrete steps echoed, obscenely loud in the dead silence of the basement, the lights dimmer, no sunlight penetrating from upstairs, just the tiny overhead lamps.

The cell was in the basement. It hadn't started out life as a prison cell of course, but we'd improvised one to keep the Anguilar I'd captured in the radio shack locked up. We'd found transparent metal windows and sealed them in place to shut off a storage area in the corner, rigging a door with another clear sheet on hinges we'd scrounged from a workshop. No plumbing, but we'd left the Anguilar two buckets, one with water, one without.

He wouldn't need either of them. The Anguilar lay flat on his back, eyes staring at the ceiling, a wash of blood down his chin like he'd taken a bite out of steak tartare and let it drool out of his mouth. Anguilar already had skinny necks, but not this skinny. It had been crushed concave. I didn't bother opening the door.

"There are cameras up in the office, right?" Dani asked. Her face had gone pale and I didn't think it was from the violence or shock at the Anguilar prisoner's death. "The Copperell didn't tear those down, too, did they?"

"There are cameras," Laranna confirmed, anger sharpening the words into daggers. "But the jammer would have killed their feed."

"I didn't see nothin' upstairs," Val said, shaking his head. "If anyone up there had noticed anything suspicious, they would have mentioned it to me."

"We have more Anguilar in the city," Laranna declared. I nodded.

"We do. And we have to figure out a way to find them."

"Go!" I hissed, motioning forward.

Dani and Laranna ducked around the corner, rifles at their shoulders. I couldn't see their faces through the visors of their helmets and as little as I liked wearing one of them myself, my visor was down. We needed the night vision. There were no streetlights in this part of the city, no housing, no workshops. This had once been, decades ago, an artisan district, where individual shops had made and sold their wares on the open market, but that had all ended when the Anguilar came, and the shops had fallen into disrepair, not useful for housing or mass manu-facturing.

Even with the night vision, the shadows were so deep that they shifted and taunted, teasing me with phantoms of motion, unseen Anguilar waiting in ambush who disappeared when I tried to look at them straight on. Real motion tugged my head to the right, not Anguilar but Strada, led by Nareena. She cut an impressive figure in the armor, taller even than most of the males, broad-shouldered and statuesque. It was easy to see why Jax had married her. Being honest, his death was probably the reason she'd agreed to command the Strada volunteers who'd joined us. I understood. Staying back there, everything would have reminded her of Jax.

She distributed her troops around the wreckage of the work-shop, moving with the stealth that Strada warriors excelled at, even in the combat armor. If I hadn't known they were there, I would have thought them another product of my imagination, shadowy specters.

By all rights, I should have let them take the door. Laranna had told me more than once that I was going to get myself killed kicking in doors and they couldn't spare me, but I didn't decide to fight this war so I could order other people to go in shooting. It wasn't much of a door anyway, just a wooden plank someone had dragged across the entrance to a cellar, which was the only intact part of the building, a foundation half-buried under tons of rubble and overgrown by vegetation.

We would never have known they were there if not for the Vanguard fighter flying overhead, the roar of its engines distant but comforting. I keyed my mic and spoke quietly, despite the fact that my helmet would contain the sound anyway.

"Gib, you sure we're at the right place? This building is pretty much a wreck."

"It may be a wreck," he replied, sounding smug since this had been his idea, "but it's still got a bunch of emergency power packs burning bright like nothing else for a square mile around it…and you ground-pounders are the only biological signatures I can read, which means they have to be underground."

"Don't gloat," I told him. "It's unbecoming." I switched frequencies. "Everyone in place, Nareena?"

"Ready when you are."

At least she didn't scold me. I motioned for Laranna and Dani to grab the edges of the wooden plank while I braced my feet against the only flat surface I could find amongst the rubble and held my heavy pulse pistol at low ready. No rifle down there, not in what was likely to be an enclosed space.

"On three. One, two…three!"

The two women yanked, and the six-foot slab tumbled away from the cellar door, light streaming up from below, a lamp they hadn't bothered to turn off as they huddled together against the night. No time to look for steps—I leapt through the opening, curled into a ball to keep from catching a foot on anything and to make myself a smaller target.

Light and shadow blurred on either side, and my stomach shrunk into a hard, cold pit deep inside my gut as I hung there in the air for what felt like forever but was barely a second. Ten feet to the bottom and when I hit, it wasn't bare ground but someone's bedroll. Still enough impact to send me tumbling forward in a shoulder roll, which I swear I'd planned the whole time and wasn't because the alternative would have been landing flat on my ass.

Information swamped my thoughts with too much detail, data I wouldn't actually put together into a coherent image until afterward. Scavenged cots, bedrolls, sheets, pillows, amidst boxes of stolen food and jerry cans of water. Pulse pistols left on the ground carelessly, though now desperate hands grabbed for them. Six Anguilar, none in combat armor. Officers, and not ground troop officers either. Their uniforms were those of technicians, engineers, the officers tasked with keeping the power plants running, the fabricators in working order, making sure the trains arrived on time—maybe literally, though it had come to my mind as a metaphor.

Not hardened in combat but bonded by a collective need to call for help, to stay alive until reinforcements came. That was as far as my assessment made it, even in retrospect, before I opened fire. The one closest to getting his pistol in action was first, though at the time it felt like instinct rather than tactics. When my handgun discharged, it caught me by surprise, as if I hadn't intended to pull the trigger, but I bet it was a bigger surprise to the Anguilar.

The first of them pitched forward, his fingers brushing against the grip of a pulse pistol before he fell away, trailing smoke and short-lived flames. I wasn't sure where I'd hit him, but it was at least disabling and probably fatal, given that he didn't move after he fell. He was the last one I was going to be able to ambush and his death gave the others time to arm themselves before I fired again.

I moved. The temptation was great to just huddle there in what felt like a safe, central location and keep shooting, but if there was anything I'd learned from Laranna, it was that movement equals life. The last thing they expected me to do was to come straight at them, so I did it, diving headfirst across the cellar, scattering ration packs in every direction, sending metal water cans bonking against the cement floor. The impact felt as if it should hurt, but the armor insulated me from the collision, like I was in football pads. I'd tried out for high school football as a freshman because the coach had encouraged me—apparently, he wanted more cross-country and track runners on the team to improve their speed. I'd played one season for the JV team in front of a crowd of about a thousand people, the families and close friends of the players mostly, before I'd given up on football because it was a huge time-suck.

I remembered the surreality of slamming my shoulder pad into a defensive back who was trying to tackle me and marveling at how it didn't hurt. The combat armor was a similar insulation against reality, a false sense of invulnerability but the only kind I had. Pulse fire struck the floor inches from my head in an eruption of flaming concrete dust that would have blinded me without the visor and I ignored the flash and the patter of debris against the side of my helmet, point-shooting without trying to aim at only six feet distance.

There was no missing at this range for either of us, the flares of crimson merging into an explosion of energy and heat that I felt this time, a blistering pain in my side, and if my shot was fatal and the Anguilar's was only a painful second-degree burn, it was only because I was wearing armor, and he was protected only by a ragged field uniform. The Anguilar officer collapsed against me. I caught him with a hand to his throat and held him up as a shield.

Energy bursts ripped into him, penetrating through and through but enough of their power was spent that I barely felt the heat, and what I did feel didn't distract me from shooting back. I'd been in so many gunfights since I'd awoken from stasis that I'd lost count, but the one thing I never got used to was the way the light went out behind the eyes. I was fighting for survival, fighting —I hoped—for the right, to save innocent people, to free the oppressed. Hesitation would have meant death, and nothing I'd experienced of the Anguilar made me regret a single one of their soldiers I'd killed, but no amount of justification would ever make me forget a single one of their faces.

Lucky for me, I didn't have to remember the other three because Laranna and Dani dropped down a second behind me and cut the rest of the enemy troops down before they had a chance to take a shot at me. I let the burned and blasted corpse fall free of my grasp to join the others. None of them were breathing and there was no other place down here for any others to hide.

I blew out a breath, staggering a step as adrenaline abandoned me and I let the pulse pistol fall to my side. An afterthought made me drop the partial mag and replace it with a fresh one, the sound of the metal clattering on the floor obscenely loud in the silence following the shootout.

"We're clear," I called up to Nareena. "Have your people check the other buildings in the area, make sure we didn't miss anyone."

"Do you think this'll solve our problems?" Dani asked, nodding at the dead. "Or are there more of them?"

"We scanned the entire city," I said, shrugging. Tired of breathing filtered, canned air, I popped open my visor and instantly regretted it. Nothing smells quite as distinctively nauseating as charred flesh and burnt blood. "If there were more of them holding out, they'd have to be right under the feet of the Copperell. I don't think we'd have missed that after all these weeks." I pulled Gib into the conversation over the comm. "Congratulations, Gib, looks like we've cleaned them out."

"I gotta admit something, Charlie," he said, quiet and hesitant, which was unlike him. "It wasn't actually my idea. Dothan suggested it to me."

I raised an eyebrow and Laranna matched the expression, her faceplate pushed up.

"I don't know what's more shocking," she said. "Dothan coming up with that notion on his own, him suggesting it to you or you admitting any of that."

"Yeah, well, I'm a big enough man to admit when I was wrong," Giblet said, somehow managing to make it sound like a boast. "He had another notion you might want to consider. We've been running orbital patrols but with the Vanguards, we could jump to the outer system and have a better view if anyone is spying on us or if…and when…the Anguilar send their force to recon this place and try to retake it."

"Not a bad plan," Laranna judged, then looked to me. "What do you think?"

"You want to run the first patrol, Gib?" I asked him.

"Naw. It was Dothan's idea…let the Kamerians have it."

Dani glanced up in surprise, as if she could see Giblet's fighter through the rafters that held up the cellar roof.

"Damn," I said, cutting off the helmet mic to keep the words between us there in the cellar. "If Gib and the Kamerians can get along, maybe there's hope for all of us."

The Anguilar corpses stared up at me with unseeing eyes, contradicting the wishful statement. Not all of us.

24

Troop ships streamed off the landing field in an unceasing train, glinting silver in the mid-morning sun. I shaped a silent whistle, watching them from the top of the wall. It was decidedly less dangerous now than it had been when I'd first climbed it. It had been repaired in the intervening weeks by the Thalassian Copperell, and Laranna had stopped trying to convince me to stay on the ground.

We'd be leaving soon enough, anyway. Strada and Copperell troops still poured out of the city, marching in formation or riding in tanks and APCs, leaving the Thalassians to see to their own defenses...mostly. The unseen parts of that defense, the most important ones, were above the clouds, being pieced together by Peboktan engineers. I'd seen video of the orbital defense platforms, even if I'd never been aboard one myself. The things looked for all the world like an oil drilling platform in space, the flat surface a launch bay for Starblade fighters, the rest of the station support for a particle cannon.

The things weren't cheap, particularly since every one of them took two power cells, each of which had to be stolen from the Anguilar, but they were a hell of a lot cheaper than starships and easier to crew. Thalassia warranted two of the deadly, if stationary weapons, and we'd just have to hope we captured more particle cannons and power cells by the time we had to provide them for the next island in the chain.

"You remind me of a Strada legend," Laranna said, climbing up behind me on the sketchy staircase, one hand resting on my shoulder as if she was still afraid of falling off. Or still worried I might.

"Is that the legend about an Earthman who broke his ribs saving the planet?" I teased, slipping an arm around her. "And as a reward, got to marry the deadliest, most beautiful woman on all of Strada?"

She laughed, though whether at the flattery or the idea I'd single-handedly saved Strada, I wasn't sure.

"Maybe, but the one I was thinking of was about the great chieftain Eristabulus. He'd managed to unite the tribes of our continent, something no other leader in our history had accomplished, and brought peace to the entire planet by negotiating treaties with the rulers of other lands. Rather than sitting back and appreciating the blessings of his achievements, though, he wandered into the hills above his fortress every evening and stared out at the stars, worrying about threats he could neither see nor control."

"As it turned out," I told her, "he was right. First you had the Kamerians to deal with and then the Anguilar."

"Not for hundreds of years after his reign," she pointed out.

"Yeah, well, my problems are a little more immediate." A nod toward the heavens and the landers climbing through the clouds to the waiting Liberator ships illustrated my meaning. "I know this was my idea, but good God, it's a huge risk. Leaving the Thalassians here to fend for themselves while we head off to Turkmenistan or whatever the hell the name of that planet is."

"Themosticlan," she reminded me, though the gentle nudge at my ribs told me she knew I was getting it wrong on purpose by now. "It's a key transport hub for food and minerals from the outer Empire to Copperell. Freeing Themosticlan from the Anguilar will strike a blow too large to ignore, one that will be recognized across the galaxy." I grunted noncommittally, which drew a glare. "Besides, we're not leaving them defenseless. The orbital platforms can hold off any enemy probing missions until we can send one or two Liberators back to support them."

"That's assuming the Anguilar don't attack in force the second we leave. They could just be lying in wait out there, ready to swoop in when the coast is clear." I was whining now and I knew it, but so did Laranna. And she knew she was the only person I could whine to when I needed reassurance, so she didn't chew me out.

"We've been running the deep patrols for weeks now," she said instead, squeezing my shoulder. "If the Anguilar were watching, we'd have caught their scouts. They've probably decided Thalassia isn't important enough to risk another defeat. After all, from what we've learned, their emperor rules via a system of honor and face, both his own and those of his bloodline, his extended family and ancestors. Even an absolute ruler can only take so many setbacks before it becomes too hard to blame it on generals and underlings. It might be easier for him to ignore the loss of one, small colony than to send a punitive expedition and have it decimated."

"That makes sense," I admitted. "It might be the first thing the Anguilar ever did that made sense, though."

I didn't want to hash it out again because we'd wind up going in circles, but now that I'd had time to think about it, there was so much the Anguilar did that didn't seem rational to me. The biggest was the *Nova Eclipse*, of course. Spending multiple planets' worth of resources on a weapon that would only rob them of *other* multiple planets' worth of resources. It was easy for most of us to just dismiss it as a symptom of the Anguilar origin as an exile race unused to ruling others, but I couldn't shake the thought that there was some deeper cause behind all this, some mystery at the root of it.

Sighing, I decided that I wasn't going to figure it out today.

"The ground troops should be on board the Liberators in an hour or two," she told me, urging me back toward the stairs. "We have to meet with Harger before Val and Nareena load up the last of the trainers."

Sighing, I followed her down the steps, hardly noticing the slick moss after weeks of traversing them daily.

"I don't like Val staying here while we attack Thermopylae," I insisted.

"Themosticlan. And you'd like it less if the militia wasn't adequately trained and the Anguilar *did* attack while we were gone. Val says he needs another month before he's comfortable with their preparedness."

"Then why don't we wait another month?" I threw up my hands in consternation. "What's the damn hurry?"

"We hashed this out already," Laranna reminded. "Over and over. You agreed with the others that the longer we wait to hit another target, the more time the Anguilar will have to be ready for us."

"Did I agree," I wondered, "or did I just let them argue me into it? Because I kind of remember being argued into it."

"You're the commander. If you want to wait another month, give the order and we'll wait another month." She shrugged, a sinuous motion that nearly derailed my entire train of thought. "Of course, that's going to create some hard feelings with the locals, since we promised we'd get our people out now that we've got everything set up for them. They'd probably think you don't trust them. Not to mention the Kamerians are going to be pissed that you agreed with them and then went back on it."

"I know, I know."

I'd thought the thing I hated the most about being in charge was that people followed my orders, however stupid they might be, and I was responsible for any death or carnage that caused. But I was finding that the hardest part about being the commander was the compromise. Not the normal compromise when there was no right answer but having to back off of positions I was one hundred percent sure were right because it was the necessary thing to do in order to keep from pissing everyone off.

"If we're going to leave," I said perversely, "I just want to get out of here. If I have to listen to Harger whine again about how we aren't leaving them enough heavy weapons, I'm going to rip my hair out."

"We have to fly the fighters up and we can't do that until the landers are stowed aboard and out of the way. And since we're here, we have to deal with Harger and his company commanders."

I turned, regarded her patient expression, and laughed softly.

"How the hell do you put up with me?" I asked her. "Hell, just listening to myself right now, I want to kick my own ass."

"Oh, trust me, I do, too," Laranna said, cocking an eyebrow. "But every leader needs someone they can trust with their doubts. That's why I'm here."

"I thought you were here to keep me from getting myself killed."

"That, too," she agreed.

Nods and waves greeted us but without the awe and effusive gratitude we'd encountered just after the defeat of the Anguilar. Still friendly and respectful, but they were used to us now. Not resentful, either, but Laranna was right, that could easily change if I went back on my word that we'd be leaving. One big difference was the lack of fear. Even weeks after the battle that had freed them, many of the civilians had still worn the expression of a dog kicked one time too many, always waiting for the other shoe to drop. Now, there was a looseness to them, a normalness, like they were beginning to accept that they were free again.

It made this whole thing worthwhile.

The gates had been reconstructed, and we went out the west entrance past a standing guard of two armed Thalassians. They saluted us as we passed by, just as Val had trained them, and I returned it gravely, fighting a silent conviction that it was playacting. They weren't soldiers, and I doubted they ever would be. At least they could handle a pulse rifle without accidentally shooting each other or themselves, though that had taken months to accomplish.

It was an ongoing process, as the recruits drilling in the fields on the west side of the city showed. Platoons marched in time, singing cadences that wouldn't have sounded out of place in an American Army basic training class anytime in the last hundred years, carrying unloaded rifles at their shoulders. Others used dummy weapons to run through tactical drills—fire and maneuver, break contact, react to ambush and anything else Val, Nareena, and I had been able to come up with. They even looked like they were becoming proficient at it.

Farther out, I knew, though I couldn't see them from here, were the live fire ranges where the Thalassians were taught marksmanship and went through those same tactical drills but with real guns. That was the riskiest part, but it was necessary, worth any possible injuries. None of the combat vets in my ROTC cadre had been fans of the current Army thinking that safety was paramount over preparedness and troops shouldn't be trusted with real weapons and live ammo except under carefully controlled situations.

Train the way you fight, that's what Sgt. Redd had told us, and even though he was probably gone now, thirty-six years later, I'd be damned if I wouldn't follow his advice now that it counted.

None of the troops broke their attention away from their assigned training to gawk at Laranna and me, though I couldn't say for sure if that was because of the discipline they'd learned or simply because they'd grown used to our presence just like the civilians in town. One or two of the trainers did nod to us, though they didn't salute. That had been my idea as well. No saluting in the field. You didn't want to give away to any enemy who might be spying on you who your officers were.

Through the thousands of trainees we walked, and I fell into the sort of purposeful stride that officers and senior NCOs always affected around their juniors, not because it was necessary but because it was important for the soldiers to believe that their leaders always knew what they were doing and weren't simply lollygagging around. It had seemed silly to me once upon a time, until I'd actually had to lead troops into battle. Belief was as potent a weapon as any hyperdrive starfighter.

The center of that belief, the wellspring that had created it, was under the canvas tent at the center of the training area where a dozen people were gathered, waiting for us. Waiting for *me*.

"Attention!" a Strada NCO called as I entered the shade of the crude structure, duplicated from my memory on an Anguilar fabricator using local raw materials.

The Thalassians inside didn't quite manage the textbook position of attention, but they did stop arguing and turn toward us, which was just as good as far as I was concerned. Val was there along with Nareena and Dani. I hadn't thought she'd want to be part of the militia training since she had no military background, but she did have some experience at teaching new sheriff's deputies how to handle a firearm without shooting themselves and had a grasp of combat tactics after the lessons Laranna and I had given her. Anyway, I wasn't about to turn down any help cheerfully offered since Val and Nareena couldn't do it all by themselves and I didn't have the time to do more than supervise now and then.

I *had* noticed that Tamura hadn't volunteered his people for nearly as many deep-space patrols since Dani had committed to staying on the ground. Not that we had any of them out at the moment. All the Vanguards were sitting outside the spaceport gate, waiting for our pilots—including Laranna, Giblet and myself—to take them up to the *Liberator*.

Two Strada NCOs were there as well, Perna and Lupo, who I barely knew other than their faces and names, but the ones I'd been dreading were the Thalassians. Specifically, Harger. Beggars, as Val had reminded me frequently in the last few weeks, could not be choosers, and none of the other Thalassians had jumped up to be the leader of the militia. Not that they were cowardly, but they had no history or tradition of military service as a culture, and they weren't all raising their hand in eagerness to be the one to start it.

It was just my luck that the volunteer was Harger. Tall and slender, the Thalassian had a long braid of shock-white hair running down his back and had rejected any suggestion that he might want to cut it to look more martial. He had, at least, shaved his goatee, thank God, because it made him look way too much like the mirror universe Spock. The main problem I had with Harger was that he was a younger, more decisive version of Novo—a nervous mother of a leader with a new complaint for every single day of the month. Even waiting respectfully for me to release them from attention, his hands were nearly wringing in worry.

"At ease," I told everyone. "Colonel Harger, I understand you wanted to see me before I headed up to the *Liberator*. What can I do for you?"

I tried very hard not to let my shoulders visibly sag with ennui at the question.

"Commander," Harger said, his tone plaintive as always, "I'm sorry to bother you…I know you have other duties and that our people are just one small detail among them." A not-so-subtle dig at our motives for being here, and one I was used to by now, easy to ignore.

"Nonsense," I responded with the same sort of dual meaning. "I'm here to help. What is it?" *Stop wasting my time*, in other words.

"Well, sir," Harger went on as if I'd opened the faucet, the words spilling out in a stream, "as I've told General McKee and Colonel Nareena…"

Val rolled his eyes at the use of the rank, and if Nareena didn't, it was only because the translation she'd been given didn't contain the cultural impact of the word. Neither of them had used any rank before, nor had any been necessary, but if we were going to be setting up a military here with ranks I'd imported from Earth, then Val and Nareena would have to be superior to the highest-ranking of the local Thalassians.

"...I don't believe," Harger went on, "that we have the proper equipment to defend this planet in case of attack. While I appreciate the weapons and training you've provided for us, I also know that the Anguilar have far superior numbers and could wash over this entire planet like a wave once you're gone."

It wasn't an unreasonable assumption, though one I was hoping the Thalassians wouldn't realize until after we left.

"We're leaving two orbital defense platforms and two squadrons of Starblade fighters," I reminded him. "Not to mention that General McKee is planning on staying with you. Would I allow my top-ranking infantry commander to remain here if I thought there was a possibility I'd be sacrificing him?"

Another good question because I couldn't shake the feeling that was exactly what I was doing.

"I've been trying to tell you, Harger," Val interjected, "that once we get a regular run going here from...our other bases"— he nearly stumbled into naming Sanctuary "that we'll be able to provide not just the heavy weapons you want but more troops to add to your defenses. We're not abandoning you here. It wouldn't make any sense for us to put all this time and effort into freeing your planet just to take off and let the Anguilar have it back."

"That's what you say," Harger allowed, "but how can we know that your priorities won't change? That you won't lose a battle and retreat back to this mysterious home base you refuse to talk about?" I winced at that, painfully aware how obvious our attempts to keep the existence of Sanctuary concealed were. "Then what would we do?"

"You have my word," I assured him. "Have I given you any reason to doubt it?"

Harger's insistent skepticism warred with respect on his face, and probably a residual wariness of insulting us even though we'd given no indication we'd retaliate for an insult. Into that hesitation, a distant, tinny voice interjected itself from the comm unit on my hip.

"Charlie, this is Lenny. Are you receiving?"

I shared a worried look with Laranna. There was no good reason for Lenny to be calling us during the loading process, but so many bad ones…

"You got me, Lenny," I replied, speaking directly into the radio instead of using the earpiece. "What's up?"

"We have a problem," he said, just as casual as if he'd called about some mechanical breakdown. "I know we've been working on the assumption that the enemy wouldn't bother attempting to retake this planet, but I'm afraid we may have made an error."

My gut clenched at the words, and my reply was hoarse.

"Tell me."

"A dozen Anguilar cruisers just entered the system at minimum safe jump distance."

25

THE ENTIRE TENT WENT SILENT, every eye turned toward me, even Laranna's, though her look contained more empathy than the others. A dozen cruisers wasn't more than we could handle, not even more than just the Liberators could handle, but I didn't want them to. Losing a Liberator was disastrous since we only had five of the ships left, but losing one packed with a couple thousand troops would be the end of us.

"How long before the last of the Strada and Copperell are aboard?" I asked, amazed at how calm the question sounded, in stark contrast with the churning in my stomach.

"The last of the landers will be docked and secure in thirty-five minutes. The cruisers will be in firing range in just under forty minutes. We will be able to engage safely by then."

"No," I said immediately. "Get the hell out. Just as soon as the last lander is aboard, I want all the Liberators to make top speed for minimum jump distance and get to the outer system. If I need you to come back in, I'll send a signal, but don't engage the Anguilar unless you hear from us, you understand?"

Lenny hesitated, which didn't happen often. He was a computer, after all, thinking thousands of times faster than a human, running all possibilities through his massive mind so he wouldn't be at a loss for an answer. But as I'd come to discover, the one thing that he couldn't process any quicker than a human was emotion. He had them. Once upon a time, I'd called Lenny "it," because I couldn't imagine a robot having feelings, but I'd learned better.

"Charlie, are you certain? The Liberators could take these ships."

He didn't say *he* could take the ships because his programming wouldn't allow him to cause direct harm to other sentient beings, but I knew where his heart was…and knew that he *had* one.

"No, I want you gone," I insisted. "We'll handle things down here. You take care of my people."

"I will. Be careful."

"What…" Harger gulped, tried again. "What are *we* to do?" He glanced out of the tent flap at the thousands of recruits still training as if everything was still normal, as if an invasion by the enemy wasn't imminent and we all might not be dead in a couple hours.

"Val, Nareena," I snapped, pointing at them, my voice harsh and demanding in a way that I never talked to anyone, because I knew no one was going to like what I had to say, "form up the militia, issue weapons and ammo and get them away from the city. As far into the wilderness as you can manage, vehicles and dismounts, everyone. I want them away from here and I want it done *now*."

"But, the civilians…," Val protested before Harger broke in, a vein about to pop in his forehead.

"You're asking us to abandon our families!" he screeched, waving his hands like a great blue heron trying to take off.

"I'm going to explain this once," I said, staring the man down, "because we don't have time for anything more. What I *hope* is going to happen is that we're going to blow those bastards out of the air before they even get here. If we don't, if any of them get through, I want the Anguilar going after you, not the civilians. If you're in the city, they'll bombard it from the air, trying to root your militia out, and they won't give a damn whether your families get hurt. But if you and your troops are away from the walls, they'll still pick up your thermal signature and send their troops after you instead of into the city. Do you understand what I'm saying? I'm willing to sacrifice you and your troops to save your families, your children. Are you?"

Harger's features firmed up, the plaintive nervous Nelly transforming into something nobler, someone who knew what he was fighting for.

"I am. I'll get it done."

"We'll make sure of it," Val told me, then offered a hand. "Good luck in the air."

Orders were yelled as Val, Nareena and Harger began chivvying their people into action, the trainers first and then the militia officers. I shut the noises out and motioned to Laranna and Dani.

"We have to get to the fighters." I eyed Dani. "Unless you'd rather stay with the ground forces. I know you don't like being my gunner that much."

"Get your ass moving, Unfrozen Caveman Soldier," she said, sighing in exasperation. "I said that *one* damn time and you've never let me forget it..."

I still had my comm out and I keyed the mic as we jogged back toward the walls, half my attention looking around for a car we could commandeer to get back to the landing field faster. The blue skies that had seemed so pleasant and inviting just a few minutes ago were now threatening, filled with the promise of terror and death.

"Gib," I called, "we have incoming Anguilar cruisers. Get all flight crews to the fighters and get them in the air now. Laranna and I will be along in a few minutes, but don't wait for us. Just get up there and intercept those a-holes before they reach orbit."

My voice broke with the effort of my jogging pace, and I stopped to catch my breath and give Giblet time to respond. Nothing. Just the puff of my breath and that of the two women running beside me.

"They could be jamming," Laranna reasoned. I didn't think they were close enough for that, but it was better than any alternative I could come up with.

"Lenny," I tried, "do you read me?"

"I'm here, Charlie," he replied immediately. "There's been no change yet…we're still waiting for the last of the troop transports to make orbit."

"Are you picking up any local signal jamming?" I asked, picking up the jog to a run, staring at the distant city walls as if the truth were hidden behind them.

"Nothing as of yet," he gave me the answer I expected but didn't want. "I believe they're out of range for anything that could affect the planet."

"Copy. Keep me up to date on the shuttles."

"Tamura, are you there?" Dani called, her own comm held to her ear like it was one of the cell phones her generation were so dependent on. "Tam, it's Dani. Can you hear me?"

I strained to overhear any answer from her comm speaker and was again disappointed. The agitated expression on Dani's face probably mirrored my own, though for more personal reasons.

"There's something wrong," Laranna said, stating the obvious but I didn't hold it against her. She keyed her own comm. "Novo, this is Laranna."

I hadn't thought about calling the Copperell elder, had forgotten we'd even given him a comm. Unlike our pilots, he replied immediately.

"Yes, Laranna, I'm here. How may I help you?" The old Thalassian sounded like he was answering the phone at an insurance agency, which told me that whatever was happening, he had no clue what it was.

"The Anguilar are here." She wasn't even out of breath and I wanted to know why, given that we did every workout together and should, theoretically, have had exactly the same level of endurance. "There's going to be a fight, and I need you to send all the civilians to the shelters as fast and as orderly as possible."

"The Anguilar!" Novo choked out and if Harger had been close to apoplexy at the news, I thought the older Copperell was going to have a stroke. "What are we going to do?"

It was, I thought, a popular question.

"Focus, Novo!" Laranna insisted. "Get the people to the shelters! Unless they're trained and armed, I don't want them to try to resist…we're doing our best to distract them away from the city so don't screw it up for us. Get off the comm and get to work!"

Then there was no more time nor breath for comms and none of us tried again, as if we'd come to a simultaneous, unspoken realization that we'd done our best to reach the others and our best hope was to save our energy for running. I'd done a lot of running in ROTC. It was sort of our favorite pastime and Colonel Danberg had seemed to think that long-distance running was a requirement to be an officer, though I hadn't noted very many instances throughout history where it had come in that handy, not counting the Battle of Marathon.

Maybe the colonel had been prescient, though, because I'd done so much damned running since I went into space, as ironic as that sounds. It was a good thing I'd been wearing running shoes when I was abducted because Lenny must have duplicated that pair of Nikes about seven times in the last year after I'd got them buried in mud, stained with blood and ripped up by rocks. I wore them now, along with blue jeans and a Chicago concert T-shirt because we hadn't been planning on a battle and I'd thought I'd have loads of time to change into my flight suit once we got back to the city.

What was it my grandfather had said?

If you want to hear God laugh, tell him your plans.

Poppa Chuck had also insisted everything worked out for the best in the end, which was a hell of a thing to say for a man who'd seen what he had in World War Two. I wanted to believe it, but racing for the city gates at a dead sprint, I was beginning to have my doubts. No smoke rose above the walls, no echo of gunfire rolled across the plain, yet still I sensed something had gone horribly wrong.

The scene inside the walls did nothing to dispel that notion. As much as we'd hoped Novo could keep the populace orderly and controlled, that had proven too much for the old man. People ran through the streets in a near panic, most of them older men and women and mothers with young children, since everyone else was in the militia and out there drilling…or they had been until twenty minutes ago.

Desperate, terrified faces rushed by us in every direction, probably not even heading to the closest shelter to their home, simply searching for the one they knew the best or passed by on their way to work, working on panic without any rational thought. I wanted to stop, wanted to help chivvy them the right direction, but a panic of my own spurred me into running faster, heedless of Dani's labored panting as she lagged a few steps behind.

She probably needed a break but we didn't have the luxury of giving her one. Every second that went by, the Anguilar cruisers were closer to orbit, closer to disgorging shiploads full of troops. If we could get our fighters into the air, those troop transports would never touch the ground.

We were close. When I'd first arrived on Thalassia, I got lost on the streets of Philos at least once a day, but by now, I knew the place better than I did the University of South Florida campus. A right turn at the next cross-street and we'd be at the gate, the Vanguard fighters all parked in the open courtyard just outside the walls. They'd be there. I kept telling myself that. They *had* to be.

That was the best-case scenario, that someone, either Gib or Tamura, had been warned about the cruisers and took off on the attack without us, that the reason they hadn't answered was that they were already in orbit, taking on the enemy. We'd get there and our two fighters would be there, mocking us for being caught with our pants down, a couple miles away from our rides when the battle came. The worst-case scenario I wouldn't even give voice to, since every other possibility was so much worse.

The civilians had thinned out as we left the main street, the shelters all located near the interior of the city, so there was nothing in our way when we reached the gate. It was open, of course, since the gates were always left open during the day, and through it, the powerful, broad-shouldered lines of the starfighters squatted impatiently, the most welcome sight I could think of.

A second wind washed away the weariness dragging at me, gave me a last burst of energy to make it through the gate, ignoring the sweat soaking through my shirt, the chafing from running in jeans definitely not built for it except to make a mental note to retire the jeans and wear fatigue bottoms from now on.

Out of the shade of the city walls and into the sun again, I was blinded by the glare for a second as we emerged through the thick, worn blocks of the gateway.

"Giblet!" I yelled, scanning the fighters, catching a hint of movement beneath them, legs going back and forth past the landing gear. "Gib, Tamura, where the hell are you?"

Laranna and Dani rushed up just behind me, and maybe there was something slightly different about Strada eyes, something that allowed Laranna to adjust to the glare a half-second before I did. She stiffened, her hand going to her sidearm.

"Oh, I wouldn't do that if I were you, little green girl. No use dying so soon before we get the chance to have some fun."

I knew the voice. I'd never forget it. Just the deep, threatening timbre of it sent shudders up my spine. I turned toward it, to my right, just out of sight to the side of the city gate. Anguilar troops swarmed out from their hiding places, pulse rifles leveled at us, and I froze, knowing intellectually that it might have been better to sell my life dearly in the here and now, while I had the chance, rather than giving myself and Laranna over to probable interrogation and execution. But I kept my hands up because while there's life, there's hope might have been a stupid cliché, it was the only thing I had to hold onto.

I winced, thinking Laranna and Dani might be willing to go out in a blaze of glory and then I'd have to join them because I wasn't going to keep going without Laranna, but she glanced sidelong at me with a look that said "I hope you know what you're doing" and surrendered. Rough hands stripped away our weapons and pulled our hands behind us, the hard metal edge of restraints biting into my wrists.

She stepped forward through the ranks of Anguilar soldiers swarming around us, dwarfing them both with her height and the broad-shouldered girth of her Kamerian armor, even the muzzle of her carbine larger than anyone else's. Her helmet was off, though, maybe because she wanted us to know who she was.

I don't know how it was possible to *saunter* in the heavy armor, but Seraph Nix, the deadliest bounty hunter in the galaxy, sauntered up to me, smiling cruelly.

"You, Charlie Travers," she said, "are a worthy adversary, and it's been a long, damned time since I've been able to say that about any of the targets I've been sent to bring in." She shrugged. "You killed my people, and for that, you'll die painfully. But I wish things could be otherwise. In another life, we might have been comrades."

"In another life," I told her, having to look up to do it since she towered over me by a good six inches, "we'd never have met, and I'd still be stuck on my planet with no idea any of this ever existed." I wanted to say something snarky, something nasty, but I had a question I wanted her to answer, and I didn't think she'd do it if I alienated her this quick. "Where are my pilots? Did you kill them?"

"There was no need," she assured me. "They're resting comfortably in the cells where you once held the Anguilar and Krinn soldiers who are *so* happy to be your hosts. Once the fleet arrives, of course, they'll reward me for each of you I turn in alive and I'm afraid they'll wish I'd put them out of their misery. Just as you will."

"How?" Laranna asked her, bitterness in her words and in her eyes. "How did you do this?"

Seraph laughed, full-throated and genuinely amused.

"I had help, of course." She nodded behind us, to the other side of the gate and the Anguilar allowed me to turn and look.

Taller and broader even than Seraph, Dothan Abur shared her amused grin. Behind him, Sainrastil Gant and Fenris Osa emerged from the shadow of the wall, sidearms in their hands.

"Blood," the big Kamerian told me, "is thicker than water. And surely thicker than promises, you hairless ape."

"Oh, shit," I murmured.

In hindsight, that whole blaze of glory thing was looking better all the time.

26

A SLEDGEHAMMER SHAPED like a fist slammed across the side of my head.

Stars erupted in my vision, blocking out the dim lighting of the cell block, spinning my world around in a kaleidoscope whirl, the dizziness and the roaring in my ears disguising the fact I was falling to the floor until my shoulder took the brunt of the fall. The brick was chill beneath me, a welcome respite from the heat, and since getting up would have been a real effort with my hands cuffed behind my back, I thought I'd just stay down there and enjoy the cool.

Dothan rubbed at his knuckles and grinned down at me.

"I was right," he rumbled. "You *can't* take a punch."

Laranna swore and lunged across the cell at Dothan, despite her restraints, but Seraph Nix swung a casual backhand that caught Laranna across the face and sent her sprawling beside me, blood trickling from the corner of her mouth.

Outrage boiled somewhere deep inside me but the buzzing in my head and the roaring in my ears combined with the pain in my jaw to keep it from bubbling to the surface. They'd taken us to the cells where we'd confined the Anguilar and Krinn officers, just as they promised, though they were much roomier now that it was just us and the Vanguard flight crews occupying them. I'd seen them on the way in, sullen fear and hopelessness in their faces. Except for Giblet.

He'd watched not us but Dothan with hatred burning behind his eyes, though he hadn't been able to offer any sardonic barbs to go with the laser-hot glare. Not with a gag stuffed in his mouth and restraints on his wrists and ankles. Red matted his feathery hair to the side of his head, showing that he hadn't gone down easy. None of the others seemed to be injured, but whatever restraint Dothan and the others had shown with them didn't apply to us, apparently.

Someone was missing, though. I still couldn't think straight, couldn't put the pieces together, but I remembered wondering why someone hadn't shown up yet. The tall, wolfish Kamerian who strode into the cell through the open door behind me answered that question, though he raised many more. Tamura Tel's visage didn't share Dothan's malevolent glee or even Seraph's smug satisfaction. Instead, I could have sworn I detected regret in his expression. But not enough regret for Seraph to have taken away his sidearm and slapped him in cuffs like the rest of us.

Dani spat at his feet, cursing to put a sailor to shame.

"You're a traitorous piece of shit," she growled at the pilot, though she didn't bother trying to make a run at him, which was probably wise given that Laranna and I were both laid out with one Kamerian punch apiece. "How could you do this to me after…"

"I had no choice," Tamura said evenly, arms crossed over his chest. "This was going to happen with or without me. And one fighter pilot wasn't going to make a difference unless they could get in the air." He shrugged. "Seraph Nix offered me the options of life or death." His mouth thinned out into a humorless smile. "I'm smart enough to know how to answer that question."

There was something odd about the way he said that, though again, I wasn't firing on all cylinders so perhaps the nuance was escaping me. A few things weren't, however. I shook my head to try to clear it, grimacing at the pain that caused.

"Seraph got here," I said slowly, favoring my sore jaw, "because Dothan and his patrol *let* her. He let the *Revenant* land somewhere outside the city and then helped her sneak in and free the Anguilar."

Dothan laughed harshly, an unpleasant sound that promised pain.

"If you can think that clearly," he said, "then perhaps I should hit you again."

"That message that got sent out," I went on, ignoring his threat. "That was you, too? And you who killed the Anguilar prisoner?"

"He was a risk." The big Kamerian shrugged. "If he'd talked, he might have blown the whole thing before Seraph Nix arrived. It was your people who gave me the idea, though. Telling stories about how you'd faced down the deadly bounty hunter Seraph Nix twice and lived to talk about it. Once they let slip she was a Kamerian, the solution to our problem seemed simple."

"Sainrastil and Fenris were in on it, too," I surmised. Then I rolled to one knee, carefully because my balance wasn't yet operating at full capacity yet, and regarded Tamura. "But not you."

"The captain," Dothan answered for him, scoffing, "is a romantic. He had visions of taking leadership positions in your resistance and molding whatever government came of it in our image. He ignored the obvious because he had the hots for this skinny rail of a girl." He jerked his head toward Dani. "But the problem was very simple to me. Why settle for being in charge of a ruined cinder that used to be Kameria when we could all be lords, ruling over our own fiefdoms in the Anguilar Empire?"

I nodded. It was about what I figured. There was only one question left to ask, and it wasn't of him.

"And what about us?" I asked Seraph Nix. "What happens to us now?"

"I should think that's obvious," she replied, taking a knee so she could look me in the eye. "Your friends are going to be taken back to Copperell, to the Anguilar HQ to be questioned very... thoroughly." Seraph shrugged. "They know you have a bolt hole somewhere, some nameless, uncharted system. Once they find it, well, your friends will be executed and wherever your sanctuary is, it'll be laid waste. And then the Anguilar can get back to the business of governance that you and your little resistance have so rudely interrupted."

"Not me, though." Her eyebrow tilted in confusion, and I expounded, my brain finally starting to work again. "You said my friends would be turned over. But not me."

"You noticed that. Yes, I've received a special dispensation from the Anguilar to take care of you myself." Seraph shrugged. "It was difficult. They *really* wanted you alive, you see. But so do I, Charlie Travers. For all that I respect you, honor demands I avenge my comrades. In return for the thoughtful consideration from the Empire, I gave them something they wanted even more than you." An evil glint in Seraph's eye reminded me of who and what, exactly, I was dealing with. For all her talk of honor, she was an evil piece of shit. "The location of that charming little world you hail from. Earth, I believe you call it."

I'M NOT the kind of guy who's ever been struck speechless. That might be one of my biggest problems, if I'm being brutally honest about myself, the fact that I just can't seem to shut up. But in that instant, all I could do was stare at Seraph. I couldn't even feel the outrage...all I felt was a lead weight of guilt that outmassed the planet. I'd done this. I'd brought her to Earth. Not directly, but I'd led her to the intelligence that brought her to Ohio searching for the beacon, for the cache of Kamerian starfighters. This was my fault.

I was the one who'd trusted the Kamerians, even after

Constantine and everyone else had warned me not to. I'd gotten us all killed, ended the resistance and now I was going to get everyone on Earth killed or enslaved by the Anguilar. And there was nothing I could do about it.

"You're a coward." The words came out of their own accord, more instinct than thought. I tucked my legs beneath me, rose to my feet, staring Seraph in the eye. "You're nothing but a damned coward. You couldn't win fighting us straight up so you got someone else to do your dirty work. You've got me here with my hands cuffed behind my back, letting the Anguilar handle everyone else so you can take off with me all trussed up and dispose of me, but you don't have the guts to fight. One on one. Right here, right now."

It was stupid, insane, pointless. I can't even say it's the only thing I could think of because I didn't think of it, it just came to me. Dothan surged toward me, fists clenching.

"Oh, I'll take that action, monkey boy. I haven't had enough fun pounding the shit out of you yet."

"No." Seraph stood, regarding me cooly. "I don't need you or anyone else to fight my battles for me."

She worked loose her gun belt and handed it off to Dothan, then slowly, methodically, began stripping out of her armor. It took way too long, and all I could think while watching her divest herself of the ancient Kamerian plating was that somewhere up in orbit, the Anguilar cruisers were taking on our defense platforms, the crews launching Starblades to intercept the landers. People were dying and I was stuck here in the dark, helpless.

"You're nuts," Laranna hissed at me, and I had to agree. Dani said nothing, still too pissed off at Tamura to even look at me.

I hadn't seen Seraph Nix without her armor before and if I'd expected her to be a lot smaller without it, I was disappointed. An NFL strong safety, that was what she reminded me of. Not bulky like a linebacker—that was Dothan. But she was over six feet and probably outweighed me by ten pounds. She circled around behind me and tapped a control on the cuffs. They fell away, clattering against the floor. I gave a half-second's consideration to grabbing for one of the guns but the Anguilar had all taken a step back as if they'd read my mind.

Rubbing at my wrists, I circled around, keeping my eyes on Seraph. Dothan moved to block the open cell door, maybe sensing my desperation, maybe just wanting a better view.

"Are you sure you want this, human?" Seraph asked, flexing her shoulders, rolling her neck like a boxer about to step into the ring. "If I take you with me, I could make it quick. Not painless, mind you—there are rituals that must still be served—but quick. I've been a warrior for longer than you've been alive, fought men twice your size and left them broken and begging."

I believed her. I'd trained in martial arts since I was a little kid, routinely fought guys bigger than me, counting on speed, surprise and sometimes, just a cold calculation that most people didn't have in a fight. But those had been in *dojang*, or sometimes in the ring. At most, I was risking a few bruises, a bloody nose. Here, I was risking everything.

"I guess if you're that certain," I told her, unreasonably calm, "then maybe you want to wager something on it. Like if I win, you let Laranna, Dani and Giblet go free. Put them on a transport and set them loose on the nearest neutral port."

Seraph laughed, the sound as sharp and abrupt as a gunshot.

"What do *you* have to wager, little one?" she pointed out. "Once you're beaten to a bloody pulp and I drag you to my ship, what could you give me that I don't already have?"

It was a damn good question, and I hadn't thought about it. There was only one thing I *could* offer her, whether I meant it or not.

"Sanctuary," I said. Laranna's eyes went wide, and I knew if Val were here, he would have shot me on general principles, but I had nothing else to bet. "Its location, stellar coordinates." I motioned at Laranna and Dani, back at the other cells out in the hallway. "You'll get something from them eventually—the Anguilar will, anyway. But some will lie, some will give you multiple locations, some won't talk at all. The Anguilar will waste time checking out different systems, different planets, until maybe we've evacuated everyone. You know we can do it. I sent the Liberators away when I got the word about the incoming fleet. If they see what's happening, they'll take off now and start the evacuation."

This time, Seraph's chuckle was honest rather than mocking...admiring, even.

"And how do I know that you won't lie to me like you say they will?" she asked.

"I'm a man of my word. Ask anyone who's dealt with me. I'm commanding a movement of half a dozen different species, some of whom don't like each other that much. If my word's not good, what else do I have to offer them?"

I hoped she hadn't heard of Machiavelli and *The Prince. A wise ruler ought never to keep faith when by doing so it would be against his interest.* Not that I considered myself a disciple of Machiavelli, but someone like Seraph would be, if his work had made it out this far.

"And consider," I went on, "just how grateful the Anguilar would be if you gave them the location of our base the second they land, a *fait accompli.*"

I still thought she'd turn me down. Despite my sales job, there was very little for her to gain by this and a lot to lose. Not that I expected her to keep her side of the bargain, of course. Just because she hadn't *read* Machiavelli didn't mean she didn't live by his principles.

"Very well," she said, spreading her hands wide in acceptance. "It's a bet. Come on, little man, I've worked up quite the lather waiting to pound you into a thin, fine paste on the ground."

I nodded, ignoring the barbs, getting my head right. I'd been in more fights than I could count now, but there was a qualitative difference between those and squaring off in a half-assed boxing match with a woman, even if that woman was a badass, cold-blooded bounty hunter.

Dothan shoved Laranna and Dani out of the circle, not trying to be gentle about it, and I wished I'd had the time and opportunity to beat his ass. Well, more likely just shoot his ass because there was no way in hell I'd be able to beat him in a fistfight. I paused, looking him up and down.

"You Kamerians have anything like a scorpion?" I asked him, dancing on the balls of my feet, trying to get into a rhythm.

"What?" he grunted.

"Little insect-looking thing. Has a poison sting. Lives on land. But there was this scorpion who wanted to cross a river, so he asked a frog to carry him. The frog says no way, you're a scorpion. You'll sting me and I'll die." I shrugged. "The scorpion says, that would be stupid. If I sting you while you're carrying me across the river, I'll drown and die, too. So, the frog does it. And halfway across the river, the scorpion stings him. The frog is dying, sinking, and he asks the scorpion why? You'll die too. The scorpion says, I can't help it. I'm a scorpion…it's in my nature."

"Is that story supposed to mean something to me?" Dothan asked, rolling his eyes.

"You're the scorpion, asshole," I told him. "And I was the goddamned frog." I sneered. "Congratulations. You can't help it."

Seraph moved, like I knew she would, trying to take advantage of me monologuing. I hadn't stared at her, but I'd kept my peripheral vision active and when the punch came, I was already moving. That was the key to fighting bigger guys in the *dojang* and in the ring, keep moving, the same as it was in combat, the same thing Laranna had taught me when we sparred.

I didn't try to duck, didn't bob or weave, just stepped and slid. Ducking and bobbing, my old teacher told me, was work, got you breathing hard, got the adrenaline pumping too soon. You wanted to make the other guy work. The punch came within two inches of my cheek, close enough for me to feel the breeze and with it a wash of fear of what that punch could do if it landed.

Don't try to block. That was another secret *sa bum nim* had passed on. Blocks were taught in Taekwondo, were a key part of the art, but he didn't believe in them. Blocks were for when you didn't have any choice, when you couldn't get out of the way. Instead, I pushed the back of her arm as the punch went by, forcing her into a step she hadn't intended, off-balance.

I didn't have much time because she was a professional killer and wasn't going to get thrown off by one misstep, so I didn't go in for a knockout blow. She thought she was in control, and if I wanted to get her off her game, I'd have to shake that notion. The roundhouse kick was a whip snap off my back foot, the impact against her thigh a solid smack. It was the lowest kick I could take but it was almost too high, and if the kick hurt her, she didn't let it affect the speed of the backfist swinging for my head.

Dodge, step, kick, dodge, step. Another strike to the back of her thigh that was like kicking a brick wall, another near miss. I was in pretty good shape, even with the near-concussion from Dothan's punch, and I could keep doing this for a while, but to what end? I wasn't going to bring her down with a leg kick, that much was obvious, and all it would take was one of those punches to land and I'd be out. I was gonna have to take some chances.

Or just stop. This isn't going to accomplish anything. She's not going to let them go and if by some miracle I beat her, she's just gonna have them shoot me in the leg.

No. There was no going back on this. She was going to pound

me flat no matter what I did, so I might as well get whatever licks in that I could. Besides…this *felt* right. Maybe my gut was reliable and maybe it wasn't but everything else was gone and this was all I had to work with. My life had one purpose now, one intense focus. I had to hit Seraph Nix. I had to *hurt* her. Whether I won the fight or not, she had to feel it.

I danced out of the range of another punch, this one thrown with more feeling. I was hoping she'd get frustrated, make a mistake, but there was a canny wisdom behind those eyes, a confidence bordering on arrogance. She wasn't going to get frustrated because she just *knew* she would win, that I was a babe in the woods, an amateur. She was a professional killer.

She was right.

"You ever heard of Murphy's laws of combat, Seraph?" I asked her, keeping my voice steady despite the exertion, letting her know that I was just as confident as her.

"Is Murphy one of you hairless apes?" she asked just as loosely, punctuating the words with a jab at my head. I bobbed away from it, the same way I'd learned when our teacher had brought in a boxing coach. Dave Abadi had strung a rope across the *dojang* and had us move back and forth, bobbing from one side of it to the other, practicing for just this kind of thing.

"Murphy was a guy who knew about life," I replied, circling to the side, then darting in to aim a hook into her ribs. It connected, but she was a side of beef, not an ounce of fat on her, and the punch bounced off like I'd hit a wall.

She barely grunted and I jumped back, knowing the counterpunch was coming. She surprised me, though. She'd shown no inclination to use her feet, much less to pull off the spinning crescent kick she aimed at my head. It might have taken my head clean off if I hadn't spent all those years training to avoid high kicks…and to counter them. I went down, turning on my heel as I did, a leg sweep.

This one caught her off-balance, took her plant leg out from beneath her, and she hit on her shoulder before slapping out, distributing the fall and rolling back to her feet. No hesitation still, but perhaps respect.

"Murphy said whatever can go wrong, will go wrong," I expounded as if the whole exchange of blows hadn't taken place, matching her calm. "But I've always thought the smartest thing he ever said was about war."

I had to do it soon. She'd had warning by now that I wasn't the pushover she'd thought I'd be. If I didn't make my move now, it wouldn't happen.

"He said," I expounded, remembering the quote from a poster on the wall of the ROTC offices, "that professional soldiers are always predictable. But the world is full of amateurs."

I did something stupid, something I knew I should never do in a real fight. A faint, first, a jab at her face that she reacted to the same way I knew she would, the same way she had this whole time. Just a slight motion away, a look to my opposite hand. I jumped into a roundhouse, the prettiest damn jump roundhouse I ever delivered, and it took her across the jaw with an impact that traveled up my leg right into my spine.

She toppled backward like a felled redwood and I lunged in before she even hit the ground, breaking another rule, hitting someone in the face with my fist, a good way to break my hand but oh, so damned satisfying. The skin over my knuckles split with each punch, but her head snapped back with the blow and if it was the last freaking thing I did in this life, I was going to make her feel the hopeless fear that we'd been feeling since the first time we met her.

Her fists pounded at my side, hard enough to make my ribs creak, but I kept punching, and the blows began to falter. I was going to beat her…

Strong fingers grabbed me by the back of the neck and threw me up against the cell wall, the breath going out of me along with hope in a flare of pain in my head and back. I slid down to a seat, staring up at Dothan. His face was twisted in a sneer, pulse pistol in his hand, pointed at my face.

"You didn't really think," he said, "that I'd let you win?"

27

T<small>HUNDER CRACKED OUTSIDE THE WALLS</small>, and Dothan looked around, his gun still pointed at me.

"What the hell was that?"

It was gunfire. *Lots* of gunfire. And it couldn't be the Anguilar landers—there hadn't been time for them to make it down from orbit. Or could there? I didn't even have my comm on me since the Anguilar had taken it, much less a wristwatch. Had I lost track of time?

"Get out there!" Seraph grunted, one hand holding her bruised jaw. After leaping up, too damned spry for the sake of my ego, she motioned at the Anguilar soldiers. "Get out there and find out what's happening, dammit!"

The Krinn and Anguilar might have been officers, might have been used to being in charge, but they obeyed Seraph as if she were their emperor, and maybe I knew why Dothan had thought she was a better bargain than counting on us to make their fortune. The armored Anguilar troopers streamed out of the prison, rifles held at the ready. Leaving us in the cell, still under the gun of Dothan, while Tamura stood to the side, arms crossed, and Seraph staggered against the wall, wiping blood from her chin.

"I don't suppose," I said, "that you're actually going to keep your word."

Seraph cocked an eyebrow and regarded me with the closest she could manage to a cruel smile with her jaw bruised and swollen. She reached down and retrieved her armor and gun belt from where they lay at the other side of the cell.

"Come now, Charlie Travers," she said. "You may be young, but you're not *that* young. Perhaps a commander such as yourself depends on the veracity of your word, but I'm a bounty hunter. I do anything I have to do in order to complete the job." Seraph shrugged. "I'm not without pity, though. I know you wouldn't have your friend and your woman"—she gestured at Dani and Laranna—"tortured by the Anguilar for what they know. Dothan." She motioned at the pilot. "Tamura. Kill them."

Tamura didn't hesitate. His gun cleared its holster in a single, smooth motion and he shot Dothan in the side of the head. The hulking Kamerian stayed on his feet for a moment, most of his head gone, out of sheer momentum before he teetered and fell. Tamura spun on his heel, turning the gun toward Seraph, but as quick and efficient as the pilot was, he *was* still a pilot…and she was a gunfighter.

Seraph's pistol was out before Tamura could move an inch,

the report of the weapon a bullwhip snap under a lightning crackle. Tamura staggered, clutching at the smoldering burn through his chest and Dani screamed, then threw herself at Seraph's legs, shoulder first. The bounty hunter stumbled at the collision, her heavy pistol clattering to the cell floor, and I threw myself at it, fingers closing around its grip just as Seraph punched Dani across the face.

I fired, but Seraph had already spun out of the open doorway and the shot blasted a hole in the door jam, coming nowhere near her. I ducked around the corner carefully, but she was gone, already out of the main entrance, left open, light streaming in from outside.

"Sainrastil and Fenris are still at the fighters," I told Laranna, moving behind her to release the cuffs. My fingers were sore, my knuckles bruised and bleeding, and it took longer than it should have. "Go free the other pilots...we have to get there before the Anguilar troops land!" Looking around, I tried to figure out where they'd stashed our comms but didn't see them...it was just as likely the Anguilar troopers had taken them when they'd scrambled out of here. No way to warn Lenny, no way to get in touch with Val or check on the situation upstairs, find out if the defense platforms had managed to hold off the cruisers. We were on our own.

Laranna nodded, rubbing at her wrists, then gave a pitying look at Dani before she rushed out to the other cells. Dani had shrugged off the punch and dragged herself over to Tamura. The Kamerian's eyes were open, fingers clenching as he fought for one last breath.

"Get these Goddamned cuffs off me, Travers," Dani demanded, halfway between a sob and a bellowed order.

I said nothing, just tapped the controls on the latch. The restraints fell away from her wrist and she grabbed Tamura's hand, held it tight, putting her cheek against his.

"Didn't…know," Tamura gasped, blood trickling from the side of his mouth as he forced out the last words. "Didn't have time to warn you…"

"I know that, you idiot," Dani told him, her shoulders shuddering as tears streamed down her face. "Dammit, why'd you have to go and get yourself killed?"

Tamura's mouth worked, but before he managed another word, he stiffened and one last, rattling breath escaped before he would breathe no more. I didn't know what to say, didn't know how to comfort Dani.

"I have to go," I told her, motioning toward the door. "You can stay here…"

"No." Dani shook her head, letting go of Tamura's hand, placing it gently on his chest. She stood, wiping at her eyes. "You're already down four fighter crews. You're going to need all the pilots you can get." She hesitated and knelt down to grab Tamura's pistol where it had fallen. "Let's go."

By the time we reached the other cells, Giblet and the others were already streaming out of the open doors, heading for daylight.

"Hold up!" I yelled, getting out in front of them, waving a hand to get their attention. "There's fighting going on out there." More gunfire, distant, from the other side of town. "I don't know what the hell's happening but none of you are going to do anybody a damned bit of good if you get killed before we get to the fighters. Wedge formation by squadrons, Laranna, Dani and me at the front. Flights, stick together."

I waved the pistol over my head.

"Follow me, Vanguard Wing."

PHILOS WAS A GHOST TOWN, abandoned by some ancient civilization and left intact for us to find, as if we'd been inside the cells for thousands of years instead of minutes. The civilians were in their shelters, hiding, hoping, praying, and I was damned uncomfortable being the thing they were praying for.

I was even more uncomfortable walking through those abandoned streets in broad daylight. Darkness was illusory shelter, but at least it was *some* shelter. Every cloud in that blue sky concealed an Anguilar Starblade waiting to rain fire on the city, or a troop transport about to disgorge dozens of enemy soldiers right on top of us. Every shadowed alcove and doorway held Anguilar soldiers waiting in ambush. Had they landed yet? I thought there hadn't been time, but I wasn't a hundred percent on that, not without some kind of sensor feed.

I only knew one thing for sure: there was fighting going on nearby and I fought an urge to run toward the sound of gunfire, knowing the best way I could end this was to get to the fighters. Laranna walked point, giving me a dirty look when I tried to take the position myself. Same old argument, but this time I let her get away with it because it gave me time to rubberneck.

That was probably why I saw Wendra before Laranna did. To be fair, Wendra saw me first and it took me a full three seconds of staring at the armored figure running our way, a pulse rifle held at the low ready, before I recognized it was her. I lowered my pistol, first checking up and down the industrial-district street to make sure she wasn't being chased by a platoon of Anguilar.

"Charlie!" she called, nearly stumbling to a halt, clearly not used to the weight of the body armor and rifle. "I was trying to find you, but we didn't know where you'd been taken!"

"Wendra," I asked, shaking my head, motioning to her getup, "where'd you get the gear? And what are you doing out here when you should be with your daughter in the shelter?"

"And who are you fighting?" Laranna added, not looking at the Copperell woman, her eyes still locked on our twelve o'clock while Dani scanned our six, Tamura's pistol held outstretched. The rest of the flight crew hung back twenty yards from us, kept in check by Giblet, since we didn't have any weapons for them. And for once, Gib wasn't talking. He kept looking at Dani, looking like he wanted to say something and deciding against it.

Wendra waved the questions away as if they were overwhelming her ability to answer.

"We're not *really* fighting anyone…well, we *weren't* until those Anguilar prisoners got out and started looking for us." She scowled. "It's hard to explain…you see, a lot of us who are mothers with young children were allowed to train with the militia, but not to deploy with them in case of emergency because we had to take care of the kids. I wasn't too keen on that, and neither were a lot of my friends, so we started"—Wendra shrugged—"*acquiring* weapons and armor whenever we got the chance."

"Stealing it, you mean," I interjected, raising an eyebrow at her.

"It's not like anyone else was using it!" she protested, making an expansive gesture with the rifle, which almost threw her off her balance. "Anyway, when the alarm sounded and everyone started heading to the shelters, me and some of my friends knew something was wrong, so while a few of us kept an eye on the kids in the shelter, the rest of us..." Wendra patted the forestock of the rifle. "And I sent someone to keep an eye on what you were doing, because I figured whatever was going on, you'd be in the middle of it."

"You saw us get captured," I surmised, and Wendra nodded eagerly.

"Yeah, by that big, ugly woman in the old armor. We also saw her set free the Anguilar and Krinn officers so we knew we had to do something. I put a scout on you and one on the troops they left by the fighters, and I figured once there were only like a dozen guards on the fighters, well..."

"The shooting, that was you fighting with the guards?" Hope warred with anxiety, my stomach churning at the thought of a bunch of single mothers with their kids waiting in the shelters for their return getting into a firefight with Anguilar troops.

"At first it was," Wendra agreed. "But that didn't last long." Her grin was smug. "They didn't know what hit them. We even got those two Kamerian traitors alive, if you want them. After that, though, we started thinking it would probably make it easier for you to get free of the big ugly girl if we kept making noise, so we just started"—her face reddened—"kind of blowing shit up, to attract attention."

I couldn't help it. Despite everything, I laughed.

"Wendra," I told her, grabbing her by the arms, "if I wasn't very happily married, I'd kiss you."

"You have my permission," Laranna offered. "Thank you, Wendra. You saved our lives…and maybe the lives of everyone in this city."

"Come on, then," the Copperell woman urged, waving for us to follow. "Let's get to your fighters!"

Knowing we had scouts out and that the Anguilar were tied up with Wendra's Mom Militia, we abandoned caution for speed, though most of us couldn't run very fast. The Anguilar hadn't been too gentle when they captured the flight crews, and I knew the only reason they hadn't executed them outright was that Seraph Nix had promised to bring them in alive for interrogation.

Me, I was burning fumes after that fight and my jaw still hurt where Dothan had slugged me. I was lucky as hell it wasn't broken and still pissed off that the best roundhouse kick I'd ever delivered and several punches hadn't done more than bruise Seraph Nix. Those Kamerians were tough bastards.

But Dothan was dead, and Seraph was in the wind…again. She was out here somewhere, probably heading for her ship, another reason we had to get in those fighters. If she got to the *Revenant* before we got in the air…

Better not to think about that. The fighters waited for us through the gate, the same view as last I saw them, and though this time we had no worries of ambush, I still slowed as we approached the gate and checked either side before waving the others through.

There was *one* difference this time, of course—all those dead Anguilar. Wendra hadn't been kidding, her people had done a number on the guards left behind. Eleven to be exact, all of them hit by what looked to me like multiple shots from multiple angles. If Wendra had looked smug, the other Copperell women she'd left behind to guard the Vanguards were absolutely beaming. I guess I couldn't blame them, and their enthusiasm was infectious. Until I saw Sainrastil and Fenris sitting with their backs against the city wall, hands behind their heads, their expressions twisted with hate. Then the smile ran away from my face.

"All right!" I yelled as the flight crews caught up with us. Some of them were hugging the Thalassian women, thanking them. "Listen up! We have four extra fighters with no crews! That means we need four crews to give up their gunner to be a pilot!"

"I'll do it," Dani volunteered immediately, but I shook my head.

"No. It's not that I don't trust you," I added quickly, "but I've seen the training and I know who's most qualified. Verander," I said, pointing at Giblet's copilot, "you've got the highest scores, you take the lead in Tamura's old squadron. Your other pilots are gonna be Carlan, Peralta and Stavros." I raised a hand against the protests from the pilots. "I know, you won't be able to use

319

your pulse cannons, but you're gonna have to deal with it. Get your fighters prepped and get in the air."

The commotion and hubbub of the crews getting their shit sorted and boarding their planes blurred into the background for me as I walked up to Sainrastil and Fenris. Seraph's pistol was still in my hand, down at my side as I approached them, though I didn't think I'd need it.

"Wendra," I said, not taking my eyes off the two Kamerians, "once we take off, I want you and your people in the shelters."

"What about the Anguilar?" she asked sharply. "We still have people harassing them, trying to keep them away from here."

"Have them break contact and make their way back to the shelters. Those landers are coming, and I do *not* want all those enemy soldiers rooting through the city and slaughtering civilians. That's why the militia is taking up positions in the wilderness, to draw the Anguilar away from here."

"All right," she murmured, clearly not happy about it. Wendra nodded toward the Kamerians. "What do you want us to do with these two?"

Good question. I wished I had a good answer to go with it.

"Tamura and Dothan are dead," I told them. Fenris looked up sharply as if I'd slapped him across the face, but Sainrastil didn't appear surprised.

"You killed them, I suppose," she grunted.

"No." I shook my head. "Tamura killed Dothan and then your friend, Seraph Nix killed him."

"You're lying!" Fenris yelled, surging to his feet, ignoring the rifle muzzle one of the Thalassian women shoved into his chest. "The captain would *never* have hurt one of us!"

"But he did. Because Dothan was going to kill the woman he loved." I nodded sideways at Dani, who was watching the exchange intently. "You see, your captain understood that things had changed, that you needed to adapt to the situation. Dothan never did."

"*Love*," Sainrastil scoffed, glaring at Dani. "A child's conceit. If the captain did believe that sort of...*bestiality* was love, then he was a fool and deserved to die."

"You're lying!" Fenris repeated, rage building behind his eyes, as if he just couldn't accept that Tamura and Dothan were gone. "You killed them! You murdered them!"

When he batted aside the Thalassian woman's rifle and lunged at me, I was ready for it, had intended to step to the side and smack him across the back of the neck with my pistol. I never got the chance and neither did he.

The discharge of the pulse pistol twice only a couple feet from my head was deafening—not quite as bad as a regular gun back on Earth, but close—and I stepped away, the concussion warring with the gush of heat and static electricity over which was the most unpleasant. The winner of that battle was being on the other side of the shot.

The first round took Fenris between the eyes, blew him backward off his feet, missing a good chunk of his skull. The second caught Sainrastil in the chest just as she was coming to her feet. The Kamerian woman *did* seem surprised this time, her features slack with shock as she slid back down the wall.

Dani lowered her gun slowly, smoke still wafting out of the muzzle, her emotions concealed behind a cold mask. Finally, she met my gaze without a hint of remorse in her eyes.

"They were going to try to kill you," Dani said with a shrug. "Besides, what *else* could you do with them? I heard what you said to Dothan about the scorpion and the frog. And you were right. They're Kamerians. Everyone seemed to understand what that meant except us."

Laranna had rushed up at the sound of the shots, her pistol at the ready, and she didn't seem in too much of a hurry to put it down, glaring at Dani as if she saw the woman as a threat. I reached out and took the pulse gun out of Dani's hand, passed it back to Laranna.

"Get in the fighters," I told both of them. "We'll deal with this later."

If there *was* a later.

28

THE FIRST THING I DID, of course, was make a call.

"This is Vanguard One to all Vanguard Wing units," I said, raising my voice to be heard above the roar of the belly jets as the starfighter rose on a cloud of dust that hid the view from the cockpit. "Please respond, any Vanguard Wing unit."

"Maybe," Dani said from the gunner's chair, "we should rethink this name." She sat back, arms crossed, regarding me coolly. "After all, you picked Vanguard Wing in happier times, when we actually thought we could make this work."

I'd thought about making her ride with Giblet, but I figured that would be too much of a distraction for him, considering. And anyway, I wanted to be able to keep an eye on her. That didn't mean I was going to be her grief counselor though.

"This is Vanguard One," I repeated, ignoring the fatalism.

"Any Vanguard Wing Unit, respond immediately. I have been out of comms range and need a status report."

The sky was alarmingly empty, both through the cockpit canopy and on sensors and that didn't make any sense.

"Vanguard One, this is Starblade Sixteen, do you copy?"

The transmission was garbled with static, somewhere at the edge of range for how low we were, around the terminator of the planet. Starblade Sixteen was one of the short-range fighters from Orbital Defense Platform Two, on the opposite side of the world from us at the moment, if I remembered their orbits correctly. Which was troubling, considering Orbital Defense Platform One should be right overhead. But they weren't talking.

"I copy, Sixteen. What's the situation?"

The city dropped below us, untouched, pristine, as if nothing had ever happened down there and nothing ever would. Everything was an illusion, and maybe Dani was right, maybe my idea of uniting the galaxy against the Anguilar was just as much of an illusion.

"It's not good, sir," the Copperell admitted. "The platforms are gone. We took down three of the cruisers before their fighters overwhelmed us. I'm the last of my squadron and I have three of their birds riding my tail."

"Shit," I hissed, checking the sensors again. Nothing. He was still too far away, bouncing his signal off the atmosphere. "Okay, Sixteen, give me your coordinates and we'll pick you up. You head our way and we can intercept."

"I don't think I have that much time, One." A long silence filled with static. "Their landers held back while their fighters cleared the way. They're on their way down from orbit now…you have to take them out. Make this all mean something, sir."

Nothing.

"Starblade Sixteen, do you read me?" I called. "Sixteen?"

Nothing, no reply, and I knew in my heart of hearts that the man was dead, that he'd given his life to fix my mistake. And he wouldn't be the last.

"We got something on sensors, Charlie," Dani told me, all business again. I followed her gesture to the swarm of red dots popping into existence on the screen as they came into range.

I didn't need the targeting computer to tell me what they were —I could tell by their speed, their sensor return. Landers. Dozens of them, heading for Philos. Behind them, dimmer in the sensors, was another wave of small ships, these moving faster, their signature tinier, dots rather than blobs. Fighters. Starblades and without any IFF return, not ours.

"Vanguard units, this is Vanguard One," I radioed, watching as Dani tapped the forward clusters of troop transports, each of them turning from a featureless dot to a crosshair reticle, waiting for one of us to come and take them down. "We have enemy landers coming in for the city with fighter cover. First and Second, you break wide and take the fighters. Third, you're coming with me and targeting the landers."

And that sure as hell wasn't the way I *wanted* to do it. I wanted to be going after the fighters, but I had the converted gunners in my squadron and I didn't want their first combat experience to be against trained Anguilar fighter pilots.

"What about the cruisers?" Giblet demanded, never one to

worry about questioning my plans right there on an open line. "If we don't take them out, they can just pound the city from orbit."

"One thing at a time," I told Gib, working hard not to snap at him despite the temptation. "They can't bombard anyone while their landers are in the air. Break off and head for orbit. You take the lead, Gib." I didn't bother with the call signs because he didn't appreciate them anymore than Tamura and the Kamerians had. "Get those damned fighters so we can take the fight to the cruisers."

"You're the boss, boss," he sighed.

"You sure about this, Charlie?" Laranna asked, wise enough to do it over our private channel instead of in front of everyone. Dani heard it though, and her eyebrow shot up. "We could take out the cruiser and leave the militia to deal with the landers until we finish up."

"That would be the smart thing to do," I admitted. "If we were worried about ourselves, about defeating the enemy. But it's not the right thing to do if we're trying to protect the Thalassians. And if we're not fighting for people like them, then what the hell are we doing this for?"

I expected an argument, but instead, she laughed softly.

"I love you, Charlie."

"Love you, too" I said. "See you on the other side."

Laranna and Giblet's birds split off from Third, arcing wide, leaving our planes behind and an empty feeling in my gut. I sensed Dani's stare and met her eyes, shaking my head.

"What?"

"You're one lucky son of a bitch, Travers," she said. And that

I couldn't argue with. Dani's eyes flickered back to the sensor screen and her expression went harsh again. "They've seen us."

They had, and they were attempting the only tactic that made sense, splitting up into clusters of three, trying to make themselves a lot of small targets instead of one big one, which was both admirable and damned annoying.

"Third squadron," I ordered, "split into elements, just you and your wingman." I shouldn't have had to remind them of that, but when we had four new pilots who'd have a hundred other things to be thinking about, I didn't want the little details slipping their minds. "Don't chase the landers, there are too many of them for that. They have to come to the city, or at least get close to it, so take up a broad patrol arc around the city at 20,000 feet and pick them off as they descend."

It didn't seem fair, but if there was a fair way to fight a war, I'd never read about it.

"Donnell, you're with me," I told my wingman. I realized I'd totally given up on the call signs but to hell with it. It had been a long day. "We're climbing to 30,000 feet and we're going to herd these bastards like cattle, drive them into the other elements."

"Copy that, Vanguard One," he said, and I chuckled at the unspoken rebuke in the reply. "Though I've never actually herded cattle myself."

"Well, there's a first time for everything."

We rose up through a bank of dark clouds, static electricity crackling off the wings, the enemy unseen by the naked eye and the optical cameras but still there on the sensor screen. They didn't want to do this. I could tell by the way they were flying, the tentative descent, the furtive maneuvers, like feathers wafting down on the wind, in no hurry to engage with us.

Not those Starblades, though. They were racing to meet their fate, burning as fast as they could, meteors of red fire even in the blue sky. Laranna and Gib and their birds arced inward toward the enemy fighters with the infinite patience of superior firepower. This was going to take a while, but I wasn't afraid of the outcome. We could do this, even without the Kamerians.

And that's when everything went to hell, of course.

"Incoming ship!" Dani yelped, her personal grief and betrayal forgotten in the sudden rush of fear. "Heading straight for us at high speed at"—she stuttered, struggling with terms she'd only learned a few months ago—"point two-six, ETA five seconds!"

And I admit that I took one of those seconds to translate the coordinates into a direction my instincts could understand, another second wasted looking at the sensor display, thinking I'd seen that signature before…

"Donnell, split right and climb!" I told him, jerking my own control wheel to the left and jamming it into a dive.

I *had* seen that sensor signature before, and when the ship came within a few thousand feet of us, close enough for the cameras to pull up a zoomed-in view of her on the tactical screen, I knew exactly where.

It was the *Revenant*. Deep-chested like a California condor, engines growling in the shadow of her heavy wings, particle cannons slung under the curved armor of her nose. Bigger than a Vanguard but nearly as agile, small enough to land on a planet but with the firepower of a cruiser, the relative power of her shields her only weakness compared to the larger vessels. She was near the apex of Kamerian technology and Seraph Nix flew her as well as any of us could run a Vanguard. Except Tamura, and she'd already killed him.

I'd hoped she chased after me instead of Donnell, and she did, throwing the massive ship into a dive to match my own, though I could only see her on the sensors and couldn't even give those much attention. Not while I rocketed toward an ice-capped mountain range, the crags and peaks gaining definition with each second, so close I felt like I could take one step out of the cockpit and be standing on one, mountain climbing the easy way.

There was nothing easy about pulling up from that dive, and Seraph wasn't going to cut me any slack. Spears of actinic lightning hunted for me in those jagged peaks, their passage only meters away lighting our shields up like a halo of St. Elmo's fire, and not the one with Rob Lowe and Emilio Estevez, either. Vanguard One shuddered and jolted, maybe from the thermal and electromagnetic energy converting to kinetic with the arcane workings of the deflector shields, or maybe from the superheated air tossing us around.

"Shit!" Dani blurted, grabbing at the arms of her chair like she was worried her seat restraints wouldn't hold and she'd be tossed out the cockpit canopy.

At least I had the control yoke to hold onto and I hung onto it for dear life, pulled up and banked away from the *Revenant*. Yet still she clung to our tail, locked onto us like a bird of prey. I kept the steering yoke twisted as far as I dare without losing control and smashing into a mountain. I kept us out of the Kamerian ship's firing arc, but barely, and I was, I knew, playing right into Seraph's hands. The more I ran, the more she chased, and I couldn't fire on her while she rode my tail.

Particle blasts spoke again, missing by more this time, just a reminder that she was still there, of what the penalty would be if I did anything stupid, like turning to fight her. Even with the inertial dampeners, enough acceleration leaked through to shove me into the side of my chair, the harness biting into my shoulder harder with each passing second. Hard enough that it squeezed the air out of me, kept me from doing what I needed to do—calling for help.

Thank God I didn't need to. The flare of the particle cannons announced Donnell's arrival better than any trumpet-blowing herald could have, and the only reason the first shot didn't take out the *Revenant* was that we were in the way. The blast grazed the side of her shields, lighting them up in an incandescent hemisphere around the starboard side of the ship, sending the *Revenant* into an uncontrolled wobble as she broke off pursuit.

"Keep on her," I told Donnell in the fraction of a second I had to breathe before I twisted the steering wheel to the left, pushing the entire yoke in the same direction.

The Vanguard screamed in protest, the superstructure groaning even with the best the inertial dampeners could do for it, and even I, an aspiring infantry soldier with no flight experience whatsoever, knew that if I'd tried this maneuver in an F-16, I'd have ripped the wings off of it. Not the Vanguard, though. She was a tough, brawny bird built to indulge in the stupidest whims of an amateur pilot like me, even if she wasn't happy about it.

Blue skies blurred around me, replaced by white and brown and green as we banked into the turn harder, the ground only a few thousand feet below. No more mountain peaks…we were flying over a huge river valley, this one dotted with farms and that tiny part of my brain that wasn't totally concentrating on keeping the fighter under control wondered idly if the people on those farms even knew that the planet had been occupied by the Anguilar. They might have been down there in the middle of the continent, isolated on a subsistence farm, living their lives happily without a clue that hundreds of thousands of their fellow Thalassians were slaving away in the mines and factories. Not too different from everyone on Earth, so completely involved in our political and military squabbles, totally unaware of what was happening around us, how it could all end in a heartbeat.

Even those idle musings faded in a burst of adrenaline as the slope-winged lines of the *Revenant* swung into view on the targeting screen, the reticle dancing around her with the motion of both our spacecraft. Dogfighting in space had been pretty straightforward, but doing it here in the atmosphere was like trying to target shoot from the saddle of a bucking bronco. While I tried to line up the fixed particle cannon with the *Revenant*, Dani had an easier time of it, since the pulse turrets moved independent of the fighter.

Crimson threads connected us to Seraph's ship for a long second, however many hundreds of rounds that was, but her shields shrugged off the attack in a spray of red sparks.

"Save your ammo," I warned Dani. "If we live through this, we'll need it for the landers." She scowled, obviously not happy with the idea of sitting and watching, but I switched my attention to Donnell. "Get ahead of her," I told him. "See if you can get a side shot or at least turn her back toward me."

"I'll do my best," he told me. "She's booking it, though...not sure I can outrun her."

He was right about that. Donnell hung off my starboard shoulder, maybe a mile back, burning hard and still barely able to keep up. If Seraph ran, if she bolted for orbit and the cover of the cruisers, I'd have to let her go, and I really didn't want to do that. Baring my teeth, I switched the radio to broadband, general broadcast.

"Seraph, you hear me?"

"Are you nuts?" Dani wondered.

"Probably," I admitted, muting the mic for a moment before switching it back on. "Seraph, I know you're there. If you run, you'll never get me. Maybe the Anguilar will, but you won't. I thought you always got your man?"

Seraph didn't answer, which surprised me, since she never seemed to miss a chance at bloviating. She didn't answer with *words*, anyway. The starfighters were more agile and nimble than a cruiser in space and had enough of an advantage in power over the Starblades to batter them into submission in an atmosphere, but the *Revenant* was almost unique out here, smaller than a cruiser but packing nearly the same size engines...and inertial dampeners.

The maneuver shouldn't have been possible in the gravity

field of a planet, should have cracked the ship's superstructure right down the spine, but she pulled it off. The drives cut out, and her maneuvering thrusters flared, turning the *Revenant* end for end before the engines flared to life again. I cursed, shooting past her, and immediately cut my own drives, yanking the steering yoke around.

The turn was rough, smashing against the side of my face like a punch from Dothan, my vision narrowing into a black-rimmed tunnel, and warning lights flashed yellow, delivering the message I already knew, that this was *bad* for the fighter. Donnell wasn't as reckless, or as fast, and I watched his fate unfold, helpless to stop it until the turn completed.

My wingman tried something more conventional, slowing down, banking into a turn, the exact wrong thing to do when Seraph already had him in her sights. I fought with the controls, wrestling them toward the *Revenant* like I could yank the nose around and line up the cannon, but physics didn't give a damn how desperate I was.

Seraph fired.

Raw, rampaging white energy consumed the Vanguard, the fighter expanding into a sphere of burning gas and metal.

Donnell was gone.

29

I COULDN'T SCREAM. I wanted to, wanted to vent my frustration and helplessness in a bellow of fury, but the battering g-force of the sharp turn robbed me of the breath, robbed me of the courtesy of vocalizing my grief and rage.

Not her, though. Seraph banked away from the burning remains of Donnell's fighter as they tumbled into the river valley, coming around to face me again, and she finally deigned to speak.

"That's what it feels like, Travers," she taunted, "when you lose one of your people."

Just another few seconds. Keep her talking.

"I know what it feels like to lose friends," I assured her, forcing myself to sound confident, unaffected despite the g-forces pushing me into the side of my chair. "I know what it's like to lose people because of my mistakes. What I don't know"—keep that damned steering yoke pegged, keep moving that reticle—"is how it feels to be so utterly incompetent that you make the same mistake twice in a row, when you underestimate your opponent so badly that you get every single one of your people killed…and then go on to get the only other Kamerians from the time of your Alliance still alive killed, too, for the exact same reason. After I kicked your ass, by the way."

That did it. The *Revenant*'s course straightened, the loss of control evident in her voice when she replied.

"You'll regret this, you babbling monkey!" she bellowed at me. "When your planet is a cinder and your people are slaves in the Anguilar mines, you'll wish you'd never laid eyes on me!"

"Oh, I already do," I told her and pulled the trigger.

The right side of the *Revenant* lit up like Christmas lights on a downtown street, her shields raging in protest at the abuse…and failing. A jet of fire crashed inward where the shields yielded to the energy of the particle blast, the right wing and the engines beneath it separating from the body of the ship in a spray of molten metal. The ship tumbled, its remaining engine flaring as she tried desperately to regain control, but from the way the nose tipped downward, the shaking and shuddering of the entire superstructure, it was obvious the *Revenant* had lost her inertial dampeners and gravity resist along with the entire right rear quadrant of the vessel. She was running on power alone, and the aerodynamics of just one wing, and she'd be lucky to make it to the ground without crashing.

I wasn't going to give her the chance.

"Hang on," I warned Dani, shoving the yoke forward, sending us into a steep dive. "We're going after her."

"Just get me close," Dani said, gripping the joystick control for the pulse turrets. "All I need is one shot at that bitch."

I hadn't kept track of how far we'd gone or in what direction as I'd been pursued and then pursued Seraph in return, but now it was obvious. We were back within sight of Philos, less than twenty miles away, and Seraph aimed her crippled vessel at the flats where the militia trained. It was, I suppose, better than the forest or the river, though not by much.

If I'd had another second, I could have caught her in the air, but Seraph knew that, too, and dipped her nose lower, risking the heavier impact to get herself on the ground quicker. I winced at the spray of soil, the wash of flame as the engines set the grass on fire just before they cut off. It hurt just looking at it, and I thought for a second that the crash might do the work for me, might break Seraph in two.

Dani wasn't taking that chance, already spraying the smoking wreck of the *Revenant* before it had even made it to a complete stop. Pulse fire ripped into the cockpit, sparks fountaining up out of the metal as the burst worked backward. The ship rumbled to a stop, billowing smoke, and before Dani could adjust fire, something popped out of the side of the hull back behind the cockpit, near where I thought the utility airlock would be. Something small, cylindrical, big enough for maybe three people to squeeze into.

A lifepod. It ejected on a burst of its onboard rockets, designed for use in space or the upper atmosphere, not on the ground, but enough to get it clear of the side of the ship and angled toward the forest at the edge of the clearing. Dani growled and tried to track the pod, but it was small and fast, its arc too short to give her a clear shot, and just before it hit the treetops, the retrorockets fired, igniting an immediate blaze around it in the brush.

And disappeared into the smoke and trees.

"Shit!" Dani snarled, aiming another burst into the woods. More fire, more smoke, and I couldn't tell if she was hitting anything.

"Stop," I told her, pulling our nose up, spinning the fighter around. "We'll land and track her on foot. She can't have gotten far."

Yeah, I did think, somewhere deep inside, that I was going too far, that I had responsibilities other than hunting down Seraph Nix. There were the Anguilar, not just the landers but the Starblade fighters and, above all, literally and figuratively, the cruisers. But the Kamerian bounty hunter had been on our asses for months now, had never let up and maybe it was panic, but I had a gut-deep feeling that if I didn't finish her off now, she'd be the death of us all.

The belly jets rumbled beneath us, the descent as quick as I could make it and still get the landing gear out. We hit with a bone-shaking rattle, and Dani was already out of her seat before I could switch off the engines. We kept pulse carbines stowed beside the hatch, and she wrenched one free of its locks with one hand and slapped the hatch control with the other.

We'd never had the chance to change into flight suits or

armor, and I was still dressed in T-shirt and jeans, which wouldn't do a damned thing to protect me from gunfire, but I followed her out of the cockpit, pistol tucked into my belt, the other carbine in the crook of my arm. I should have been searching the tree line, but instead my eyes were drawn upward by the scream of atmospheric engines. Anguilar landers fell out of the sky, coming not for the woods where the militia waited but straight for the city.

"Dammit." They hadn't taken the bait. I suppose I should have known that the Anguilar were more interested in using civilians as hostages than fighting the militia. I reached for the comm that should have been on my belt and realized I didn't have one.

"Over here!" Dani called from somewhere on the other side of the smoke.

Flames crackled all around us, licking up from dry underbrush, threatening to consume the thinner trees, the heat not painful yet but oppressive. I coughed reflexively at the smoke as I ran through it to where I thought Dani had yelled from, keeping my rifle at the ready. Seraph could be anywhere, waiting for us in ambush in the midst of this conflagration.

A human shape loomed in the white haze, and I swung my rifle around to cover it for a moment before details clarified as the smoke cleared and I saw it was Dani. About twenty yards beyond her, surrounded by the splintered remains of small trees, was the escape pod. Scored and scorched, laying askew on its side, the door still shut.

The hackles rose on my neck. She had to be inside. Maybe injured. We could take care of her now...though that didn't feel right. If she was injured, helpless, could I actually kill her? As ruthless as Seraph was, I hadn't quite reached that level yet. Then again, I doubted she'd surrender, so maybe I didn't have to worry about it.

I motioned Dani forward, bringing the carbine to my shoulder. She tucked her own weapon under her arm and grabbed the handle, then looked at me for confirmation. I sucked in a deep breath and nodded. Dani grabbed the eternal hatch lever, yanked it downward, and pulled. The hatch stuck for a maddening three-count, but then it creaked open, and I shot forward, sticking the barrel of my carbine inside.

Nothing.

The interior was empty, not a blood stain, not a scrap of evidence that anything had ever been in it except a light coating of dust.

"Shit!" Dani exclaimed, turning back the way we'd come. "She's back at the *Revenant*! She has to be!"

Before I could say anything, she turned and ran through the smoke again, and I cursed, trailing her again through the fire. It was obvious what Seraph had done, in retrospect. She'd launched the escape pod to draw us away from the wreckage of the ship, then waited until we'd gone after the pod before making a run for it. Anger burned in my chest, more at myself than her, but still bright enough that I wasn't concerned too much anymore about taking her prisoner.

Back through the smoke, coughing uncontrollably this time, unable to see a damned thing, and now that we *knew* Seraph was behind us, it was highly likely she was waiting in ambush. I wanted to yell at Dani to wait, but that would have given our position away even more than the coughing. Irrational fears tugged at my nerves, that I'd get turned around in the smoke, run deeper into the fire, die ignominiously of smoke inhalation or, worse yet, burn to death, which was pretty much my lowest on the rung of ways to die, ranking just below getting torn apart by wild animals.

But then I was through again, gasping for breath, blinking tears out of my eyes, the trees behind me, metal monsters ahead. The fighter was where we'd left it, but Dani was running toward the wreckage of Seraph's ship, her face twisted in a fierce grimace.

"Get out here, you bitch!" she screamed, firing off a burst of pulse fire into the open airlock of the ship. "Come out here and face me! You killed him, and I'm going to rip your damn throat out!"

I risked a look back at the city, at the air above it. The rest of my squadron still zoomed by, pursuing Anguilar landers, but they hadn't been able to get them all, and at least a dozen of them descended below the city walls even as I watched, joining the others I'd already seen touch down.

"Dani!" I yelled. I'd learned how to pitch my voice to carry from the very best, former drill sergeants who'd bellowed like dying buffalo, and she turned at my call, though the reluctance was plain to see in her face. "Get back in the fighter! We have to go!"

"No," she snarled, gripping her carbine like she meant to choke the life out of it. "She's out here and I'm going to kill her for what she did to Tamura."

"The Anguilar are landing in the city," I shouted back at her, pointing toward the walls, to the troop transports descending behind them. "We have to give them air support! I need my gunner, dammit!"

Her lip twisted into a snarl and with a scream of frustration, she aimed another burst into the *Revenant*'s airlock before turning and running back to the Vanguard. I took a moment to lock my carbine in place, then rushed to the pilot's seat, pulling up the comm board as I strapped in.

"Vanguard elements, this is Vanguard One, sitrep."

"Vanguard One, this is Two," Laranna came on immediately. "Are you all right? I got a report you were attacked by Seraph."

"I'm okay," I told her. "Vanguard Sixteen is gone." The words came out bleak, and as much as I liked Donnell as a person and appreciated him as a pilot, if I was being honest, part of that bleakness was from the loss of the starfighter. "The *Revenant* is down, but Seraph escaped. We're heading into the city for air support. What's the situation up there?"

The whine of the engines powering up threatened to drown out her answer and I was okay with that…I dreaded what she was about to tell me, imagining a dozen different ways things could have descended into disaster while I'd been tied up fighting Seraph.

"We're still tangled up with the Starblades," she told me. "We haven't taken any casualties but they're keeping us running around up here….and the cruisers are hanging back, waiting to see who's going to win the fight. I get the feeling once we've mopped these guys up, they're going to close in fast and try to negate our hyperspace capability."

Yeah, that sounded exactly like what they'd be doing, particularly since Seraph had to have warned them about the Vanguards.

"They're trying to flytrap us with the Starblades," I decided. "Vanguard Three"—which was Giblet, and hopefully, he'd answer to the call sign—"take your squadron out of orbit, get to minimum jump distance and harass those damned cruisers."

"Roger that," Giblet said, the words almost a snarl. "It's about time we stopped playing around with these bastards."

"Gib," I said, watching out of the corner of my eye as Dani got strapped in, "do *not* become decisively engaged with the cruisers." I punctuated the order by yanking the Vanguard into the air, the sudden burst of acceleration pushing me down into the seat, a sensation both thrilling and terrifying at once, like riding a rodeo bull. "I want you to keep them occupied, hit and run, keep them from firing on the planet until we can mop up down here and get all our fighters up there. There's only one squadron of you and if you get tangled up with one or two cruisers, the others are going to pick you off. You get me?"

"Yeah, I get you," he grumbled. "I don't like it, but you're the boss."

Which was as good as I hoped to get from him. I switched frequencies as I banked the fighter out over toward the city, hoping to hell that Val and Nareena were paying attention to what was going on.

"Val, it's Charlie." No call signs now, not with the old cowboy.

"I hear you, Charlie. The Anguilar aren't coming this way." Maybe I imagined the rebuke in his twang, but probably not.

"You noticed that, did you?" I asked between gritted teeth, the Vanguard fighting me as I took it lower, wanting to climb instead, like the machine knew its capabilities were being wasted down here. "Get the militia to the city. I've got the enemy air support tied up and we're doing our best to shoot down as many landers as we can, but it's not enough. I'm gonna try to keep them busy until you get here."

I didn't wait for a reply. Columns of smoke already rose above the walls. I wanted to be everywhere but this was the one place I *had* to be. The Thalassians had believed my promises. If I let them down, it would only be after I died trying.

30

"LEFT," Dani snapped. "Take me left."

I tried my best. The Vanguard was meant for space, meant for bigger battles than this, and I was using her for a knife fight in a phone booth, down below the level of the walls. If I had one thing going for me, it was that the Anguilar soldiers seemed as lost as I was, looking for someone to fight, hostages to take, but not knowing where the bunkers were, where the civilians were sheltered.

Which meant most of them were busy running from *me*. Or, more accurately, running from Dani's guns. The particle cannon was a thousand-pound bomb, more useful for blowing cities up than for saving them, but the pulse turrets moved down the streets and alleyways like surgical scalpels, excising the Anguilar infection. Crackling threads of crimson walked backward from the front to the rear of a squad of armored troopers, scarring the pavement with their remains, and I pulled up, trying to get a bird's-eye view of the city for the next gun run.

The only trouble with the turrets was…

"I'm getting low on ammo," Dani said,

Yeah, that. I could fire the particle cannon until it wore out, but the pulse guns fed thermal cartridges, and a fighter this size could only carry so much of it. I checked the sensor screen, hoping I'd see the rest of my squadron coming down to help, but all it showed me were landers trying desperately to get past them and my pilots doing exactly what I'd told them, staying within visual range of the city, not letting the enemy draw them away.

A touch on the controls zoomed the screen out, showing Laranna's squadron in the upper atmosphere—some of them, anyway, the ones not around the terminator of the planet. The Starblades were doing what the landers couldn't, though their attempt was just as fueled by desperation. Laranna's planes were spread out by elements, chasing a dozen short-range Anguilar fighters all across the continent.

Of Giblet and the cruisers, I was totally in the dark, that battle far beyond the range of the Vanguard's sensors. The upshot of it all was that I was the only friendly force inside the walls, if you could call it that, until Val and the militia got here, which was going to take a while. It was only two miles from their position to the walls, but getting thousands of barely trained militia across that ground in some sort of tactical order was a job I was glad I didn't have. Unless having it meant I wouldn't have to be in charge of this whole, giant fiasco because that sounded pretty good about now.

"How many rounds?" I asked, not looking away from the front screens, the nose dipped slightly downward, belly jets roaring their defiance of gravity.

"Less than a thousand."

That sounded like a lot, but the reality was, the turrets could fire those off in a few seconds. As if to show me that all pulse ammo was soon fleeting, a fusillade of red streaks speared up from an intersection three streets over, converging on the underside of the Vanguard's nose. The defense shield glowed an angry violet in response, in no danger of failing, just letting me know it wasn't happy about the abuse.

"Bring me around," Dani said, traversing the turrets.

"I thought you only had a few hundred rounds," I protested.

"Yeah, but it's just as well spent on these guys as it is on the next set."

Unable to argue with that, I kicked us in the ass with the belly jets, raising higher to get a better shot at what looked to be a platoon-sized element taking cover behind construction vehicles left behind from repairs to the buildings in the area. They weren't making it easy, moving from vehicle to vehicle, forcing me to swing the nose around, slewing us sideways in the air. Dani cursed, finger hovering over the trigger.

"You gonna shoot 'em or not?" I wondered.

"I only have a few hundred rounds, you said it yourself." She shook her head. "I waste them blowing up those tractors, there'll be nothing left for the Anguilar." Another red halo as they shot at us from behind in the cover of an alleyway. "We're taking more fire."

"Not a big deal." I shrugged, turning the fighter to see if we had a clear shot at the infantry behind us. "As long as they don't have…"

I should have learned by now not to say things like that, not to even *think* them. The flash was brighter than the sun, bright enough that even through the filters and dampeners, it left blinking afterimages across my vision. The afterimages weren't nearly as bad as the wave of heat that penetrated both shield and cockpit, forcing the air out of me in a gasp, sending the Vanguard tumbling to the side, the jets screaming in protest.

I fought with the yoke for control, blasting the belly jets, trying to climb out of range, but something had taken damage and we skewed off to the right, smashing our starboard wing against the side of an apartment building.

"What the hell was that?" Dani yelled over the blare of warning buzzers and the uneven blast of the engines, and I only answered her because it gave focus to the effort I was putting into keeping the steering yoke steady.

"Plasma gun," I grunted. Strain tugged at the muscles in my shoulders and forearms, the fighter wanting badly to flip over, to slew to the starboard again. It took everything I had to even out her course, turning the main drives on their gimbals and blasting them straight downward. "The last time I saw them was on Strada…they usually only have them in fixed defenses because they're heavy and awkward to move."

The fighter kept slewing starboard and when I tried to give it more power, it only got worse, nearly throwing us out of control. There was only one thing left to do, as loathe as I was to admit it.

"Shit, I'm gonna have to set her down." Speaking the words was like saying *Bloody Mary* three times while looking into a mirror, letting loose chaos and evil...or, in this case, another plasma blast.

This one wasn't a clear shot, punching through the upper floor of a nearby building before it hit us, which was the only reason we didn't crash immediately. The shield collapsed with this further insult to its integrity, and sizzling heat washed through the cockpit, nearly enough to rob me of consciousness. Forcing my eyes open against the lack of oxygen trying to drive me into blacking out, I pushed the yoke downward, barely remembering to extend the landing gear.

We thumped hard and I nearly fell right out of my chair. I didn't remember hitting the quick-release for my restraints, but I must have because the next moment, I leaned against the airlock door, pushing it open to let in a rush of cool air. *Relatively* cool. The fighter still radiated heat, the skin glowing red in places, and it was a testament to Kamerian workmanship that the thing wasn't shredded like cheese on an uncooked pizza.

I had to suck in air for a few seconds before my brain started working right, before I remembered to check on Dani. She hung out of her restraints, eyes open but unfocused, face beet red from the heat in the cockpit. I slapped at her quick-release, then cursed and sucked at the burn on my fingers. The metal on the buckle felt like it had been left in a car with closed windows during an August heat wave in central Florida. No problem if I'd been wearing combat armor and the gloves that went with it, but again...civilian clothes, like I'd wandered into a cheesy science fiction movie and won the fighter pilot slot by getting the high score on a video game.

I pulled my shirt sleeve over my fingers and used it to cut loose Dani's restraints, catching her before she fell out of her seat and hauling her toward the airlock. I nearly had her out when movement tugged at my peripheral vision and I looked around just in time to yank her and myself back before a spray of pulse rifle fire splashed across the fuselage, another wave of scalding heat.

The floor of the plane's interior banged against my shoulders, with the added weight of Dani across my chest. Not quite dead weight…she'd begun to regain consciousness, moaning softly… but enough to smack the back of my head against the deck. The air had cooled enough that I could breathe, though it wasn't pleasant, and I took a lungful to gather my strength before I pushed Dani off me. The carbines were still in place in their racks, and this time, I took the opportunity to retrieve a spare drum from the cabinet beneath them and reload Dani's weapon. I hadn't fired mine.

Another blast of pulse fire near the lock, and this time, some of it splashed inside, striking the opposite wall and leaving a blackened streak on the dull gray. The Vanguard was pretty tough on the outside, but if one of those rounds hit the controls…

Holding a rifle in each hand, not counting on Dani because she was still out of it, I tucked one under each arm, braced them in tight with my elbows and rested the barrels against the curved bottom of the airlock's lower hatch. This was more something I would have expected to see Ah-nold doing in an action movie than me doing in real life, but accuracy wasn't job one here, suppressive fire was. I leveled both barrels in the general direction of the oncoming horde of Anguilar and pressed down both triggers.

The great thing about pulse weapons was also the sucky thing. Each round from the rifles was a tracer, turning air to plasma and providing a ready-made sighting system to help me guide the rounds on target. The problem with that, as detailed in the Murphy's Laws of Combat that I'd mentioned to Seraph, was that tracers worked both ways. I played the two carbines across the line of Anguilar soldiers charging into the intersection where I'd crashed the fighter, mowing down at least four of them in less than two seconds and sending the others scrambling for cover. All I needed was to grab Dani and get her out of the fighter, get out of the area and try to find a shelter.

But there was still that damned plasma gunner.

I didn't see him until it was too late. No excuse, sir, as I would have said to Colonel Danberg, but I wasn't wearing a helmet with a visor or even enhanced vision goggles, which meant the incoming and outgoing pulses of scalar energy dazzled my eyes with every shot. Not enough to blind me, but plenty to turn the Anguilar running back and forth across the road into featureless silhouettes. Until that giant muzzle swung over the shoulder of the Anguilar trooper leaning around the side of a rowhouse, still glowing a faint red from the last time it had fired.

"Oh, damn," I said mildly, then dropped both guns and pulled the airlock hatch shut.

I didn't see the blast, didn't hear it, really. I just felt it. Felt the heat first, of course. The ever-present, stifling heat, hot enough that it burned my hand where it touched the floor, hot enough to rob me of my breath again. Darkness closed in around the corners of my vision, but I was still awake enough to feel the vibration through the skin of the Vanguard, hear the shriek of anguished metal when the rear landing gear on that side collapsed, pitching the nose into the air at an angle and us with it.

Still half in a daze, I rolled back to the rear of the cockpit and thumped solidly against the rear firewall with Dani hitting me in the chest again. She cursed this time, which I took as a good sign since it meant she was back to alertness. Although, at this point, all that meant was she could be awake when she died.

Except…that plasma gun took a while to recycle before it could fire again. A carbine had rolled to the back with me and I grabbed it, lunging for the airlock. The hatch had been blown off by the plasma blast even though the impact point had been to the rear of it by at least ten yards and the entire side of the fighter was wreathed in smoke from what smelled like melted pavement. I couldn't see more than a couple yards in front of me…which meant they couldn't, either.

I jumped. I couldn't see the ground, either, but I knew it was there and it hit about when I thought it would. If someone had told me a couple years ago when I was going through Airborne School that learning how to do a Parachute Landing Fall would come in as handy as it had despite never again parachuting out of an airplane, I might have laughed at them. But it saved me again—balls of the feet, calf, thigh, buttocks and pull-up muscle in the back, the legendary five points of contact.

Rolling onto my belly, I snugged the stock of the carbine against my shoulder and waited for the smoke to clear. An eddy blown by the wind opened an observation window for me and revealed a pair of Anguilar soldiers way too close together, close enough that I could almost hear Sgt. Redd yelling at them that one grenade would've taken out the both of them. I didn't have any grenades, but I was able to put a short burst into each of them without moving the muzzle of my carbine more than a fraction of an inch.

I rolled three feet to my right just as return fire tore up pavement where I'd just shot from. I'd never been a sniper and never would be one, but I remembered what I'd been taught by a trainer in an ROTC camp. Another Vietnam vet because all the best stuff I'd learned had been from people who'd been in actual war, he'd told me that a sniper working alone should take one shot, two at the most, before moving positions. I guess that was doubly true when shooting something that provided a big, flashing neon sign telling everyone where you were.

It worked both ways, though—I'd seen where the shots had come from that had just targeted me, their sources materializing into slightly darker shapes in the smoke. Another burst took out two more of the enemy before I rolled off the shot again. It was too good to last. An unwelcome breeze through the alleyway chased the smoke away, revealing far too many of the enemy still standing, still closing in on me.

"Come on, you bird-brained bastards!" Dani snarled from

above me, firing from the airlock hatch of the fighter. "Come and get it!"

Two more went down from her shots, but the rest hadn't run, just ducked behind cover, still pouring suppressive fire at the hatch, forcing her back out of the line of their shots. I took advantage of the distraction to scramble behind the cover of the collapsed landing gear, squirming around the mass of twisted metal, trying to find a good firing position.

Before I could, the barrel of the plasma weapon stuck out around the corner, the Anguilar gunner finally braving the free-fire zone again to take another shot at us. I shifted to the side of the landing gear, ready to put him down before he could fire again, but a wash of sparks and a hail of fragments off the landing gear sent me tumbling backward, a dozen tiny needles of pain flaring to life in my neck and face. Rolling onto my side, I tried to force my eyes open, had to wipe blood out of my face and wished to hell I'd put on a helmet because I wasn't going to be in time to stop that plasma gunner from blasting us both to ash.

No plasma blast came, though, just a deafening fusillade of pulse fire. I'm not sure how I knew that the flurry of pulse-gun shots weren't from the Anguilar troopers because it was another two or three seconds before I could see a damned thing. Maybe it was the acoustics, the way the *snap-crack* reports echoed off the buildings, but when I managed to get my eyes open and wipe the blood away, I wasn't surprised to see the plasma gunner down and the Anguilar retreating.

I *was* surprised to see who'd come to our rescue. I expected Val and Nareena to charge around the corner with their militia in tow…but the one leading the charge through the intersection was a lot shorter and thinner, even in the smallest armor they'd been able to find for her, wearing no helmet, just a wild, ferocious grin.

"Wendra!" I blurted, climbing painfully to my feet. "What the hell are you doing here?"

Now that I knew it was her, the rest of the armored figures shifted in perspective, and I realized that she'd brought along the same Single Mom Militia who'd taken out the Anguilar guards at the fighters.

"Saving your ass, Charlie," she said. "Again. We saw your fighter go down and decided we had to go help out."

"I thought I told you guys to go back to the shelter," I said, blinking away blood again. It wouldn't stop dripping, and finally, I just ripped the sleeve off my right arm and tied it around my forehead to staunch the flow from the tiny cuts there.

"It's a damned good thing for us they didn't," Dani opined, dropping down from the hatch. She looked the Vanguard up and down, her expression bleak. "Because this bird isn't going anywhere."

31

"You look," Dani told me, "like a pre-steroid Rambo."

"Really?" I asked, keeping my eyes on the buildings around us, but painfully conscious of my newly sleeveless T-shirt and makeshift headband. "Because I feel more like the guy playing the fife in Willard's *Spirit of '76*."

Dani looked at me blankly.

"What?"

"Oh, good God," I moaned, shaking my head. "What the hell happened to your generation? It's that internet shit you keep talking about, isn't it?"

"You sound like my father," Dani scoffed.

"That's probably because we were born within a couple years of each other."

"Are we supposed to talk this much in combat?" Wendra asked tautly, jogging up to the two of us. She hadn't been happy when I'd insisted on walking point, but as much as I appreciated her platoon bailing us out, I still believed more in my experience.

"Not normally, no," I admitted. "But in this case, we actually *want* the enemy to know where we are. We're trying to draw them away from the shelters."

"Maybe we should sing a sea shanty," Dani suggested. "Or something you're more comfortable with, Charlie…Madonna, maybe."

This time, I did look over at her, scowling.

"I'm not a big Madonna fan," I told her, "but I'd take her a hundred times over the trash from the twenty-first century you played for me on your phone. What the hell is a Justin Bieber?"

Dani turned on me with anger flaring in her eyes.

"Hey now, Travers, you leave Justin alone!"

"There," I snapped, the banter suddenly forgotten, nodding ahead and to the left, through the remains of the industrial parking lot.

It was still charred and blackened from the diversionary bomb Dothan had set off to draw us away from the holding cell when he'd murdered the Anguilar soldier, the construction vehicles we hadn't been able to salvage hunched morosely like the skeletons of ancient beasts. We'd come this way on purpose, away from the shelters, on the hope that they'd follow us and now it seemed as if they had…assuming I wasn't jumping at shadows.

"How long before Val gets here with the rest of the militia?" Dani asked, eyes narrowing as she tried to find the movement I'd spotted.

"Probably another ten minutes to get to the gate. Then…

well, it's a city. They're going to have to sweep through it methodically, which doesn't do a damn bit of good for the here and now."

The roar of engines overhead and a distant explosion illustrated why we couldn't expect any help from the rest of my squadron. The Anguilar landers had taken back off after they'd dropped off their troops, intent on providing air support with their pulse turrets, and my guys were busy hunting them down. I'd found all that out when I'd made one last call on the fighter's radio before we'd abandoned it, and with it, our only means of communication.

I was beginning to understand how Dani felt about her cell phone. I'd been spoiled with instant communications all the way to high orbit and beyond, but now, I was worse off than a 1980s infantry platoon, lacking even a PRC-77.

I didn't stop moving, not wanting to let on that I'd spotted the enemy, instead leading the platoon around to the right side of the parking area, circling the burned-out hulks. The rest of the lot had been cleared out after the fire, the construction vehicles distributed around the city as they'd been needed for rebuilding, leaving too much open space on all sides of the center cluster of blackened metal. I wanted to keep it between us and the possible hiding spaces at the other end, where warehouses completed the three-sided enclosure. The movement had been furtive, in the narrow alleys between the storage buildings and after another thirty seconds of nothing, I thought maybe my mind had been playing tricks on me.

Until the rear guard opened fire.

"Dammit!" I grunted, turning and running back the way I'd come.

Wendra's private militia platoon had, at least, absorbed some of the training I'd passed down through Val and Nareena, namely tactical movement. The streets were too narrow for squad wedge formations, with each squad in an arrowhead shape and the squads themselves spread out in an arrowhead for the platoon. Instead, I'd gone with a staggered file, half of the platoon on one side of the road, half on the other, with ten meters between them. Which was about the only time I was going to use the metric system.

They'd also learned how to peel back and reform when facing a threat in the opposite direction, so when Dani and I headed to the rear, the rest of the platoon followed right along with us like a zipper unzipping. The rear of the formation, which had just become the front, had taken cover behind one of the burned-out wrecks, another good tactical decision, but they were pouring automatic fire at the enemy with little regard for conserving ammo.

"Controlled bursts!" I yelled, sliding in beside the third squad leader, the young woman who'd been in charge of the rear guard. "Don't waste your ammo! We don't have that much!"

She looked abashed and turned to yell the order to the rest of her squad while I leaned around the back of a burnt truck bed, then pulled back when a burst of pulse fire hit only a couple yards away from me. I'd seen enough. The Anguilar were hunkered beneath the half-open curtain doors of a long freight loading dock, no more than a squad of them...which didn't make any sense. They wouldn't attack a platoon with a squad—not even the Anguilar were that stupid.

"They're circling around us," I told Dani and Wendra, waving them back. Grabbing the squad leader's attention with a hand on her shoulder, wishing I knew her name, I pointed at the loading dock. "Short bursts. Keep their attention. We're going around the buildings. If you think you're getting pinned down, break contact and move back to the next cover."

I could have sat there for ten minutes giving her instructions, but I'd have to trust that she and the rest of them had absorbed enough during training to do the right thing. I caught up to Wendra just as she reached Second Squad.

"Take your Second Squad," I told her, "and head for that gap." I indicated a break between the buildings straight ahead. "Those guys back on the loading dock will have a shot at you, so move fast and don't stop. Dani and I are taking First Squad and circling this way." I pointed at the other end of the chain of warehouses, the direction I expected the attack to come from. "We're gonna catch them between us."

And that was more time than I had to explain things.

"What's your name?" I asked the First Squad leader, a pale, slender woman who didn't look older than her late teens.

"Talia," she said, her voice shaky. Not everyone was as gung-ho confident as Wendra.

"Get behind us," I told her, gesturing at Dani and myself. "When we contact the enemy, head left, find cover and start laying down fire. I don't care if you hit anything as long as you don't hit us."

She nodded, but I was already sprinting away with Dani close on my heels. Running again. Too much damned running. My mouth was full of cotton, and I simultaneously felt an overwhelming urge to pee and might have given into it if I could have relaxed enough. I needed water, I needed a shower, I needed rest, and more than any of that, I needed this all to be over. But it was only going to end if I made it.

I didn't pause at the corner of the building, knowing what to expect and knowing with even more certainty that my only advantage was that they wouldn't be expecting me. I was right about half that equation. The Anguilar squad moving stealthily forward about thirty yards shy of the corner hadn't been expecting Dani and me, but *I* hadn't been expecting what I saw at the center of their formation, leading them.

Seraph Nix.

She hadn't run. I should have known she wouldn't, not with an army of Anguilar landing to back her up. She'd made a bead for the city before we'd even made it to the woods and hooked up with the first Anguilar unit she found. I had a split-second glimpse of the Kamerian, long enough to see that she wasn't in any better shape than I was. Her armor was scorched and scarred, blood matted in her hair, and her left arm limp at her side, but one hand was plenty to hold her carbine, and she triggered a blast straight at my face.

Something hit me, knocking me to the ground just as the wave of heat and crackling static electricity washed by over my head. There was a weight across my legs—Dani, I thought. She'd saved my life. I squeezed out from under her, pulling the trigger of my carbine before I had it lined up, sweeping the muzzle right to left across the oncoming squad of Anguilar. Eight to a squad, small compared to American infantry but I wasn't complaining since it was also small compared to *our* squad. And they hadn't forgotten how to shoot.

A swathe of red streaks went over where I'd been standing a moment before and the entire front rank of the Anguilar squad went down like bowling pins, the second four scattering like cockroaches. And Seraph Nix with them. She'd abandoned the other Anguilar, ducking through an open door into the warehouse.

"Don't shoot me!" I yelled back at the Thalassian squad, scrambling to my feet and squeezing sideways through the side door as it began to swing shut.

Darkness swallowed me up, the change from the bright light outside leaving me blind momentarily, and I ducked to the side, taking cover behind a row of cargo crates, listening and letting my eyes adjust. A clunk of metal on metal, gentle but loud enough to make it past the whine in my ear left over from one firefight after another. Off to the right.

Dark shadows revealed their details as my eyes adjusted to the dim light filtering through shuttered windows and I took a deep breath before spinning around the other side of the stack of crates, running toward the sound. Finally, my choice of clothing proved an advantage, the Nike running shoes padding silently on the concrete floor, unlike Seraph's armored boots. She was moving at a slow, cautious jog rather than sprinting, which she would have done if she'd known I was following.

Trying to control my breathing, I cat-footed after her, rifle to my shoulder, wishing I had a handgun. I'd heard someone say once that you never wish you had a smaller gun, but I did now. The quarters were close, the aisles between the stacks of crates narrow, and a handgun would have been perfect. No handgun, no comm, thanks to Seraph. Just a rifle and no spare drums, God alone knew how many rounds were left because I didn't have time to check the counter on the side, couldn't take my eyes off the aisles between the rows.

The place was a maze and the only reason I knew which way was out was the dim glow through the cracks in the window shutters, but I figured Seraph had to be following the curve of the building back around to the other end, away from the firefight, away from the Anguilar she'd abandoned. Looking for an exit. I put on a burst of speed, sacrificing stealth for a chance to get her before she got clear of the building.

There. Movement ahead, bulky armor scraping against the crate on the right side, knocking the empty container askew. I fired and the crate exploded into flame, wooden fragments blowing outward, ricocheting off the walls and the other boxes, sending a billowing cloud of smoke across the aisle, all the way up to the ceiling. Pulse fire flashed back at me from the haze of smoke and I threw myself to the floor.

My blue jeans and newly sleeveless T-shirt didn't do much to cushion me from the rough concrete and the impact nearly knocked the rifle loose, but it was better than getting shot. Seraph's fire stopped and I pushed to my feet with the butt of my gun and raced after her again.

I had to slow her down and I knew the best way to do it. The bounty hunter tried to act like the strong, silent type, but she just couldn't resist a good taunt.

"Come on, Seraph!" I yelled after her. "You always get your target, right? I'm right here, the only one you couldn't kill. Come get me."

"You're a pain in my ass, Travers," she yelled back, "but I'm not stupid. I don't *have* to kill you here, in this warehouse. You're not getting off this planet...all I have to do is wait you out. Maybe I won't kill you right away. Maybe I'll keep you alive until the Anguilar take your world...I could take you there and let you watch while your people are sent to work in the mines, while they starve working on farms for the Anguilar. Would you like that? Would you like to watch the death and destruction you've brought to them? Because the Anguilar would never have known they existed. Isn't that right, Charlie? You led death to your own people. By the end, you'll be begging me for death!"

I'd kept moving while she talked, skirting the edge of the corridor, counting on the smoke to conceal my approach. Just a few more feet and I'd be able to see her past a cluster of boxes stacked floor to ceiling. I took one more step, and she lunged out at me from behind the boxes, too close for the damned rifle, pushing it aside as her hands went for my throat.

I had less than a second to act, and instinct brought my hands up to catch hers, dropping the rifle. It clattered to the ground between us as I caught her wrists, but the strength behind those hands and the weight of her and the armor pushed me back a step. Training told me where to strike but logic stopped me. That armor would make kicks useless, and I couldn't punch her while she was pushing her hands against mine. She bared her pointed teeth as if she meant to sink them into my throat, her breath rank like rotten meat.

"Maybe," she growled, "I *will* kill you now, while the last thought through your little monkey brain is going to be that not only will your world die, and that you caused it, but you also won't be able to do a damned thing to stop it."

There was one thing left I could do, a move that she hadn't seen last time we'd fought. Let loose of one hand, grab the other, and twist, putting my leg in front of hers. She had me on weight even without the armor, but all that weight and all that armor came at the cost of a buttload of momentum. The impact against my hip was like slamming it into a brick wall but it worked— Seraph toppled over my leg and hit the floor flat on her back. No way for her to break that fall, not with all the weight of that Kamerian suit, and the metal crashed like a trash can rolling down a driveway.

The next move would normally have been to go for a mount, finish off the opponent, but again with that damned armor. Instead, I launched myself back toward my rifle…but she caught my ankle in a grip like a vise and yanked me off my feet. I went down hard on my side, the blow driving the breath out of me, vision disappearing in an explosion of light. Helpless, and when the stars faded, Seraph loomed over me, a wickedly curved knife held in her hand, poised to plunge it into my chest. I suppose she'd decided about the whole kill-me-now or kill-me-later thing.

"Yo, bitch!" The exit door slammed open, and Dani

Campling burst through it, her rifle leveled and death in her eye. "You shouldn't have killed my boyfriend."

The rifle discharged with a crimson flash, and Seraph Nix stiffened, the knife clattering to the floor just before the bounty hunter collapsed backward to join it. The most dangerous bounty hunter in the galaxy lay dead on the bare cement floor of a warehouse of a backwater system no one cared about, killed by a county sheriff's deputy from rural Ohio.

Dani offered me a hand.

"Come on, Travers. The squadron's landing outside. We still got work to do."

32

I WAS STILL a lot more infantry than I was a fighter pilot, but I had to admit it felt good to be back in the cockpit of the Vanguard. Not *my* Vanguard, of course. That bird might fly again, but it would need some serious repair.

Peralta wasn't as happy to be kicked out of the pilot's seat and back into the gunner's position in Stavros' fighter to make room for Dani and me in Tamura's old Vanguard. He'd have to deal with it. I was too busy to worry about hurt feelings, climbing up through the atmosphere.

Things down below were under control. Val and Nareena had led the militia through the gates a half an hour ago, and with the landers all shot down, finally, they'd take care of the rest of the Anguilar ground troops. My worries were all above me.

"Vanguard Two, Vanguard Three, this is One," I called into

the fighter's comm system, then swore softly. Forget it. "Laranna, Gib, it's Charlie. What's the situation up here?"

"Charlie!" Laranna exclaimed. "Oh, thank the gods! I heard from your squadron that you'd been shot down!"

"I was," I admitted. "I got better. On the bright side, Seraph Nix is dead. Tell me something good."

"Wish I had better news, but once we took down the last of the fighters, the cruisers started moving in from cislunar space."

I could see it on the sensors now that the blue skies of a Philos afternoon had given way to the deep purples and blacks of space. The twelve Anguilar cruisers were drifting toward a tactical formation as they approached the planet, and the reason for their spread was just as evident. Giblet's squadron hung right at minimum safe jump distance, coming together into a wedge formation even as I watched.

All the cruisers were still there, but on the bright side, so were all of Giblet's fighters.

Unfortunately, the cruisers were already inside safe jump distance from the planet, which meant the biggest advantage our fighters had was gone. I could see the battle unfolding inside my head, twenty-two of us against twelve of them, and we could either gang up on one at a time, leaving the rest free to snipe at us, pick us off one by one, or bombard Thalassia out of spite, or we could harass them, keep them busy. Distracting them was a short-term solution, though.

Command decisions, that was what Danberg had always called moments like these. One of the rare gems in the piles of shit he'd told us. Moments like this were the ones where disaster or victory were a hair's breadth apart, and the one who made the call was going to have to deal with being the architect of defeat or triumph.

"Lenny, do you read me?"

There was the possibility he wouldn't. He'd said they'd wait out past the asteroid belt, in the outer system, but he might have seen what was happening on and around the planet and decided not to risk his ships by sticking around. It was hard to tell, particularly given what we knew about his half-truths and manipulations.

"We're still here, Charlie." If a sentient AI could sound relieved, Lenny did. "I wasn't sure if you'd call."

"We need you in the fight," I told him. "We're going to engage the cruisers, but we can't take them all, not this close to the planet. We're gonna pull their coat over their head and you're going to kick their asses."

A pause and I imagined rather than saw the affected look of consternation on that metallic version of Michael Keaton.

"Should I assume that's some sort of metaphor?" he wondered, "or do I need to mix up a new batch of translator nanites?"

"Just jump back here, both ships, and tell your crews to wait for an opening." I switched frequencies with a flick of a finger. "Gib, you read me?"

"I'm here," he grunted, not sounding happy about it. "You're a big freaking tease, you know that, Charlie? We could have blown a couple of these things straight to hell while you were screwing around down on the planet."

"Well, you're gonna get teased some more. Get your asses back over here and into formation."

The last gasps of Thalassia's atmosphere faded behind us, the curve of the planet visible in its green and blue glory, the moon the size of a basketball hanging in space near the terminator. Sometimes, when I could take a second and not worry about someone trying to kill me, I was struck by how beautiful it was out here. Then the Anguilar cruisers came into optical range and spoiled the view.

Not that they weren't impressive in their own way. Grudgingly, I had to admit that the artificial mountains were just as beautiful as the moon and the planet, monuments to the height of technological achievement, office buildings thrown into space, sailing the gaps between stars faster than light. Raw power glowed at their tails, snarling and snapping and clawing, tyrannosaurus rex lumbering for its prey on some Cretaceous battlefield.

And here I was in a fighter about the size of a C-130 if you shortened the wings by half, less than a tenth the length of one of those cruisers, protected from the vacuum and the cold by a few inches of metal, from the weapons of the enemy by something even less substantial, a deflector shield based on principles of physics I'd never fully understand. Oh, and I was beat all to hell, dressed in a blood-stained, sleeveless Chicago T-shirt and blue jeans. And it was cold.

At least I wasn't alone. Not that Dani looked much better than I did, a bruise already darkening on the side of her face, her hair matted by sweat and burned at the ends. Her eyes were hollow, the resolve gone out of her now that we were in the fighter again.

"Does it feel any better?" I wondered. She glanced a question at me, and I went on. "Now that she's dead, does it feel any better?"

"A little," she admitted. "It doesn't…" A spasm of pain passed across her face. "It doesn't fill the emptiness but at least it closes the book."

I nodded, getting that. I'd felt something similar when I'd killed Mok-La on the *Nova Eclipse*, not satisfaction, just relief that it was over, that I'd never have to deal with him again. No matter that the Anguilar Empire was still a massive evil hanging over all our heads, at least the personal enmity of that particular evil wasn't aimed at me anymore.

"Tamura loved you, you know," I told her. "He did everything he could to keep you safe, even when it meant killing his best friend and getting killed himself. He didn't betray you."

For the first time since we'd left Tamura's body in that cell, Dani showed an emotion other than rage. Her shoulders shook, tears squeezing out from eyes tightly shut.

"Later," she said, shaking her head, wiping her face. When she opened her eyes, her expression was set and stolid again. "Later, when it's over."

The rest of the wing gathered around us as they came into visual range, as if they were showing their support for Dani. Tactical diamond formation, with me in the lead this time. Maybe Gib was a better pilot than I was—well, no, there was no *maybe* about it—but if I was the leader of this crazy show, I was going to do it from the front. The cruisers were only minutes from weapons range, and the plan formed in my head about two seconds before I broadcast it.

"Listen up, Vanguard Wing," I barked in my best drill sergeant imitation. "Here's the deal. The cruisers are in a globular formation. We're going in from the relative east, away from the firing arcs for their particle cannons. They're going to try to swing toward us, and when they do, we split into squadrons, east, west and south—I'll go south, Laranna to the west, Gib to the east. Leave north open as long as they take that avenue of escape and get to safe jump distance….then we pursue that direction. Don't become engaged with any one cruiser. Fire as you bear, then pass them by and head to the interior of the formation and we'll swing around and do it again. Our goal is to keep them away from the planet. Even though we're splitting up, use me as your guide, keep following in that direction forward. Everyone clear?"

"Clear," Laranna said, and Giblet muttered acknowledgement.

And that was all the time we had for preparation. The cruisers described the glittering silver outline of a Christmas tree ornament, their blunt noses pointing at the planet, and, by coincidence, us. Time to change that. I nudged the steering yoke to the right, twisting the wheel as I did, the ship's fly-by-wire systems transforming the motion into a bank to the right, mirroring how it would work in an atmosphere as best they could with the gimbaled drives and maneuvering thrusters.

However the fighter did it, whatever arcane combination of

applied physics worked together to carry out my commands, we curved around to the right of the Anguilar formation, relative east as I'd labeled it, still burning toward them even faster than they approached us. Whatever bad things I could say about the Anguilar as military commanders, one thing they had in plenty was a sense of self-preservation, and the captains of those ships knew we were trying to circle around them, get out of their line of fire, and attack from the flank. They weren't about to allow that.

The entire formation of cruisers turned as one, as if they were a mobile hanging from the ceiling, connected by wire and spinning with some random draft of an air conditioning vent. The red lines that showed the range of our particle cannons and theirs on the tactical screen were getting closer, and in seconds, the cruisers would volley fire, trying to catch us in a web of particle cannon blasts.

"Break!" I ordered, and pushed the steering yoke downward.

So much more sound than I ever expected in outer space. All of it was inside the cockpit, of course, vibrations through the metal, the rhythmic banging of the steering jets, the roar of the drives, the high-tech starfighter awash with a constant background noise like a World War Two bomber. Dani nearly had to yell to be heard over the din.

"They're still turning," she warned. "Trying to match us...but I don't think they're gonna be in time."

"That's a hell of a thing to guess at," I said, grunting as some of the acceleration slipped past the compensators and thumped me against the seat, then threatened to pull me out the top like a dip on a roller coaster.

Somebody fired. I don't know if it was the ship directly in front of us or one of the others close by, but a crackling stream of energy with the power of an exploding star passed only a few dozen meters from the cockpit, close enough that the defense shields lit up with a faint glow as if extolling us to caution.

I'm being as cautious as I can without getting killed, I assured the fighter silently.

Then we were past the cruiser's firing arc, not just me but the other fighters in my squadron. Only six of us with my fighter wrecked and Donnell gone. Stavros was my wingman now, though I didn't trust him the way I had Donnell. At least he'd kept close during the maneuver...maybe too close, since the proximity warning kept blinking yellow on my starboard wing.

White fountains of energy fountained from the maneuvering thruster banks at the ventral rear of the cruiser, still trying to turn it to bring its cannons to bear on my squadron, but before they had the chance, a large swathe of that belly laid itself bare for us. Oh, point-defense turrets still spewed red dashes of scalar energy at us, but the fighters' defense shields shrugged off their fire as if it weren't there.

"Fire as you bear!" I ordered, leading by example, jamming down the trigger for the Vanguard's particle cannon.

At this range, less than two hundred yards away, I couldn't miss. The cruiser's shields did their best, but we were too damned close for them to diffuse the fearsome power of the cannon shots and the gleaming silver of the hull passing beneath us turned black and red as pustules of damage rose and burst, spewing out vaporized metal. Not deep enough to do critical damage to the drives, not at the angle we had for our shot, but enough to make that Anguilar captain panic.

The cruiser's main drive flared like a supernova and the massive ship surged away from the formation, abandoning discipline and tactics in a desperate bid for survival. The next cruiser to the relative south of the one we'd hit was only a few miles away on the downslope of the globe, the Argentina to the Panama of our first target. She had more time to react and her captain, whether he was braver than Panama's, was definitely smarter. She'd already been turning toward our original direction of approach and, rather than cut the steering jets and try to turn her nose back toward us, the captain of the Anguilar Empire Ship *Argentina* just kept that spin going the way it had started… and aimed her drive toward us.

The defense shields on the Vanguard fighters would stop a lot of threats, could even survive—sort of—a grazing shot from a particle cannon. But they couldn't hold up to the close-range exhaust of a cruiser's plasma drive.

"Break right! Break right!" I yelled, yanking the controls to match my command.

I could *tell* the Vanguard to move that abruptly, and with the excess power the fighter had, it could even try to comply, but even the funky gravity-defying technology of the Anguilar and Kamerians had to obey *some* laws of physics. The fighter shuddered and rattled and tried its dead-level best to shake itself to pieces—and us, right along with it. Warning lights flashed, telling me, essentially, not to do that again, but I wasn't going to make any promises.

We'd gotten out of the way of the exhaust plume, but at the cost of any sort of organization. My supposed wingman, Stavros, had jetted off nearly fifty miles from me, and the other four birds were strung out over two hundred miles of outright gaggle. What was worse than that was *where* we were. We'd gotten clear of the immediate threat, but off across the other side of the Anguilar formation, Gib and his squadron had harassed two of the cruisers into breaking the sphere and making a run forward.

Right into us. I couldn't *actually* look straight into the maw of an Anguilar particle cannon from the cockpit of my fighter, but it sure *felt* like I could.

"Third squadron, scatter!" I yelled, about to yank the controls in a desperate hope of getting out of the cruiser's firing arc, yet knowing I wouldn't be able to do it.

I'd gotten so damned caught up in the maneuver I was leading and the status of the rest of the wing, I'd let myself forget about the Liberators. Thank God they hadn't forgotten about us.

Twin beams of pure destruction sliced through the Anguilar cruiser at a downward angle, bisecting the hull, white fire pouring out the ventral hull as the drives fed back through the reactor and into the crew sections.

The *Liberator* chased her particle blasts across the firmament, Monstro the whale crashing through a shiver of sharks. And yes, a group of sharks *is* called a shiver. I had to look it up for zoology class. Except this wasn't just one whale, it was a pod, five of them, storming in from their hyperspace micro-jump, weapons seeming to rip apart the very fabric of space and certainly doing a damned good job of ripping apart the Anguilar cruisers.

The Anguilar had to know they were outclassed, and they tried to run, turning ponderously away from orbit, heading back to minimum jump distance. I wasn't prepared to let them get away that easy.

"Vanguard Wing!" I called, pulling my fighter into a tight turn back toward the closest of the enemy ships. "Form on me! One cruiser at a time, and aim where I aim!"

I knew even then I was going to hear it from Gib about why I didn't have the Liberators come in from the beginning, but the truth was, with only one squadron to support them, I couldn't have guaranteed that we wouldn't lose one of the big ships.

Now, we were going to make up for lost time. The rest of the wing lined up behind me, my own squadron taking the longest to get in line after being scattered, and we raced after the cruisers... the seven of them that were left. Five had already fallen to the surprise attack of the Liberators and their remains drifted like a giant spaceship graveyard. The remaining cruisers weren't in any sort of ordered formation, just spread out in a line at least five hundred miles long, engines burning at max acceleration.

But not as max as ours. The Kamerian fighter engines weren't as powerful as the Anguilar cruiser drives, but they had a lot less mass to push around, which meant that, although the capital ships could outrun us in a marathon, we could kick their asses in a sprint. I pushed the throttle open, the abrupt shove into my seat somehow satisfying, like pushing down the accelerator of a sports car.

"You know," I told Dani, "the only sports cars I've ever driven have belonged to other people."

She stared at me, brow knitted.

"Well, I guess this is better than a Corvette, huh?"

"So much better," I agreed, fingers curling around the steering yoke, thumb hovering over the firing stud for the particle cannon.

That red line floated ahead of us, but this time, I didn't care about the red line from their weapons because those were facing the other direction. That's the thing about running away instead of retreating—when an army retreats, they cover each other's backs. When they run away, they're just begging to get cut down. The line intersected the stern of the rearmost cruiser and I touched the trigger.

The cruiser's shields coruscated with dispersed energy, but not all of it. Some shot through, enough to put a spike of white fire through the drive bell of one of the engines. The warship slowed with the sudden loss of power and my Vanguard shot past, making room for the next in our formation. I kept one eye on the rear cameras as the rest of the wing came into range behind me, each of them pouring one shot into the engines of the cruiser like a company of Parthian archers firing a barrage as they galloped past lines of enemy infantry.

Fire and clouds of sublimated metal poured out of the engines, brighter and more intense with each wave, each barrage, rocking the huge vessel, sending the stern drifting downward. Laranna and her squadron brought up the rear and by the time the last shot was fired, the cruiser had tumbled into an uncontrolled roll.

I didn't turn back to finish her off. She could wait. The next one in line was the target, the purpose to do as much damage as we could to the entire flotilla before they got away. Every ship they didn't have was one more ship that couldn't come back here, couldn't go to another system and enslave more innocent people.

But before that red line reached the next cruiser, the first ship in the cluster disappeared, surging forward into a hole in space through a rainbow ring that closed around it. As if the jump had started a chain reaction, the rest of the surviving Anguilar warships lurched toward escape and safety, one after another, getting away clean.

That red line advanced too slowly, but just as the last of them reached safe jump distance, there was a split second when the line intersected the ship. I jammed down the trigger, and the searing burst of charged particles hit the stern of the cruiser even as the hole in space opened ahead of it. The shield flared and…something happened. The shield or the shot or something interacted with the hyperspace portal, and it collapsed around the nose of the cruiser, slicing it neatly in half.

The ship's atmosphere poured out, and I thought I could see tiny figures tumbling away from it as the back half spun away into space.

"Damn," I said. "Never seen that before."

"Commander Travers," a steady Copperell voice with a hint of self-satisfaction in his tone echoed over the cockpit speakers, "this is Chief Kamen." Bridge crew chief of the *Liberator*. "Do you need any assistance?"

Pulling back on the throttle, I sighed, settling back into my seat.

"No, Chief. I think you guys assisted the hell out of us already."

33

Smoke climbed high into the night sky, a dark haze across the moon.

Gathering the woodpile outside the city walls of Philos had taken two days, not for the cutting and the hauling, but to organize it into the intricate patterns Lenny insisted were part of the Kamerian ritual for the dead. I guess it could have been worse. I'd read about some cultures where the dead were left to rot on open platforms until the vultures and worms picked them apart. Burning was quick, clean.

At least Tamura's body had been wrapped in a ceremonial shroud first. I didn't know who'd done that, I was just glad I hadn't had to look into his eyes while Dani and I had carried him to the platform. Of all the people I'd shot, all the ones killed around me since I'd come out here, I'd never had to handle a dead body before. There was something unreal about it, like what was inside that shroud couldn't have ever been a living thing.

Dani stood silhouetted against the flames, motionless, staring. I wanted to say something, wanted to tell her that it would be okay, but I wasn't sure I could promise that. Laranna's fingers tightened around mine, and she leaned her head against my shoulder.

"You've seen the Strada ceremonies for the dead," she said softly. I had, when Jax died. "You know what to do if it happens to me."

"Don't say that," I snapped, looking sharply at her. "It's not going to happen."

"We're fighting a war, Charlie. People die in war. No matter how badly we want them not to." She met my eyes, hers glittering in the firelight. "What about you?"

I shrugged, not comfortable with the subject. But since she'd asked, I gave it a moment's thought.

"I don't really care what you do to my body after I'm done with it. Just toss it into space and have a party."

"Me," Dani said, and I started, not realizing she could hear our quiet conversation, "I want to be buried at sea." She didn't turn around, just stared at the fire. "You can burn me up first, but I want the ashes scattered in the ocean."

"Why the ocean?" Giblet asked. He hadn't said a word during the ceremony, had barely said a word to any of us since we'd landed after the battle. Now, Dani did turn and looked at him. He regarded her with an expression of honest curiosity. "I thought you lived somewhere inland. Before, I mean."

It was just the four of us tonight. Val had begged off, saying he didn't know Tamura that well and didn't want to intrude, and I'd thought Gib might have skipped the ceremony as well, but he'd even volunteered to drive the truck that had taken us and Tamura's body out to the edge of the forest.

The corner of Dani's mouth twitched upward in an aborted attempt at a smile.

"I am. But I've always loved the ocean. I always wanted to live on the beach, by the shore, but before, I didn't have the money. Now…" She motioned around us. "Now, I don't know if I'll ever get back to Earth. But if I go and you guys are still around, take me back there. I really like the idea of going back to the ocean."

"I don't want to hear this crap," I admitted.

I pulled Laranna closer, then extended an arm to the others. Gib sighed and rolled his eyes but reluctantly let me grab him around the shoulder and pull him into a hug. Dani looked at all of us dubiously but surrendered to the inevitable when Laranna motioned for her to join. We held each other for a long moment before I let loose of them, not wanting it to get awkward.

"You're the best friends I've ever had," I told them. I wasn't about to cry or anything, but if the last year had taught me anything, it was that none of us could be sure we'd be able to say what we wanted to before it was too late. "I'm not letting any of you go."

I hesitated, casting a long look at Tamura's shrouded body, engulfed in flame, the white covering spewing smoke.

"And you *are* going to go home again, Dani."

"What?" she asked, wiping at something in her eye. "You've decided I've got a screw loose and you're going to dump me back in Ohio?"

"Not quite." I waved at the fire, still spreading over the platform. "I wasn't going to say anything till later, didn't want to interrupt the ceremony…"

"Charlie," Dani chided, "if anyone would understand, it would be Tamura."

Yeah, I figured he probably would. The Kamerian had been nothing if not pragmatic.

"Seraph Nix is dead," I told them, "but the intelligence she handed over to the Anguilar is still out there—along with the information that Dothan gave her. The genie is out of the bottle." And not the sexy Barbara Eden kind of genie, either. "That plan we had about island hopping and striking into the interior of the Empire…they know all about it. And I don't know that we have either the people or the firepower to make this work if they're waiting for us."

"Then what the hell can we do?" Giblet wanted to know. "We don't have any way to get more people *or* more weapons. The Strada can't afford to give us any more troops, and we couldn't feed them if they did. No one else even *has* a military. We're alone."

"Not quite," I corrected him. "There's one power out there that's got a huge military, a big population, and just as much incentive to fight the Anguilar. They're not as advanced technologically…but they're the only world we know of that's developed space travel independent of Lenny's creators and the Anguilar."

"Oh, Charlie," Laranna breathed, shaking her head, "you don't mean…"

"I do. We don't have any other choice. Seraph Nix was right. The Anguilar knows they're out there, knows they can grab *millions* of slaves and loot the planet for everything it's worth. Unless we warn them. Unless we tell them what's really going on, tell them the truth and ask for their help."

Three sets of eyes stared at me in disbelief.

"We've got no other choice. We're going back to Earth."

Amazon won't always tell you about the next release. To stay updated on this series, be sure to sign up for our spam-free email list at jnchaney.com.

Charlie and the rest of the crew return in HOME OF THE BRAVE, available on Amazon.

CONNECT WITH J.N. CHANEY

Don't miss out on these exclusive perks:

- Instant access to free short stories from series like *Backyard Starship*, *Sentenced to War*, and more.
- Receive email updates for new releases and other news.
- Get notified when we run special deals on books and audiobooks.

So, what are you waiting for? Enter your email address at the link below to stay in the loop.

https://www.jnchaney.com/taken-to-the-stars-subscribe

CONNECT WITH RICK PARTLOW

Check out his website
https://rickpartlow.com

Connect on Facebook
https://www.facebook.com/DutyHonorPlanet

Follow him on Amazon
https://www.amazon.com/Rick-Partlow/e/B00B1GNL4E/

ABOUT THE AUTHORS

J. N. Chaney is a USA Today Bestselling author and has a Master's of Fine Arts in Creative Writing. He fancies himself quite the Super Mario Bros. fan. When he isn't writing or gaming, you can find him online at **jnchaney.com**.

He migrates often, but was last seen in Las Vegas, NV. Any sightings should be reported, as they are rare.

Rick Partlow is that rarest of species, a native Floridian. Born in Tampa, he attended Florida Southern College and graduated with a degree in History and a commission in the US Army as an Infantry officer.

He has written over 40 books in a dozen different series, and his short stories have been included in twelve different anthologies. Visit his website at **rickpartlow.com** for more.

Printed in Great Britain
by Amazon

48306988R00225